*The Quick
and the Dead*

The Quick
and the Dead

Selected Stories

MÁIRTÍN Ó CADHAIN

TRANSLATED FROM THE IRISH

INTRODUCTION BY LOUIS DE PAOR

YALE UNIVERSITY PRESS ■ NEW HAVEN & LONDON

A MARGELLOS
WORLD REPUBLIC OF LETTERS BOOK

The Margellos World Republic of Letters is dedicated to making literary works from around the globe available in English through translation. It brings to the English-speaking world the work of leading poets, novelists, essayists, philosophers, and playwrights from Europe, Latin America, Africa, Asia, and the Middle East to stimulate international discourse and creative exchange.

Yale University Press books may be purchased in quantity for educational, business, or promotional use. For information, please email sales.press@yale.edu (U.S. office) or sales@yaleup.co.uk (U.K. office).

Set in Electra and Nobel types by Tseng Information Systems, Inc.
Printed in the United States of America.

Library of Congress Control Number: 2021936480
ISBN 978-0-300-24721-3 (hardcover : alk. paper)

A catalogue record for this book is available from the British Library.

This paper meets the requirements of ANSI/NISO Z39.48-1992 (Permanence of Paper).

10 9 8 7 6 5 4 3 2 1

CONTENTS

INTRODUCTION

Máirtín Ó Cadhain is the outstanding prose writer in modern Irish and a significant figure in twentieth-century world literature. While his posthumous reputation rests largely on *Cré na Cille* (translated both as Graveyard Clay and The Dirty Dust; 1949), the only novel published during his lifetime,[1] his shorter fiction is central to his achievement as a writer and indispensable to any critical consideration of his work. It might even be argued that his reputation will ultimately depend on the best of these stories, in which he attempts to reconcile the sprawl of his own recalcitrant imagination with the limitations of the European short story.

Although Liam O'Flaherty claimed to have been so taken with Ó Cadhain's debut collection, *Idir Shúgradh agus Dáiríre* (Half-Serious, Half-Joking; 1939), that he returned to Ireland from America specifically to meet the author, that book gives little indication of Ó Cadhain's potential as a writer of substance.[2] Given that he was already a committed left-wing republican and political subversive at the time these stories were being prepared for publication, their blandness is surprising. Having been dismissed from his post as a primary school teacher at Carn Mór in east Galway in 1936, Ó Cadhain moved to Dublin where he was appointed Commanding Officer of the Dublin Brigade of the IRA and eventually elected to the Army Council in 1938. His decision to join the IRA before he had ever

---

1. Two novels were published posthumously, *Athnuachan* (1995) and *Barbed Wire* (2002).

2. Costigan and Ó Curraoin 1987: 69.

heard of Karl Marx or James Connolly, he says, was a response to
the hardship and hunger he witnessed in his early years in Conamara.[3] Ó Cadhain was arrested in September 1939 and detained
without trial at Arbour Hill Prison until December that year. He was
rearrested in April 1940 at the funeral of his friend Tony Darcy, who
had died on hunger strike protesting the lack of political status for
republican prisoners, and interned from 20 April 1940 until 26 July
1944 at Tintown, the Curragh military prison.[4]

During his time in 'Sibéir na hÉireann' (Ireland's Siberia),
Ó Cadhain read voraciously, taught classes in Irish language and literature, and developed a style of writing that is radically different
from his first collection of stories. In keeping with his conviction that
psychology is the litmus test of modern fiction, he argued that his
period of internment deepened his understanding of the human condition: 'Fuair mé an oiread eolais ar an duine is dá mbeinn céad bliain
ar an saol' (I learned as much about humankind as I would if I lived
to be a hundred).[5] He also credited the work of Maxim Gorky (1868–
1936) as a precipitating influence in his development as a writer:

> Lá amháin fuair mé seanchóip d'irisleabhar Fraincise ar phínn
> sílim i siopa leabhar i sráid Aungier i mBaile Átha Cliath, rud a
> bhí in a oscailt súl domsa cho mór is a tharla don Naomh Pól ar
> bhóthar Damascus! Casadh aistriú Fraincise liom inti ar scéal
> le Maxim Gorky: lá buana imeasc Casacaí an Don. Gheit mé
> suas den leaba a raibh mé sínte uirthi dhá léamh. Níor léigh
> mé a leithéid roimhe sin. Tuige nár inis duine ar bith dhom go
> raibh scéalta mar seo ann? 'Bheinnse i n-ann é sin a scríobh,' arsa
> mise liom féin. 'Sin obair a níos mo mhuintir-sa ach gur malairt
> ainmneacha atá orthu.' Tháinig mar bheadh cineál ocrais orm,

---

3. Ó Cathasaigh 2008: 18.
4. Costigan and Ó Curraoin, 48–50.
5. Ó Cadhain 1969: 26.

ocras ba do-fhuilingithe go mór ná an cineál a bhíodh i mo bholg scaití. Thosaigh Cois Fharraige ó bhreaclach go carraig mhaol, go caoláire, go sruthán, go loch, go sliabh, go haghaidh fir, mná agus linbh, dhá cruthú féin thiar ar chúla m'fhoraí dúinte. Bhí an t-irisleabhar sin i mo phóca agus ba bheag eile a bhí ann an lá ar gabhadh mé.

One day I found an old copy of a French magazine, for a penny, I think, in a bookshop in Aungier Street in Dublin, and it was as much of an eye-opener for me as happened to Saint Paul on the road to Damascus! In it I came across a French translation of a story by Maxim Gorky: a harvest day among the Cossacks of the Don. I sat up straight in the bed where I had been lying down reading it. I had never read anything like it before. Why had no one told me such stories existed? 'I could write that,' I said to myself. 'That's the kind of work my people do, only they have different words for it.' A kind of hunger came over me, a more unbearable hunger than the kind I sometimes felt in my stomach. Cois Fharraige, with its stony ground and bare rock, its inlets, streams, lakes, and mountains, the faces of its men, women, and children, began to take shape behind my shut eyes. There was little else besides that magazine in my pocket the day I was arrested.[6]

By revealing the economic inequalities that distort the lives of individuals and communities, Gorky's 'revolutionary romanticism' provided a justification for political action. While many critics have made a careful distinction between Ó Cadhain's creative writing and his polemical work, his fictional portrayal of rural life distorted by economic inequality and an urban world dehumanised by bureaucracy is in keeping with the indictment of official Ireland in his political writings.

The dramatic change accomplished by Ó Cadhain during his in-

---

6. Ó Cadhain 1969: 26.

carceration, from a linguistically gifted apprentice to a writer whose work is characterised by deep empathy and insight into the emotional lives of women in traditional rural communities, is evident in *An Braon Broghach* (The Cloudy Drop; 1948). The outstanding stories in this second collection reveal the psychological distress and resilience of women in Gaeltacht communities as they struggle with economic hardship and emotional frustration: the dislocation experienced by a Conamara woman following an arranged marriage in 'An Bhearna Mhíl' (The Harelip); the rupture of a relationship between mother and daughter through emigration in 'An Bhliain 1912' (The Year 1912); the collision between romantic love and the economic pressures on a newly married couple in 'An Taoille Tuile' (Floodtide); hunger and the suicide of a husband in 'Ag Dul ar Aghaidh' (Pushing On); the physical toll of the road to and from the weekly market on a pregnant married woman in 'An Bóthar go dtí an Ghealchathair' (Journey to a Bright City).

Ó Cadhain's particular brand of psychological realism is further developed in the 1953 collection *Cois Caoláire* (Beside the Bay). 'Ciumhais an Chriathraigh' (The Edge of the Bog) reveals the loneliness of a woman in her late thirties whose repressed sexuality has been awakened by a fleeting encounter with a drunken soldier at her friend's wedding. 'An Strainséara' (The Stranger) tracks the physical and nervous collapse of a childless woman under the emotional strain brought about by the arrival of her nephew to help her aging husband with the farmwork. Ó Cadhain's trademark ability with dialogue is to the fore in 'Fios' (Knowing) and 'Clapsholas Fómhair' (Autumn Twilight), where skewed relationships are animated by spite and mutual suspicion, the inevitable downside of life in a close-knit community where people live in claustrophobic proximity. In a rare moment of agreement with his critics, Ó Cadhain acknowledged the facility with dialogue as his greatest inheritance from the oral culture of his own community: 'An uirnís liteartha is fearr a fuair mé ó mo mhuintir an chaint, caint thíriúil, caint chréúil, caint chraicneach a thosaíos ag damhsa orm scaití, ag gol orm scaití, de mo bhuíochas' (The best literary device I got from my people was their talk, rough, earthy, salty speech that starts dancing on me sometimes, crying on me other times, whether I like it or not).[7] Virtuosity with dialogue is central to Ó Cadhain's most celebrated work, *Cré na Cille*, a tour de force that contravenes the conventions of the traditional novel. The characters are literally all talk, a collection of corpses in a graveyard eager to interrogate each newly interred body for news of the world above ground. Their exchanges are dominated by envy, spite, vanity, mutual suspicion, begrudgery, and endless malice. Taken together, *An Braon Broghach*, *Cré na Cille*, and *Cois Caoláire* provide a scathing critique of the economic injustice inflicted on Gaeltacht communities at a time when those communities continued to provide a rhetorical ideal for Ireland's self-fashioning in the aftermath of revolution.

There is a fifteen-year hiatus between the publication of *Cois Caoláire* in 1953 and *An tSraith ar Lár* (The Mown Swath) in 1967, during which Ó Cadhain's writing saw a radical change. Although he continued to explore aspects of rural community life, the outstanding stories in *An tSraith ar Lár* and *An tSraith Dhá Tógáil* (Binding the Swath; 1970) focus on the predicament of urbanised men asphyxiated by bureaucracy. In a 1952 radio lecture, Ó Cadhain anticipated the dramatic shift in subject matter, explaining it as a matter of writerly responsibility:

> Is faide an t-achar i mBaile Átha Cliath anois mé ná bhí mé i mo cheantar dúchais ariamh. B'éigean dom eolas an-bharrainneach a chur ar an gcathair, eolas níos barrainní ná tá ag go leor d'fhíormhuintir na cathaireach féin uirthi, le linn dom a bheith i mo chomhalta feidhmiúil in Óglaigh na hÉireann. Is mó de mo dhlúthmhuintir i mBaile Átha Cliath ná sa mbaile. Tá go leor

---

de mo chomharsanaí agus as mo thaobh tíre in a gcónaí gar go
leor dhom. Is cineál ghetto muid b'fhéidir. B'as an nghetto Kafka
agus Heine gan ach beirt a bhfuil eolas agam ar a saothar a lua.
Cho fada agus is léar dom is ghettos ar fad é Baile Átha Cliath
[. . .] measaim freisin nach cóir do mo leithéidse arb i mBaile
Átha Cliath atá formhór mo shaoil caite agam, Baile Átha Cliath
a fhágáil in a pháipéar bán.

I have been longer in Dublin now than I ever was in my native
place. While I was an active member of the IRA, I had to ac-
quire detailed knowledge of the city, more detailed knowledge
than many people have who were born and bred there. More of
my immediate family live in Dublin than in Conamara. Many
of my neighbours and others from my part of the country live
quite close to me. Maybe we are a kind of ghetto. Both Kafka and
Heine were from the ghetto, to mention only two writers whose
work is familiar to me. As far as I can see, Dublin is completely
made up of ghettos . . . I also think that someone like myself who
has spent most of his life in Dublin should not leave Dublin a
blank page.[8]

While there is an obvious parallel between Kafka's work and
Ó Cadhain's later urban stories, he himself identified a less remote
source of inspiration:

Níl uair dá siúilim i gcuid de na sráideanna nach bhfaighim boladh reoite na súmaireacht fhola seo—fuil Bhaile Átha Cliath
agus na tuaithe araon—as na scórtha oifigí, idir chinn rialtais
agus eile, i mo thimpeall. An té a bhfuil eolas aige ar an domhan
sin—agus tá roinnt agam féin—is doiligh dó a ligean ina ghoire
scaití gur den phlainéad seo ar chor ar bith é. Níl d'fháth aige
bheith ann, shílfeá, ach le dúil ar a dtugann an gnáthdhuine

---

8. Ó Cadhain 1969: 22–23.

páipéar a adhradh. Gheobhaidh tú boladh an phárlathais naofa seo i ngach bus ar a deich ar maidin agus i ngach scuaidrín ag an cúig tráthnóna.

Every time I walk in certain streets I get the frozen smell of this bloodsucking—Dublin blood and country blood—from scores of offices, government offices and others, all around me. Anyone who knows this world—and I know a little of it myself—finds it difficult to admit that it is part of this planet at all. You imagine it only exists for the worship of what an ordinary person calls paper. You'll get the smell of this holy paperocracy in every bus at ten in the morning and in every queue at five in the evening.[9]

And yet, he said: '[D]'ainneoinn gach ní tá giobail den daonnacht ar sliobarna as nach bhféadann an párlathas féin iad a mhúnlú. Mar sin is scéal é is fiú a inseacht' (In spite of everything, there are flitters of humanity clinging to their story that even the paperocracy cannot shape. For that reason, it's a story worth telling).[10]

Ó Cadhain had direct experience of the psychological and spiritual suffocation endured by his characters. Following his release from prison in July 1944, he worked at a variety of labouring jobs, stockpiling turf with other ex-prisoners in Phoenix Park during a fuel shortage and serving his time on building sites in Dublin and in England. He continued to collect words from the Conamara dialect for a new dictionary of Irish and began work as a part-time translator for the Government Publication Office, An Gúm, a form of intellectual labour he found inimical to creative writing. He also taught at the Institute of Technology in Parnell Square and the National College of Art before he was finally appointed as a junior translator in Rannóg an Aistriúcháin, the government translation office—'istigh i gcraos an

---

9. Ó Cadhain 1978: 80.
10. Ó Cadhain 1978: 80.

bheithígh féin' (in the belly of the beast itself) — in March 1947.[11] He
continued to work in Rannóg an Aistriúcháin until he was appointed
lecturer in Irish at Trinity College Dublin in 1956. In 1967 he became
Associate Professor, and he was appointed Established Professor of
Irish in 1969, a year before his death in 1970. 'His final apotheosis as
professor of Irish in the oldest and most revered of the British colonial
universities he accepted,' Seán Ó Tuama says, 'with great humility
and the wryest good humour.'[12]

It might be argued that the thematic shift in Ó Cadhain's later
work is less dramatic than it first appears, that he has simply transferred his imaginative sympathies from the rural women who in-
habit his early stories to the male urban characters of the later work.
There is, however, a satiric edge to the urban stories that mitigates
the reader's sympathy with characters whose impotence is as much a
function of their own inherent weakness as it is of the dehumanising
environment in which they live and work. The two most impressive
stories in *An tSraith Dhá Tógáil* indicate the extent of that change.
Tomás, the central character in 'Fuascailt' (Release), is obsessed with
the thought that his failure to go to the rescue of a swimmer in difficulty has left him sexually inadequate, unworthy of his wife Bríd.
'Fuíoll Fuine' (The Dregs of the Day) chronicles the failure of N. to
make the necessary arrangements for his wife's funeral as he wanders
from one meaningless encounter to another around the streets of
Dublin, endlessly deferring the moment when he has to face up to
his responsibilities and go home. His meandering through the city in
a kind of existential daze leads eventually to a drunken spree with a
foreign sailor who, he imagines, will take him to the end of the earth.

In his 1952 radio lectures Ó Cadhain argued that a radical change
in technique would be required by his new material: 'Is gá cumas ar
leith chuige agus teicníc úr, b'fhéidir, nár féachadh sa nGaeilge go

---

11. Ó Cathasaigh 2002: 108–14.
12. Ó Tuama 1995: 215.

fóill' (It requires particular skill and a new technique, perhaps, that has not been attempted previously in Irish).[13] One of his sternest critics, Seán Ó Tuama, explained the challenge as follows:

> There are almost insuperable literary difficulties in dealing with modern urban life in a language which is not a current urban community language. Ó Cadhain certainly showed that most parts of this life could readily be *translated* into Irish. But in such translation one experiences only the denotative sense of language, rather than the connotative, so that it is quite dubious if Ó Cadhain ever manages to create verbally the mood of the city and its people for his readers.[14]

The poet Seán Ó Ríordáin, on the other hand, insisted that Ó Cadhain had grafted the Anglophone world of his later fiction onto the patterns of Irish, leaving no trace of a linguistic scar on this new literary dialect:

> Bhíodh sé chomh mall, útamálach ag rá nithe ar uaire—go háirithe nuair is ag aistriú saoil ó Ghaeilge go Béarla a bhíodh sé—go dtuigfí duit go bhfeicfeá é ag cumadh, go bhfeicfeá na focail Bhéarla ag fágaint a gcathaoireacha agus ag géilleadh slí (saoil) do na focail Ghaeilge. Ach d'fhan a chuid Gaeilge neambéarlaithe cé nach raibh d'eiseamláir aici ach eiseamláir an Bhéarla chun go sealbhódh sí chuici féin liomatáistí a bhí go dtí sin i seilbh an Bhéarla amháin in Éirinn.

> He was so slow and awkward saying things at times—especially when he was translating a world from Irish to English—that you imagined you could see him composing, that you could see the English words leaving their chairs and giving way (world) to the Irish words. But his Irish remained unanglicised even though

---

13. Ó Cadhain 1978: 80.
14. Ó Tuama 1995: 217.

English was the only exemplar it had in order to appropriate areas that until then had been the exclusive possession of English in Ireland.[15]

While Ó Tuama's argument is difficult to contradict in its general application, the extent to which Ó Cadhain's synthetic Irish represents the speech and thought patterns of his urban characters is one of his more impressive achievements. A number of factors contribute to the success of this urban literary dialect. Since the establishment of the Free State in 1922, Irish speakers, including Ó Cadhain and his colleagues in Rannóg an Aistriúcháin, had been adapting the language to the demands of their bureaucratic work environment. That the central characters of 'An Eochair' (The Key) and 'Fuíoll Fuine' (The Dregs of the Day) are clerical workers lends a degree of verisimilitude to the mix of rural idioms and office-speak that characterises the artificial, but nonetheless plausible, dialect they speak and think. Equally, the move to a more nonrealistic style of writing in stories such as 'Cé Acu?' (Which One?), 'Ag Déanamh Marmair' (Marbling), and 'Ag Déanamh Páipéir' (Becoming Paper) reduced the need for the kind of linguistic realism that is a feature of his early style.

This selection of Ó Cadhain's work includes alternative versions of five stories from *An Braon Broghach* (1948) previously translated by Eoghan Ó Tuairisc and published in *The Road to Brightcity* (1981): 'An Taoille Tuile,' 'An Bóthar go dtí an Ghealchathair,' 'An Bhliain 1912,' 'An Bhearna Mhíl,' and 'Ag Dul ar Aghaidh.' Ó Tuairisc's pioneering work remains a landmark publication, a watershed in the history of translation from Irish to English. It has its own integrity of style and its own particular register of English, the response of an unusually dexterous bilingual writer to a fellow citizen in the republic of words. Ó Tuairisc's engagement with Ó Cadhain is an extension

---

15. Ó Ríordáin 1978: 115.

of his own determination to confront the legacy of a fractured tradition, the traumatic aftermath of the nineteenth-century language shift that set Anglophone Ireland adrift from Irish. His introduction to *The Road to Brightcity* draws attention to the particularity of the Irish language, its oral and literary traditions, its linguistic and cultural history. Irish, he says, is 'subtle, sinewy, unobtrusive, modern in every sense,' inclined towards 'verbal extravaganza' while maintaining 'its unique mixture of the muck-and-tangle of earth existence with a cosmic view and a sense of "otherworld".' The lived history of the language, he says, has left its mark on the inherited patterns of Irish and on a particular attitude evident in Ó Cadhain's work: 'some dark, disjointed, manic intuition of reality. [. . .] It is like being confronted with a Rouault Christ where one had expected to see a Jack B. Yeats Blackbird Bathing in Tír-na-nÓg.' He compares Ó Cadhain to Joyce:

> Both men were realists with mythic minds, they were intoxicated with words, both had a sense of life at once comic and compassionate and saw mankind as forever in exile blundering about in worlds half-realised. I'm not sure whether in fact Ó Cadhain won't yet be seen to be *il miglior fabbro*, having learned in the last resort to keep his myth to himself.[16]

While the final judgment may be a little contentious, it is a generous tribute from a writer whose own work is characterised by a high degree of formal and linguistic experiment. The new versions offered here of stories included in *The Road to Brightcity* might be taken as a tribute to both Ó Tuairisc and Ó Cadhain from another generation of translators.

Máirtín Ó Cadhain's work is uneven, marked by a number of radical shifts in subject matter and style as he seeks to articulate his own insights into the repression and resilience of women in tradi-

---

16. Ó Tuairisc 1981: 10–12.

tional rural communities and the diminished lives of bureaucratised urban men. The unevenness is a measure of his ambition as much as it is of his limitations and, indeed, of the vicissitudes of a life committed to revolution.

The longer stories, and indeed the novel *Cré na Cille*, are the result of a persistent struggle to reconcile the formative influence of the oral traditions of the Conamara Gaeltacht and the acquired forms of the novel and the short story with the needs of his own imagination.[17] The best of the early stories reveal the complexity of Ó Cadhain's understanding of women, whose life choices are determined by the brutal realities of a world in which the inescapable laws of custom and tradition place the survival of family and community in a subsistence economy above the individual's need for self-realisation. In Ó Cadhain's Cois Fharraige, the heroic triumph over adversity so central to Ireland's self-representation is replaced by a sense that endurance is the last refuge of the disenfranchised, less a moral virtue than an economic necessity. As the focus shifts to a Gaeltacht community in transition, infiltrated by modernity and Anglicisation, the preoccupation with fertility and reproduction becomes central to Ó Cadhain's representation of a world in which women adapt to changing circumstances while men appear paralysed by uncertainty and insecurity. The predicament of an unmarried woman on the brink of middle age ('Ciumhais an Chriathraigh') and an older woman whose stillborn children are buried, unblessed and unnamed, in unmarked graves ('An Strainséara') are treated with deep tenderness as Ó Cadhain exposes the economic as well as the emotional and psychological consequences of childlessness in a peasant society. In contrast to the treatment of frustrated female desire and infertility, there is a more jagged edge to the representation of a man persuaded to marry for economic advantage who finds himself locked in a childless marriage to a woman who rejects his sexual advances. The tone

---

17. Ó Tuama 2008: 81.

of the narrative in 'Beirt Eile' (Another Couple) is ironic, distancing the reader from any sense that the male protagonist is worthy of sympathy. In the urban stories, male characters continue to be preoccupied by a failure of agency, a fundamental anxiety that leads to both social and sexual dysfunction. At the heart of Ó Cadhain's vision of the 'bloodsucking paperocracy,' there is a sense that the dehumanising impact of modern bureaucracies has led to a compromised masculinity incapable of responding to a crisis in self-definition. While women are more peripheral in these stories, they are less confused in their reactions to a bureaucratised world than their male counterparts. The move to more surreal and fantastic narrative modes, and from the relative stability of the third person to the uncertainties of the first-person narrator, correspond to a transition from revolutionary optimism in Ó Cadhain's earlier political writings to an 'increasingly bitter polemic in the early 1960s' in which 'the virtuosity of the prose is exceeded only by its vitriol.'[18]

Seán Ó Tuama has argued that 'Ó Cadhain wrote the most consciously-patterned and richly-textured prose that any Irishman has written in this century, except Beckett and Joyce.'[19] The poet Seán Ó Ríordáin put it more bluntly than that: 'Ar deireadh shílfeá gur leat féin Éire agus nár le Bord Fáilte' (In the end you felt that Ireland belonged to you and not to the Tourist Board).[20] A half-century after Ó Cadhain's death in 1970, his international reputation continues to grow. As his work in translation reaches new audiences in other languages, the response of readers and critics confirms his stature as a writer whose significance is not limited by either the language in which he wrote or his country of origin. If the tyranny of rural poverty and the transition to a bureaucratised urban modernity in mid-twentieth-century Ireland provided the immediate context for his

---

18. Mac an Iomaire 2017: xiv–xv.
19. Ó Tuama 1995: 213.
20. Ó Ríordáin 1978: 115.

work, Ó Cadhain's representation of a beleaguered but undefeated feminine and of masculinity in crisis makes its own contribution to European and world literature. In a world still dominated by the inequality and injustice he struggled against in his life and his writing, his voice demands to be heard from beyond the graveyard clay.

LOUIS DE PAOR

WORKS CITED

Costigan, An tSiúr Bosco, and Seán Ó Curraoin. 1987. *De Ghlaschloich an Oileáin: Beatha agus Saothar Mháirtín Uí Chadhain*. Conamara: Cló Iar-Chonnacht.

Mac an Iomaire, Liam. 2017. Introduction to Máirtín Ó Cadhain, *Graveyard Clay/ Cré na Cille*, translated by Liam Mac an Iomaire and Tim Robinson, vii–xxxiii. New Haven and London: Yale University Press.

Ó Cadhain, Máirtín. 1969. *Páipéir Bhána agus Páipéir Bhreaca*. Baile Átha Cliath: An Clóchomhar Tta a d'fhoilsigh do Chumann Merriman.

Ó Cadhain, Máirtín. 1978. 'Saothar an scríbhneora.' In Seán Ó Mórdha, ed., *Scríobh* 3: 73–82. Baile Átha Cliath: An Clóchomhar Tta.

Ó Cathasaigh, Aindrias. 2002. *Ag Samhlú Troda: Máirtín Ó Cadhain 1905-1970*. Baile Átha Cliath: Coiscéim.

Ó Cathasaigh, Aindrias. 2008. 'A Vision to Realise: Ó Cadhain's Politics.' *Canadian Journal of Irish Studies* 34, no. 1: 18–27.

Ó Ríordáin, Seán. 1978. 'Útamáil Uí Chadhain.' In Seán Ó Mórdha, ed., *Scríobh* 3: 115–16. Baile Átha Cliath: An Clóchomhar Tta.

Ó Tuairisc, Eoghan. 1981. Introduction to Máirtín Ó Cadhain, *The Road to Brightcity and Other Stories*, 7–12. Dublin: Poolbeg Press.

Ó Tuama, Seán. 1995. 'A Writer's Testament.' In *Repossessions: Selected Essays on the Irish Literary Heritage*, 212–18. Cork: Cork University Press.

The Quick
and the Dead

FROM *AN BRAON BROGHACH*
(1948)

Bríd was woken by the sound of the cock crowing. She yawned and turned over. She stretched, then settled her head back into the pillow. But her husband was awake too. He nudged her. 'That's three times the cock's after crowing,' he said. 'You'd better get up.'

It was hard to peel off the cosy covers, but after stretching a few more times and wiping the sleep from her eyes, she sprang out of bed. She had her new frock on, the candle lit, and was raking the ashes from the banked-up fire when her husband appeared behind her on the hearth.

'It was good of you to get up,' she said. 'You're time enough.'

He made no reply but went to fumble at the dresser.

'How could I have got it so wrong?' he said, picking up the clock and putting it to his ear with a shake. 'I was obsessed with winding it, and then what did I do but go to bed and forget to do it. It stopped at ten past two.'

'A rattling curse on that rattling thing! It's four o'clock now.'

'If it's not later.'

'I'll have to be off the minute I've smartened myself up.'

'You'd be time enough leaving at five and allowing yourself four hours. I'll slip over to Tomás's, and if Taimín isn't up yet I'll wake him. He'll be good company for you seeing as Peige Shéamais isn't heading to the Bright City, nor any of the other women from around here.'

'There isn't a hope in hell that Taimín will shake a leg for another hour or two, seeing as he has a customer for the turf. I'll get a lift home with him unless . . . '

'Unless you get a better offer.'

'What I was about to say was,' said Bríd in a tone as quarrelsome as her husband's, 'unless I find that I'm ready for home before then and some other cart offers me a lift.'

'A cart from the Currach. You think that crowd are bathed in honey.'

'Well, I still know them a lot better than I know anyone around here,' Bríd said mildly.

'I haven't lived here five years yet.'

Her husband was sorry then for picking on her like that.

'It's a hard journey to the Bright City for the little you get out of it.'

'I'm just worried that I won't be getting much out of it at all in future. Three of the hens stopped laying this week, after all my molly-coddling, and what the yellow cow gives will barely do the tea. I'm afraid I won't have enough to churn again for a week. Even a fortnight from now I'll be hard-pressed to come up with anything I can sell.'

'You could do with a break,' her husband said carefully, as if wary of where it might lead if he overdid the sympathy. 'You're worn out, going to the Bright City Saturday after Saturday. It's an awful trudge, unless you're like Máire Sheáinín and can take a jaunting car.'

'It is a trudge, I suppose, but I don't let it get me down,' she said carelessly. Her husband sympathized, but still he didn't like to hear her talk like that. A young strong woman, barely thirty years old! You'd never hear the older generation of women saying things like that. It would have been nothing to his own mother to go into the city twice a day with a tankard of milk when she worked as a serving girl for Liam Chathail, and there was never a chance of a lift home for her. Or his grandmother, who'd bring a hundredweight of meal on her back from the Bright City before milking time, only stopping twice along the way for a rest. Women today had only to bring up some water from the well and they were doubled over with pains the next day.

'I'll be all right if the woman from Bóithrín an Léana keeps out of my way,' she said, continuing her own train of thought and taking no notice of him or his sudden silence. 'Only for that I wouldn't be half as rushed—trying to get a head start on everyone else. She'll hold me up from getting to the market and I won't get home till all hours.'

'Don't be rushing home until you have everything done. I'll look after the house.'

'Like you did last Saturday—the children nearly burned to a crisp from the kettle left on the fire, only for Neil Shéamais happened to be passing? Don't you stir out of this house today till Neil gets here or I'll have your guts for garters. She said she'd be here around ten and that she won't be in any hurry home until after dinner. I'll have to buy her a bit of a present at Christmas if God throws a few pennies my way. You have sticks to sharpen for thatching, don't you? Just concentrate on that. Don't leave a pot anyplace precarious. And if Citín starts crying, give her a drop of warm milk in the bottle.'

'Right,' the man said brusquely.

'And leave the dash down with Neil in Peadar's place. Don't forget now. She'll be churning today. And move the calf from Garraí Gleannach up to Barr Thuas. But, upon all you hold dear, don't leave the house, even if the field starts sprouting gold, unless there's someone here to mind the children.'

'I won't,' the man said, irritation simmering in his voice.

'I'd better look lively,' she said, knocking back the dregs of her tea.

'Make sure you bring something with you to eat.'

'I won't need anything, if the woman from Bóithrín an Léana gets hold of me. She took me into her kitchen this day last week and insisted on giving me a cup of tea. It was great tea. A lovely golden colour. She's a kind woman, not always trying to lord it over you like the rest of them. Her husband's a peeler—a sergeant at that. She's from Longford.'

'I left a creel of turf at a peeler's house along that road one time before I sold the horse. She tried to ply me with tea but I wouldn't take any. I didn't have enough English to be making conversation.'

'Was she pale in the face and not very tall?'

'Sure how would I remember that? It was nearly four years ago.'

The man swallowed the rest of his tea and went outside.

'The moon will be up for another hour yet,' he said when he came back in. 'I can tell from the stars that it's not a second past four. The sky looks cloudy, but still I think it'll be a lovely morning. There's not a light anywhere. There must be no one at all heading for the Bright City.'

'Only the ones with turf. Everything else is used up. Remember, it's outside the laying season.'

'I'll leave you up to the top of the road, or as far as Taimín Thomáis's house and I can wake him up.'

'There you go again, itching to get out. Talking about leaving the house and—God forbid—but who knows what might happen to the children.'

'They're sound asleep. I won't be gone two seconds.'

'Go on back in and get a few more hours' sleep. I'll be right as rain.'

She went into the back room. The two children were tucked up in their little bed, snoring softly. The mother was careful not to disturb them as she sprinkled a drop of holy water around the bed and made the sign of the cross on herself with it.

She lifted the strap of the butter-creel that she had got ready the night before and slung it around her neck. The man settled her shawl over the top of the creel and she stepped outside.

A rough, rubbly path led up to the road through the village. Water oozed under her feet and her left foot felt damp inside its shoe long before she reached the firmer ground where carts could travel. Bríd was amazed that there were no lights in the village houses. She had thought that, with the strong southerly breeze, people would be up and about 'catching' the red kelp from the shore. Máire Sheáinín's house was in darkness too, but she'd be in plenty of time getting up in another few hours, since she could afford a jaunt.

No matter how many times Bríd travelled this road, in the predawn hours, on the same errand, the eeriness of the sleeping village always struck her anew. At least the feeling wasn't as strong as when the scattering of houses lay in complete darkness. Tonight, shafts of moonlight defined houses and sheds, and sent scrawls of scary shadow trailing from the gables. Bright rays of moonlight streamed down on grainy granite scree, lending it a cold, gaudy sparkle, like the eye of a snake going to ground. The clear pure light of the moon as it gradually leached away was like the final glamour of the fairy folk as they faded to nothingness at cockcrow.

For now the barking of Tomás's dog was the only living sound in a village that would be alive with bustle and noise in three or four hours' time. The dog's bark seemed like the voice of Nature itself, warning in some obscure language that the master and his mistress, night, were sunk in sleep still, and were not to be wakened. In the lull of the wind the dog's protestations reverberated from houses and small fields. The sounds bounced across stretches of stony ground, scaling the heathery, rocky heights above the village. Echoes fluttered slowly from cliff to cliff, were stretched thin across hard places, and dwindled, finally, to a peevish whimper on some desolate, distant bogland.

A vein of shadow ran from Tomás's carthouse across the track. A quick glance sideways showed the cart propped on two forked sticks, but there wasn't a breath of smoke from the house yet. The memory of her husband's annoyance at her refusal to wait for Taimín Thomáis was still fresh in her mind. As well as being a neighbour, Taimín was her husband's first cousin once removed. She couldn't convince her husband, not if she wore her tongue out trying, that it wasn't snobbishness that made her avoid Taimín and jump at the chance of a lift with a cart from Currach — her own townland — five miles west of this parish, Saturday after Saturday. Then again, maybe it was snobbishness of a different kind.

Although she'd been married five years now, she found the people of the area a bit odd. She didn't understand them. Maybe she never would. Maybe she wasn't cut out to understand people. But whatever the reason, she had no wish to spend any time with Taimín Thomáis. He had been at her matchmaking. She remembered clearly the gleam in his eyes as he grabbed her hand when he drank her health. From that day on she couldn't bear him to lay eyes on her. She felt his gaze held hidden layers. A veil of ash, and behind it a fire of anger, greed, and venality. She could never hold a conversation with Taimín Thomáis without feeling that glowering fire scorching her. She didn't really understand it. All she knew was that when he looked at her, she felt as if his eyes were burning her skin.

Before turning from the village road out onto the main road, she stood for a while and listened. No sound of cartwheels or footsteps. It must be earlier than she thought. Otherwise somebody somewhere would be stirring. Still, she'd better be moving along. The Bright City was all of nine Irish miles away and it would be better to get there in good time.

The moon was sinking west over the islands, its streaky glow meeting a million silvery drops across the surface of the bay, to conjure a bridge, perhaps, for the fairy host to cross to Beag-Árainn. But despite the moon's merry dazzle, she looked for all the world as if she were weeping up there in the lonely sky, and her showy jewellery only served to emphasise the depth of her sadness. Bríd couldn't wait for the moon to set. She preferred a cloak of darkness. She felt freer in the dark. The danger that a person might lose her grip on her own eternal being and melt into the transient, material world all around her seemed greater by moonlight than by day.

Bríd liked the dark. It allowed her mind to flow outwards to the world, instead of having light and shape impinge on her thoughts, reminding her of the world's harshness. She seldom had a chance to think; she was always so busy grappling with the demands of family and others. And although she resented the journey, if she had to make it, she would rather do it at her own pace than have to adapt to someone else's. She couldn't bring herself to talk about it with her husband, but since she had given birth to that last stillborn child, she wasn't anything like as strong as she had been, and lately the long walk had been wearing her down. And if she was on her own when she got nearer to the Bright City, it was ten to one that she would get a lift from someone she knew, and that would save her two or three of the hardest miles of the journey.

She told herself that if she was anywhere near Coill na Maoile before the jaunts started passing, she'd have a good chance of getting a lift the rest of the way, since the jaunt drivers would be getting too close to the city to be on the lookout for another fare. But it was unlikely a jaunt would take two, and if he chose one out of two—which wasn't all that likely—she probably wouldn't be chosen. And if it happened that someone she was walking with got a lift, she was afraid she would be more disappointed, having come so close to getting a lift herself. Lately, the exhaustion seemed to hit her just when she was within a mile or two of her destination.

Wasn't it well for the women with enough spare cash to spend a few shillings on a jaunt. There was Máire Sheáinín, jaunting up and down the road any old Saturday she pleased. But there was no point in Bríd comparing herself to her. Máire Sheáinín had been raking in money since the war began and, furthermore, was getting fistfuls of it, night and day, from America. Bríd had done her damnedest to save every ha'penny she had from last Saturday, to make a shilling for a jaunt halfway today. But during the week the shilling followed all the other shillings—into the till at the shop.

Still, unless she was clean out of luck, she'd be sure to get a lift for the last bit of the journey. Máirtín Mór, her own neighbour, would pick her up. He only ever had the same three. Didn't he pick her up the Saturday of Hallowe'en? Or Seán Choilm. Though if he had four, he wouldn't be inclined to squeeze another one in. He was always grumbling that he didn't want to overload the horse. But there was no way that Peaid Neachtain would go by her on the road. He always called in to play cards once the visiting began. Cóil Liam was the best on the road for giving lifts. She hadn't a hope with Mike from the shop. It was hard enough to get credit from him, never mind looking for a lift as well. Right enough, he would usually only have himself and his brother's wife, and whoever else he picked up along the way. He took only those who would pay well or someone that he was hoping to entice away from some other shop to his own. And Micil Pheige always passed her by. He used to be very good about giving lifts. There was none better. But something had got hold of him lately. He was mad into some crowd he called the Sinn Féiners, and anyone that wasn't a Sinn Féiner was ruled out for lifts. Bríd often wondered what sort of crowd these Sinn Féiners were. Pádraig Thomáis Thaidhg was in with them and they took him away last year, that time there was some sort of a skirmish in Dublin and the Achréidh area. But 'the Earl' got him out again, even though the Sinn Féiners were agitating against him. The Earl could save a man from the gallows. Rumour had it they used to be drilling at night with hurley sticks and that they were all set to make war on England. They had a meeting in Baile an Draighin a while ago and they ended up at loggerheads with the parish priest there. But poor people didn't get involved in that kind of thing. What would they get out of all that? A poor man just has to struggle on.

Bríd passed through the village. Although there was a light in one or two of the pubs, there wasn't a soul about, apart from two policemen standing with their backs to Geraghty's yard, and not a budge out of them. Maybe they were watching out for turf carts with no lights, although they didn't usually bother with that. Maybe they were keeping an eye on the pubs. What were they talking or thinking about? What would policemen have to be talking or thinking about, since they didn't have to slave on the strand or in the fields or bogs but had a grand old life drawing their salary.

Crossing the Dumhcha she heard the noise of a cart coming up the side road from Baile Dhonncha and she hesitated over whether to wait for it or not. The hill of Ard na Fearta lay ahead. In the moonlight, the stones, flat and tall, stood to attention in the marshy fields on each side of the road, like heroes of old summoned from sleep by the trumpet's blast. If there was any truth in the old tales, the sound of the trumpet meant a great slaughter was underway. But a woman who had to go to the Bright City time and again in the dead of night all by herself when sometimes it was the last thing she wanted to do, such a woman could not afford to dwell on ghost and fairy lore.

Bríd was so used to banishing all thoughts of that story, and so adept by now at suppressing the fear it used to stir in her, that the only concession she made to it was to quicken her pace slightly as she tackled the hill.

In reality, there was nothing to be scared of on that strange stretch of the road, unless you counted Liam the Tailor, with some young lad she didn't know tagging along beside him. Bríd recognised Liam's gravelly voice right away. She had often heard him—as had half the countryside—kicking up a din in the middle of the night after drinking in the village. The second Bríd heard his voice she slowed, then stood still for a while. But now not a sound could be heard, no one driving or walking, not even the cart she had heard a little while ago. She owed the tailor money—the price of the homespun suit he had made for her husband the previous year—and she had made and broken so many promises to pay him that not for love nor money would she choose to walk by him now. But she would have to do it, because they were only idling along and there was about a mile and half to go to their turnoff. She greeted them.

'By the holy,' Liam exclaimed loudly to his fellow traveller, 'when I was your age I wouldn't have missed a chance like this. A lovely young woman . . . '

'Sure my card is marked already,' said Bríd, speaking as lightly as she could. Liam gave that old drinker's guffaw of his. 'You'll never get the better of someone from the Currach,' and began to hold forth on the ready wit of the Currach people. Bríd thought it best to be moving on. She knew she was in no real danger. In a situation like this, a woman was more likely to be robbed than to be assaulted in any other way. But Bríd wasn't in the mood for loitering or chatter, especially since she would be embarrassed if the subject of the money came up again with the tailor. Still, it was hard to put him out of her mind. Just her luck to meet him, of all people, on the road. She wondered if he was regaling the other fellow with the tale of her outstanding debts. But he wasn't that kind of person. He was easy to deal with and seemed able to keep things to himself. But then again, you never knew with a drinker. Well, come what may, she would have to pay him by Christmas. It wasn't as if her few measly shillings would make that much of a difference to him anyway. He earned a good living, except that he spent most of it in the pub, leaving his wife and family at home struggling to get by. It was a funny old life.

Bríd was nice and warm now, having walked more than two miles. She could take her shoes off and carry them over her arm. One shoe was chafing her foot a bit where the water had seeped in earlier. She pushed her shawl back down over the top of the creel, and that freed her up. She was really hitting her stride now. The blood pumped, powerful as organ music, through her veins. She hardly felt the road fly by under her feet. She enjoyed the ease of it. It made her feel equal to life's challenge.

Once she cleared the Leitir side road, there were lights in all the houses that lay scattered sparsely at the sides of the road, and there were turf carts all over the place. Sometimes five or six carts in clusters, with two or three of the drivers strolling in step in front of one of them. An odd one with the driver perched up on the front-board. Lots of women with creels and baskets on the road too. Some of them walked in groups, others travelled in twos. Still more walked in among the turf carts. Bríd had only a passing acquaintance with most of them, and not even that in the case of others, since most of them were from places well to the east of the village and she had grown up five miles to the west of it. She had never had much to do with them either, since, up until today, she would usually have had companions of her own. But it costs nothing to be civil on the road. So Bríd nodded a greeting to each of them but steered clear of lengthy conversation. It wasn't that she wouldn't have welcomed the company, but she was afraid that some of them would get so carried away chatting to a new friend that it would be hard to shake them off. The groups of women usually broke into pairs as the journey wore on and however much she might have enjoyed the group chatter, she didn't want the kind of conversation two people might have. The length of the journey itself deterred Bríd from taking on company. Nine miles was a long trek and gossiping would only sap her energy.

She was also afraid that if she took up with another woman the conversation might take too intimate a turn. Her mind had its dark thoughts and her heart its poisoned arrows. Bríd believed it was best not to grumble about life's trials and hardships. Even the fact that Mike from the shop would quote three different prices for the same article, depending on whether the person was deep in his debt, could make good on credit, or could afford to pay up front, she didn't count that as grist for complaint. She wasn't one to blame mankind for the substantial woes that kept her wrestling with hardship and want, forced her to trudge barefoot to the Bright City every Saturday, and condemned her to so much worry and toil . . . She was sorry that it had to be so, the heavy lot of those in this Vale of Tears. It all stemmed from the fateful bite of the Apple. But she didn't see it as a personal cause for complaint, any more than she would take it personally that she, rather than another, had to suffer bad weather, misfortune, death, or a long walk in the dark. Although Bríd knew the meaning of 'good luck,' 'bad luck,' and 'misfortune,' she wasn't well acquainted with the notion of 'happiness' or 'joy of life.' One thing she did know was that she was far from easy in her mind. If forced to explain, she would have said that life seemed to press upon her continually, blotting out the sun, until sometimes she felt her heart would explode from bitterness . . . Now that she had the two children she could no longer visit her own people, and on the rare occasion when one of them dropped by she never got the chance to have a proper chat because her husband and neighbours would be there, butting in and prying. Bríd often thought she'd give a lot for a woman friend she could really talk to. Still, she didn't believe that the privations of the heart could be cured by baring her soul. Her listeners would only take it as licence to meddle. They'd add to the story instead of hearing it out and accepting it as it was. But it would be a relief to get things off her chest. And she would rather do that with a stranger, someone from a far-flung spot who would pay no more heed to it than they would to the whispers of the wind, than with a local who would only use it as an excuse to tell their own convoluted tale of woe, and then afterwards peddle it as gossip. Today, she didn't find her usual comfort in the thought that there were many walking the road who were suffering just as much as she. Her mind felt so filled with dark thoughts that she was sure if she began to speak she would never be able to stop. Her simmering sorrows were close to boiling over. She was afraid she would start to weep . . .

So far, she'd had no trouble passing people by. But a woman with a basket at the Ionnarba turnoff proved almost impossible to shake off, despite the fact that Bríd didn't even know her to see. As she was only carrying a light basket, she had no trouble keeping up. Bríd stepped up her pace to the point that the woman asked where was her hurry, and she said that she had to be in the Bright City by eight o'clock to bring butter to a customer who wanted it for breakfast. Afterwards she felt bad for not staying with the woman, who had seemed anxious for company, just as she had been herself on other Saturdays . . .

Gleann an Aonaigh. Ard na Cille. Coill na hAille. An Sruthán Geal. They seemed to float towards her with agonising slowness, like oases to a thirsty traveller in the desert. At Bearna na nEach she took a rest. She rested again at Cloch an Choiléir a little farther on. Bríd had never before felt this bone-tired so early on in the journey. She was worried that she had made too much of a sprint at the start and that her will to finish was flagging. Once daylight broke, she would die of shame if she had to take a rest at every turn. She could imagine what they'd all say. A fine figure of a young woman. Only two children so far. When there were women who'd had twelve children making short work of the journey.

She rested again. The strap of the creel was chafing her shoulder a bit because of all the red kelp she had carried during the week. But at least now the moon had set and the thick dark of night's last phase had descended. It would be easier now, since no one would be able to see who she was as she overtook them. Then she had the idea of tucking her skirt up around her thighs. This would free her stride, as sweat was streaming down her legs. It wasn't decent for someone like her — a young mother — to do this, so she was glad of the darkness which would shield her from comment.

But before long she was struggling again, trying to hold off taking a rest until she'd got over the next rise in the road. When she caught herself guessing how many footsteps to the next rise after that, she thought she was going mad altogether. Every rise and tilt and twist and turn in the road required of her the defiant courage a child needs to face a harsh father. Every step was on a par with the great feats in the old stories: the feat of Watcher's Ford, the stout-heartedness of the boys of Ventry, Goll's ordeal on the rock, the heartbreak of Deirdre of the Sorrows. For Bríd, and for many another Bríd like her, every mile was a Via Dolorosa, every step a Gethsemane, every stone an Apple from the Tree of Knowledge, to be paid for in blood, sweat, tears, and humility.

At last, she took a rest at Droichidín na Saor. This was the halfway mark. She still had over four Irish miles to go. She wondered how long she'd been walking. Bad luck to that trickster of a clock. How long until dawn? Already the morning star was rising in the east, rosy tinges yielding to grey, and one or two early birds were up.

She had never been so worn out at the halfway point before. Her body burned from the fast pace. She stumbled and stalled. When she stopped to rest, cold shivers ran through her hot, sweaty body. Her legs above the knees were trembling. Cramps had set in, low in her womb. She knew well what was causing the pain. Lately she'd been finding heavy weights hard to carry.

She set off again at an aggressive pace. She was so glad of the darkness. It was a sanctuary. If she felt faint she would have to throw herself into the ditch along the grassy edge of the road where she wouldn't be found until it was day. She remembered only too well that Neile Mháirtín was found dead like that in the ditch at Bun an Tortáin. At the inquest they said she'd already been dead for two hours when she was found. The doctors said she had died of hunger. It had been lashing rain and the morning was black as pitch, and the ditch where she'd met her death had cradled her snugly. Still, it was strange that not a soul out of the many who had passed by that place noticed her body. She left a good few children behind, all close in age.

God forbid, but if the same thing was to happen to her the house at home would be a shambles. What would become of her two children? If her husband couldn't manage to mind them the one day of the week she had to be away from home, what on earth would he be like seven days a week? Eibhlín had nearly scalded herself with boiling water last Saturday, even though he had promised faithfully before she left that he wouldn't go out and start pottering about until little Neile Shéamais arrived to mind them. Would he be as feckless again today? Would he never learn? She wondered if they were awake yet and had they started to cry. They often did in the very early morning. Would he remember to replace the milk that had gone cold in Citín's bottle during the night with a warm drop?

Bríd gained a certain bitter satisfaction from the knowledge that her husband would be useless at minding the family if she were to go. But he'd marry again, of course. The children would have a stepmother. She'd ill-treat them and thrash them if they got up to mischief or were peevish. What else would a stepmother do? It was hard enough for Bríd herself to resist giving them a good slap sometimes. Children were hard going. Bringing them into the world was an ordeal. The two stillborn children she had borne had put paid to her girlish figure and filled her bones with the lethargy of middle age. She hadn't been herself since. Would she have to give birth to another dead baby? God forbid. It would put her in the ground for sure. But the will of God be done. And what if she never had another child . . . Would she and her husband be as close as they are now? Would the clamour of children give way to a seething, cold resentment between them? Would her husband bother to get up on a morning like this to see her off on her journey if there was no need to assure her—even doubtfully, as he did today—that he thought he could manage them while she was gone? You only had to look at Nóra Anna and her husband. They were like the two arms of a tongs with no spark between them when they closed, just a dull clack. Those two bickered constantly, and yet at the same time each was lonely, or so local gossip had it anyway. Bríd had neither bickering nor loneliness to contend with, just the children's whingeing.

They were never done whingeing and acting up. Half the time she got no sleep. To make matters worse, whooping cough and measles were rife at the moment and the schools were closed. Hard times would never pass her door without dropping in. If they caught whooping cough or measles it would be a whole month before they shook it off and she'd be much the worse for wear . . . Would she be able to give them an education? She'd have to, since they were bound for America. Everyone was saying that America would open its doors again once the war was over. They'd have to make their own way, because she had no dowry to give so that they could marry near home. It would be hard to keep the older ones at school once they started to give a hand around the house, but they were entitled to their chance, so she would just have to keep slaving on . . . Would they be good at sending money home? Or would they be like her own sister, who promised to help her three times a year and then hadn't sent a ha'penny since the first year—unless she wrote this Christmas. A few pounds would be a godsend. There was good money to be made on everything—if you had things to sell—but then the buyer had to pay four times the price. Pigs fetched the best price of all, but at the moment there was an outbreak of the staggers and pigs were falling like flies. She wondered if they'd be able to forage for themselves.

This was Bríd, always fearful of what lay ahead. She paid more attention to the troubles that might be on their way to her than to her current ones. It would be an awful blow if anything happened to the pigs. She was going without food herself to fatten them for the big Christmas fair next month. If all went well, they would be good and plump . . . She had a hefty bill in the shop, her shawl was threadbare, her shoes were letting in; she owed money for household goods, money to the tailor, and manure money. On top of everything, the cows were going dry and the hens had stopped laying. After all her hard work, all the pinching and scraping to make ends meet, she'd have nothing to bring to the city anymore. From now on, whatever she had for a week would have to stretch to a fortnight.

But these disasters were nothing. They were real. She could handle them. They had shape and form. You could fight them. People had struggled for centuries against far more deadly blows than these. All you needed was flesh and blood and heart and thrift and hope to fight them. But it was the new, as yet unknown twists of fate that had yet to inflict themselves on this suffering race that worried her most. Who knew what shape they would take or how severe they would be. The world was in mortal danger and who knew what would happen. Bríd had heard the old people say that the end of the world was coming. The prophecy about the clash of foreign nations had come true. There was talk of conscription. What if her husband were taken away and killed? So far no one from around here who had joined the war had survived. And if only a single shot were fired, Bríd was certain it would be her husband who would fall. It would be just their luck . . .

Things were precarious even here in Ireland. She had heard there was some kind of commotion over beyond the other day. Food was getting scarce even if you could pay up front. There was a rumour that soon flour, tea, and tobacco, even brown sugar, would run out and that next year soldiers would seize animals and crops if the war continued.

In that case, how long would she have to keep going to the city? A year, two years, five years, twenty years . . . Until her eldest daughter could go in her place. She would be middle-aged by then and still having to make the journey. Would the superhuman effort it took be etched on her face and figure by then, plain for all to see? Would carrying the creel have made a hunchback of her? Would her feet be worn to the bone, as she lolloped along like a horse? Or marched like a martinet. Her profile honed sharp and bleak as the prow of a currach. Her cheeks leather scored by the feet of a thousand crows. The glint of steel in her eyes. That's how most of the middle-aged women she knew looked: once-soft features turned to iron by the weekly wrangling and the gruelling trudge on Saturdays.

And would her own children have to go through all this? If they could get someone to send them the money to go to America they'd be well out of it. But like everything else, you wouldn't know whether they'll be letting anyone into America anymore. The worst thing that could happen was if they could scrape together enough of a dowry to marry a man close to home. Then they'd have the weekly wrangling and the long trudge on Saturday to contend with too. But who knows what will happen. Maybe life will have changed by then. Only the really rich had jaunts in the beginning, but now the better-off country people had them and the rich were tearing about in motorcars. It could happen that country people would have motorcars too, like 'the Earl.' And it's not too long since bicycles came on the scene, but already some of the men and one or two of the women around here had one. Not that it mattered to her. Bicycles weren't for married women or country women. But it's a wise woman could predict anything in these changeable times. Maybe by the time her daughter had grown up every woman would have a bicycle . . . What use was a bicycle anyway? You couldn't carry a creel or a heavy basket on one, although she'd seen messenger boys carrying wobblier loads than that on them in the Bright City. They were all right for short distances. A motorcar, that's what a woman with a butter-creel needs. She'd never see the day. And most likely neither would her daughter or her daughter-in-law.

Would her daughter-in-law, the wife of the son she hadn't yet had, be good to her? Would she bring her nice things to eat from town and her breakfast in bed? Or would she abuse her like Úna Chaitlín's daughter-in-law does? She'd probably be nice enough until the children came along and started their whingeing. When her son got married the whole cycle would begin again, housework and kids and whingeing. But it would be her daughter-in-law's problem then. Even so, it would all be going on and she would have to do her bit the same as everyone else. But anyway, it would be great to have the odd few pounds coming from America, from the rest of the family, and herself and the old fellow wouldn't sign the house and land over outright to the son until they were getting the pension. Once she got the pension, she'd be her own woman. She could do whatever she pleased with it. There'd be a new generation in the house, battling with everything she had to battle with now. But she wouldn't have to worry about all that, since it would be someone else's responsibility. She'd have time to go visiting, to sit and chat. She could linger as long as she liked in a neighbour's house. But the time would come when she wouldn't be able to leave the house or maybe even her bed anymore. Bríd was certain she would cling to life. Even so, death would come . . . But Bríd didn't pursue that particular line of thought. She was taking a grim satisfaction in mulling over her trials and tribulations. Those faraway, later stages of life seemed so much more clearcut than the conundrum of this present one.

At Ard na Ceartan she stopped for a rest. While she'd been thinking the journey had flown by, and she wasn't feeling particularly tired. But her body ached and she was famished. She was glad now that she had taken some food with her, and she set about eating it. Usually, she didn't feel hungry until she was on or near the outskirts of the city. The darkness was thinning now and the grey of the eastern sky gradually growing pale, but there was a heavy mist and a touch of rain on the wind. She worried it might start to pour. If it did she'd be like a drowned rat before she got near the city. Which wouldn't matter except that she had to get to the market. Her clothes would dry on her skin and she could get an awful dose out of it. Then she started to relax a bit. She was as far on before daybreak as she'd been any other Saturday. Not much more than a mile from An Mhaoil, and the jaunts usually caught up with her around there. But she'd better get to the far side of the village because anywhere up to there a jaunt with a seat left would still be hoping to pick up a paying customer. The hunk of dry bread gave her a bit of energy but also a fit of hiccups that made her chest rattle like the tide sucking at a stony shore.

She'd forgotten the hiccups by the time she reached the side road to Aille an Bhroic, because she had started to think about Labhrás na hAille. Bad luck to her father who wouldn't let her marry Labhrás when he asked. It would have knocked six miles off the journey to the Bright City and she wouldn't have had half the drudgery. Or if she'd married Páid Concannon from Páirc an Doire she'd have the city on her doorstep, and all she'd have to do would be to get up fairly early, milk the cows, sit up on her donkey cart, and away with her into the city with the milk. Ah but to hell with that for a thought, it wouldn't have worked. He was too old. And anyway, she wouldn't have wanted to be shuttling in and out of the city twice a day—nor once a week either, if she could help it. What a pity she hadn't gone to America when she had the chance instead of deferring to her parents' wishes.

At Carraig na Loinge there was a powerful wailing going on. A sign of bad weather, a woman from those parts had told her, one morning as they walked together. A squally wind whistled through the gaps in the wall and the telegraph wires were screaming shrilly. Bríd roused herself to sing a song out loud. It was a song of Pádraig Choilm's: *Tá mé i mo shuí ó d'éirigh an ghealach aréir* (I've been up and about since the moon rose last night). But she only knew two verses of it. Then, to relieve the monotony, she started on the Knight with the Dark Laugh, a story her uncle Micil Mháirín used to tell. *An áit ba te ba teann. Rinne siad cruán den bhogán agus bogán den chruán nó gur chroith siad an talamh i bhfoisceacht naoi n-iomairí agus naoi n-eitrí díobh, gur thugadar toibreacha fíoruisce aníos trí lár na leice glaise le neart a gcuid coraíochta.* (A hot and heavy spot. The earth shook and tremors travelled the length of nine furrows, across the nine ridges, turning soft ground hard and hard ground soft, forcing springs of clear water to burst from sheer rock, so wild was their warfare.) Tantalising echoes of the tale swirled about in the nooks and crannies of her mind, but she didn't know the whole of that story either. She was surprised at how bad she was at retaining stuff like this, seeing as she hadn't done too badly at school. She hadn't listened carefully enough to all those songs and stories. She would have to buy a newspaper today, if she had a few pence left over after putting aside the price of a pint for whoever would be driving her home. She'd read it aloud to her husband tomorrow and let him know how the war was going. But it was so long since she had picked up a book or a paper, she wasn't sure she'd still be able to read. She'd be able to make out the price of pigs anyway, and that was all he would want to know.

From the top of Ard an Léana the houses of An Mhaoil loomed towards her, blurred, ghostly shapes wafting up out of the mist and dark. It was never her favourite thing, going through that village alone in the dead of night, even though she had done it a few times. The place had long been notorious for robberies, although she hadn't heard of anyone being molested there for ages. An Mhaoil had done its penance and kept its nose clean for two generations now, but that didn't suffice to clear its name. Anyway, if there were a hundred robbers on the go, it wasn't the likes of her they'd pick on. It was just that the houses seemed to huddle high up to the side of the road like a knot of vultures waiting to swoop on their prey, that was what scared her in the depths of the night.

Her stream of thought was suddenly interrupted. There was someone up ahead on the road. A woman—a woman with a creel. Bríd was so immersed in her own thoughts by now that it gave her a shock to see someone else. She had walked such a long stretch without meeting a soul. This was Peigín Nóra from the next village to hers. She stood like a pillar in the middle of the road, waiting. Bríd had about as much chance of getting away from her as a rabbit had of escaping a weasel. Her heart sank. After managing to avoid companions all morning, she now had the one she wanted least. Peigín Nóra, of all people. A woman who never stopped talking and whom nobody liked. A woman the jaunt drivers despised. She would often take a jaunt and haggle tirelessly to shave the price to the bone. Or at least that's what Bríd had heard said about her. She was in a right fix now. No cart would take two anyway, never mind that Peigín Nóra was one of them.

Peigín Nóra immediately started talking nineteen to the dozen. In an agony of reluctance, Bríd was forced to listen. No subject was too great or too small to be grist for Peigín Nóra's mill. The price of goods bought. The price of goods sold. Conscription coming. The big American ship that had sunk with its cargo of Christmas letters, tea, and tobacco. The staggers and the whooping cough, which were rife in her own area since the day before yesterday. Fever again in Leitir Gaoithe. Mike at the shop had announced that certain people would get no more credit unless they cleared their debts by Christmas. A daughter of Tom Beag's was on her way home. No one knew yet for certain who the man was. The priest would be thundering mad tomorrow . . . Although Bríd was forced to hear it, she took no pleasure in this last piece of gossip. It made her think of her own two stillborn children. Bríd thought it was a remarkable woman who could get through something like that unscathed. Anything to do with birth was the stuff of tragedy to her now.

When they got to Mairéad's pub, Peigín invited her in. A half-tot of whiskey would cheer them up no end. But Bríd knew she couldn't afford to stand the second round, and anyway she didn't drink apart from the odd glass at a wedding or a christening. It did cross her mind, though, that maybe a half-glass of punch, if she had the price of it, might help with the tiredness. She told Peigín to go ahead and get her own, and that she would wait outside for her. But the other woman refused to go. Bríd was embarrassed to come between Peigín and her bit of comfort, even though the same one was known to be a bit too fond of the drink. Peigín had less to say now as they walked along, side by side. Bríd's thoughts were free to wander, straying far and wide like wild animals. On top of everything else she was worried that her feet were wearing out. She was afraid more than ever that she wouldn't be able for the last three miles. She would have to put her shoes on when they reached the outskirts of the city, and she worried that they would skin her feet on the last bit of the journey. It was turning wet as well. The wind had changed and a sneaky drizzle was falling that would drench you before you knew where you were. It was only when she looked back to see if any jaunts were coming that she remembered to let down her rolled-up skirts, something she should have done long before she got to An Mhaoil. The dark was slowly melting away and daylight was seeping through the murky cocoon of mist that swirled around her in Coill na Maoile. There wasn't a breath of wind in the wood today. The air beneath the trees felt sultry and dead and fat drops of rain fell from the treetops as if the branches were spitting slobbery, evil curses.

Farther on, at Gleann na Coille, the first jaunts went by—three of them, one after another. Two of the drivers didn't spare them a glance, but Bríd wouldn't have expected it, as she didn't know them from Adam. The middle driver was Máirtín Mór, looking as if he could hardly believe his eyes that there were two of them. He stared hard at them, as if willing them to be just one person who would fit on the single empty seat up on the box. He looked back and forth several times from Bríd to the empty seat behind him, but then, after some hesitation, he gave the reins a shake and urged the horse on up the hill. A minute or so later, Cóil Liam passed with only two and himself. Bríd knew he would have made room for her had he not detested the woman she was with. Máire Sheáinín was on board this jaunt. She barely nodded to Bríd, and Bríd could have sworn there was a hint of glee in her eye when she realised Liam Cóil wasn't going to pick her up. A bit further on, Micil Mór picked up Peigín. If you travelled the whole of Ireland you wouldn't find a better man for giving lifts than Micil, and although he would rather have taken Bríd, he felt the older woman had the greater need. 'You're fine and strong and young, and able for the road,' he said to Bríd. 'If I could take you, I would.'

Once she reached the fork in the road and chose the upper way, she knew she was ruling out the chance of getting a lift. Most of the jaunts took the lower road. There were more houses along it and more chance of paying customers. She'd spent quite a while deliberating whether to take the lower road, but the memory of the cup of tea she'd been given a week ago today was an oasis in the desert, drawing her on. There was nothing like a cup of tea after a long journey. It warmed you up for the day ahead, instead of having to wait until one or two o'clock after the market and going to the shops. By the time you'd get a cup you'd be so hungry and tired you could hardly drink it.

She hadn't gone far up the rise when she heard a donkey cart trundling up behind her, creaking with the strain. It was a cart from that townland at the edge of the city, laden with all sorts of produce: potatoes, cabbage, root crops, a basket, a tankard of milk. The driver was a lone woman, straining forward, her muscular legs dangling, lashing the donkey's behind with the reins as she drove it up the slope. Bríd was about to ask for a lift, but the woman clearly had a lot on her mind and had no time to talk. She didn't spare Bríd a glance.

Then a donkey and cart from the same locality came towards her, having made the morning milk delivery to the city. You didn't have to prod that donkey; he was trotting along nicely. A woman was sitting on an empty milk can, a full-figured, long-legged woman, looking sleek and well fed. She would have been close to forty. Although she was sweating and straining to control the cart, you could see to look at her that she had peace of mind and her share of the good things in life. Bríd didn't know her, not even to see, but she decided there and then that this was Páid Concannon's wife, the woman he married after Bríd had refused him . . . Another jaunt was coming. She longed to look back but was too embarrassed. It was Seán Choilm. She recognised his growly 'hup' long before he caught up with her. He would definitely pick her up. Even though he had four passengers already, there was so little of the journey left that surely he wouldn't judge it a strain on the horse to put one more up on the box. But he passed her without a word or a look. She was surprised to see him on the upper road. But she remembered now that she had told Cáit Cheaite, who was up on the cart, where the woman who had given her the tea a week ago lived. Cáit was clever enough for anything.

She had barely started up the hill when she heard another jaunt coming at an easy trot. Despite herself, she looked around and her heart leaped. It was Peaid Neachtain. He had warmed himself at her fire many a time since the season for cards began, although she hadn't seen him this past fortnight. And he only had three passengers. It was hardly worth her while taking a lift now, with just about an Irish mile to go to Bóithrín Buí. On the other hand, it would be worth it. That was the worst mile, the long tedious trudge uphill. The horse was drawing level with her now, pace altering as she breasted the hill. But Peaid didn't so much as turn his head in her direction. He shook the reins and urged the horse to full stretch so that she passed Bríd at a gallop and disappeared up over the hill. Bríd nearly dropped. She wouldn't have believed it if she hadn't seen it with her own two eyes. She would give her right arm not to have looked back . . .

Bríd trudged on up the hill. She tugged her shawl more tightly around her as the drizzly mist came seeping in. Although the fog had lifted, dark skies glowered above the wind and it looked like it was going to start lashing down any minute. She'd be soaked to the skin by the time she had done all she had to do, had got her bags of shopping, and was sitting down to a cup of tea in the eatinghouse . . . She might have to sit for ages in her wet clothes until she found a cart driver to give her a lift back.

At long last she crested the hill at the hill at Coill an Choláiste. She was into the suburbs now, flanked on both sides by large, elegant houses, the outer streets of the city itself just a little further on, and an Bóithrín Buí only about a quarter of a mile away. An easy walk downhill now to the edge of the city centre. Bríd put her creel in the shelter of a high hedge. She would have to put her shoes on. As she was tying her laces the thought foremost in her mind was the cup of tea she might get, and how refreshing it would be after the strain of the journey, if the peeler's wife waylaid her again. But maybe some-one else would have got there ahead of her. Unlikely though. Why had she gone and told Cáit Cheaite about it? That one could worm her way in with anyone. She'd give it a try anyway, first off, though it would add to her journey and she might end up with nothing to show for it but sore feet. No point in delaying.

Bríd rolled the cloth back off the creel to check that all was in order. The swirl of butter lay there, demure as the Sleeping Beauty waiting for her prince to wake her. A little water lay in the print, but the butter was good and firm, not the melted mess it becomes in sum-mer. She lifted the straw and paper off the eggs and counted them again. All there—three score of them—gleaming pale and clean, white, brown, pale blue. She hadn't arranged them in any particu-lar way, but still she knew from which hen each egg had come. This one was from the little grey pullet. That white, delicate one was the speckled hen's. The crested hen's were brown and big as duck eggs. She often fancied one of those, and since the laying season was over she contemplated boiling one for herself, but she didn't like doing things on the sly. They were strange poor creatures, hens, God love them. She had to dance attendance on them, otherwise they'd have been gone long ago. Bríd wrapped the eggs up again and settled the straw around them. She drew the cloth back over them and was ready to set off again . . .

The drizzle had stopped now and the air was clear. To the southeast the sun had put a gold edge around a huddle of big, dark, brooding rain clouds, and was breaking through them in a dazzle of beauty. Its rays glanced off a jewellery of wet leaves and raindrops on the road. The sunrise was a triumph, victory over night's dull torpor and all its burdens, dangers, hardships, and shame. Bríd looked around at the road she had just travelled. She looked back along those nine long and winding miles that had taken so much out of her. She knew that she would have to walk them again and again. She would walk them until she was weather-beaten and spent and had a hard glint in her eye. But today's miles were behind her and her mood had lifted. Blood pulsed in her veins and her heart sang. Energy bubbled up in her. The spirit of a young, wild thing possessed her. Her body was sharp as a scythe and ready for action. Whatever challenge life might throw at her, she would rise to it. She seized the strap of the butter creel . . .

TRANSLATED BY KATHERINE DUFFY

THE HARELIP

Nora Liam Bid spent the night much as she had spent the night before, making tea for the wedding guests. But now the foggy dawn light of the early February morning was snaking its way into the half-deserted parlour, and as she had cleared up after the last round of tea and was now released from work, the unease of it all came back to nag at her again. Unease with the marriage, the change, the unfamiliar East Galway plain: that same sharp pang that stabbed her the night her father came home from Galway Fair and whispered to her mother that he had set Nora up with a bigshot from the flat East Galway plains. Seeing her husband and his sisters for the first time last week at the matchmaking had done nothing to shake that feeling off. Like a gravid salmon stuck in a putrid, choked upriver branch, destined never to reach the clean spawning beds upstream, Nora had entered into the yoke of marriage in Ard chapel yesterday midafternoon. And now, finding no solace in her mother's gentle words, her father's drunken blether, her husband's tranquil placidity, or in the chattering of her sisters-in-law, who were as fawning as they were friendly, she went down to the kitchen to the group of neighbours who had come from Ard with the wedding party.

The dance shed outside had been empty for some time and the kitchen was heaving with people who fell silent whenever she appeared. It was as though the silence was personified in their boozy, panting breaths, the wisps of tobacco smoke, the specks of dust rising from the concrete floor in a cloudy haze — and was heading for her, like a spectre trying to get her to say the words that would free its tortured soul. It was that morning-after-a-wedding time when a lad could go looking for trouble and find no one to bother him. The drunken talk had lost its edge, the laughter faded. It seemed to Nora that the young ones had little enthusiasm for the jigs they danced and just wanted to stop the married couples and 'auld ones' from using the silence that was taking hold of the house as a reason to say it was time to go. And though the young ones from Ard were no strangers to revelry or interminable drudge, they all now looked and sounded as tired as they were weary of foot. The only one who still had feet of flames and cheeks ablaze was Bartleen, her father's servant-boy.

Nora bowed her head and let a flame spark her mind, a flush dart through her soul, until she was dead to the silence and the unease. She remembered their frequent, harmless courtship, snatching dulse from him in summer or, in the autumn, the two of them down on the flags in the yard cracking the nuts he had brought to her from the Lios hazel grove, nighttime fireside chats when the old pair had gone to bed and she was waiting for her brother Patrick to come home from a visit. The young girls from Ard, the ones who were at the wedding tonight, often used to tease her about Bartleen. The funny thing was that tonight was the one night no one would say he was the one for her, and yet it was also the one night it wouldn't have bothered her if they did. Bartleen had a way with words that would take the melancholy edge off her laughter when her father and mother were trying to make a match for her. Nora's wound of regret was only surface-healed, regret that she had been so slow to speak, so ill-inclined to find fault with God's works that day when Bartleen told her her old fella was off making a match for her again and that you wouldn't get a look in unless you were a shopkeeper or a young buck from East Galway.

It wasn't to spite Bartleen for what he had said that she commented on his harelip that day. What she had meant to say was that she'd go off hotfoot with him—there and then. But at the end of the day, it wasn't his lithe, lean body, or his grey-sky eyes, or his foxglove cheeks that had caught her eye or captured her heart and her lips; no, it was the repulsive birth defect that he didn't even try to mask with a moustache. And if disgust had less often trumped desire, the web of her young life might be more than the lifeless grey-green crust it was today. Even now she could see the harelip coming at her like a lamprey through a grey sea-lough, and though Barley was harping on about how the East Galway crowd had taken over the house all night with their reel sets, she couldn't listen to him until the pair of them were out in the middle of the floor dancing the local plain set.

'So you have the yoke on you at last?' he said, as though trying to be witty now that his irritability had waned.

'God help us,' she answered. It was then something dawned on her for the first time that neither match, nor marriage, nor the wedding itself had given her clearly to understand.

'Don't be sorry. You're much better off there; you'll have plenty of everything and you'll be your own boss on the flat plains of East Galway instead of facing heavy rocks and hard labour over in Ardbeg — not to mention looking after your old fella. We'll send you the odd load of seagrass and the odd bottle of poitín, and a bag of nuts in the autumn.'

Nora felt something close up against her heart. It was only now she remembered that there was no seagrass, no nuts, no poitín here.

'I was looking for you all night last night, Bartleen, to get you to sing "Derrynea, Costelloe" for me, but there was no sign of you in the crowd. You'll sing it after this dance. Go on. I'd love to hear it again . . . '

But Bartleen had barely cleared his throat when her mother and her husband's sister came and carted her off again to the parlour.

'It is high time we headed off,' said the mother. 'Look, it's bright already, and your Martin has been up since the night before last. You two are at home, God bless you, but look at the journey we have ahead of us.'

'Eleven miles to Galway,' said Martin Ryan, the new husband, in a stiff, curdled voice rendered all the more unfriendly by his East Galway accent. 'And another fifteen back west, isn't that it? That's what the labourer I had here for a year, from Ard, used to tell me.'

Despite their talk of the long miles and the fussing over coats and shawls, Nora didn't admit to herself that her family and neighbours were leaving. She didn't admit it until the Ardbeg girls came over to her and kissed her, telling her not to be lonely, that they'd be over to see her from time to time. Nora recognised each and every roar from the Ardbeg boys, racing back west along the Galway road on their bikes, making her feel even more removed from the East Galway folk who were bidding her farewell in the dim misty light of morn. They sent cold shivers down her back and a sense of loathing through her veins, with 'Mrs Ryan' rolling off their every honeyed tongue. The cars that had brought some of the Ardbeg crowd were revving out on the road, drivers tooting their horns. And as she had often done before, going home at the end of a wedding, Nora put on her coat and walked out onto the road. Bartleen was the last one to be bundled into her family's car.

'God help us, Bartleen,' she said. 'Keep a fistful of seagrass for me.'

And though she felt herself getting weak, Nora heard the sorrow in the words that he squeezed out through the hairlip gap, the collar of his raincoat turned up against his mouth.

'Don't worry. And I'll bring you a bag of nuts too, in the autumn.'

'There's any amount of nuts in the creigs around here,' said her husband, by her shoulder.

Nora stood at the gate, rooted to the spot, watching the car until it had gone back west over Ardeen Cross, yet letting on not to having heard her mother's parting shot, not to be lonely, sure she'd see them again soon.

Lonesomeness, is that what you call the unbreakable grapnel that anchors an exiled soul to its native harbour? She wasn't lonesome. She was being tossed about on the waves, at the whim of God's hand, having released the anchor chain of her soul, the last link with

heredity broken now that Bartleen had left. She headed off like a lost
ship and drifted over to Ardeen Cross. Galway was as near as she had
been to this part of the world, and even if was dark when the wedding party drove over here last night, it wasn't to view the surrounding countryside that she had come to the top of this grassy tussock.
The only thing on her mind was how to get to the top of the nearest
hill and avoid being smothered by waves of past and future tense. At
that moment she couldn't tell whether Martin Ryan was to the left
or right of her, she paid no heed to his pipe stem tracing shapes in all
directions in the air, the unusual and unfamiliar names it mapped out
only adding to her alienation and spite. And she didn't notice Ryan
leaving her to go back into the house.

The fog was furling and unfurling, then thinning and spreading
out in sorry grey strakes towards the edge of the plain. Nothing but
vast flat fields as far as the eye could see — not a stone or rocky patch
in sight, the stone walls straight as a die, except where submerged
here and there in swollen winter lakes. A wood grove here, a cop-
pice there, and the odd barren patch down below her, like knots of
wood in a white-deal table that had been bleached and scoured. But
where she stood was the freshest hilltop in these fat, unfeeling lands.
The houses were not sprung up together here; the nearest, hesitant,
plume of smoke seemed to be a mile away. All the houses looked the
same. All the same build. The same space around them. And the
same team of trees sheltering the walls of the haggards. Nora could
only liken them to a massive house that had come apart during the
night, its hostile components separated as far as they could be from
one another. She looked over at her husband's house. It wasn't unlike her father's two-storey slated house in shape and in style, except
that her father's house looked newer, faced the sea, and backed onto
round-top hills; the house itself was as though sculpted from a block
of granite cut out of the barren rock, standing like a mighty menhir
over the cluster of thatched cottages that was Ardbeg. But that was the
least of the differences between them. The two houses were as differ-

ent as water and new milk. Like the countryside around it, her new abode had a stupid arrogance about it that reminded her of the smug smile of a shopkeeper who had just looked over his books. Its arrogance reminded her that this house had not sprung up overnight — it was permanence personified. Nora knew it was a 'comfortable' house. She knew her father wouldn't have sent her there if it wasn't, with all the young bucks he had turned away from her and the fine dowry that she had. She shuddered to think that from now on she would be just another of the house's modern conveniences.

There was no stretch of mountain or sea here to fetter restless feet or snare the dreams of a wandering mind. There was nothing but the smooth flat plain to engulf people's desires and traits and warp them into a cold single-thread cloth, just as the sea drowns every little drop of water in its own grey image and likeness, regardless of its colour or kind before it is caught by her womb. From now on, whatever little contact she was likely to have with the place she called 'home,' her role in it would be no more than that of a flimsy thread in a close-woven fabric.

There was a chill in the morning air, though it wasn't exactly cold — not unlike her sister-in-law's frosty friendliness — and she went inside. She felt nothing much had changed in there. After all the high jinks the kitchen wasn't untidy enough to be called 'homely,' not to mention native Irish. She had often seen their own kitchen in a much worse state after a few hours of a house dance. Apart from the two tables that were still lined up in the parlour, the servants had put everything back before they left, and there wasn't a thing out of place that would remind you that the day before had been a red-letter day and that two lives had been joined body and soul by the yoke of cohabitation and copulation that would ensure an everlasting source of life in the house. The fateful events of life were no more than skimming stones on the sleepy surface of this countryside.

She sat down and looked at the kitchen around her, something she hadn't had a chance to do since she came to the house. From the saucepans scoured clean to the two large straw-coloured cupboards, everything around bore the hallmarks of the thriftiness that is hand-maiden to longevity. It might have reminded her of the vessels set out in burial chambers never to be moved or used until eroded by time, but since Nora knew nothing about archaeology, all she asked herself was how Ryan, on his own, had kept the place so spic and span. This house did not lack a woman's touch. But what Nora found oddest of all was that there was neither hearth nor fire to be seen, just a metal range, brazen and unwelcoming, the last spark after dying inside in its belly.

'Where's the turf, I wonder,' she said to herself getting up, for to transform the frostiness of alienation into flashes of glowing famil-iarity she would have to put down a roaring fire that would set the steel stove ablaze and prove to her that flames and warmth could overcome solid cold iron.

'I only use coal,' he said. 'Would you not be better off not leaving the fire and lying down on the bed for a while?'

She was frightened. She hadn't thought of bed until then. She felt the pressing authority of the sleepy voice send a wave of disgust through her veins, yet she knew there would be no denying the au-thority of the voice if he felt like bringing things to a head.

'I'm not tired,' she said at last, but her husband had gone out for coal. He soon returned and threw a shovelful of it into the mouth of the stove. Nora was sickened by his jabbing with the poker at the embers. It was like a soul being weighed on the scales of temptation by the devil, trying its damnedest to save itself, the cracking embers breaking and trying to burst into flame. She'd give all Ireland now to have a father-in-law, a mother-in-law, a prattling sister-in-law, or even a dumbstruck creature at the hearth. The smoke from Ryan's pipe was rising up to the loft in measured puffs, free and easy as you like. The smoke from her father's pipe, and from Bartleen's, formed curly and crotchety streaks that always looked like they were wrestling with something in the air. There were no wild moors—none of the wild

oats of her homeland—in her husband's speech. He could hardly
have been so precise and accurate except that his entire mind was a
smooth plain with no heights or hollows. The seldom time he made
a joke, and his taut hooked nose broke into a smile, he reminded her
of the god of wisdom trying to seek out pleasure for a little while. The
more accustomed she got to the local turn of phrase, the stranger and
more meaningless it sounded to her. Her courage slipped away. She
longed for a cloth woven from different threads: different people,
different days, different times, nighttime again, or anger in his voice
instead of the dead gentle drone that was filling her ears.

She got up and went as far as the doorway to get some fresh air.
Though the fat hens had just been let out, they had headed straight
for the flower beds on either side of the path that leads from the steps
to the front gate. The few flowers that had poked their heads through
the earth had been trampled last night. It would have been hard for
her not to recognise Bartleen's footprint—as often as she had checked
him for leaving it before, in the peaty soil, on land and on sand. She
was scrutinising the trace of the shoe when a heavy-footed man wearing a countryman's soft hat and corduroy trousers passed by on the
road. Nora recalled that he was an eccentric neighbour of her husband's; he had been given special treatment in the parlour the night
before. Without ever slowing his step and with just the slightest turn
of his head, he greeted her grudgingly and laconically, as though each
syllable he uttered was costing him a penny's rent. The fog had come
down again in a murky mantle over the plain with only the odd chink
of visibility. Still, she would probably not have gone in so soon if an
obese hen hadn't vexed her by scratching the footprint from the soft
shapeable soil with her clumsy claw.

She sat back on the same chair by the range. With the heat of
the fire and exhaustion, her husband had fallen sound asleep—his
snoring dull and measured, unconcerned and effortless, like a veil
of gossamer sea on a stony beach in the calm of summer. She took a
good look at him for the first time. It was as if she had left him until

the end, this insignificant item in her new life. Long-limbed, square-shouldered man. The strong body, sinewy neck, and sallow rough-complexioned face sealed with centuries of sun and storm, soil and hardship. Black hair edged with grey, a sign of strength. Slow, dead eyes in which Nora could never imagine a twinkle of laughter, a flash of anger, or the look of love. Flaring nostrils that couldn't be too fastidious about fragrances. A jet-black moustache which she figured — from the odd glimpse she had got of it — badly needed a trim. And it was then it occurred to her that the thick seal-tufts had no harelip to hide.

TRANSLATED BY ÚNA NÍ CHONCHÚIR

THE YEAR 1912

'The trunk.'

Although the mother spoke the word lightly, there was a touch of resistance in her voice. She had refused to go to the Bright City with her daughter the previous Saturday, to buy the trunk. It made her blood run cold to see it there, enshrined like an idol on the ledge of the kitchen dresser, the children making it the centre of their play, opening it, closing it, peering at it from all angles. She didn't want to upset her daughter during her last week. Only for that she would have shoved it right out of sight under the bed in the back room. And tonight, although the daughter was as eager as ever to have the expensive item on show before the gathering of friends and family, the mother got her own way as the night wore on, with the excuse that the trunk could get damaged or scratched if it stayed where it was.

The trunk was a black mark, a scar on life's complexion, especially tonight of all nights. Occasions of good cheer were rare enough under her roof. The combined glamour and utility of the trunk was a chimera, a supernatural trick to steal away her firstborn, the apple of her eye, while the drinking and dancing, the music and revelry, were at their height. Yet seven weeks ago, before the passage money had arrived, she had been on tenterhooks just as much as Máirín, waiting for it.

That Máirín should be off to America was no surprise, any more than the departure of her own eight sisters, some of whom she still missed sorely, had been a surprise. Life's many blows had taught her to damp down her heart's desires and to strangle her motherly love, as Eve should have strangled the serpent of knowledge. But it had all flared up again when the passage money arrived. Voices murmured in her mind, giving repressed emotions free rein. Tongues of flame from the banked-up fires of her heart were burning holes in her reason, making her deplore emigration as an injustice on a par with the sacking of temples and the scorching of land.

But the call of destiny must be answered. The fateful day had dawned. Patch Thomáis had gone to get the jaunt. The merrymaking down in the packed little kitchen had reached a crescendo, as if the survivors of a disaster, a people for whom tomorrow held no hope, were abandoning themselves to one last night of wild carousing . . . Máirín had better look lively.

A ha'penny candle burned on a small press by the kitchen wall, its light wavering in the breeze that skimmed through the papered-over broken window pane. By the light of the guttering flame the trunk's brass knobs seemed to hold the secret of vast, mysterious depths. It took the mother a moment to remember where it was she had seen the exact, pale yellow shade of its timber: on the face of a corpse after a long wake in sultry weather. And her revulsion at the thought of looking into it was the same feeling that had often made her avert her eyes from a corpse in its coffin.

'Have you got everything?' she asked her daughter, looking away from the trunk in its pool of light. It contained a multitude of things: a sod of turf, a chip off the hearthstone, locks of hair, a bunch of shamrock, even though it was autumn, grey homespun stockings, a handful of dulse, clothes and travel documents. The daughter took her shoes, coat, hat, and dress out of the trunk and laid them out on the little press ready to put on. She had done this many times this past week, but her mother hadn't approved and, earlier tonight, had half-begged, half-threatened her not to put them on until morning came.

The mother closed the trunk again and threw the bedcover over it 'to keep it clean.' Her greatest fear was that when her daughter was dressed for America she would have the same look of strangeness as the trunk itself. Máirín stood barefoot, wearing only a long white shift which she had arranged carefully earlier in the evening and which would not now be removed until she had reached the house of a relative on the other side. She was like a vision that the mother had dreamed up and brought forth from her own mind, the single dream of hers that had retained its original beauty and clarity. A dream that embodied the sadness of a paradise lost, and that brought the story of the Apple and the Fall to life again: the plucking of a mother's first fruit. She had a million things just on the tip of her tongue ready to share with her daughter, from the store of endearments that is a mother's heart, those words that swim upstream like salmon from the moment a mother feels the first stirrings in her womb until the light of eternity quenches this world's dim glow.

She had spent this last month peppering their conversation lightly with such things: that she wouldn't have cared if everyone else in the house left, if only Máirín could have stayed . . . that the whole house would miss her, but most especially herself . . . that of all the children, Máirín had never caused her a moment's sorrow . . . that she lent a lovely presence to any house. . . . But all of that was just the barest tip of the iceberg. She was like a lady-in-waiting who was busy fastening a necklace around the queen's throat when it broke apart and the precious beads scattered, rolling off into oblivion. She felt as if some enemy within was sifting her words and preventing her from baring her soul, taking that sweet release away from her. She knew that from now until she died she would never again have the chance to say what was on her mind without having someone else write it down for her, in a language whose patterns and substance were as strange to her as the speech of a ghost from the fairy hill. A letter was a withered straw when compared to the warm rush of words exchanged by mouth and the joy of eye contact. The mind's impulses and the tides of the heart would be dammed up by the dry act of writing.

It was unlikely that she would see Máirín again for years and years. She would have to pay her passage money back, then earn the passage for one or two more of the family, as well as sending a bit home. Maybe the child she carried in her womb would see Máirín sooner than its mother would. That American coat might as well be a shroud. From now on when someone said 'God speed her' when her name was mentioned, they might just as well say 'God have mercy on her soul.' Children often mixed up those two different blessings. And when the time came for 'God speed' to change to 'God have mercy,' it would be a passing without proper rites and ritual. No mother would hold the grave-clothes, unfolding them now and again to assuage her grief. No name would be carved for posterity, on a rough bit of board down by the sea's edge. The voyage—that vast, cold crossing would erase her from the family's living history. She would be gone the way of the wild geese.

Although all these thoughts lay in a bitter sludge at the back of the mother's mind, she didn't accept that she would never see her daughter again. Sense and logic told her that this was the case, but her heart, her hope, her courage argued otherwise. And she had decided to listen to her heart. But she knew that if she did see her again, she would be nothing like the innocent, young country girl she was now at nineteen, her beauty like morning sunshine on a hillside in paradise. Her lips would have touched the bitter fruit of the Tree of Knowledge. Envy would have weaselled its way into her heart. Life's hard lessons would have riddled her thoughts with the worm of cynicism. Her expression would be steely and cold. She would talk with a strange accent, as if a wicked stepmother had wreaked havoc on her speech. That was what all returned Yanks were like. She must reveal her true self to her daughter now, as a mother might have done back in the time when every foray beyond the cave for food was a matter of life and death. She must reveal her true self before her age and ignorance made a laughingstock of her and before a difference in beliefs could drive a wedge between their two minds . . .

Start with the money: she judged that the best approach. She produced a cloth purse from her bosom, extracted the small change that her daughter might need in the Bright City, and handed her the purse. The daughter put it around her neck and settled it carefully at her breast under her blessed scapular. 'Make sure you mind that well now, child,' the mother said. 'Most likely you won't need it at all, but if it happens that you don't find work immediately, it's best not to be a burden on your aunt Nora. She has a houseful of her own to look after. Keep the rug tucked tightly around you on the ship. Don't take up with anyone unless it's someone you know. You'll be fine once you get to Nora's house. Don't kill yourself working, even if it means earning a bit less . . . You'll be back home to visit in five years time . . . Well, ten years at the most . . . You'll surely have built up some savings by then . . . My . . .

Up until that point she was managing to speak cheerfully. But when she tried to go deeper she faltered, and stood rooted to the spot, staring wordlessly at her daughter. Her hands fidgeted with the folds of her apron. A flush that was part smile and part sorrow burned on her cheeks. Her face contorted with grief. Her forehead creased with distress and became a web of lines struggling for composure.

The daughter was nearly ready now, and asked for the small change that she would need in the Bright City. The mother had been so busy talking that she had forgotten to bring out the little purse for it. She got completely flustered now, as she turned to find it, and forgot she was clutching the money in her fist. It fell and scattered all over the floor. The mother had planned to first find the right words and have her say, and then to bestow the money on her daughter like a sacred gift, and finally to embrace her and kiss her . . . Instead the precious offering was ripped from her hand . . .

As the daughter put the change purse in her coat pocket, she felt an envelope. 'A lock of your hair, mama,' she said. 'I thought I put it in the trunk with the others.' She held the dark curl up to the candle-light, and her blue eyes softened like a child's. She wanted to say something to her mother but didn't know exactly what. Her thoughts crashed about in her head like a stranger stumbling across a treacherous bog on a dark night. For her to say what she needed to say, the two of them would have to be lying in the same bed with the lights out and a ray of moonlight slanting through the tiny window like a magic wand, guiding her to speak. She looked into her mother's eyes for inspiration, but her mother remained inscrutable, a dark hillside that concealed a roil of emotions in its depths, blazing but unable to break the surface.

The daughter put on the light, loud coat and the wide-brimmed hat. It was like getting ready for battle, she thought, trying the hat this way and that, although she was at a loss to find the best way to wear it. Little did she know that the width and angle of the hat brim did nothing for her looks, nor that the tan shoes, black hat, and red coat combined to create a motley ensemble that swamped her fresh complexion. But she was ready: hat, coat, low-heeled shoes, and lady's gloves—this was what she would wear from now on. Like a butterfly realising for the first time that it has left its cramped caterpillar body behind and that it can now sail away on wispy wings through wide, untrammelled spaces, she felt the unsettling, lonely shock of the new, but also some of the dizzy pride of the butterfly . . .

The mother didn't realise until the trunk was closed and locked that she had forgotten to put a bit of hen-dirt in it, or in any of her daughter's clothes. But she wouldn't unlock it again for all the world. She couldn't bear her daughter to make fun of her, this morning of all mornings, accusing her of silly superstition. She splashed her with holy water, and while she was putting the stopper back in the bottle, the daughter, bubbling with excitement, had gone down to the kitchen to show off her American clothes.

The jaunt hadn't arrived yet. There was a thrum of dancing, and Tom Neile, standing by the closed door, was giving a drunken rendering of 'The Three Sons,' drowning out the music:

'It's many the fine young man, nimble and strong, sails over
    the o-o-ocean and never returns.'

'Keep it down,' the mother said to Tom. But she'd have given a lot, at that moment, to be able to sing an air like Tom, to express all that was in her heart in a stream of song. The young girls clustered around her daughter now, scrutinising her outfit, even though they'd spent most of the last week doing just that. They cut the mother off from her daughter. In her eyes, they were standing in the way of love, with as little thought for it as the cold waste of the ocean itself.

The young women were all excited about America. Excited about the life they'd all share soon in South Boston. It was their lot in life. The American trunk was their guardian angel, the emigrant ship their guiding star, the broad Atlantic their Red Sea. Bidín Johnny reminded Máirín to ask her first cousin to hurry up with the passage money. Judeen Sheáin told her, on her life, to make sure to tell Liam Pheige about the shenanigans at old Cáit Thaidhg's wake.

'Don't forget to tell our Seán that we've sowed potatoes in the mountain field again this year,' said Sorcha Pháidín. 'When he left he swore there wasn't a man born who would manage it once he was gone, it was so hard.'

'Máirín, tell my fellow that I'll be over to him shortly,' said Nóra Phádraig Mhurcha in a whisper that all the girls heard.

'By the hokey, it won't be long till I'm knocking sparks out of the pavements of South Boston myself,' said a redheaded young fellow who had plenty to say for himself after a few drinks.

'God help the rest of us who have to stay at home,' said old Séamas Ó Curráin.

The whiskey was doing the rounds again. 'Ah here, take a sip, it'll do you good,' said Peaitsín Shiubháine, who was doling it out— thrusting the glass at Máirín with a hand so shaky that he spilled some on her coat. 'A mouthful won't do you a bit of harm. It's a hard morning for going on a sidecar. Divil a drop of poitín you'll get where you're going.'

There was a catch in his voice, for he was thinking of his own six daughters, who were 'over there.' One of them had been gone thirty-five years. He would never see any of them again . . . 'I'll drink it myself then. Your good health, Máirín, and may God bring you safely to your journey's end.'

Neither Peaitsín nor anyone else at the party thought to add 'God bring you safely home again.' The oversight sparked the mother's banked-up anger again.

'Five years from this day, she'll be back home again, you'll see,' she snapped.

'Please God,' chimed Peaitsín and Scáinín Thomáis Choilm, in unison.

'And she'll marry a rich man and settle down here with us forever,' laughed Máirín's mother's sister Citín.

'I doubt I'll have that much money after five years,' said Máirín, 'but sure maybe you'll marry me, Seáinín, penniless and all as I'll be.'

' . . . Don't be getting the accent, anyway,' said a young boy-cousin of hers, 'and don't be going around saying "I guess" this and "I guess" that like Mícheáilín Éamainn, who only spent two months there and came home across the fields with nothing but half a guinea and a new waistcoat after all his travelling.'

'And don't be asking, "What's that, mammy?" when you see the pig.'

'You'll send me the price of my passage anyway, won't you?' said Mairéad, the next daughter down, her eyes sparkling.

'And me mine,' Nóirín, the other sister, reminded her.

It seemed to the mother that that pair's wheedling was taking ten years off her life. Years of delay were being heaped on her daughter's visit, like shovels raining clay on a coffin. The time of the visit would be stretched to Judgement Day. Her own flesh and blood were the worst enemy she could have.

She made more tea for Máirín, although she had only just finished drinking some. The mother longed to get close to her again. She needed to break bread, have a farewell communion, bind her daughter to her with the intimacies of a final supper. She would tell her straight out that, as far as home was concerned, this parting meal was not a funeral supper: that there would be an Easter before the Judgement. But they had no time alone. Her sister Citín, her daughters, and some of the young girls crowded in at the table by the wall and in no time at all Máirín was lost in amongst them.

Máirín couldn't eat a bite. Her cheeks were flushed with excitement; longing, panic, awe, and anguish, each was written on her face. Máirín had never been farther than the Bright City before. But tales of America were mother's milk to her. South Boston, Norwood, Butte Montana, Minnesota, or California, those names meant more to her than Dublin, Belfast, Wexford, or even places that were only a few miles out beyond the Bright City, in Achréidh. Her life and thoughts had been moulded by the glamour of America, by its riches and pastimes, by the gnawing longing to get there . . . And although she was homesick leaving now, the feeling was shot through with delight, hope, and awe. At last, she was standing on the threshold of fairyland . . . Wild seas, tall masts, glittering lights, silvery streets, dark people, their skin gleaming black as beetles—beside all of these, field and hill, rock and strand paled into insignificance.

Tonight her mind was a leaky sieve, barely able to hold the scraps of memory she would later cast like wrack onto the waves as she sailed away. She was so distracted that she allowed herself to be led out into the centre of the floor to dance, even dressed up as she was in her good clothes for America. Anyway, she hadn't the heart to refuse Pádraigín Pháidín.

She reproached herself for spending so little time with him this evening. At the beginning of the dance she was a little bit shy, but the beat of the music—music that was prized even in the fairy fort—got under her skin, and soon, in her motley ensemble, she was frolicking like a lone young fawn in high spirits, with the other youngsters of the herd frisking about her, egging her on to take the limelight and show what she could do, while the old-timers sat around in a circle, lost in thought. The mother was thinking that if she lived to see her again the hard knocks of life would have broken that dancing spirit. The fierce rush of blood that made her reach for the stars as she danced would be gone and the grey weight of passing years would have bowed her defeated bones down to earth.

But now the mother's attention shifted from her daughter to Pádraigín Pháidín, her dancing partner. Instantly, she put two and two together. Anyone could see it. Most likely neither had ever spoken a word of love to the other. Maybe no word had been spoken tonight and maybe it never would be. But she knew they would be married in South Boston, in a year's time, or in five or even ten years' time . . .

She was flabbergasted. So that was what lay behind Pádraigín's sudden urge to dance. What she had failed miserably to say in words, he was spelling out in his dance. His limbs and body spoke a poem full of life and movement, strength and skill, building up to the moment his hobnailed boots knocked a spark out of the hearthstone as the final note sounded. Some people would have put it all down to a bit too much drink taken, but the mother knew better. That spark was the perfect climax: a flourish of triumph. Then without missing a beat, still breathless from dancing, he began to sing in a steady voice. And the mother stopped thinking about her daughter as she listened:

'The garden's gone wild, my dear, and I'm all alone,
No fruit and no flowers, no blossom upon the blackthorn,
The harps are all silent, the birds will not sing in the trees
Since my own darling flower departed to Cashel O'Neill.'

His song was urgent, a fledgling spirit rattling the bars of its cage. By now the mother hated the sight of him. An evil spirit, pawing at her treasure . . .

Then came a jangle of harness and the clatter of the jaunt on the path outside. In an instant, the music and merriment died, except for the warblings of Seáinín Mac Tuathláin, who lay in a drunken stupor against the closed door:

'Óra, mhóra, mhóra. When I land over there it'll be on the south side of the New York quay . . . ' This was the only bit of a song Seáinín could ever manage.

'You'd be some gift to America, all right!' cried a young fellow, losing patience with him. 'I wish you bloody well were on some quay over there, instead of hanging around here annoying us.'

'Take that out and tie it up on the jaunt,' the mother said, as the trunk was lifted down from the room and hefted onto the table like a golden calf.

'It might get bashed. Leave it there until I'm ready to go myself,' said Máirín. That trunk was her badge of respectability, licence to wear an elegant hat and gaudy coat instead of a drab shawl. Without the trunk her 'lady's' outfit would seem somehow profane. She was afraid that if she let it out of her sight for a minute her vivid clothes might turn to ashy rags on her skin.

Now Máirín began saying her goodbyes to those who were too weak to escort her up to the main road. Old-timers in bad shape who could barely manage to shuffle across the street, and who might never again get to leave their firesides to go to a social gathering. They were the first link in the chain to be broken, and her first inkling of how hard and how heartbreaking parting could be. Whatever might happen with others, she was seeing these people for the very last time.

Despite her fluster and hurry, she stopped to drink in the sight of them, consigning their precious features to memory. It was only when she came to her grandmother, who sat by the fire, that emotion overwhelmed her. She loved her grandmother as dearly as she did her mother; they had always been the best of friends. And the love was returned manifold. Never a week went by but the old woman would save a little bit of her pension for her, whatever else might fall behind. The old woman was as still and silent as if she was already six feet under. And in a way she wasn't far off it, for she had one foot in the grave and was just waiting for the grim reaper to call. Her mouth was closed and dry as a coffin nailed shut, and except for the fact that she blinked now and then and seemed to focus on the here and now again for a moment, Máirín would have sworn that she had no idea what was going on.

'I'll never see you again, mammo,' Máirín said, the tears that had finally broken distorting her words.

'God is good,' said her mother, with a touch of defiance. Máirín moved away then, as if out of the austere depths of winter and into summer sunlight, as she went to kiss the little children and the baby in the cradle. To be near them was balm to her senses. It was like escaping the chill of the grave.

The mother took her off to the back room again. But they had hardly any time there before Citín and Mairéad swept in to get their shawls for the journey to the Bright City with Máirín. The mother could have killed them. Their intrusion had made her sorrow congeal to a hard lump in her throat once again. All she could find to say to Máirín was that she knew she would earn plenty, that she hoped the weather would be good for the crossing, and that she must promise solemnly to get her picture taken over there and send it home.

'My precious girl,' she said, picking a speck of fluff off her lapel and giving the hat a quick little tweak which her daughter promptly undid, setting it back as she'd had it before. She took a long, last look around the house, and then she was ready to go.

The jaunt began to trundle awkwardly over the rough village track, the huddle of men, women, and children trailing after it. It looked for all the world like a sacrificial procession: the jaunt a funeral pyre up in front, the plumes of the men's tobacco smoke hanging like incense above it in the clear morning air, and Máirín with her outrageous clothes and flushed face the high priestess, presiding over it all.

The mother walked side by side with her daughter and offered to carry her rug, but Bríd Shéamais grabbed it and insisted on carrying it. The mother had intended to have Máirín to herself for this last bit of the way, but her own Citín and Mairéad got in the way again. All the young girls were pushing in close to Máirín, some whispering and laughing, some lost for words with loneliness, and plenty more full of envy, wishing they could change places with her. The mother's sadness gave way to a seething resentment towards these ninnies who were stealing her daughter away before she was even out of her sight. She resented the jaunt too. It clattered along at speed as if racing a corpse to the graveyard. She was sure that the trunk, sitting up there on the box of the car, its timber pale as corn in the early sunlight, was spurring the horse to this breakneck pace. Words deserted her . . .

The sun, not long risen, had a soft, pink glow. Drystone walls flashed toothy grins. In the mean little fields, stubble bristled like Samson's head, freshly sheared by Delilah. A sailboat that had just left harbour with the wind behind was tracing a bright wake out through the narrow inlet.

At the crest of Aille an Chuillinn, Máirín stopped to look back at the house. From now on it, and the few houses clustered around it, would be lost from view. A line at the apex of the roof, where last year's fresh thatch met the black and withered stuff of previous years, seemed to demarcate days gone by from the days to come. The village looked like it had slipped back into sleep, as if it had only woken up for a moment, just long enough to spit into the sea, where the sailboat would cover the traces . . .

The jaunt stopped at the end of the track. People clustered in a circle where it joined the road, cutting the mother off from her daughter. She was lost in the crowd, just another stray stone in the pile. More than ever now she envied Citín and Mairéad, who would be going with Máirín all the way to the Bright City. When the farewells began, the women swooped in for kisses like noisy scavengers. They jostled their way to her daughter, squeezed her hand, and snatched a flurry of kisses, like starlings pecking at the sweepings. The men shook hands with her quickly and shyly, somehow conveying that if it had to be done it were best to get it over with quickly. Pádraigín Pháidín seemed to do the same, but unlike the others he raised his head just a fraction, and the mother saw the eyes of the couple interlock for a split second . . .

At long last her turn came. She hadn't kissed her daughter since she was a little girl. But although her lips were starved for the kiss, she was unable to put all her longing and sorrow into it. Hadn't Máirín just kissed all and sundry? Didn't everyone else get first pick of the caresses ahead of her? Her daughter's kiss felt cold and flat, all feeling drained from it by the fact that it had been sampled so many times by others. Máirín's body was cold too—she felt cold and insubstantial as a fairy from the hills. And what spoiled the kiss most of all for her mother was the fact that she couldn't tear her eyes away from the trunk, which seemed to be taunting her, saying:

'No kiss from this world can break the fairy spell whose trick is to bathe her in pleasure and travel and forgetfulness, whose trap is a golden one of young love and desire among the green, faraway hills . . . '

By now, Máirín was sitting up on the jaunt, Mairéad on one side of her, Citín next to the driver on the other, and Pádraigín Pháidín tying the trunk up firmly on the box between them. To the mother they were three evil spirits: the damned trunk; Mairéad, greedy for her passage money; and Pádraigín Pháidín, on fire to get to America and win her daughter's hand. All three of them mad to get their claws into her beloved firstborn . . .

Pádraigín finished his task and people stood back to make way for the horse. The women started to sob; their sobbing swelled to a wail with no real emotion in it, the mother thought, nothing but noise and crocodile tears. They couldn't even give her space to grieve. She herself didn't shed a single tear . . .

'I'll see you before five years are up,' she said in a faltering voice. She couldn't meet her daughter's eyes, not if the sky was to fall.

'You will,' the daughter sobbed as the cart began to move. But now the mother's heart as well as her head told her that it would never happen. Pádraigín Pháidín, the young girls from the village, her other children, right down to the one she carried in her womb, they would all see Máirín before she would. The mother knew now that this was just the first of her brood to spread her wings and leave for the land of summer, a wild goose gone, never again to return to her home.

TRANSLATED BY KATHERINE DUFFY

FLOODTIDE

Mairéad stretched her limbs and made a fork of her first and ring finger to rub the sleep from her eyes. She felt the cold of dawn in her wrists. Taking pleasure in her failed attempt to rise, she shrank back again onto the warm edge of the bed which Pádraig had left a minute before.

The month since she had come home, plus the three weeks since she had got married, had been a rude awakening. She thought of those ten years in New York when she used to be out on the floor at the first call of the clock before the dawning of the day, for the sake of . . . for the sake of this day — a day when she could lie in or get up as she pleased.

'Are ye up yet?' her mother-in-law's quivering voice came from the back room, through the door that Pádraig had left open behind him.

'We are,' said Mairéad and rubbed some more sleep from her eye.

'They had said,' she told herself, 'that Pádraig would not have the patience to wait for me until I had paid the passages over for my three sisters. They had said that since he was an only child, he would have given in to his mother and married some other woman years ago . . . They had said that given how young I was when I went over, I'd put him out of my head, marry beyond, and that it was unlikely . . . '

'Get up, Mairéad. Lydon will go mad . . . Time and tide wait for no man . . . '

The irritability she sensed for the first time in the old woman's voice startled her out of her daydream. It announced that the eternal battle between a son's mother and his wife was about to begin. In the dusty light she pulled on the most comfortable clothes she could find and remembered the rumour that was going around, that the old woman was complaining about the scant dowry she had brought with her into the house. A ten-year wait; putting up with big knobs and hotshots in America . . . Her shoelace broke in half in the second hole from the bottom. She felt the seeds of spite take hold in her heart.

'It's a long time since anyone got up so early in this house! Spring is close at hand at last . . . Now Mairéad, a drop of tea would make a young man of me again . . . '

Pádraig had put on a roaring fire and the kettle was humming to the boil by the time he brought a handful of oats out to the horse that stood harnessed beside the door. With the cheer in his voice, his face breaking into an affectionate smile as he spoke her name, Maireád's irritation melted on the spot. For the sake of all this, she'd be well able to put up with the old woman's contrariness. There'd never be a cross word between herself and Pádraig, or if there was, she was sure it would be her fault . . .

It wasn't exactly what you would call bright as they were leaving home. Lydon's two daughters were sitting on a pair of upturned creels at the top of the boreen that led down to the shore, and Lydon himself was pacing up and down along the edge of the shingle bank, champing on his pipe.

'I declare to God,' he said, half in jest, half in earnest, 'I thought we wouldn't cut a strip of seaweed on the Cora today! I have yet to see a newlywed couple too keen to get up in the morning!'

The two daughters smiled, and Mairéad gave a great shout of laughter.

'The tide has gone out a bit,' said Pádraig sheepishly.

'Gone out a bit! It's practically at low water! It's the second day of the spring tide, and if we don't make the most of it today and tomorrow there won't be another ebb this year good enough for cutting the deep ridges of the Cora.'

'There's a spring tide?' said Mairéad, simply. Because she had gone to America so early in life, she had little real knowledge of some of the domestic concerns whose names were woven into her memory.

'A spring tide,' said Lydon, with all the appearance of a bishop in whose presence a shameless blasphemy had been uttered.

'The great spring tide of the feast of Saint Bridget! You're not used to the spring tides yet, my dear, you have other things on your mind.'

He winked at her and nodded over towards Pádraig, who had gone on ahead, down along the stony beach with Mairéad's creel tied onto his own and slung across his back.

Mairéad was reluctant to say much at that point. It was enough for her to think about the job that she had to do that day. For the past week the old couple had been banging on about the spring tide, but Mairéad hadn't been one bit bothered about going 'to the beach,' until now, when she found herself at the edge of the shingle bank.

Mairéad was born and bred on the edge of the great bay. She had already gathered periwinkles and sand eels, laver, dulse, and carrageen. The spring before she went 'over' she had helped her father cut seaweed on the upper part of the beach. But she had left before she was fully inured to the slavery of the seashore. Her hands had quickly become wrinkled from washing, scrubbing, and cooking, instead of acquiring the leathery skin of a foreshore forager. In the ten years during which the sea would have put salt in her blood and mettle in her bones, Mairéad saw salt water little over ten times.

But as they became exposed to the sea, the salt wind in from the deep sea breathed new life into her veins.

'Aren't there plenty others like me in the parish,' she said to herself, 'who spent twenty years in America and who are as used to this slavery today as if they had never left home? And sure the slavery of the sea is only part of the slavery I'll have to get used to again? Is it any worse than slavery on the bog, slavery in the fields, the slavery of cattle and pigs, the slavery of bearing and rearing children, if God grants me any . . . '

All the same, Mairéad would have preferred not to have had to gather seaweed on the Cora with the Lydons. Would Nóra and Caitlín Lydon tease the greenhorn, and would news of her ineptitude reach her mother-in-law at home? 'Isn't it just typical,' she said, 'that the Cora had to be jointly harvested on my very first day out? I wish it were just Pádraig and me.'

She intended doing her best, for Pádraig's sake, but she knew he'd only allow her to do half her best for fear she'd overstrain herself, being unused to the work. 'For God's sake, mind your back,' he'd say, even if there were only two potatoes in the cow's tub. Right now, Mairéad would prefer if he abandoned his reservations and waited before giving her a hand. The smooth and shifting stones of the shingle bank were a major challenge to her, crunching under her feet and becoming even more slippery as she tried to tread lightly across them.

'There's a big difference between this place and the streets of New York,' said Lydon as they were breaking it down to the end of the shingle. 'You should have put on hobnailed boots. You'd be better off barefoot than with those light little "toy toys" on the beach.'

'First ones I laid my hand on this morning,' said Mairéad, laughing, though this time against her will.

Down on the exposed strand, the crisp and solid sand lifted Mairéad's heart and she dashed over towards a cluster of whelks and periwinkles that the tide had left on the strand overnight. She stuck the tip of her shoe under them and kicked them over to Pádraig, hitting him on the calf of his leg. But still he didn't wait for her. Mairéad found it tough, going over the hollow they called the *cosán*, between the outer strand and the low-water mark, that successive generations of Lydons and Keadys had promised and failed to turn into a horse track. She made her way over much of this rocky passage by clearing the tide pools in bounds. When she came as far as large rugged masses of rocks, she slid sideways along them, grabbing onto a boulder. Neither her breasts nor the acorn barnacles benefitted from her passing. At one point, she would have fallen but that a sea anemone's tentacle brushed against her and kept her on her toes. At another point, a little kingdom of periwinkles on a rock face rained down into the pool. The bright laughter of the working party echoed in the clefts and recesses all along the shore.

The Cora was the furthest point along the strand: a rocky ridge extending into the water, gaps and divots carved out of it by the constant erosion of the open sea. The Cora was never entirely exposed, but you could harvest it at the low ebb of a spring tide, if you didn't mind getting wet. Pádraig tucked the ends of his *báinín* jacket into his waistband and waded up to his hips in the narrow arm of sea, reining himself back in when he felt himself being drawn out.

'We had better start on this black seaweed here,' Lydon said, as though channelling his irritation with the Keadys towards the sluggish ebb tide. 'Isn't that dreadful?'

'Not worth killing ourselves for a year's growth,' said Pádraig, but since all the others had stooped to work, he himself started. It pained Mairéad to see the salt water dripping from his clothes. She looked over at him again and again so that he might see how sorry she felt for him, but Pádraig never once lifted his head. Mairéad understood that since the spoils were to be split equally between the two households, Pádraig was trying to do the work of two men, seeing that there were three Lydons. It didn't take her long to realise that he was actually doing the work of three men, that she might as well not have been there. She was slipping on the oily slabs, and the tufty year's growth was so tough that she skinned her knuckles trying to strip the rough coating off the stones. It didn't matter how often she edged her sharp-pointed knife, it made no odds. She cut her finger on a blade of seaweed. She stared at the blood streaming down onto the rock, not wanting to complain, until Caitlín Lydon noticed it and bandaged it with a strip of her calico bodice, which the salt water washed away again before long. Her fingers were numb, and dark blue blotches started appearing around the knuckles on the back of her hands. She had to rub the back of one hand against the palm of the other. But the real embarrassment came when she had to go wading.

Pádraig glanced sideways at her from time to time, vexed, Mairéad thought, vexed that partnership was forcing her do work that he himself would never have asked her to do.

'The nip of February is still in the morning air,' said Caitlín Lydon. 'It probably feels strange for you to be on the shore?'

'Ah, not really,' said Mairéad. 'It's a matter of getting used to it, I'd say.'

'It's a sorry way to make a living,' said Nóra Lydon. 'If I were in America, God knows I'd never leave it. My passage money will come this summer.'

'You never have a good word to say about life at home,' said Caitlín to her younger sister. 'But you might miss it yet.'

Caitlín spoke in the adult tones of the *bean an tí* who was to inherit the Lydon house, land, and strand. But it seemed to Mairéad that her voice was a little more venomous than necessary in her defence of the home. Mairéad stopped short of telling her about the Brooklyn shopkeeper who had been asking her to marry him until the day she left America. They would just end up laughing about it in all the rambling houses of the village that night. Was there ever a hussy or whore came back from America and didn't claim that some millionaire or other wanted to marry her beyond?

By going waist deep in the water, the men could now go out onto the Cora. The women would stay where they were until it had ebbed some more in the arm of sea.

Lydon, out on the Cora, issued a constant stream of orders to his daughters: 'Strip the stones down, they won't be reaped again for another two years.' But Mairéad knew the orders were aimed at her, even if his eye never once rested on her. After a while, the women edged over the channel by the exposed bank of red sand. Mairéad stood staring at a crab that was wandering about in a pool, before it took refuge under a stone. It took all her strength to dislodge the stone, and what came out from under it but a tiny speckled fish that escaped her claws and went into a nook between two standing stones. Her heart jumped. She thought of how she had loved crabs and rock-fish when she was a girl. Her father would never come home from a seaweed strand without bringing back some shore-gleanings. If only Pádraig wasn't so busy, she'd ask him to catch a handful of crabs and rockfish for her.

The flat stone beside her was covered in limpets. She vividly re-membered the very rare occasions she had served limpets and cockles as a delicacy. You couldn't beat a batch of shellfish roasted on the embers. She got a craving for limpets. They might also appease the old woman at home. She thrust her knife in under the edge of a lim-pet that had slightly loosened its hold on the rock. At first she was loath to come between it and the rock. She couldn't help but think of her mother-in-law coming between herself and Pádraig. But the limpet came away so readily that she had no further scruples. 'It's a pity I haven't got a little can or a bucket,' she thought. Then she re-membered that if she gathered up the coarse apron she had on over her American dress and tied it behind her, it would hold plenty. She could put them into the creel when they had finished on the beach. 'Slowly but surely,' she told herself, 'I am developing some sea acu-men.'

'Don't be driving yourself daft with those limpets, Mairéad,' said Lydon. 'Top-shore limpets have twice as much meat in them as low-water ones, and besides, limpets are not right until they have had three drinks of April water.'

Though what he said was true, she took the hint. She was there to cut seaweed, not to pick limpets.

Mairéad edged her way further along the strand with the two

women. She liked the little lagoons that had been exposed by the ebb. Her thoughts were captivated by the faint murmur of the waves in the mouth of the channel. The saltwater gossamer breaking against the mini-strand charmed her mind, and she laid into the work. She didn't find it so brutally difficult either. Though the most abundant weed here was serrated wrack, the blackweed here was lusher than over on the rougher ridges. It was interspersed with top-shore weed and soft tufts of knotted wrack, like golden locks in the rays of morning sun. For Mairéad to touch the tufts was even riskier than going at the limpets a short while ago.

Lydon's temper was now stirring in his voice.

'Of course, ladies, you don't think that my old rough-crop field can digest serrated wrack! The earth will have moulded every single stipe into its own shape by next autumn. I wouldn't ask you your business if I was sowing the loam at the bottom of the village. The tidewater is shallow enough now for you to come out here.'

Caitlín Lydon went out barefoot as far as a boulder under the Cora. Nóra took her boots off and went out onto another smooth stone. Mairéad did likewise with her own boots. She flinched as she was about to pull up her dress, and looked over, shamefaced, at Lydon and Pádraig. All she was wearing underneath was a flimsy American petticoat. It surprised her at first how unconcerned the other pair were about pulling up their skirts, until she remembered that they had never left home. Her feet contracted with the cold of the water, and she walked over, as gingerly as a cat crossing a puddle.

Suddenly she was afraid that she would be swept away by the rippling waves that were breaking in white flakes across the raised rock in the channel. The soles of her feet were ticklish on the gravelly bottom. She frowned, as it felt like the Lydons were laughing at her. She looked longingly out at Pádraig, who had his back to her, cutting as fast as he could, racing against the mouth of the wave. He didn't even lift his head.

She was out now on the exposed Cora in front of the rocks

where strapwrack grows. Its rich fronds infused her with greed. She was filled with a desire to plunder. Desire to scrape the rock faces clean as a plate. She took pleasure in the squeaking of the long trails of it releasing their grip and the hiss of the bundles falling down into the rocky hollows. In spite of the cold and wretchedness of the salt water, she felt her blood rush, something she hadn't felt for ten years . . . She came to a gently arched shelter, in under the camber of the Cora, where there was a downy growth of carrageen on the jowls of the rocks. The bunches of carrageen Nóra Sheáin Liam brought to America had often jolted her mind back to the edge of the great bay, to the lovely beach where her heart's desire had remained. She remembered her mother-in-law and turned her attention to picking carrageen.

'One might say,' said Lydon, the urgency of the sea now in his voice, 'that you ladies are not doing too well. This reef is not even half stripped. You must be afraid ye'll get wet. And salt water never hurt anyone.'

Mairéad gave up on the carrageen, though Lydon's voice didn't bother her anymore. She was sure she could do her share, that the sea had tempered her skin and slavery had strengthened her arms.

Lydon was prophesying doom once again:

'The tide is flowing. Look, Carraig an Mheacan is almost under. Hadn't the ladies better start returning to shore? They'd be better off doing that just now.'

For the first time that day, Pádraig lifted his head and looked Mairéad in the eye. He tried to say something, but his lips shut tight again before the speech came. Mairéad could see clearly that he would stop her from doing that work if he could. The strong hold of the partnership had tamed the heart that was flashing through his eyes at that moment. He needn't worry. Mairéad intended showing him that although she might appear to be soft-spun, there was a tough weave in her too. It was because he was so good to her that she was going to do her utmost for his sake.

They began filling from the furthest part out. They'd be able to collect the nearer part until the tide had come a good bit in.

For hands that had been ten years in the murky heat of a narrow kitchen, it was refreshing to feel the stiff slime of the seaweed sticking to them as she pushed the creel. The first creel didn't knock much out of her, though the path was rugged and the water from the seaweed came streaming down her back.

She heaped as much on top of the second creel as either of the two Lydons. And she wouldn't have slipped except that a bundle of the heaped load hanging over the edge of the creel fell off as they were coming out on the edge of the Cora. And even though she did slip, she wasn't hurt. She grabbed on to a rock behind her and kept such a grip on the creel that only a few bunches fell off the top. She would have preferred if the two Lydons had gone on instead of leaving their creels down on the stones and coming back to help her gather the fallen sheaves. From the third creel on, she felt that the Lydons were slowing down so that she could keep up. The journey from the low-water mark to the seaweed spreading bank, nine or ten yards above the high-water mark, was getting longer with every creel. Mairéad thought it was like trying to bail out a full tide.

All over her body, she felt the rolls of sweat take the sting out of the chill of the salt water. The strap began to give her blisters on her palms, the salt water starting biting into her knuckles . . . Her back was stiff, and as for her legs, best leave them out of the equation. They seemed to belong to someone other than the person who had come down the boreen so quick and lively that morning. Afraid that at any minute she'd go over on her ankle. The soles had come clean off her flimsy shoes. Every time she stood on a sharp pebble she pulled back her foot, arching the upper part of her instep toward the shoelaces. She was like a horse with a nail in its hoof, quickly lifting her foot off a pointed periwinkle or a limpet shell. She was also ravenously hungry. She had eaten very little that morning. For ten years she had been in the habit of having a cup of tea in her hand at eleven o'clock every day. But fasting was child's play compared to this crushing and scald-ing work. In America, there would be a break or a change of activity after every shift. But the same journey, from lower to upper shore, over and over again. . . .

Lydon's temper was brewing, in unison with the rising tide.

'You're slow, ladies! I think we'll have to leave this reef uncut and start returning to shore. If we're depending on you, the flood tide will take some of what we've already cut.'

Now that the men were retreating, the race was on. The rocky shore didn't bother them one bit. Caitlín Lydon, barefoot and all, was just about able to keep up with them. Pádraig was emptying his creel on the spreading bank by the time the others had reached the tidemark, all except Mairéad, who was still above the lower edge of the sand.

She had no feeling left in her feet. Sometimes when she came to the upper edge of the sand she closed her eyes to shield them from the painful sight of that last stretch. Now, she was numb to all pain. She ploughed along as though goaded by someone inside her. Her body was rigid and so was her mind. Her thoughts were disjointed fragments: 'The partnership . . . If the seaweed was left to myself and Pádraig . . . Slavery is something a body has to get used to . . . The flood tide . . . '

She slackened her pace going to the top of the shingle, and hadn't the strength of mind or body to open her eyes properly. Be-fore she knew it she was into the tidemark, covered in shells and periwinkles, masses of oarweed holdfast, bits of barnacle-encrusted boards, strands of wrack and the remains of red tangle that had been thrown up by the spring tide from where it had lain rotting during the neap. It was a slimy strip of red tangle that made her slip. Feeling her feet going from under her, she let them go. It was a relief to release the strap of the creel; Pádraig filled the creel and took it to the top.

Mairéad felt the look of laughter in the Lydon girls' eyes, despite their talk of 'treacherous stones' . . . 'a distance that was too long.'

To think she had left the comfort of America for this. But that wasn't Pádraig's fault.

'There's no call for you to go down anymore, Mairéad,' said Lydon. The three of us will gather what's left, we'll do it in one go, and Pádraig will have no trouble filling a creel with what's left down at the channel, Pádraig, young lad, come on, or the tide will have every last stipe taken.

But now Mairéad was determined to go back down. Isn't it well they didn't ask Nóra or Caitlín Lydon to stay up above? She'd go down, if it was only to spite them. If there was only a single clump of seaweed left, she'd make two halves of it. She had made her bed and she would lie in it . . .

In spite of Pádraig's haste, she was neck and neck with him on the way down, and when they reached the low-tide mark she was no more out of breath than he was. It gave her some satisfaction to have him to herself for the first time since they had come to the shore. She dismissed the idea of gathering her share of what was left into her own creel: there wasn't a creelful's worth when all was said and done.

One would think, the way it was angrily erupting, that the flood tide regretted being caught out that morning and intended taking full revenge for what it had exposed earlier in the day. It pushed into the channel, nudging the pebbles with its cold snout, sniffing into fissures with its snorting nostrils, fumbling with its long fingers far up onto the red ebb-strand, lunging voraciously at the bundles of seaweed that had been left uncollected. It had already hauled off a few large heaps, and Pádraig was put to his knees trying to save a thicket of strapwrack from its gullet.

The sense and starvation of the sea sat well with Mairéad's troubled mind. The rush of the sea gossamer was like a lullaby to her troubled heart as it tousled the serrated wrack on the stones and then broke despondently, though it had not yet displaced the little sandhill deposited by the ebb. But before the scattered gushes of the first wave had been absorbed by the sand, the force of a new wave came to topple the sandhill once and for all. Mairéad stood in the cold pool on the edge of the bare strand until the backlash of the wave that had taken the sandhill drenched her to her knees. A velvet swimcrab came out of a crevice, prospecting from the crested shoulders of the wave. A periwinkle went from the rock playing catch-me-if-you-can with the surge of sea water rushing for the last gatherings of weed. Mairéad went out to the edge of the wave to retrieve a handful—a shiny handful of yellow-weed.

'Leave my way!' said Pádraig, who was up to his thighs stealing the last of the spoils from the ravenous sea. Mairéad stood up straight, her mind startled by the voice. A harsh, alien voice. A voice from a kingdom far removed from that of lonely letters, sweet nothings, and pillow talk. Stunned, she burst a little bladder of seaweed between her fingers and squirted a dull red splatter of it up onto her cheek.

The dark shadow she saw on Pádraig's features at that moment was as churlish and low-spirited as the black streaks that the rising wind was leaving on the bristled locks of the flood tide.

TRANSLATED BY ÚNA NÍ CHONCHÚIR

PUSHING ON

She would have taken a bite of the burnt crust herself, but self-denial trumped starvation. And it wasn't the six-year-old's eyes, wild and frightened, that caused her to keep her fast, but the withered hand the youngster held out between crust and mouth to grasp a life that was slipping away from him before he could grab hold of it. She put the half-mug of milk, a morning's worth of milking, on the edge of the table beside her husband. But he just glanced out the corner of his bloodshot eye at the mug handle, hawked up a stringy gobbet of phlegm which he spat into the fire, opened the door, and walked out into the yard. Distracted by the look in her husband's eye as he closed the door behind him, she didn't stop the young lad from grabbing the milk. For a minute, she listened to the mouthfuls of milk rattle in the boy's greedy gullet. She was about to tell him that the crust would taste better if he dipped it in the milk, but it wasn't worth her while now, for all the milk, for all the crust, that was left, and since she hadn't bothered to tell him at the outset, when it would have been easier. Her tongue was as dry as a smith's boiling bellows.

She took a handful of oat scrapings from the bottom of the grain bin, shook them on the floor, and opened up the old wicker chicken coop in the corner. And it was only when she called 'chuck, chuck' and got no squawk of a reply that she remembered they had picked the last hen's bones clean the day before. Going out to fetch a can of water, she felt her mind freeze over as though stuck in yesterday, and there was nothing she could do about it. Coming in over the gap on the way back, she left the can on the goose pen opposite the wall of the well-field, as she always did when she was carrying a can in each hand. She couldn't work out for the life of her if it was yesterday or a week yesterday or a month yesterday that that pen last had geese in it. And with the way life had been treating her for the last three months, and the weeks and the days melting and merging into one another in her mind, she was down on her hunkers and had unhinged the little door of the pen before she remembered that there couldn't possibly be any geese in there. Her husband was going from the dunghill to the cowshed door, a torn shit-smeared strip dangling from the tail of his bawneen jacket, as though some exorcised demon had pegged itself to his back. Lifting the door latch he glanced around the yard, and for a second his tormented eyes met those of his wife. But the tortured look failed to pierce her heart. For a minute she didn't recognise him. She forgot they were married, that they shared a home. She knew all along, though, that he was going in to harness the donkey and bring a load of manure to the potato field at the top of the village, as he did every morning. She was about to tell him he needn't bother since there were no seed potatoes left, but why should she, he knew that too.

She poured water into the small pot and hung it over the fire, for no reason except that she used to boil up a mess of cabbage stalks for the hens at that time every morning. No sooner had she put the pot on the fire than it occurred to her she now had neither hen nor pullet to her name. She went out to drive the cow down to the shore meadow as she always did once she had the young lad ready for school. Her husband had got to the shed before her and had let the donkey out into the yard. He came out from the donkey's corner to untie the cow as well. It was he had tied the cow the night before, which was a rare thing, and had made a double knot instead of a running loop as his wife would have done. The knot was too tight, and rather than undo it he decided it would be easier to take the halter off the tie-stick altogether and throw it up with the donkey's halter over a crossbeam until it was needed again in the evening. Neither of them asked what the other was at. It occurred to her that the husband had usually left the yard by that time of the morning. But before she had the next fleeting glimmer of understanding—there was no seed to sow—the thought had vanished completely from her mind.

As always, she kept pace with the cow, who knew her own way down to the shore meadow. Coming out onto the king's highway, she remembered that she had put the small pot on without stoking the fire and that she hadn't got the young lad ready for school. She tried to quicken her step, and as she did her mind erupted into a raging cauldron of boiling water; images of school, young boy, pot and cow bubbling up maliciously, one after another, over here and over there. And each cursed bubble quickly begot another: the fair; her long-exhausted credit; having to hide her plight from the neighbours; the seed that was gone; the 'committee flour' that had been promised but never came; and the poorhouse. Then the globules of memory became so confused in her mind that she could no longer tell them apart, and so she pushed on.

The cow trundled more slowly than usual that morning, but she made no attempt to hurry her on. Even as they came out onto the king's highway and a car blew a sharp, fierce blast of its horn, neither she nor the cow moved any quicker towards the path to the seashore to avoid ending up under it. She was jolted into involuntary awareness as the whirlwind of the car wrapped around her, brakes screeching by the cow's chest. What if the car had killed the cow, and the fair only two days away! It was then it occurred to her for the first time that they could kill the cow themselves and eat her. Otherwise they'd be dead by fair day, after six relentless months of hardship and suffering. She tried to make sense of the situation, but her mind was like the tiny eye of a needle being poked with three or four threads at once, with so many thoughts cutting across one another that none could penetrate. Her senses were numbed, not so much by the morning fast as by the perpetual thought of it, of credit, of the committee, the fair, the cow, supper, breakfast. And since she had failed to find the makings of breakfast anywhere that morning, her mind could now also be let wither, abandoned like an old cargo ship at the bottom of the harbour having put its last load ashore.

It was a great comfort to her that she had lost all emotion, that her senses were numb. Each time she tried to process a thought, her body was wracked with spasms of satisfaction. They started as sharp twinges in her womb. Pricked her palate and tongue with sharp pangs of burning desire. Her forehead breaking out in a sweat, ideas bursting into a thousand airborne bubbles before her eyes. Her bodily senses were wrestling hard against one another as though only the most scaldingly painful could survive. Sometimes she thought all the sounds of the world were being played out in her ears, not a familiar sound among them. Other times she went stone deaf, all sound replaced by a vision, infinite and impersonal, its shapes blurred and unstriking. And later again her taste buds were aroused by the salty tang of every sea and the taste of honey gleaned from all the world's beehives dancing on the tip of her tongue . . .

It was a mild late-February morning. A fragrant steam rose from the earth. Buds were burgeoning on trees. Leaves on shrubs were lush and green and brushwood was breaking across stone walls. A blackbird's mating call, a lone lamb bleating, waves pounding on the shingle at spring tide like some kindly creator making flesh of its word, incarnate of the virgin Nature. But to her it was a world far removed from human senses. A world without beauty, scent, sound, or taste. A world without length or breadth or depth or substance or feeling. A world without mysteries or gospels, birth certificates or last things. It was like a world casting off its old familiar traits which had not the strength to shoulder its altered appearance.

She hadn't chewed a blade of grass or juicy leaf or slip of hawthorn as she had always done with delight every morning until now. She also had a habit of lingering at the gap into the glenside field. Every morning, driving the cow in at the gap, she'd go pulling cress in the watery pools by the boundary walls. She used to cut across there at night to dig up some of their own early-harvest seed potatoes from the small plot and boil them up unknown to her husband. The pools still had cress in them, the small plot still had ridges untouched, but she had neither will to live nor life force enough to pick it. After a while, gently tapping the cow wrenching coarse grass by the wall, she pushed on.

She moved on towards the shore meadow with the cow, as she had done yesterday and the day before and the week before. Shore meadow was etched in the walls of her mind and soul, along with the fair, the mealtimes she could remember, the meals she had to go without. The cow ambled, tearing up clumps of roadside grass, grinding one part of the tuft between her teeth and swallowing the other, half chewed, to be turned into cud. The grass was coarse and green and juicy, and would remind you of fresh milk slurped down to warm the cockles of your heart. At one stage she tried to grab a green fistful of grass from inside the cow's mouth, but left it alone when she realised its jaws were not going to let go.

'Daddy!'

She didn't take her hand off the cow's rump, and the young boy had to tug at her apron before she looked down at him. 'Da-ddy!' he said, gasping in panic between each staccato syllable. 'Out in the shed . . . halter round his neck . . . hanging from the beam, eyes turned in his head. Mommy! Mommy! Go home quick, quick.'

'Good boy . . . hanging from the beam.'

The words knocked sparks off the walls of her mind, just as the car brakes had done earlier, and she stood still . . . And she realised then that she was driving the cow down to the shore meadow as she did every morning. She tapped the cow again a moment later . . . it was just as easy to push on. Like a spider's web spun by the wind in a darkened room, her thoughts streamed back and forth, and she kept step with the plodding cow, pushing on . . .

TRANSLATED BY ÚNA NÍ CHONCHÚIR

FROM *COIS CAOLÁIRE*
(1953)

THE EDGE OF THE BOG

'What's come over me at all?'

Muiréad hadn't drained the butter mixture properly. When she was putting it in the bottom of the dresser, it spurted onto the pat and dribbled over her fingers.

'What's come over me at all?'

She repeated the question so she could hear the crankiness in her voice. It took a while for the echo to be swallowed up by the big, bare kitchen . . .

She had forgotten to replace the lid on the churn after shoving it in by the closed door.

'Same as a cold,' she said as she sat on the stool, 'it'll have to run its course.'

Muiréad hardly ever sat down out of tiredness, but the crankiness of the last few days had forced her to rest several times. This crankiness was worse than anything else life had inflicted on her until now, seeping down into the wild roots of her being. Her only sister had died in America; her brother had drowned; her mother's death ten years earlier had left her alone on the edge of the great bog.

Sorrow had eaten its way into her happiness like maggots through ripening fruit. But it hadn't stopped her planting in the Spring or harvesting in the Autumn, looking after pigs and fowl, cattle and churnings, and working the edges of the bog. She was still young when she was left to soldier on. Shut up as she was in her outpost, any offer of a helping hand, any advice, was treated like an incursion from enemy territory. So much of the last ten years had been spent digging straight ditches in the bog that her mind was a pool of dead water bordered by the straight shores of Spring, Summer, Autumn and Winter . . .

It was the late night she had spent at Neainín Sheáin's wedding that made her realise the pool could have a different shore. And she had been thinking of that shoreline ever since, playing gently with bits of odd fantasies she had stolen from the storehouse of moors, hills, and lakes she kept in her mind . . .

Spring, Summer, Autumn, Winter. Cattle. Pigs. Churnings. Ditches. Ten years . . . A female salmon, trapped in a pool for ten seasons . . . And clear fords upstream . . .

A pullet squawked into the house and Muiréad got up to put it out. The bird changed tack on wings neat as sails, scattering ashes as far as the ceiling before landing on the edge of the churn. 'Damn you, you hoor! You've pickled the butter in ashes, after all my slaving . . . ! What's come over me . . . !'

Her mother used to say churning on Monday was unlucky. Muiréad had no time for that kind of old nonsense. And yet she never went near the dash-churn on Mondays, even in summer when the cow that had just calved was shedding milk . . .

Today, for the first time, she realised that her weekly trip to the shop was a necessary part of her life . . .

She hadn't made butter on a Monday for ten years . . .

From the recesses of her mind, a filthy torrent had poured out, bringing with it all the rubbish of her annoyance. The sluice gate at the highwater mark of her mind had delayed the churning for an hour . . .

The trip to the shop was a liberating pilgrimage that brought her to a windswept mountaintop, releasing her from the narrow hold of her day, the blind bog of her week . . .

Her mind leaped across the great bog to the sack of bran she usually sat on in the window of the shop at Bun Locha. It was nice to sit there in the half-light, feeding off the dreams of those who had more than enough to spare . . .

Spring, Autumn, cattle, churnings, ditches . . .

The women of Cill Ultáin and Ceann Thiar who brought their children to the dispensary in Bun Locha talked about those things too. Listening to them chattering in the shop, Muiréad never imagined the Spring, cattle, and ditches they spoke about were anything like hers. Their talk belonged to a bright, happy time before she was born, before the magic wands were shattered . . .

Mcaig Mhicil would be in Bun Locha. She'd wait for Muiréad, and Muiréad would wait—as usual—until the other women were finished. Then she and Meaig would walk home together, as they did every Monday. But today, as she hurried to the dispensary with her mollycoddled child, Meaig didn't have time for the usual chat at Muiréad's gate. She'd drive the shop demented with her talk of the child and be so wrapped up in him on the road home, she wouldn't notice Muiréad's face darkening with annoyance, any more than she did every other day . . .

Five to eleven . . .

Muiréad got up to see if she needed anything from the shop. The little bag of bran sat hunched in the press, almost as full as the day the lorry had left it in the yard. The half-empty bag of oats reminded her she had meant to buy some yellow meal last week. It was cheap, healthy food that filled the hungry gap between the last of the old potatoes and the new ones that weren't worth digging yet . . .

She'd say it was for the hens, or the pigs. She'd wait until everyone else had been served. But there was always a customer in the shop. Of course, Cáit an tSiopa knew that Muiréad bought from the lorry. Her lip would curl maliciously:

'Thinking about going on the stirabout, Muiréad . . . ?'

No one, except for the odd old woman here and there, had eaten stirabout for donkey's years. And she not forty yet? A female salmon . . .

The shelf in the bottom of the dresser was as full as the press.

Neainín Sheáin's wedding was the reason the last purchase from the shop hadn't been touched yet . . .

Neainín was her brother's daughter. But that wasn't why she was fond of her. Muiréad herself wasn't exactly sure why or how much she liked Neainín. Every Sunday, from when she was a little girl, Neainín would come over to visit. They'd do the rounds together, looking at the pigs, the hens, the fields, or the latest patch of sodden bog Muiréad was draining. Sometimes, Neainín might bring a couple of friends with her. Those summer days, they'd go down to Poll na hEasa to look at the salmon basking in the mouth of the stream, or up to Leitir Bric to see the lakes, like shining ringlets in the hollows of the hills . . .

Then Neainín took a notion to go and marry a soldier — a soldier she would only see once a fortnight. A week yesterday, she was here visiting as usual. As they walked the land as far as Poll na hEasa, she said the chickens were doing well, that the early sowing had hardly been worth it. When she turned away from the still pool, she said all the fish had gone upstream . . .

Hens, potatoes, fish . . . And not a word about marrying . . .

On Tuesday she was back again, to tell Muiréad she was getting married on Thursday. No word of a lie! And she only twenty-three years old . . . !

The piece of pork Muiréad had bought for Neainín's dinner was still in the dresser, raw as a wound. You could count Neainín's visits on the fingers of one hand from now on . . . The pork wouldn't be eaten on Sunday. It was the only thing that couldn't be got from the lorry, so she had no need to go to the shop on Monday for the Sunday following. Monday would be like Sunday, Sunday like any other day, and so on like a string of rotten eggs . . .

The pigs were squealing in the sty, and the half-door couldn't stop the hens' wings and screeches from turning the kitchen into a cauldron of noise. Muiréad ignored them, and didn't bother with the usual late-morning cup of tea in her hand that would take the edge off her hunger until lunchtime. She went up to Páircín na Leice to weed the potatoes she had planted at the start of the year . . .

There were more weeds than she expected: redshank, chickweed, sow-thistle, and snarls of borage tangled around every stalk, weakening their stems, blocking the sun. Muiréad attacked the rebellious lowlife. There were far more weeds than last year, after all her hard work digging trenches. It was five years since this patch had last been planted with potatoes. It had been coarse moorland then, but the crop that first year was better . . .

Cáit an tSiopa would be saying if the shop was too dear for certain people, then there was always the lorry . . .

Jude from Cill Ultáin would tell Ceaite from Ceann Thiar that the priest with the beard had said her little Cóilín would be saying Mass in Cill Ultáin yet . . .

Ceaite from Ceann Thiar would tell Jude from Cill Ultáin that Cuimín Mhurcha's wife had told her she'd have twins this time around and that the doctor wouldn't take anything less than twelve pounds—five pounds per child and two pounds lance money . . .

There was no borage on the new growth at the north end . . . Her own hair was the same colour as the borage . . . Ten years ago . . . Her mother used to say it was a sin—the sin of pride—to look too often in the mirror. That's what Lucifer used to do. He had a comb of sunbeams for his golden hair! Then he stuck his tongue out at God . . .

Meaig Micil would hand the child around from one person to the next. She hadn't slept a wink on account of him . . .

Muiréad had fertilised the ground well with coarse sand, and cottony cow dung collected from the hill above. The ditches deepened . . .

Meaig Mhicil wasn't even twenty. She had told them her age the last time she was here with Neainín. Every Sunday since then, she told them again how old she was . . . She wore a tight, flimsy blouse the night of the wedding. You could see her breasts, like two ripe apples with the stems still in them, just plucked from the tree . . .

And the way she had pressed herself against him . . .

It was a shithole of a bog and it would stay that way until the sun mounted the moon . . .

Neainín kissed her soldier shamelessly in front of her. They shoved open the door of the shed into the dark. They couldn't even wait till the crowd had gone home . . .

There shouldn't be any borage at the bottom here, or in the north-facing patch . . . Spring. Autumn. Churnings. Ditches. A female salmon . . .

The young girls were no sooner out the door than they were grabbed from all sides. Each of them gave a little scream as she was grabbed, and then laughed. They were still laughing as they went into the bushes at the back of the sheds and down the twisty old lane. The sound of the accordion in the wedding house drowned out the screams and the laughter . . . The musicians knew well what they were doing . . . The two in front playing together . . .

This bloody borage! It should be in the thin growth, near the rock, instead of here at the bottom!

Then one brazen young fella had grabbed her in his arms. He pulled her so close that, although it was dark, she could see his rough, sallow face. The cigarette in his mouth lit up his eyes and the pimple on his face. His warm breath smelled of drink and he slurred his words. He knocked over a bucket of water by the corner of the house as he came after her . . . But it wasn't her scream that stopped him. His arms were reaching for her as his face came closer. Then he recognised her and slunk away.

There weren't half as many weeds on the hill, where they should be. No coarse sand or manure had been spread there, only the dry droppings of the donkey . . .

A minute later, she heard him laughing at the gable end. It was definitely him. Telling the other lads that he almost . . . The nerve of him . . . !

The potatoes had failed in the Buaile last year; that's why she had none left . . .

There was neither sight nor light of him in the wedding house afterwards. How on earth did she not recognise him? Because she didn't mix with people—was that why? Blazing eyes. Rough, sallow skin . . .

A shithole of a bog; as withered and dry as an old bone on top and soggy underneath.

Her scream had been meant to push him away . . . She complained to Neainín about it afterwards, hoping she'd find out his name. The soldier had answered her:

'Divil a bit of harm a good strong squeeze ever did any woman, Muiréad . . . '

A good strong squeeze . . .

'What's come over me at all?' said Muiréad as she yanked clumps of weeds from the ridge, clay and all.

'How will I tell the priest? How will the girls who were at the wedding tell the priest? I wasn't round the back of the sheds, where no one could see, only the stars above . . . '

'Poxy borage,' she said, spitting the words out through the beauty-gap in her teeth.

All the same, deep down she didn't hate the rampant weeds as much as usual. She brought an armful of straw from below up to the cairn on the stone slab. She didn't check for the smell of blight as she walked back along the trench. Every evening this time of year, she'd walk the potato patch to make sure it hadn't taken hold. There were small red spots on the leaves and traces of white scum on the top of the cairn. Muiréad felt nothing as she looked at them.

Some wisps fell from the armful of straggly straw. When she bent down to pick them up, she noticed they were potato stalks. One of the stalks she had wrenched from the earth had a healthy potato at the end of it. Muiréad gave a hollow laugh as the same question surfaced again, under her breath:

'What's come over me at all?'

She threw away the stalk, surprised the untidy state of the potato patch didn't worry her more. There was a cloud, a dark, shapeless cloud, lying over the bog. Muiréad didn't know what it meant. At that moment she didn't care whether it meant the withering of crops, or blight.

Muiréad had always thought it was well for those who could throw off whatever baggage they were carrying and straighten their backs in the clear air. She had thrown off her own worries now . . .

She'd love to wander off across the bog this time of day: to stalk the edge of the water like a heron; to be like the moorhens, sleeping and waking in the heather; to cry a while and laugh a while, depending on whether Gleann Leitir Bric was sunny or in shadow; to walk slowly down the hill with the little stream, accompanying its brave music against the rocks and sighing when its final trickle drained into the mire; to go murmuring with the grasshopper from hummock to hummock during spells of fine weather; to follow the salmon to the bright fords upstream . . .

She was surprised at how fierce her breathing had become, how everything seemed clearer since she had emptied the dead water from her gills. The pure water refreshed the waterfall of her senses. Since she had thrown away her sterile cares, the screaming and laughing of the wedding was a clear bell ringing in her ear. She heard the same tune in the irrepressible thrum of the grasshopper and the happiness of the condemned mountain stream . . .

Blazing eyes . . .

Muiréad started, and moved quickly away from the discarded straw towards the house . . .

It would be easier to tell the priest you were with a boy . . .

Meaig Mhicil was going down the road, holding the child by the hand, stopping every now and again to rub its face with her apron. If Muiréad wasn't already halfway to the house when she saw who it was, she'd have stopped for a chat. There was no need to hurry; Meaig was as blind as a bat . . .

Suddenly, Muiréad was jealous of the other woman. Wasn't it well for her that nothing could come between her and her precious child. For the rest of her life, Meaig would be the same as Muiréad had been for the past ten years: Spring. Autumn. Churnings. Ditches. Worry . . .

She wondered if the back that stoops under the weight of love also carries the hope of love . . . Where there is hope, there is worry—love-worry . . . Does the back throw off that weight as well?

The clear lines of the last ten years had been wiped off the moor by the limp wings of the grasshopper, while Muiréad kept rewriting them as question marks on the silent, unchanging sky . . .

She had never wanted anything but her own selfish happiness. Sometimes, however, her fortress was unable to keep out the clear light of other people's lives. Then Muiréad would look out on the world, anxious to show that there was room for heroism and sacrifice in her heart too. And because the bog was the nearest monster at hand, she attacked it fiercely, but for no good reason.

To dry it; make something of it; make the world speak of it as if it were a bright daughter or a heroic son. That her struggle might be remembered like the songs of some mad poet from long ago were remembered today. That she herself might become a lasting dreamsong written on the face of the bog, to be read by all who passed by . . .

Then her hopes would rise up like two arcs of a rainbow from either end of the moor. But they always stopped, like broken pillars under the vault of the sky, the great bog like a filthy wedge always pushing them apart . . .

Today she realised she needed someone else to shoulder some

of her worries. She could never weld the broken arcs into a perfect arch on her own, or turn the foul water of the raw bog into the giddy white wine of hope . . .

A rough face . . . She'd know him again . . . If she saw him; but she wouldn't. He'd be off gallivanting in England, or in the army, or married.

Muiréad went into the room, to the large mirror she hadn't looked in for years, except for Sunday mornings before Mass . . .

Heavy, lustrous hair still as yellow as the borage. A pretty face, sensual as ripe fruit . . . Cheeks lined with straight furrows . . . Hips and buttocks stretching the old dress . . . A female salmon . . .

Some devil was tempting her . . .

The cow needed milking. She realised she hadn't scrubbed the milk cooler after the churning. It was the bloody churning that had started it all off! She wouldn't churn on a Monday ever again. Maybe it was the folly of youth that had made her ignore the old people . . .

She carried the cooler out to the haggart wall to scour it with sand. She didn't see Pádraig Dháithí until his greeting made her look up from her work. She was surprised he hadn't stopped at the stile. She watched him all the way up the road, irritated by his brisk walk. The entrance to her yard was the same as any other now for Pádraig, just another stepping stone on the way back to his own place . . .

She scrubbed so hard she tore splinters off the side of the cooler. Wasn't Pádraig Dháithí in an awful hurry? Couldn't he stay and have a chat, like he did whenever she met him on the road . . . ?

Hot water splashed from her hands over the sides of the cooler, scouring the sun-baked earth from the cobbles in the yard . . .

There could hardly be another baby arrived at Pádraig's? Meaig Mhicil would know, if she had the manners to stop awhile, on her way up or down, and talk to her. Was that why she was in such a hurry this morning? Maybe, after all, she had never brought the child to school. What could have kept her so long? Hanging around until it was time for the kids to go home! What was she up to?

Married women were in their element in any house that had a newborn baby. She used to hear them in the shop saying they drove the doctor demented.

'Are you in labour too?' he'd ask if one of them got in his way.

Then all the women would burst out laughing; their cackling filled the dark little shop, like a large exotic bird flapping its wings in the half-light. As soon as they stopped laughing, they'd pair off and start whispering to each other. Muiréad could never work out why they were laughing or why they were drawn to houses with newborn babies. She would always be a clumsy swimmer clinging to the surface of the bog, looking up at the birds as they spread their wings at the tip of the rainbow, singing their secret songs in the sun's ear.

She stared at the puddles of hot water she had spilled in the gutter by the side of the road, remembering all the nights Pádraig Dháithí had spent talking to her, over at the stile and up at the school wall. Like a magic garden that suddenly sprouted from the blind bog before disappearing again, she remembered the last of those nights, when he told her he was going to ask Nuala Hiúí to marry him, if Muiréad wouldn't have him . . . And he and Nuala were after having their ninth child today . . . !

Muiréad was barely in the door, cooler in hand, when the dog rushed in after her. He jumped up on the chair and ran his tongue anxiously across the table, licking up the breadcrumbs she had left there after her dinner. Then he started sniffing and scratching at the dresser door. He devoured the hunk of bread Muiréad threw him, then stood on his hindlegs and leaned against her, hoping for more. When she gave him another piece, he made for the door, but Muiréad grabbed the leash from the wall and tied it round his neck. She ignored his howling and dragged him around the back of the house. If she tied him up in the kitchen, she wouldn't sleep a wink all night with the noise.

The hens had settled in the henhouse. She couldn't leave him there, or in the pigsty. The cowshed was empty, but Bile Beag still hadn't brought the new door. A dog howling in a shed with no door was as bad as one in the house. She had to do something with him, at least until the cow was milked.

To hell with the dog! She thought she'd get some peace when she sold the donkey. That bloody donkey! At the first sunny whisper of a grasshopper, he'd prick up his big, lazy ears; no rope or spancel could keep him in once the bright summer entered his heart and blood . . .

She locked the door of the henhouse and tied the leash to the hasp.

'Where were you, you bitch, when the cows were headed for the swamp yesterday? And today, when the sheep were at the hayseed . . . ?'

Muiréad kicked him in the belly with her nailed boot. He didn't whimper but lay flat on the ground, his ears laid back, his upper lip twitching, as if he were asking forgiveness. She'd never treated the dog like that before; now she wished she hadn't.

A big lump of his ear hung loose, and there was a fresh, red weal on his hindquarters. He was limping, his eyebrow a mass of clotted blood, hiding his bright eye. It was his first trip to the house in two days . . .

Muiréad loved milking at this time of year. Her heavy hair brushed the cow's flank, while the milk flowed in diagonal spurts as quickly as threads run from a spool by nimble fingers. The thick generous milk of summer . . .

A noise from the yard startled the cow. She took no notice of the armful of hay or the 'Só bhó bhóin' Muiréad sang to try and soothe her. She would have gone to the house to get a chain but she realised there was hardly any milk left. Bad luck was harnessed to the bog—locks, ropes, halters, and chains . . .

The cow's hoof knocked over the bucket, spilling the fresh milk down the parched hillside as far as the seeping cow dung.

She stared at the lazy slick till the last glint of bright milk had disappeared . . .

Out on the hillside, the playful stream was choking in the quag-mire. Here, the best milk had been swallowed by the dungheap, down into the darkness, among the worms and rotten corpses of ancient trees. The stinking belly of the bog would swallow anything—a per-son's sweat as soon as a cow's milk—and turn it into stinking swamp-stuff, quagmire, and mould . . .

That milk should have produced something beautiful—shoots sprouting in the clean wind and sun . . . It should have made her pigs' backsides as soft as fresh breadloaves; or made a prize bull of the black hill-calf, so that cows would be brought to him from far and wide. It should have brought a bright glow to a child's face . . . It was milk like that which gave Meaig's children their ruddy cheeks . . .

Although she was nearly forty, Muiréad's body was stronger and more able now than it had been ten, even fifteen, years ago.

But the exhausted stream had drained to a trickle in the swamp. The proudest tree that blossomed under the sun was now a stump of bog deal submerged under the moor. A cranky old stump . . .

Who knows how long Muiréad would have stayed there blaming the bog for all its shortcomings if she hadn't heard the sound of cry-ing. A woman was coming up the road towards her. Muiréad made for the house, so she could get there ahead of the stranger, who went right past, without glancing at the wicker gate or the stile . . .

A tinker. Muiréad didn't like tinker-women. She sent them on their way with as little as possible for their trouble—a handful of po-reens, usually. They were all thieves as far as Muiréad was concerned, although they had never stolen anything from her. But she wasn't in the habit of leaving things lying around . . . She always locked the door facing the road, even if she was only going to the shed at the back of the house. The dog had been trained to keep a look out at night, or when she was away from the house . . .

The tinker-woman went down the path to Meaig Mhicil's.

Meaig would get rid of her with a few poreens too . . . Hardly. The tinker-woman knew her business. Meaig would take pity on the squalling bundle in her arms; a woman with a child was always welcome in a house where there was another child.

Meaig had little interest in any child except her own. As soon as she'd hear the practised scream of the tinker-child, out she'd go, dragging her own child by the hand, to show him off, telling the other woman how she hadn't slept for a month on account of him . . . She'd tell her his age to the day, reciting every ailment he'd had from the time he was the same age as the tinker-child . . .

It was milk that gave him those ruddy cheeks.

The tinker would get a generous helping of milk for her child . . . She knew her business all right—no point in going to a house where the best milk had been swallowed by the greedy, stinking bog . . .

Muiréad walked back along the lip of the bog from where she had watched the woman. A few hens were still running around behind the house, half terrified. Then she realised what had startled the cow: the dog was gone—he had ripped the hasp from the door and taken the whole lot with him: hasp, lock, rope, and all! She had no other hasp or lock for the henhouse. Or a dog to keep watch. And the tinkers camped up by the sandpit at Trosc na Móna! She'd have to put them up in the loft, like she'd had to do a few times before, and nurse her bitter worries in her arms again . . . Let them stay where they were . . . Even the tinkers would think twice before coming to her now . . .

Muiréad brought the milk bucket inside and sat down on the stool . . .

She was too set in her ways to take a rest this early in the evening. She needed an armful of nettles for the hens and pigs . . .

She went out again, up around the Leacachín, and attacked a thick clump of them by the west wall . . . Nettles were healthy food for hens. And pigs. They'd have to do until the new potatoes were ready . . . If she saw him . . . Even if she did . . . What would she say to him? I told myself, Father, if I saw him, I'd tell him . . .

Muiréad tore the sock from her hand . . . Better to let herself go completely once and for all than to keep stroking a wild dog in the recess of her mind, like she was doing now . . . Hell is full of people who did less . . .

She turned towards the foxgloves, little ears listening along the eastern wall. She picked one and burst it between her fingers. The night of the wedding, during the set-dances, the boys made a snapping sound like that with their fingers as a sign to their partners that it was their turn to dance . . . No one asked her to dance. If they had . . . She hadn't danced for at least ten years . . . She was never one for dancing; the houses on the sullen moor were too far apart . . .

If she had been asked out, how would she have refused the invitation? That her shoes were hurting her? That she had twisted her ankle a couple of days before? That her light shoes were being mended? She couldn't say she wasn't able to dance . . . She'd be bumping into people on the dance floor, making a show of herself . . . But no one asked . . .

Her feet moved, and her lips murmured rhythmically . . . Down like this . . . Up again like that . . . Across . . . Around . . .

Muiréad burst all the blossoms on the stalk and it gave her a strange satisfaction, like nothing else she had done all day; the same satisfaction she'd get from lighting a cigarette, she thought, from pursing her lips and blowing long strings of smoke into the air. But she had never put a cigarette in her mouth. The young women took them from the men the night of the wedding, hiding their heads between the boys and the wall so their parents wouldn't see them. But no one offered her a cigarette. If they had, would she have refused? She pursed her lips . . .

She attacked another foxglove. Soon, the edge of the field was covered with the shattered lights of the fairy-lamps. The old people used to say there were magic lanterns in the foxgloves that allowed the fairy-women to see in the night dew the face of the man they would take with them to the other world . . .

Let them cool off in their fairy-skins; it was hard enough to find a man in the real world! Or did the fairy-men skulk away from them too in the darkness and burst out laughing?

She'd recognise him, without the light of the foxglove or the dew . . . She didn't have to wash her shirt, like those other óinseachs, up where the three streams came together in Gleann Leitir Bric . . . A rough face; a pimple; blazing eyes . . .

Dusk had almost fallen on the long day when a late bee landed on her hand, exhausted from the futile search among the shattered foxgloves . . .

Muiréad walked back and sat on the large, bare slab in front of the house. She didn't feel like drinking tea or milk again; she'd done so three times already today. Neainín and the girls said drinking tea after supper kept them awake.

She couldn't remember the last time she had been outside so late. Even in the middle of summer, she'd have the bar on the door and the lamp lit while it was still light. For the past five weeks she had got up and gone to sleep again with the sun, without ever lighting a lamp. Pity she hadn't remembered it sooner! There wasn't a drop of oil left in the house . . .

Even if he only came to her once a fortnight!

The light was fading from the bog as the long, cold fingers of night crept around the shoulders of the mountains, dragging them down into the blackness at the foot of the sky . . .

Muiréad listened carefully in the light breeze: there wasn't a peep from the tinkers up at the sandpit. All she could hear was a hollow wheezing, like an old man in his sleep. The bog always wheezed like that at this time of year, its stinking belly parched by drought . . .

She must have been blind not to have noticed it before now: the yard was infested with docks! Thistles grappled with fuchsia by the wall — a fine parade of them, smooth seedpods at the ready, marching up to the window ledge! Rushes — the straggling beard of the moor — stood to attention at the southwestern corner of Garraí an Tí . . .

Pádraig Dháithí was right: that's where she should have planted the potatoes this year. It was better than the worn-out soil of the Leac . . .

The hilly clumps on the bog were like animals — huge beasts lying low, waiting until the light died before attacking . . . There was still some daylight brooding on Tulach an Fhéidh. She noticed something bright passing through the narrow light . . . Maybe it was Gilín, the pet lamb, returning from the fold. From the time he was born around St Bridget's Day, he had never moved away from the house until this morning. If he had been with her this evening, the two of them would have been inside the house while he nibbled sugared bread from her hand. The lamb was company for her on these endless summer evenings. But Gilín felt more independent these days. Every day for the past week, he was up on Aill Mhór sunning himself, listening innocently . . .

She was nice to the donkey, to the dog and the lamb, but it made no difference. Sooner or later, they pricked up their ears and left . . .

Again, the mountains seemed to be closing in on her. Their true shape was clearer in the dark than during the day — big, hard warts on the moor's thigh. Out there, between two hills, there was a bright hole in the black clouds at the edge of the air; that was Meall Bán. From there, Neainín would watch the road, one evening every fortnight, waiting for her soldier to come home. She'd spot him two miles away, she said. She'd see his buttons glinting in the sunlight. She'd run inside and put the kettle on, then walk down the path to meet him at the top of the road . . .

Docks. Thistles. Rushes . . .

It wasn't today or yesterday or the night of the wedding these ugly scabs had appeared. They had sprouted from a weedy patch she didn't know was in her until now. All that had happened was a blanket of fog had lifted from the bog for a second, and she saw the quagmire she was drowning in . . .

The bog begrudged every spell of fine weather, to the stream, the grasshopper, to everything. If a patch of land was prised from its clutches one year and sprouted golden ears of corn, the following year it would stiffen its barbarous mouth and vomit rushes and stagnant water back up through it . . .

For all that, she had kept a tight rein on the bog until now. In the past year, faded blotches had appeared on her door; she could see them clearly, even in the failing light. She should have listened to Pádraig Dháithí and put a few strakes of thatch by the chimney at the start of the year, where the soot marks ran down the wall . . .

Even if he only came once a fortnight, she'd shave the moor's stubbled jaw and empty its stinking belly while he was away . . . A visit every fortnight would be better than Neainín on Sunday or the shop on Monday . . . She'd look out for him from Aill Mhór; polish the buttons of his uniform with the tip of her finger; put unsalted butter on the pimple . . .

Ó bhó bhó, how could she go to the priest with her fine story?

A jacksnipe flew overheard, its cry spilling over the bog, mingling with the sound of Meaig Mhicil's singing on her late visit to the well. There was no trace of Meaig's joy in the plaintive voice of the bird. If it was daylight, she'd see the jacksnipe dragging an outsize shadow across the face of the bog. She heard the loneliness in its call, a restless loneliness that was rooted, maybe, at the other end of the moor, where there was joy, fragrant green fields, a home it had left behind . . .

Neainín's soldier leaving, once a fortnight, after a day and a night at home . . . In the smallest room in his wife's people's house . . . Neainín was hoping, the night of her wedding, that Muiréad would offer them a room in her house: 'I wouldn't spend a night alone in that house, Muiréad, even if they put me in charge of the whole army! Men coming and going, the tinkers up at the sandpit every other fortnight, and the fairies drilling on the hillside at night! A dog wouldn't put up with it!'

Muiréad answered from the selfish ark where she had spent the past ten years:

'It has good doors and strong bolts . . . !'

A stinging gust of wind came in from the sea, over Cnoc Leitir Bric, knocking the heads of the thistles together in the fuchsia. She felt pins and needles in her thighs from sitting on the hard slab . . .

She pulled a bunch of keys from the wide folds of her dress . . . The door wasn't locked! She had forgotten to lock it when she left the house. It was open all the time she was milking. The bloody dog was to blame!

She should bank a few sods in the fire. There wasn't as much as a spark left in the ashes. She'd find it hard enough tomorrow morning lighting the fire without a drop of oil in the house . . .

Muiréad bent down to the ashes and raked through them roughly with the tongs, bringing a few dead embers to the top. She went back into the room, without gathering them together or banking them for the morning . . .

She hurried through her prayers by the bed. Her mind was like a rock pool filling with seawater; she couldn't catch the minnows that kept swimming in and out between the rocks . . .

Hearing a noise outside, she got up off her knees: the dog whimpering, maybe, or the tinkers prowling around the back of the house. She had forgotten to put the bar on the door . . . Going into the kitchen, she noticed she hadn't even bolted it . . .

She felt no fear as she went out into the yard, and around the back of the house . . . Neainín with her tinkers and ghosts . . . !

The roosting hens were wheezing in their sleep. The cow was by the dike, happily chewing the cud . . .

It wasn't a dog, or a tinker, or the wheezing bog that made that sound . . . Maybe it was the wind funnelling the noise of the tide through the lake behind Leitir Bric . . . Or the splashing of the stream being smothered by the marsh . . . There was no need to check it out. It was probably one of life's little mysteries, something as simple and as strange as her own breathing, the peaceful snore of the living, growing world resting and renewing itself in hope for what tomorrow would bring . . .

The grass in Garraí an Tí would grow again tomorrow; the thistles by the house would grow stronger; the cow's udder would fill with milk; the hen would be ready to lay another egg . . . Hope. Life . . .

Muiréad turned back towards the house. It sat there like an enormous blister on the sallow skin of the bog. The bog should be allowed to grow and blossom as it pleased . . .

She went back to bed without barring or bolting the door . . . What did she care if the door was wide open . . .

If he came . . . Looking for a light to fix his bike . . . On his way back from the pub . . . The open door would welcome him in . . .

What would she say to him . . . ? That he smelled of drink . . . That she recognised his eyes, the pimple on his face . . .

Who's to say he wouldn't come? To apologise for the other night? For turning away from her? And bursting out laughing?

Who's to say? People do things like that . . . If you could believe the songs . . . Spending the night crying at a sweetheart's house . . . A cold sweat on his face in the morning . . . After the heat of love . . . He'd compose a song, then, with her name in it . . . People like Meaig would sing it on the way to the well, or soothing her child, and she would be remembered forever . . .

If he came . . . His foot on the stile in the morning when she woke up, his hair damp from the night dew . . . She'd laugh with him . . . A laugh that would prick up the ears of the moor and sweeten its stinking belly . . . Like the laughter at the wedding . . . A woman's laugh . . .

If he came . . .

Muiréad felt pins and needles in the side she was lying on. She turned her face to the wall . . .

But he wouldn't . . . Her whole day was a lie, trying to make a rainbow from the failed things of the bog—the miserable stalks in the field, the suffocated stream, the grasshopper that winter turned to dust on a clump of rushes . . .

She hadn't left her stagnant pool today, any more than any other day. A breath of clean wind from the angry sea had crossed the swamp and set the water trembling. Like a passenger on a boat with no crew to make the most of the flood tide, she stayed where she was, anchored in the calm of the harbour . . .

And that was all she had done today—ripped the lid from the forbidden well of her heart so she could swim in the dark flood that poured out of it; frustration; furious desires; a new kind of fear; terror as shapeless as a splash in a river at night, when you don't know if it's a fish, a rat, a skittering stone, or a withered leaf falling into the water . . .

But it was a special day, the first day of her life! Not a Spring day or an Autumn day or a hen day; or a Monday listening silently to Meaig and the other women in the shop, or telling them about her ditches on the mountain, with their absolute beginning, their certain course, and absolute end . . .

She had a story after today, her own story . . . As good as any woman's story, a small, happy rose in a vast swamp of sadness and filth . . . Clear and airy like the waters of the stream, the chirp of the grasshopper, new and golden like the plaits of the rainbow . . .

Maybe she could make a poem from it, something she could never do with the bog. Songs had been written about less . . .

Muiréad turned towards the window, already touched by the midsummer dawn, her mouth crooning softly:

'Níl mé críonna, a's faraor nílim
Ach mealltar daoine a bhíos glic go leor . . .
Sé críoch gach baoise—'*

How would her own story end . . . ?

Maybe it wouldn't. Maybe the only way her beautiful, true story could end was by being decapitated in the swamp, or broken like the arches of the rainbow over the moor, forever apart . . .

---

* I'm not old, and 'tis a pity I'm not / But even the clever are led astray . . . / The end of every foolishness—

A simple end, mysterious as breathing maybe . . .
'What's come over me at all?'
How would she tell it to the priest . . . ?
She couldn't . . .

TRANSLATED BY LOUIS DE PAOR,
MIKE MCCORMACK, AND LOCHLAINN Ó TUAIRISG

KNOWING

There were three of them there, crouched down in the nook of the corner of the ditch by the shore, the first one arse-ways on his hunkers, the second guzz-eyed leaning over, and the third crick-necked hugging his knee.

'It's just as well for some people now that the tide's going out,' Crick Neck says. 'We can take it easy.'

'The stuff that's coming in with the swell will be as high as a mast,' Arse Ways says. 'It's the first day of the spring tide in full gush.'

'I never saw as much tangled seaweed thrown up this early in May,' says Guzz Eye. 'If the wind whips up over there, it'll rot on the shore. Nobody to lift it.'

'Nobody to lift it.'

'Nobody to lift it, bejaysus.'

'It can rot to fuck, as far as I'm concerned,' Arse Ways says, 'I have tons of the stuff, enough to do the job, enough for a few corners of mangels. Do you think that I'd bother me bum to start stacking it up and drying it like the Walshes. I'd sooner get fucked by the devil. Let it rot . . . '

Let it rot as far as I care,' Guzz Eye says. 'I got enough mangels and Swedes today anyway . . . '

'Let it rot, all the way, as far as I care,' says Crick Neck.

'If only the wind shagged off to the north soon,' says Arse Ways.

'Let it be,' says Guzz Eye.

'Let it be and more,' says Crick Neck. 'You'd think it wanted to ride up its hole just now.'

'It'd be worth it. The Walshes would have fuck-all seaweed to stack up then.'

'Isn't that what I'm on about, you thicko,' says Guzz Eye.

'And me too.'

'And me like all the rest.'

'That would give great pleasure to us and to the neighbourhood.'

'You can say that.'

'You can say that again.'

'The wind would never have enough sense to do it.'

'But you'd never know.'

'Who'd ever know that?'

Crick Neck turned around and leaned on his other knee. He tucked the end of his sweater in behind Arse Ways to protect the matches that were being snuffed out by the gusts of wind just as they were about to light his pipe.

'It looked like yourself and Old Walsh were going to get stuck into one another down at the Inlet,' Crick Neck says to Arse Ways.

'God forbid that himself or anyone belonging to him has any luck,' Arse Ways says, squatting back down as best he could. 'A shower of shites! Those bugger scutty Walshes from up the country who left every mouse in their barn famished with hunger. Would you believe, he spread out some of my strings of seaweed . . . ! I'm telling you, he did!'

'He did?'

'Did he really?'

'I'm telling you by all that's holy, he spread it out and over to himself! "Hey, what's this you're doing?" I says to him. "Spreading May seaweed smack bang in the middle of the day. Spread it away and go stuff yourself! I'll take my own even if you spread it a hundred times!" I made him shift pretty quickly from the Inlet. And then he fecks off over to the Ridge in front of Martin Ted . . . Who cares, but it's only a few heaps anyway. Damn him and drown him!'

'Damn him and drown him again!'

'Damn him and drown him yet again!'

'The sea is a bitch, you'd think with all it throws up, 'twould drown him too.'

'Oh, a bitch.'

'A real bitch. She drowned many others less deserving than him.'

Arse Ways had to huddle himself in behind Guzz Eye as the swirling wind coming in off the edge of the ditch kept quenching his matches. Crick Neck went onto his other knee.

'Walsh's two daughters were swiping the stuff from me down at the Shingles. Each one on either side of me up to their arse in the sea.'

'Up to their arse in the sea.'

'That's the way to tell it: Up to their arse in the sea.'

A spout of smoke was rising up from Guzz Eye's pipe, leaning over this time: 'You spotted the way that the Walsh boy went outside me, back there on the strand . . . ? He was shoulder high in the tide, his fork ready to grab every clump that was mine. I hope he snuffs it, morning, evening, and night! He didn't take a gnat's notice of me until I stuck my fork in the tangle of seaweed straight at his chest. I have no idea now or then why I didn't plunge it right into the middle of his gut . . . '

'I have no idea either,' Arse Way says, looking him straight in one of his eyes.

'Nor me no idea neither,' says Crick Neck, looking straight into his other one.

'I'm telling you now,' Guzz Eye says, 'it's not like someone wouldn't want to do it . . . "May God fluck you and foul you," I says, "you heap of shit. There wasn't one bundle of seaweed that came in last year that you and that bunch of thieves in your house didn't grab. You have it splayed out before the break of day, and the breath of noon, and the going down of the sun. If you had an ounce of shame between you, you wouldn't dare to show your faces here today. You'd leave the few wisps that are left over to the rest of us, those of us who haven't had a smell of a snatch of seaweed, except what you lot have stacked up. Don't you have all of the shore stacked up and cleared out already, so why couldn't you leave the few clumps that happen to stick to our palms without swiping them? Fuck off out of here like snot off a shovel, or I swear to Jesus I'll gut you all the way from your balls to your oxter . . . " That's what I said, no word of it a lie.'

'Your health!'

'Your health, and a long life.'

'I'll give you one guess,' says Crick Neck, 'what the old one, the Walsh woman, wanted from me just a while ago: she wanted a corner of my patch to dry her seaweed in. "We're totally screwed here without any strip of land beside the shore," she says. "We have no choice except to crawl from here to the Yellow Sod humping a haul of seaweed all the way. All you have to do is to stand in the tide and spread it from the fork out on to the ground." "Every one of us has only his own small bit of land," I says.'

'I said the exact same sweet words to her,' says Arse Ways. 'She asked me for a strip of that sand bank over there.'

'Me too,' says Guzz Eye. '"You have three chunks of land right up kissing the shore," she says, "and you're happier seeing magpies flapping backwards and forwards over it than to spare your neighbours the long journey to their own bit of seaweed. I hope they'll be dancing a jig on your grave before long!" she says.'

'She said that?'

'She really said that?'

'She did, no word of a lie.'

'She's very quick with her effing and blinding!'

'She's not afraid of God, or man or beast!'

'Isn't she the right whore!'

'Hag!'

'Harpy!'

'Harridan!'

'They say that the Walshes' blood would boil out in the middle of the sea. Herself and the lot of them in the deepest hole out there!'

'The deepest hole out there.'

'The deepest hole there is.'

Arse Ways settled himself back another bit on his hunkers. Guzz Eye leaned more over on his right-hand side. Crick Neck switched to his other knee.

'The Walshes themselves aren't the worst, not as bad anyway as that piss artist of Patch's who gave them a strip for spreading over near the Marsh.'

'A strip for spreading?'

'A strip for spreading, bejasus.'

'Watch your mouth now! Here he comes! The piss artist!'

He went down on his two knees between Arse Ways and Guzz Eye. He gave a few little coughs. Three pipes were looking at him simultaneously, the thick smoke swirling through his gasping breath.

'Anyone have a match?' he asks.

'A match! I suppose the Devil himself had a pile of them stashed away before the War,' Crick Neck says. 'I haven't, anyway.'

'Nor me.'

'Nor me neither.'

'No hope of a light so between here and the houses,' Piss Artist says, looking ruefully at the three mouths puffing away passionately as if they were part of some kind of ritual—an accursed one.

'Blast it anyway that I didn't bring a light with me. I'm gasping for a puff.'

Crick Neck took the pipe out of his mouth. Cupped it in the palm of his hand. Squashed the tobacco down with his thumb. Tapped it out on the crap of the seaweed and mire on the rough surface of the rock. A glob of half-burned tobacco plopped down on to his thigh. Looked down at it again:

'I thought if I dumped out the dregs there might still be enough left there to tickle your tonsils,' he says. 'But the glimmer is completely gone. Many blazing matches were drowned in that hole out there these last few years.'

Arse Ways whacked the dottle of his own pipe onto the rock.

'Don't the Walshes have any matches anyway?' Guzz Eye says, emptying out the guts of his own pipe. He winked at Arse Ways. Arse Ways winked at Crick Neck. Crick Neck winked at Guzz Eye. Guzz Eye winked each eye one after the other at Piss Artist . . .

Piss Artist got up and slouched along the stony beach towards the edge of the Marsh . . .

'You can feck off now.'

'You can feck off now.'

'You can feck off now, for fuck's sake.'

'Looking for a match on a windy day.'

'And they're so scarce.'

'And tobacco so dear.'

'We got great fun from that.'

'All he'd want is that we'd have matches and tobacco ready for him in the palm of our hands.'

'He can get them from the Walshes, as he's so fond of them.'

'I've wasted a whole gobful of tobacco because of him, but I'd rather that than give him the satisfaction of having even one puff,' Guzz Eye says, scrabbling away with his fingers trying to grab at the dreck from which sprigs of smoke were curling out behind his buttocks.

'I'd rather that too.'

'I'm with you all the way in that.'

'Of course, he'd have got a match and the light of his pipe if he had cooperated, and if he hadn't given the Walshes a place to spread their seaweed down by the Marsh. He went against the neighbours. He gave the message that we're all a shower of wasters.'

'He made us all into a shower of wasters.'

'He made us all into a shower of wasters, no doubt about it.'

Crick Neck tucked the corner of his sweater down under Arse Way's side to save his match from the gust of the brisk breeze.

'I got no joy at all from my smoke just now.'

'Nor me.'

'Nor me just like both of you.'

'It's great to have a smoke with no hassle.'

'Too true for you.'

'Too true for you about that.'

'I suppose we should do another bit of work?'

'I suppose we should.'

'I suppose we should. We should indeed.'

Guzz Eye straightened up from being crouched down and looked back. Arse Ways straightened up from being hunkered down and looked back. Crick Neck straightened up from being on one knee and looked back:

'The Marsh will be covered with seaweed soon.'

'Soon, definitely.'

'Very soon, definitely.'

'It's no problem for the Walshes, they have five big lumps over there lashing away at it.'

'Five big lumps, no lie.'

'Five big lumps, without a word of a lie.'

'The Piss Artist's stuck in the ditch over there gabbling away with the mother and daughter.'

'With the mother and daughter?'

'With the mother and daughter, God's truth.'

'Bad luck never nibbled at his arse until he started messing around with the Walshes.'

'That collection of cunts will wipe the silly grin off his face as they did so often before.'

'It's not that long since he hated their guts.'

'And bringing them to court in a flash. Their cattle trespassing and wrecking his place. Not a day passed without them destroying his land.'

'He swore to me by all the devils in Hell that they didn't leave him as much as a sod of turf, and he'd have to be up and out on the bog before dawn with his eyes glued.'

'And that they stole his potatoes from the shed and that he'd have to survive on bread alone until the autumn . . . Watch out! They've spotted us looking at them . . . '

Arse Ways turned his side around back again to face into the wind. Crick Neck turned his head in a slant towards the houses. Guzz Eye turned his gaze in a wide arc that took in the daughter, Mrs. Walsh, and the Piss Artist:

'You'd never know how he took a fancy to them all of a sudden. He refused them his car only last week.'

'And a shovel.'

'And a grain of sugar, and a grain of soda, and a drop of buttermilk.'

'Last Friday he called the father a crook.'

'And his son a bollocks on Saturday.'

'And the mother a bitch and the daughter a seedy slut on Sunday.'

'You'll never really understand this world.'

'It's often been said, man. You'll never really understand this world.'

'Nobody will ever know exactly what it is between the Piss Artist and themselves,' Arse Ways says.

'That's exactly the way to put it: nobody will ever know exactly what it is between the Piss Artist and themselves,' Crick Neck says.

'I know,' Guzz Eye says all of a sudden, twisting himself around towards Arse Ways, who was facing southwest into the wind, and towards Crick Neck, who was facing northeast in the direction of the houses. His eye was like a precious stone that emitted a mysterious glow from one part, while the rest of it was still half buried in the earth. It winked at Arse Ways. It winked at Crick Neck. But Arse Ways didn't wink any eye at Crick Neck, nor did Crick Neck wink any of his back at Guzz Eye. The two of them just stood there—southwest against the wind and northeast towards the houses — hoping for a flash of revelation from the starred eye.

Guzz Eye turned and strolled along the line of seaweed marking the edge of the high tide where coils and clumps rolled in from the sea beyond the reach of those who could harvest it. When he came to the edge of the stony beach he turned around to the two others who still stood there facing southwest and northeast.

'I know. I know it only too well,' he says again in a confident authoritative voice: the voice of knowing.

TRANSLATED BY ALAN TITLEY

THE STRANGER

1.

Nóra hadn't slept a wink all night. She heard the plop of frog-spawn in Garraí an Locháin, the screech of a startled thrush in the bushes beyond the road in Páirc na Buaile.

The cock crowed for the first time — a smouldering cinder hurled through the black hole of sleep. The second call was different — persistent and arrogant, its harsh cry a steel beak pecking at her chest. For the rest of the morning the noise in her head and the palpitations in her heart would not go away. She didn't feel like getting up until it was well past the usual time.

She put on her wrapper. It was cleaner than the red dress that was frayed at the hem. She had no call to put on her Sunday clothes on a weekday.

Usually she went barefoot until after breakfast. Today she put her shoes on as soon as she got up; she'd tie the laces later.

You could see her face and shape more clearly as she bent down to pick up the tongs, her nervous body taut as a coiled spring, ready to snap.

You'd notice her face more than anything else — blotched, and uneven, like mortar divided into panels with a trowel, each panel so dry the skin would come away if you scratched it. And if that comparison occurred to you, her glazed eyes might also remind you of shiny shells that are set into mortar. Her hair was grey and wispy as the thin ribbon of smoke from the dead fire.

She brushed the hair from her eyes and put down the tongs, then stood for a moment in the middle of the kitchen looking around, each wrinkle on her forehead writhing like a painful wound:

'I don't put it on until milking time . . . '

She took the patterned shawl, as she called it, from the dresser and wrapped it around her.

She picked up the tongs again and cleared away the ashes, then banked the glowing embers. She took a few sods of turf from the pile along the wall, broke them, and placed them around the live coals. Like an ugly moth emerging from its hiding place, a thin wisp of smoke seeped from the new fire . . .

As soon as she had made the breakfast, she sat in the chimney-nook coaxing the smouldering fire.

The ashes scattered on the hearth were like the dried dung of some large animal. A film of dust on the floor. Shitscrapings from shoes, potato sproutings with bits of fluff on them. There was a puddle of water by the keeler and buckets near the closed door, with sops of straw, mangolds, and a waistcoat that had fallen from a hook on the wall scattered around it . . .

Every morning she had breakfast before sweeping the kitchen and putting the ashes out.

When she looked up from the chimney-nook today, the house seemed dirty in a different way than before. She couldn't stand it. She grabbed the brush and scraped the heavier dirt vigorously towards the fire, ignoring the awkward places under the press and by the shut door until later.

She got the stumpy shovel with the broken handle from the gable, and threw water on the ashes that had been there for two days. Five shovelfuls; five trips to the mound in the yard. There was no need for such work on an empty stomach, she told herself . . .

When she came back in, Micil and the Young Man were up.

2.

Micil gripped his boot tightly with both hands as he struggled into it.

'How well it was me got stuck with this rotten relic of an old cow!' he said, grunting.

It was the same tune every morning from Micil as he tried to squeeze into the tight boots.

The Young Man was on the other side of the fire, watching a trickle of sooty water seeping down the whitewashed wall . . .

'A drop of castor oil will ease them out for you,' he said, turning to Micil.

'I put butter on them but it was no use . . . '

Nóra dropped the knife she had been wiping on her apron. She ignored it and turned around to pull the half-full keeler from the closed door. She had lifted it on its side, with the water lapping against the brim, when the Young Man got up to take it from her.

'What'll I do with it?'

He had to ask again before Nóra could wrest her eyes from Micil's boots, before she could unlock her tongue to reply:

'Put it out in the yard.'

There was no need to bother with it in the first place. She'd only have to bring it back in later anyway. It was all his fault . . . ! All that talk about castor oil . . . ! In a house where there was never a drop of the stuff . . . !

'Can I give you a hand with anything else?' asked the Young Man when he came back in.

'Stay where you are,' said Micil. 'A man shouldn't lift a finger till he has his breakfast eaten. That's what I say anyway.'

'I'm well used to work on an empty stomach,' said the Young Man. 'Many's the time I had a load of turf drawn in from the Rua Thamhnaigh before breakfast! During the lobster season we hardly ever get to eat a bite until we come in after checking the pots.'

'Madness, boy. Sheer madness!' said Micil. 'You should never work on an empty stomach. A mug of tea's your only man! I wouldn't put a foot outside the door without it. When the priest is hearing confessions here in the village, I nearly drop with the hunger . . . '

Micil went on and on, but Nóra didn't hear him any more. The Young Man's talk had left her confused, as though new rocks had sprouted around the house during the night . . . So that was what women bought castor oil for . . . To put it on shoes . . . ! Going hungry to the bog. A creel of turf on your back on an empty stomach . . . At least that wasn't as bad as carrying a currach, like a cap on your head, down to the sea . . . The boat creeping towards the cork that marked the lobster pot, like a beetle crawling towards a button in the folds of a bright dress. The fisherman still fasting . . .

Nóra knew nothing about lobster fishing. Nobody had bothered with it in these parts until recently. The first time she saw anyone doing it was a fisherman from the West who came over every summer for the lobster season. Sometimes, when she was down on the shore, she saw him working. From the south side of the house, she could see him heading for the pier, then pulling on the oars as he made his way out to check the pots. It never occurred to her that he hadn't eaten . . . ! They had strange notions in the West . . . !

'The bog isn't far from ye over there,' said Micil to the Young Man.

'Nearer than it is to ye anyway. Rua Thamhnaigh is only about a quarter of a mile from us. I'd say it'd nearly be cheaper for a man that's on his own over here to buy coal and the bog so far away.'

'Even if it was outside in the haggart, we wouldn't cut turf on an empty stomach . . . !'

It was Nóra who had spoken, defending her husband's easygoing habits, the habits of her people, which had to be protected from the newfangled ideas, the aggression and hardness that was second nature to the people who lived in the islands and inlets back there in the West . . .

3.

'Your breakfast is ready,' she said to the Young Man.

Micil had already pushed his stool in to the table.

She put Micil's egg straight onto the table, and the Young Man's in an eggstand beside his teacup.

She had given him a cup and saucer. Micil had a mug. If the tea was too hot, he'd get a saucer off the dresser to cool it. Nóra huddled over the fire with her own mug.

The two men went on talking. Twice Nóra spoke to stop the hem of conversation from unravelling into awkward silence.

She listened closely . . .

His tongue was quick as a fish. Darkskinned words from out West! 'Crayleagh' for ashes, 'slack' for a weakness, 'mire' for bog hole. 'Lobsterhole,' 'wrack,' 'boltrope' screeched like strange birds in the kitchen . . .

The night before, one of the neighbour's girls, Máire Jim, came in with her messages from the shop. The Young Man chatted with her. She started imitating him, saying 'swine' instead of 'pigs.' Her own Nóirín, the Young Man's cousin, would be just as bad. Nóra would have to give her a clip on the ear to stop her. It would end in tears. She'd no sooner be out of sight with the rest of the young ones than she'd be at it again. You couldn't be up to them. Maybe the Young Man would hurt them. They'd get more than a clip on the ear if he took his hand to them. Who could blame them for imitating his strange talk . . . ?

Currachs and boats! 'Na Rosa' and 'Na hInsí'—his talk was full of them! Ever since she was a child, Nóra had heard about those places, that were less than twenty miles away.

Twenty miles to the West. Half a mile from the house, you could see the lobster pots in the shallows along the shore. Twenty miles would shrink to half a mile; half a mile would stretch to twenty. The two places were black holes that remained invisible and unknown to each other.

Her sister Bríd, the Young Man's mother, had often written to invite Micil and herself over for a visit. She promised she would, but couldn't bring herself to go. She had never been to the West. Micil went—once . . .

4.

Micil capped his egg as gently as if he was drawing back the covers on a child to see if he was asleep.

The Young Man stirred his tea, then drove his spoon through the middle of the egg, cutting it in half—the blade of an oar slicing a wave.

Nóra had meant to cut the bread herself but forgot all about it until Micil handed the cake to the Young Man:

'Here you go. You've a steadier hand than me, God bless you!'

Micil cut thin slices for himself as carefully as if he were shaving. He put the bread straight into his mouth, pushing it to one side. Because his teeth weren't great, it seemed as though he was reluctant to chew it.

The Young Man gartered the bread, cutting wedges right through to the middle of the cake. Nóra thought of the sharp prow of a currach, the straight stern.

He buttered both sides of the bread. Instead of shoving it straight into his mouth, he held it a couple of inches from his face, then plunged his teeth into it. Such bright, healthy teeth! Like a trout taking bait from a hook. He had spent the previous night regaling Micil and Nóra with stories of dangerous fish—of lobsters' claws, the snap of dogfish and congers . . .

Micil was calm and unhurried as a cow chewing cud. The Young Man ate ravenously, greedy as an eel, watchful as a fox, suspicious as a dog with something in his mouth. He ate as though his food were dipped in blood and eaten fresh after a kill . . .

5.

Micil wiped his mouth with the sleeve of his bawneen and left the table.

'I was never any good for work,' he said, tearing a piece of paper from the sugar bag in the window to light his pipe, 'until I had a smoke.'

His back was against the table, his legs crossed, and his face between puffs of smoke, sluggish from sleep, like soggy dough.

'Where's your pipe? . . . Here . . . ' He handed a plug of tobacco to the Young Man.

The Young Man pulled a pouch from his pocket.

'I've plenty here. And a pipe. Anyway, I never take a smoke till later on. My stomach is a bit salty—'

'Sea salt,' Nóra murmured to herself.

'Tobacco is too severe on a full stomach. Last winter I hardly ever took the pipe out until I went visiting at nighttime.'

'Fair play to you!' said Micil. 'It gives me all I can do to stay off it when the priest is here for confessions . . . '

It was true. Any night he was off the pipe in preparation for the morning, he slept restlessly and didn't get up until she was back from the shop.

She used to see her father hurrying off down the road before the neighbours, with his pipe in his fist. Her brothers too . . . There wasn't a man in her family, or in Micil's, who would wait 'till later on' . . .

She stared in astonishment at the Young Man.

6.

He had arrived late the previous evening. Nóra had things to do. Then Máire Jim came in. The Young Man sat in Nóra's corner; she couldn't see him properly from the other side of the fire without making it obvious.

He had been to the house once or twice before but didn't stay long. Why would he, with only Micil and herself for company? Although he ate with them and spoke with them, his visits made no more impression on her than the odd glimpse she had from the door of sailboats passing by in the bay. Today was the first time she had paid any attention to his conversation, his face . . .

A fresh, young face; flushed cheeks; black, bushy eyebrows; rough, sallow skin: his father's colouring . . . and that growth in the hollow of his cheek!

A hard, dark growth! A mole!

Neither Micil nor anyone belonged to him had a mole. She didn't have one; neither did her father or mother, or any of her brothers and sisters. Bríd certainly didn't have one. How could she . . . ?

But Bríd's husband, the Young Man's father, had the same dark mole in exactly the same spot.

7.

Micil noticed the Young Man looking at the sootstreaks on the wall.

'I don't suppose you're any good at thatching? The rain comes in on top of us.'

'I'm not too bad at it,' said the Young Man.

'I've been watching and helping thatchers all my life, but I never had a go at it myself. The thatchers these days would rob you blind.'

'True for you.'

'Don't I know it. Nine bob a day. I needed a bit done over there on the south side of the house last year, so I got Ó Droighneáin from Tamhnach to do it. Two days it took him. No hurry on him, only three strakes a day! He's very tidy, but still . . . '

'If you have the straw,' said the Young Man, 'it's no bother for me to fix it so it won't leak . . . '

'God bless you! It isn't everyone could do it.'

'We can all do a bit of thatching in our house.'

'Fair play to ye. Putting a roof on a stack of oats was as much as any of our crowd could do. I wouldn't go as far as the ridge board, not if I heard the angels of heaven up there singing. God forgive me! I'd get dizzy . . . '

'I'd think nothing of climbing a ship's mast.'

'There you are now! Each to his own. I never saw anyone from Nóra's family up on a roof either.'

'So my mother tells me. My father often said that his own father, Réamonn Mór, reckoned he was the first person in his family that wasn't born in a boat. 'I was born on the roof of a house,' he'd say, 'with a mallet in my hand.''

Nóra scalded the milk bucket with boiling water . . .

8.

Micil harnessed the donkey.

'I'll throw five or six loads of manure into the field beyond,' he said. 'Where's that line that was there a minute ago, Nóra? I have to spread those heaps of black seaweed.'

'I'll do it for you,' said the Young Man.

'You will not! There's plenty of time yet for donkey work. Anyway, you'd be wasting your time trying to lay out the ridges in the east corner until you know the lie of the land. I'm fifty years at it and I still miss the line of the ridge and the furrow from time to time . . . '

There was pride in Micil's voice: at last he had a riddle the Young Man couldn't solve.

'Sure I'll have a go at it anyway. You can show me how to do it. All I have to do is spread the seaweed in ridges?'

'It's not as easy as it looks. The field is full of cairns, and every ridge has to be in exactly the same place as every other year. We'll start at the bottom, and I'll need to make a few croobawns where the water drains away . . . '

'Croobawns?'

'Now!' said Micil triumphantly. 'There's a big difference between boatmaking and building houses. You're the man for catching
lobsters, but I have the measure of Garraí an Tí . . . '

9.

'God bless the work!' said the Young Man as he stooped his head
into the shed where Nóra was milking the cows. 'Micil put the run
on me,' he said, laughing.

'Did he?' she said, amazed. The shawl slipped from her shoulders, the end of it trailing into the bucket.

'If he had to leave it fallow, he wouldn't let me next or near the
east end of the field!'

'That's Micil for you,' she said. She sounded exhausted, but her
voice was gentler than it had been during breakfast. The Young Man's
good humour had softened it.

'Micil would be as jealous of that corner as an eel guarding its
young!'

Her own words brought a half-smile to her wrinkled face. She
glanced up at him to see if he had noticed her mimicking his fishtalk
from the night before.

'Can I give you a hand with anything?' asked the Young Man.

'Like what?'

'Anything at all, seeing as I'm idle. Is this one milking at all, bless
her?'

'The yellow one . . . She is. She calved two months ago.'

'Have you another bucket, and I'll milk her for you?'

'You? Milk her? She wouldn't give a drop to anyone only myself.
Do you know how to milk?'

'I do of course,' said the Young Man easily, without noticing the
edge in her voice.

'You don't take after your mother then! I remember at home
long ago when we were young, Bríd had no mind for the milking,
God bless her!'

'My father teases her; he says all the cows must be dry over here. Himself is better than any woman at the milking.'

'You won't catch Micil milking a cow! Nothing will do him, only digging. Even the mention of it would be enough to put a puss on him! My own father was the same—the Lord have mercy on him. And my three brothers . . . '

10.

When Nóra came back after driving out the cows, the two men were trying out new spades in the house.

'Yours is too light,' said Micil, gripping the Young Man's spade tightly with both hands, cutting the air expertly with it. The bright wood-grain was straight in the smooth handle of the new spade. The wood seemed stiffer than the gleaming metal blade licked by the sunlight that came in through the open door.

'Too light, I'd say. It would be all right back in your place, but you need something heavier over here. This place is full of stones and hard soil, boy . . . God bless your innocence! It isn't half wide enough for the likes of Garraí an Tí . . . ! The bottom of the handle is too spindly. Look for yourself! Who put it in for you?'

'I did it myself the night before I came over. It was easier to carry with the handle in.'

'God, you're a handy man all the same! I could put a handle in myself only I'd make a hames of it. I prefer to get Taimín below to do it for me . . . Right then! We're off! Up to the field . . . '

They headed away, Micil with his spade in one hand and a basket of seed on his shoulder.

The Young Man leaned his spade against the stone fence and took a set of bicycle clips from his pocket. He gathered the ends of his trousers together and clipped them, then lifted his spade across his shoulder and followed Micil . . .

From inside the door, Nóra watched him warily as he went through the gap in the yard and out towards Garraí an Tí . . .

She thought she was seeing things. Bicycle clips! For planting potatoes! Like the policeman wore when he was searching for unlicensed dogs! . . .

No one around here wore spancels like that except the crowd from the mountain, and they had bog holes to wade through.

Micil often had a torn hem of his trousers trailing after him, but he'd as soon tear it off altogether as tie it up like the Young Man had done. Maybe he'd get Micil to buy a pair of them for his own trousers! . . .

11.

It was only then she realised she hadn't said her prayers; the breakfast had put it out of her head. She set the chair against the table and knelt down in front of the picture that hung by the window, facing the sun. She had bought it years ago at a mission stall.

Nóra said her prayers religiously. These days, she hardly ever stumbled like she used to in the days when it was all she could do to answer the Rosary for Micil. Now, when she felt herself falter, her eyes latched on to the picture.

The cross exposed on the shoulder of a hill. Gentle eyes. The kind head haloed in light and tilted to one side. Blood dripping from where the nails had entered the flesh. The woman in the heavy cloak at the foot of the cross looking up at her Son as the man with the frenzied face pierced His side with a spear . . .

At first, when she looked at the picture, she was overcome with envy and spite towards the woman who could at least see her Son, even if He was being crucified . . .

After a while, flowers bloomed in the stony soil of her mind . . .

There was Mary, the Mother of God. The hem of her flowing cloak was a sanctuary for all who were troubled and in pain. The gentle eyes, sweet face, and halo were a cure for all misery. The wine-blood on the nails and spear eased every pain. The picture brought the balm of prayer to her parched heart and frostbitten eyes.

But today when she looked at it, her eyes were dry. All she could see were flushed cheeks, bushy eyebrows, rough skin, and a mole. There was a mole on the cloak, on the tip of the spear, on the holes made by the nails, on the gentle head, on the brow of the hill, on the wings of the angels above . . .

'Hail Mary, full of grace. The Lord is with thee. Blessed art thou amongst women . . . '

She tried to keep going, but it was no use. Every stone on her rosary beads was a mole . . .

12.

She headed over to the field where the two men were working, Micil laying out the ridges, marking them with the line, turning the sod with his spade, while the Young Man spread the black seaweed that was scattered in heaps at the bottom of the field.

'They wouldn't waste their time with the likes of this at home,' said the Young Man, grabbing a fistful of seaweed and throwing it impatiently on the line.

He straightened up and looked out to the sea, which was less than half a mile away. He could see the scattered rocks, with their dark coats of thick seaweed, sticking out of the dripping blanket of the ebb tide. Although the flood tide had been going out for a couple of days, he could see fingers of the shoreline laid bare a long way out—rough, ugly fingers like something spawned by the hostile earth.

'You'd think there'd be plenty of seaweed below there on the shore.'

'There is too,' said Micil, looking down at it. 'There's a whole forest of strapwrack out there on Carraig Bhuí, but what use is it when you can't get at it on foot.'

'What use!'

'You could get as far as the Scothach out there when the flood tide is out but you'd have to let the seaweed go again with the wind and the tide. It's too tricky for a horse or a donkey out there. The seaweed is shared, but for every man that'd be willing to draw it, there'd be two more that wouldn't. There hasn't been so much as a handful of it cut in twenty years.'

'Twenty years!'

'That's right. The ones that are going now aren't as tough as the crowd long ago.'

'Small wonder ye're short of fertiliser!'

'The best of the black seaweed at the top end is mine. That's some of it there—two years' growth. You can't get seaweed like you used to.'

'Didn't you say yourself there was a forest of strapwrack—'

'Black seaweed, I said. It's worn out. Something wrong with it . . .'

'Small wonder and ye skinning the same few rocks all the time! If I had a currach, I'd have a mountain of strapwrack on it . . . Not to mind the killing you could make on the lobsters!'

'As if you haven't enough to do!'

'It's a nest well worth robbing, boy, at twenty-four quid a dozen!'

'I caught a small lobster the other day when I was cutting seaweed. Myself and Nóra had it for dinner.'

'If I had my currach, ye'd have them every day of the lobster season. And pollock, mackerel, and cod as well, and fish to salt for winter . . . I can't believe there isn't a single boat here at the mouth of the sea!'

There was a hint of a smile in Micil's eye, as though the Young Man had said something funny.

'Sure there isn't a boat or currach in these four villages.'

'Wait till I see now: there's five, six, eight, nine altogether in our place.'

Nine dark shadows swam into the corner of Micil's mind inhabited by vicious dogs, stoats, bulls, and soldiers . . . 'I never set foot in a boat. God ordained that we should avoid misfortune.'

'Isn't God on the sea as well as on land?'

'I've watched the sea for more than sixty years and I tell you she's a troublesome mistress—quiet as a girl one minute, a raging hag the next! Bad blood! Fickle as a woman . . . '

'What harm? If you're used to her ways—'

'Are you telling me there's no harm in drowning! . . . '

'If your time is up, you'll die anyway. There's more people killed on dry land than at sea . . . '

'God love you! Wasn't everyone belonging to you drowned? Stay away from the currachs, I'm telling you . . . '

'I'd rather be up there in the prow than in the finest car ever made: to hear the laths straining under the canvas with the strength of the oarstrokes; the gunwale level with the water; the gripe cutting the sea and the high waves hurling you down like a hat swept away in the wind. I'm telling you, boy! As soon as . . . '

'This is no place for boat talk,' said Nóra. 'Our Micil was never in a boat, nor me, nor my father . . . '

13.

'Hi! Go easy!' said Micil to the Young Man, 'we have to put croobawns there.'

'I never heard of croobawns back in our place . . . '

'Of course you didn't! . . . Watery, soapy spuds is all you'd get from that wet hollow without them. Wait now! We'll run them down as far as the bottom from this side of the ridge . . . Like this . . . '

Micil marked out the shape of the croobawns for him with his foot and the stick he had tied to the end of the line.

'I see now. I noticed some of those in the fields by the road on my way over—little ridges like teeth in a rake . . . '

'That's why I asked you not to mark the ridges this morning,' said Micil happily. 'Next time this field is planted, you'll remember to put croobawns in here. By that time I'll hardly be up to it anymore. But you'll get the hang of it if you watch me . . . '

'Is it because the ground is waterlogged that you put in the croo-bawns?'

'Of course. What else?' said Micil, looking pityingly at the Young Man. 'All the water from our side and a fair share from Baile an tSruthāin as well flows into the drain in this field. It floods in winter.'

'Do you know what I'd do with it . . . ?'

Micil looked uneasily at him.

'I'd make channels.'

'Channels?'

'That's right. When the field is fallow.'

'God bless your ignorance! The cows would soon make a mess of your channels.'

'I'd line them with flags.'

'Flags!' Micil's voice was shaking with indignation. 'You'd be wasting good land . . . The best of land . . . '

'I wouldn't waste a single sod. I'd cover them over with scraws. The Potato Man would give you a grant for it. We got fifteen pounds at home last year from him.'

'More luck to ye! The Potato Man here gives money to the crowd beyond, but we don't bother much with that kind of thing around here. We go our own way the best we can like we've always done . . . Whoa! Wait up! Hold on till I put down the line . . . '

The Young Man had spread a thin layer of seaweed along the edge of the ridge without using the line to mark it . . .

'Do you use the line for every one of them?'

'I do of course.'

'Think of all the seaweed you'd have spread in the time it takes you to move the marker and set it again! If you were on your own, you'd be up and down the whole time!'

'What would you do so?'

By this time Micil wouldn't have been surprised if the Young Man said he'd sail a currach in the ditch, put a roof over the potato ridges, or go fishing for lobsters among the cairns . . .

'I'd spread the seaweed without any line. Why not? I can make a ridge straighter than any line. I was in the army for a while . . . '

'Is that so?'

Micil took two steps back and dropped the line.

'I thought you knew that. Watch this . . . Take aim as if you were firing a gun.'

'A gun,' said Micil in a choked voice.

'Aim your hand at the ditch. Then look for another mark halfway down. Use that pointy stone there as your mark . . . Here! You try it now . . . ! Stand here . . . '

'Some other time,' said Micil, moving away towards Nóra, who was spreading seaweed below them at the bottom of the field, with her back to them. 'Wait till Taimín and Jim are here . . . '

Micil walked up and down the ditch winding and unwinding the line.

'Are you serious? Would you really do it without a line?'

'Half the time we never bother with it at home.'

'That place . . . !'

The crust of laughter in Micil's voice didn't hide the pith of insult in his words:

'As for ye lot! Didn't I hear a man from back there tell me the land is so worn out and useless that ye shove seeds in sods of turf and plant them in old boats . . . !'

'Would you believe me if I told you we sold a ton and a half of potatoes last year . . . '

'Only for you telling me yourself, I wouldn't credit a word of it. The last time this field was planted — six years ago now, we got eight — '

'I'll bet you anything you like you never sold a ton and a half from this field.'

'God love you! This is a great field, a great bit of land altogether. Look at that fine, loamy soil! When I was your age, the blessings of God and His Mother on you, she looked finer to me than the most beautiful lady . . . '

'Go away out of that; sure this land is as dried up as the tits of an old hag, and it planted since the time of Adam. We planted our potatoes in a reclaimed patch of bog and didn't even spray them. I was away in the army; Colm and the old lad were too busy at the fishing and the lobsters . . . '

'There you are. One foot on land and the other at sea and you end up with neither salt nor honey in your mouth. The land goes to waste unless you look after it. There isn't a day goes by but there's something that needs doing on this place.'

'So I see!'

The broad grin on the Young's Man face reminded Micil of a fish . . .

'I'll bet you get as good a crop from this field by doing it my way, Micil. My father used always to say that corn grows just as straight on crooked land.'

'People talk a lot of shit, so they do,' said Micil, flushing with anger for a moment.

'The line is only for show, for the neighbours. The crop is what it's all about. You can make ridges until the field is full of them, it'll still be no better! That's what I say . . . '

Micil looked as though he'd been struck deaf and dumb.

'Wait till you see how straight this ridge will be without any marker.'

The Young Man started trimming the ridge again.

'For God's sake!' said Micil after watching him for a while. 'You have it as crooked as . . . as the gunwale of a currach!'

He pushed the marking stick into the earth beside the ditch. He hurried to place the other stick at the head of the ridge, pulling and freeing the line behind him as he went, as if he was trying to tie down the field to stop it running away. The line got caught in stones, in the seed basket, in the dog's legs, in the Young Man's bicycle clips . . .

'Maybe you're right . . . Maybe . . . I don't know. I've done it this way for fifty years,' he said, backtracking to free the line as he straightened it. 'I never saw anyone around here do it any differently. This is how my father did it. And my grandfather . . . '

'My people used a line as well . . . ' Nóra's open mouth was raw as a cut between the two men.

14.

They covered a large strip of land with seaweed. Then they started spreading manure, leaving Nóra to do the planting.

'Just a touch will do it,' said Micil to the Young Man. 'It's been well fertilised before . . . Don't leave it in lumps like that; you'll have it choked with manure.'

They had four ridges covered in the time it took Nóra to plant two.

Micil leaned against a cairn and took out his pipe. Coming from the bottom of a ridge, the Young Man kicked a round stone ahead of him along the ground, then picked it up in his left hand and hurled it over his shoulder onto the stoneheap by the fence.

Micil was right-handed. When he threw stones at sheep, they curved lazily through the air and always missed. Nóra reckoned he'd need a line to hit anything. The stone took root in the Young Man's fist as though it had grown there. The crowd from the West would take the eye out of your head with a stone . . .

The Young Man settled down beside Micil against the cairn. He pulled out his pipe. It had a large bowl and a silver ring on the stem.

His knife was big too, with a yellow ring on the end of the handle and a lip that had to be pulled out to open the blade.

He cut a pipeful of tobacco with one stroke and crumbled it with his hard nails. He kept his finger pressed tightly on the mouth of the pipe while he smoked, as if someone was trying to snatch it from him.

'When that claw gets hold of something, it won't let go of it easily,' said Nóra, watching him out of the corner of her eye.

Because Micil was crouched below the cairn, the Young Man

appeared taller than him. She recognised the familiar smoke from her husband's pipe: small, slow puffs coiling along the ground, curling as they were blown by a soft breath of wind. The other dragged thick gusts from his big pipe; his smoke made hooks and claws that tore at Micil's in the air . . .

The two men were silent . . .

It occurred to Nóra that they were beginning to understand each other.

The cairn was surrounded by a large balloon of smoke, but the spring air and earth beyond were fragrant and pure as incense.

A truce, for the time being, maybe . . .

Sooner or later, the balloon would burst . . .

15.

'You're left-handed, God bless you!' said Micil to the Young Man, taking off his bawneen and putting it down on the edge of the cairn. 'I'm right-handed. Every last one of my family before me was the same.'

'Of course they were,' Nóra said softly, as though talking to herself.

'The old lad at home would have you in stitches telling about the time he had to buy a right-handed spade for my mother . . . '

The Young Man pulled off his woollen jacket and flung it towards the cairn. In his hurry to get to work, he didn't notice that he had knocked Micil's bawneen onto the ground. Only Nóra saw the edge of a sleeve sticking out from under the jacket at the bottom of the cairn . . .

'When there's a right-hander and a left-hander together over here,' said Micil, 'each man digs his own furrow.'

'When myself and the old lad were planting those potatoes I told you about last year, the two of us worked together, one on each side of the ridge . . . '

'The man on the open side has the best of it that way, instead of each man digging his own.'

'What harm? Leave this side to me! I'll do it.'

'Fair play to you. We'll each of us do it our own way; we won't be trying to best each other anyway. You're young yet, God bless you, and your hands won't mind the blisters!'

Nóra noticed the edge in Micil's voice. The Young Man was planting a strange new life in the familiar ground of Micil's world . . . ! She knew no good would come of making ridges that way in Garraí an Tí.

It wasn't long before the good humour was back in Micil's voice:

'Let's get to it then, boy!' he said, heading towards the end of the ridge. 'We'll soon see what you're made of . . . We won't be long getting through this lot!'

They started tossing back earth together, Micil inside by the fence, the Young Man opposite him on the other side of the ridge. Gradually, two untidy heaps grew up from the hard skin of the earth, two dark hems on the striped blanket of ground.

Nóra used to say that Micil 'tore up the ground.' But he'd turn the sod as gently as if he was helping a sick friend to his feet. It was like watching someone put his arm around a woman's waist, to see him set his right foot under the spade, then lean to the right as he lifted and turned the sod. As soon as he had turned it, he'd cut a cross in the fresh earth.

He had a feel for this stretch of land. Small wonder: the Céidigh had been digging it for nine generations.

He was dead right when he said earlier that the head of the Young Man's spade was too narrow. The earth ran off it into the furrow like water off the blade of an oar. He'd straighten his back, push forward with his left foot, gripping the handle tightly in his left hand, then tense his whole body for the attack. After turning the sod, he stabbed the earth as fiercely as if he was twisting a bayonet in a beaten enemy . . .

Watching the backs of the two men as they drew closer to her, it occurred to Nóra that they were not, and could never be, doing the same work . . .

The square back, the short neck hunched into the shoulder blades, looked nothing like Micil. He didn't take after his mother at all! Everything about him said he had his father's blood in him, the boatman her sister Bríd had married in America!

As he drew nearer to her along the ridge, her eyes skimmed over his back and face, over the haggart, until they rested like exhausted birds on the fence between the haggart and the north side of Garraí an Locháin . . .

Without another look at the two men who were gashing the smooth skin of the earth, she moved away as far as the gap in Garraí an Tí and went into the yard . . .

16.

She made bread for the tea, then made dinner, cutting the heads off the herring before roasting them on the tongs. Usually, she and Micil ate from the same plate, but today she put out three plates. She took one of the two large earthenware dishes down from the dresser for the potatoes.

Usually she would only do that on Christmas Day, but her thoughts had been a confused heap for the past four days. She couldn't stop thinking back to last Thursday night when Micil smoked two pipefuls as he sat by the fire after saying the Rosary.

'Why don't you got to bed, Micil? You must be tired after working the flood tide.'

'I am tired. I'm worn out, not that I'm complaining against God about it, but I am very tired!'

'Is something the matter, Micil?'

'No more than usual, Nóra. I'm tired, that's all . . . I really am . . . There was something I wanted to say to you, Nóra . . . We're not getting any younger, and the land here is going to waste. It's a shame really, the finest bit of land around . . . '

'True for you, Micil, it is too.'

'It is. My own father, Lord have mercy on him, often said it! When he was near the end he said to me:

"I'm leaving the land to you, Micil. You're the ninth generation of Céidigh on it, the best land in the village, in the whole parish. You can let go your wife, Micil, your horse and cow, the shoes on your feet, your belt or your shirt. But never let go the land of the Céidigh, even if you have to hold on to it with your teeth from the grave!"'

'Did he say that, Micil?'

'God grant that I not make a liar of a dead man, Nóra! If he saw the weeds in the Garrantaí Gleannacha for want of drains, or the heaps of briars taking over in Páirc na Buaile . . . And then there's the pool . . . Do you see the sooty dribble down the wall there . . . '

'True for you, Micil.'

'To make matters worse, I have no mind for planting this year, even though there's little enough to plant.'

'Are you that bad, Micil?'

'I am and I amn't. I'm able enough for a day's work, but I don't feel the same grá in my bones anymore for the spade . . . I'd prefer to just give a hand to someone else.'

'We'll pay a man to do the work, Micil. We have enough to pay a labourer.'

'An old boar would do a better job than that crowd! And they'd rob you into the bargain. 'Twould be cheaper to buy potatoes. The potatoes aren't the real worry in any case. It's the land that nine generations of the Céidigh have sweated over I'm worried about, going bad as the Garlach Coileánach.'

'You wouldn't know what to do, Micil.'

'What I was thinking, Nóra, is if we don't do it now, we'll have to do it in a few years' time . . . '

'You wouldn't know what to do, Micil.'

'You would not. True for you. There isn't a Céide left in Ireland we could leave it to. None of the crowd in America will come back. They were asked often enough. That leaves your sister Bríd in the West. What about that son of hers?'

'A fine strong young man, but . . . '

'But what?'

'No buts at all . . . '

On Friday morning, Micil got a lift in a lorry to the West and signed over the land to his wife's sister's son.

He had been to the house two or three times before and spent a few hours of a Sunday afternoon with them, bringing the bustling shadow of the world outside into their quiet life.

From now on, she'd have to conceal any resentment she felt towards the Young Man who'd be under the same roof as her.

Twenty times since Thursday night, she told herself she'd love him like an aunt should.

From Thursday night to Sunday night the thought of him was a beam in her eye.

He had come last night before dusk, dragging the darkness with him into her house . . .

17.

After the dinner she went to make the beds.

As soon as she went into the room, the Young Man's Sunday clothes on the back of the chair caught her eye. He'd left them where they'd be seen anyway! You'd know he was here to stay!

And they were so neatly folded! She was always giving out to Micil. He'd leave his clothes any old way. She was a fine one to talk, as he said himself! She often left her own in an untidy heap . . .

Where was the deep furrow that Micil's head left on the pillow? . . . It was as though it hadn't been slept on at all! What business would a boatman have with a pillow? The short neck hunched between his shoulder blades! . . . Perfect for sleeping on a plank! A light sleep, so light it wouldn't disturb the covers . . . any more than a drowning disturbed the surface of the sea! . . .

Nóra had no idea how the bedclothes could be so neat—in one smooth mound like a wave in the Caoláire during bad weather. When she folded them down, the bed was smooth and unruffled as a calm sea . . . !

She was about to leave the room when she noticed an envelope that wasn't there before, shoved in behind the mirror.

She pulled it out and two pictures fell from it. One was a picture of a hooker tied up at the pier, his father's boat.

The second picture showed a house with fish drying on the thatched roof; oars leaning against the wall; a marshy field stretching beyond the house to a stony fog-drenched hill. His father's house . . .

There was a woman there as well. A young woman; her back and her behind arched like a hook, grinning . . .

Nóra raised the picture to the light . . . A conger eel would laugh like that! A brazen woman, without a gentle bone in her body . . . A woman from the West . . .

There was a third picture: the same woman; and a man. Dark eyebrows . . . It was him; with his arm around the woman . . . !

So that's how it was! He was great with a girl from the West! She was the one bright apple of his eye. The match she and Micil would make with Máire Jim, or Jude Taimín, or some local girl wouldn't be good enough for him . . . !

He'd bring a stranger from the West into their house in spite of them! A woman who would rear a brood of strangers around them. A bitch of a woman who would claw Micil and herself . . .

Nóra threw the pictures down by the window . . .

18.

She was still flushed even after she had finished tidying up.
Now she could go back to Garraí an Tí to lend a hand.

From the yard, she could see the two men had turned the field as far as the brow of the hill.

Her eyes moved as quickly as they had before dinner, as they had for the past four days. As soon as Micil had set off for the West, Nóra's eyes had looked to the north side of the haggart and kept returning there like a bird to its nest . . . Such a struggle for the past four days to stop her legs from following her eyes! Last night, she couldn't stop them any longer . . . !

Micil could see her from the field, hesitating at the gap in the fence. She went back into the house to cut some more seeds . . .

Last night, when Máire Jim was going home, she had gone as far as the gate with her. Afterwards, she couldn't bring herself to go straight back in. She went into the haggart and headed along the fence of Garraí an Locháin. The high fence cast hunched shadows from the low moon into the field, making her hurry past; that and her fear that Micil would come looking for her . . .

If she joined the two men now, she would have to work on the hill, and Micil would notice her eyes drifting away to where she had gone last night . . . The hill swelled like a hard, pregnant belly, higher than the surrounding fences. The haggart, part of Garraí an Locháin, and part of the boundary fence with Baile an tSrutháin to the east, where she came from, could be seen from the hill . . .

Garraí an Locháin. The boundary fence. The cairn . . .

She'd be better off cutting seed potatoes. She couldn't help her feet following her eyes . . . in spite of Micil.

19.

Micil came in and lit his pipe.

'The flame went out on us,' he said, 'I'll have to take a sod out with me.'

Nóra looked straight at him, the panels of her cheeks drawn together as she smiled. She said nothing.

'You've enough seed there for four days, Nóra. If you could come out and plant some of them for us . . . '

'I need to cut plenty, now there are two of you,' she said weakly.

Her husband looked away. He looked around him awkwardly, then looked right at her:

'The Young Man is a great worker, Nóra. The best! No word of a lie! He's handy anyway!'

'A man that would dig ridges without a line!'

'Well, maybe he's not as neat as the next man. The spade is the real problem; it's too narrow. I told him that. Of course, he has his own way of doing things; each to his own, as they say. He'll soon get the hang of our ways. One thing's for sure, he won't let the land go to waste . . . '

Micil took a seed potato from the basket, examined it and wiped the dirt from it with the tip of his finger . . .

She said nothing but flung a dud potato into the basket . . .

'He says he'll cut a few seeds this evening,' said Micil, picking up where he had left off. 'It won't be long till you can leave the lot to him, Nóra!'

She threw another dud in the basket.

'And he can use a scythe as well, and make baskets. We won't have to depend on Taimín anymore to make a few baskets for us. And Seán Thomáis had me robbed last year when I got him to do the reaping down by the Cladach . . . There was no eye in that one you put in the basket just now, Nóra!'

'Let him do it so, since neither of us is any good at it, Micil!'

She put the knife down on the lower part of the dresser and sat by the fire.

'He has the right knife for cutting them too.'

'A fisherman's knife; they all have them when they're fishing for lobsters.'

'Mind he doesn't stab you with it! He was in the army, Micil!'

'Lots of men join the army!'

'He'll bring a woman from the West into your house . . . '

'Ara, God help you, woman!'

'He'll kill you with a stone. He has the same bad blood in him as the rest of the crowd back West.'

'Ara, will you have sense!'

'He'll make you go out in a currach so you drown . . . '

'God bless you, woman! Do you think I'd set foot in a currach for him? Anyway, the good man wouldn't ask me to! He's the most obliging man you could meet. What have you got against him, Nóra? I can find no fault with the lad . . . '

'But Micil . . . '

'But what?'

'The mole!'

'The mole?'

'On his cheek!'

'He can't help that. God put it there.'

'Not God, Micil; his father. He takes after his father and his father's people, every inch of him.'

'That's no disgrace, God bless him; whoever he takes after, he's a great worker. The best! He's so handy . . . Here, Nóra, get a move on, and head over to the field . . . !'

They walked outside to the end of the house.

'I don't suppose you're finished on the hill yet?'

'How could we, and it full of stones like a quarry? My father, God bless him, used to say it was Conán's pouch. "It was that hill in the east side of Garraí an Tí," he'd say, "that put blisters on the Céidigh's hands." He should know! If you go over now, we'll have it turned by this evening . . . '

All that was left in the north end of the haggart was a small stack of wet, miserable hay, the leftovers of winter . . . Micil turned his head.

'The hill is tough as an old mule. Even my father said so. It would take two good spademen a whole day sweating until nightfall to get through it . . . '

His hurried speech made the worry in his voice more obvious . . .

'Maybe you'd better cut some more seeds after all. It won't take long for two to plant them. He's a great hand with the spade . . . '

He stumbled as he went through the gap and the sod fell from his hand. He left it there. The flame had gone out . . .

20.

Something was wrong with the house: the house where nine generations of Céidigh had been reared: the house that she had married into—one of the Catháins from the next village over: the house that had been left exactly as it was for thirty years, as long as she and Micil had lived together—she couldn't believe it was the same house.

Something was wrong with the house today . . .

Nóra put her hand on the chair, the table, the dresser, the keeler . . . She looked up into the rafters. She routed the cat from the fireside and banished the dog out to the yard . . .

There were things happening that the Céidigh and Catháins had never done:

A currach tacking in the keeler with Micil at the oars: Micil thatching on top of the dresser, reaping on the table, marking ridges in the ashes without a line . . .

The twisting serpent of the 'Cuigéil' was coiled around the ridgeboard. The sharp-toothed dogsnout from the 'Rosa' was sucking the sootstreaks from the wall . . .

The cat jumped from the 'crayleagh.' 'Between the devil and the deep,' she hissed as she fled across the fire away from Nóra's boot . . .

She didn't recognise the dog stretched on the floor. He had black eyebrows and . . . a mole . . .

It was a stranger's house . . .

She had put on her shoes and the patterned shawl this morning in a stranger's house. Before breakfast, she had taken out the ashes from a stranger's house. In a stranger's house, she had cut the heads off the herring and set a cup and saucer, an eggstand, and an earthenware dish on the table . . .

The Céidigh and Catháins never did anything like that, not even for their children . . .

Her own children wouldn't go to the bog on an empty stomach . . . She'd give them their tea in mugs . . . The bottoms of their trousers would be trailing when they went to the field . . . Her sons would laugh at her if she suggested they milk cows or cut seeds . . . They wouldn't make baskets . . . They'd have no time for currachs . . .

The last thing they'd do would be to dig ridges without a line . . .

She wouldn't need to watch what she did and said all the time. They'd have the same faults as herself. She'd pick a local girl with the same faults for Micil Óg and she'd see another Micil Óg in the house before she died . . .

No she wouldn't. All she would see were the children of a boatman from the West . . .

21.

She sat down again to cut more seed potatoes. Once or twice she rubbed the left side of her head. The same clicking noises that kept her awake last night were bothering her again. She didn't try to stop the secret voices in her head any longer. They were almost a comfort to her—dark as the cry of a thrush, the plop of frogspawn, the humped shadows of the low moon last night in Garraí an Locháin . . .

Garraí an Locháin. A cairn. Shadows . . .

There were five of them: Micil Óg, Nóirín, Pádraig, Colm, Peige . . .

Micil Óg. He was my firstborn, the hardest one of all. Michaelmas Eve of all nights. I felt a pain in my heart. I thought it must be the cock I had for dinner . . .

Pádraig was born in March. Garraí an Tí was planted that year. I remember Micil was at the east end of the field. It was after dinner.

God knows how I managed to get as far as the door to call him . . . What am I saying? It wasn't spring; it was Christmas. The pain was terrible. That's how I remember. The stabbing pain in my chest . . .

The darkness of her troubled mind pushed through her thin skin, smoothing out the wrinkles on her face. She couldn't tell which was which. Always, in the end, she had to name them in the order she wished they had been born . . . Micil Óg, Nóirín, Pádraig . . .

Today the pretence was as useless as shattered spectacles . . .

How could she tell whether they had been boys or girls . . . ? Was the first one a boy at all . . . ?

It was all made up—Micil Óg, Nóirín, Pádraig . . .

All lies from start to finish, her dreams pretending to be real, blinding her . . .

They were born dead; all five stillborn; not one of them born breathing.

If only she could have seen them alive, even for the blink of an eye, and heard a baby cry under the blanket! Or felt the soft gums even once on her breast! To have hugged a baby—a warm, living bundle—even once before it died!

She heard nothing, felt nothing, hugged nothing . . .

Like unhealthy limbs, like a diseased part of her own body, they had been spat out of her like the gallstone that had nearly killed her. Gallstones . . .

If they had survived until they were grown up: so she could see her husband's eyebrows, his arched back, and slender neck on the boys, her own mother's tapering fingers and blonde hair on the girls. Micil's bright face, his homely talk and easygoing ways . . .

Had they lived. Even for a year. A week. A day. Even a minute . . .

At least she could have grieved for them; spoken their names without fear or shame; prayed for them with a clear conscience; chatted to the neighbour women about them . . .

Cite Thomáis, and Cáit and Muiréad were lucky . . . Their children had died as well! But at least they saw them; kissed them. The memory of their dead children would be a bright sunroom in the wilderness of their pain forever . . .

A ray of sunlight knelt down outside the window . . .

Mary, the Mother of God, was lucky! Her Son was being crucified; but at least she could see Him! . . . And she would see Him again . . .

Nóra envied them all. That's why she was so reluctant to visit her sister Bríd in the West. Bríd had her children around her. And she never stopped talking about the ones that had died . . .

Nóra didn't even get to name hers. She was afraid to even mention them. Useless threads . . .

They were taboo in this world and the next. Whenever Cite Thomáis spoke of her own dead children, she'd say they'd all be waiting for her when she died, with candles in their hands to light her way to heaven. Each one of Cáit's little ones would be an angel 'bright as a new shilling,' calling out to her, 'Mother, Mother,' at the gate of heaven . . .

Too unclean to be saved; too clean to be damned . . . A displeased God, not an angry one . . . The diseased black sheep of eternity . . . Chained to a pillar, unwanted by God or the devil—'in a dark place without pain.'

No matter where she ended up, she would never see them again . . .

Still separated in the hereafter . . . But at least her dust and theirs would be together at last . . . !

Even that was denied her. She'd be buried in the consecrated ground of Cill an Aird. They were buried in the boundary fence between Baile Chéide and Baile an tSrutháin, in ready-made boxes, secretly in the night, unseen by all except the stars, cold, poisonous stars that never shed a tear . . .

22.

She rubbed her head again, gently, as if she were touching a wound . . .

Five pregnancies, five illnesses, five hard labours, five awful defeats . . . Frustration . . . Hope . . . On a see-saw between the two all those years . . .

The fifth time had nearly killed her . . . The doctor said she couldn't conceive again . . .

God was deaf to her prayers . . . Micil was sullen:

'Down there . . . Over there . . . Up there . . . Put them out of your head, for God's sake . . . '

He wouldn't tell her where he had buried them; that was the hardest blow of all . . .

The first hint she got of Micil's secret was like a gift of sunlight in her memory. It was shortly after the last labour. She was in the yard, away from the open door, listening to the gentle lapping of water in the bay. The Dublin priest with the beard was writing down Micil's old sayings, as he did every night since he came to visit . . .

'One more thing before I go, Micil . . . '

In an instant, Nóra forgot about the lapping of the Caoláire, her ears pricked up like dogs scenting a bone as she stood inside the door . . .

'Where did ye bury unbaptised babies around here?'

God forgive him, even if he was a priest. What a question to ask!

Micil had to repeat his answer three times before the priest could make the words out from the tangled bandages of his hoarse voice . . .

'In the boundary fence . . . Between two villages . . . Like you said . . . Between two townlands . . . '

A boundary fence!

Nóra had heard that too. She knew from Cite, Cáit, and Muiréad where all the unbaptised babies born in the two villages were buried. But it never occurred to her before now that her own could be in the boundary fence too. She always imagined they must be in some out-of-the-way place:

The moors above the village where the lambs kept bleating in August after they were weaned . . . The edges of the mountain lakes among the reeds, the clover, and the water lilies, where grumbling ducks took flight from strange sounds late at night . . . The corner of a stone fence where the animals might shelter, and a calf that had just been bought could be heard lowing sadly for his own yard . . . An exposed sand dune by the Caoláire . . .

But she was wrong. They were right there in the boundary fence between Baile Chéide and her own village . . .

Right by her own door . . . Maybe . . . on her own land . . . Maybe even in Garraí an Locháin. It was the only one of their fields that bordered on Baile an tSrutháin . . .

Nóra took another bundle of seed potatoes from under the bed in her room . . .

Her smile was as hollow as the potatoes she had just cut as she thought back to the day Micil moved the cairn from the middle of Garraí an Locháin and piled it up again by the boundary fence between their land and that of the Curraoins in Baile an tSrutháin. That knocked the husk off Micil's secret!

As soon as she saw what he was up to, she realised. Every other grave site the women told her about in the two villages had a cairn marking it. People had always piled stones over the dead . . .

'That's where they are, Micil! In the boundary fence . . . !

The large round stone fell from Micil's hands.

'Go on away home,' he said, his narrowed eyes small as two bright flies in his head, 'and don't let the Devil make a fool of you with your carry-on . . . The stones were using up good land . . . My father used to say if it wasn't for the stones and the pool it would be the best hayfield he had. I'll drain the pool as soon as I get a chance . . . '

The knife went right through the potato, cutting her hand. The blood kept dripping as though her finger was trying to scratch her thoughts on the white surface of the seeds . . .

Micil's lame excuses about the stones, the day she discovered the secret burial place, made her want to laugh . . .

Who'd have thought they were right there outside the door? She could visit them every day; any time she wished, she could see where they were buried. She'd salute them on her way to the well, to wash clothes, or milk the cows. They would be a bright stream of quicksilver through the rough, stony ground of her days, through the grey drudgery of her life.

The wound of grief would bleed forever in her heart, now there was a marker right in front of her eyes where she could relieve her sorrow. A hundred times a day she could remind herself that she was a mother . . .

23.

By now, the late afternoon sun was a red plate in the southwest over the Caoláire, shining though the window and the open door. Sunlight poured down on Nóra's grey hair as though it were determined to ripen the thoughts in her head . . .

Sweet memories of Garraí an Locháin . . . For years after she had discovered Micil's secret, the field was kept as a meadow, its fences pointed with no gap for a cow or a person to get in to interfere with the cairn or disturb the stones.

After the first few years, Micil no longer objected to her having it to herself. The cairn by the boundary fence was hers, the cowslip that peeked out from underneath it, the hip shoots that pushed their way through the stones, the warbling of the tits and sparrows that settled on top of it, gently making themselves at home . . .

Today, the time she had spent in the shelter of the cairn by the fence, darning a sock for Micil or sewing a jacket for herself, was a stream of sunlight in Nóra's heart. Other times, she'd lean against the pile talking to the Curraoins on the other side of the fence, chatting about anything at all, for as long as they wished. Mostly she just sat there, looking and listening:

To the plop of frogspawn in spring on the flag-covered bank of the pool; watching caterpillars in summer, with their dry, agile skin, crawling to the tip of a blade of grass; or listening to mice scurrying from the old haycocks in the haggart. In autumn, she'd see steam rising from the scummy water of the pool in the warm sun, and on dry winter days, clouds straggling across an empty sky.

They were all hers, the frogspawn, the caterpillars, the mice, the steam, and the clouds—threads in the fabric of her dark consolation.

Nóra put down the knife . . .

She could hardly believe now that she used to chase the children of the village out of Garraí an Locháin; they loved going there to float their flag boats on the pool. She begrudged the parents the happiness of their children. After she discovered where her own children were buried, she was delighted when they came. As she sat by the cairn, their cheerful noise from the hollow by the pool set lightbells tinkling in her heart. They were hers now, and she spoke to them in her own voice, the soft gentle voice of her own mother:

'That's enough now! If ye trample the grass, Micil will have a fit.'

But as soon as they came skipping towards her, with their flushed cheeks and muddy feet, out of breath from running, the old bitterness took hold of Nóra again, a black, smouldering shadow darkening her eyes. They were not her children.

The bitterness passed as quickly as it came:

'My Micil Óg hasn't come back yet . . . He's hiding beyond the hill . . . And you tell me Nóirín is floating flag boats on the pool. Where did you leave Pádraig and Colm and Peige, Jude Taimín . . . ? Come over here to me, Máire Jim. How old are you . . . ? Ten. You're big for your age, God bless you! You say you're a year older than Jude Taimín. Off ye go and play now like good girls, and don't let my

Nóirín get her bib ruined in the pool. If Micil Óg flattens the grass, tell him his father will take the stick to him this evening . . . Máire Jim and Micil Óg are the one age, and my Nóirín is just a month older than Jude Taimín. Nóirín is taller, though. She takes after my mother. She was a tall woman too. What she doesn't have in height, Jude will make up for in width. All Taimín's family were stocky . . . They're two fine good-natured little girls — Jude Taimín and Máire Jim. In time, God willing, either one of them would make a good wife for Micil Óg . . . '

24.

A potato she was about to cut fell from her hand, rolled as far as the door and out over the worn threshold into the yard. Nóra went after it . . .

In the blinking sunlight, she caught a glimpse of the steel spades, quick teeth devouring the earth and a light cloud of dust rising from the powder-dry hill of Garraí an Tí . . .

Before she sat down again, she turned the stool so it was facing away from the closed door. She felt a slight chill in her back. The sun had faded from the door and window, and the floor was flecked with dark shadows which seemed to have a life of their own in the quiet, empty house . . .

Nóra would never forget the salt tears — the worry, the pain, the sin — that forced their way up through the bright fields of those memories of Garraí an Locháin . . .

The children taking stones from the cairn to mark bases or play Ducksey; wiping off the dung of the cattle that grazed there in winter until the new grass was ready; taking away the rubbish the Curraoins threw on top of the cairn, without anyone noticing; flinging black snails as far as she could over the boundary fence . . . Trampling ugly, hairy caterpillars into the earth, then taking to the bed for three days after, sick to the pit of her stomach . . . Micil complaining during the summer that the young ones from the village were flattening the grass in Garraí an Locháin . . . He got some satisfaction giving out like that . . .

She remembered clearly how agitated she was when part of the cairn fell down, as she waited for a chance to fix it unbeknownst to her husband . . .

It was very wet one day.

'I'll go down to Taimín's to get him to put a couple of half-soles on my boots for me,' said Micil.

After a while, Nóra hurried through the haggart behind the cocks and the stack of hay. Micil was there, in the howling gale, re-building the fallen pile . . .

'Did you get your boots soled,' she asked when he got back to the house.

'He didn't have a last.'

'You're drenched to the skin. How did you manage to get so wet between here and Taimín's?'

Micil looked at her. His cheeks were flushed. He looked away from her and spat out of the corner of his mouth into the ashes . . . But he was in foul humour for a week after.

Micil also had good reason to remember the time they were making a road through the village. It was his fault that he didn't wait half an hour at the house until the road gang had moved on. Nothing would do him only to go straight to the other end of the village:

'Come on! Those sheep have to be spancelled. That eejit over the road has just warned me this minute to keep them away from his . . . '

'Another half-hour, Micil.'

'Half an hour! It'll be dark by then. The day is short . . . '

'But . . . '

'But what?'

'The road gang.'

'What about them?'

'The cairn,' she said, in a choked voice. 'They'll take the rocks! I've been watching it since they arrived . . . We need those rocks ourselves, don't we? For a new shed . . . '

Even now she couldn't tell whether it was anger or pity she saw in Micil's eyes, or a hint that she should stay behind. He left straight away and had the sheep caught and spancelled by the time she arrived.

When they got back, the cairn was gone, grafted onto the body of the road, among the mute stones from the fields all around . . .

That night she went out to look at the road in the moonlight. A waste of effort. Every stone was the same on the raw, new road . . .

All that was left of the cairn in Garraí an Locháin were some small pebbles which hadn't been worth collecting and loading on the workmen's barrows. Nóra gathered them into a small pile, which was still there to this day, a cold, lonely heap sheltered by the fence, like fallen masonry in the corner of a ruined church . . .

What she remembered most clearly—like a huge, dark bird puncturing the thin skin of the years—was Micil's surly silence, which lasted for a long while after the stones were taken away . . .

But Nóra could say nothing.

That was what tormented her most—that she had to remain silent forever about the cairn and the five children. She could say nothing to Micil, or he'd lose his temper; nothing to Cite Thomáis, to Cáit or Muiréad; not a word while they went on about their own dead children: how long they lasted, what killed them, how well they looked after them; the year, the day, the time they died, the graveyard where they were buried; how they grieved for them; how they went to the cemetery to say a prayer for them; how they never forgot to ask God's blessing for them during the Rosary every night . . .

And the things the women said to her:

'I'd pray for yours too, Nóra, you poor thing, but it wouldn't do them any good. They say there's no use praying for unbaptised children. They're sent to a dark place with no pain. God help us!'

Every word, every syllable, every sound they made was a festering sore in Nóra's heart . . . She began to avoid the other women altogether. What a terrible thing to say—that it was no use praying for them!

How many times had it been on the tip of her tongue to ask Micil, as they sat by the fire at night before the Rosary, would it be a sin to say a prayer for them? She was certain he'd say it wouldn't. But she said nothing. The very mention of them was enough to put him in foul humour . . .

She began to lose faith in prayers; it wasn't long before she stopped praying altogether. That went on for years, her days like a series of frames with no pictures, her heart as dry as the inside of a nut, until she had to go to hospital to have the gallstone removed and the priest questioned her during confession . . .

Nóra put down the knife and put a hand to her head . . .

How she'd struggled to do as the priest told her . . . to put the women's talk out of her head . . . to avoid what was left of the cairn, and Garraí an Locháin altogether . . .

She had tried her best ever since. She didn't go to the north side of the haggart anymore if she could avoid it. The fence was built up high where the step from the haggart into the field had been. Micil promised to drain the pool, to keep the young ones from the village away—the same empty promise made year after year by the Céidigh, from one generation to the next. She made herself go to Taimín's well for water, wash clothes in the little stream in the Buaile, milk the cows in the Tuar, away from the house . . .

Ever since then, the black hole in her heart had been closing, bit by bit . . . Her prayers set a peaceful lullaby singing in her heart, and hope rushing through her mind . . .

Until today . . .

Today, there was nothing in her mind, only a huge mole; nothing in her heart, only a small heap of stones sheltered by a boundary fence . . .

25.

Today, her mind had flung off the warm sheet the priest had wrapped around her and huddled down once more by the smoking ruin of her thirty years in the house . . .

The two men returning from Garraí an Tí dragged her back again, reminding her that the spring evening was far from finished, that it was time to prepare feed for the cattle and do the milking.

Micil went to bring in the cows. The Young Man sat by the fire and lit his pipe. Nóra noticed him looking at the sootstreak on the north wall again.

When she had finished the milking, she came in to find the dog playing with the Young Man. His front paws were on the Young Man's knees as he tried to lick his mouth. She hooshed him away crossly and he headed for the yard.

'Making up to a stranger like that,' she said, following him out.

She took the feed to the calf. Micil was at the gable end, leading the donkey to the stable.

'Take the stranger with you when you go visiting,' she said.

'Mind he doesn't hear you! What's wrong with you at all, calling your sister's son a stranger?'

They stayed in that night. The Young Man cut seeds until it was too dark to see the eyes. Then he asked for a last and hammer, settled himself on a stool, set a candle on the table beside him, and began mending a pair of Micil's old boots.

Nóra was by the fire knitting a sock, her eyes absorbed in the fluent movement of the needles. She didn't look up until it was time to heap the fire. The Young Man was bent over the boot, the candle-light on one side of his face making the other side appear even darker.

She concentrated again on the sock, her fingers working the needles even faster. All she saw was a mole . . . five moles . . .

She left the sock on the window ledge. She would have to un-ravel part of it . . .

'Where are you off to?' asked Micil.

'I think I might have left the door of the henhouse open. The fox might . . . '

'Wait a minute!' said the Young Man, getting up and going to his room. 'There's a flashlamp in the pocket of my new jacket, in case it's dark outside.'

He came back almost immediately with the lamp: a sleek, slippery thing in his big, strong fist. He pushed the button and shone a blade of light onto the window.

Nóra took the sock with her to her room.

'Where did you get that gadget?' asked Micil.

'I bought it.'

'The only people I ever saw with a yoke like that were the police. One night I was coming from Taimín's place, the fat policeman was at the top of the road shining it onto the cyclists.'

'They have them in all the shops back in our place. They're very handy if you have to check on the cows in the shed on a dark night.'

'I use a lantern and candle,' said Micil.

'This is much quicker'—he switched it on again—'take it,' he said, handing it to Nóra as she came back to the kitchen.

'I want nothing to do with it,' she said under her breath, backing away out through the door.

26.

The door of the henhouse was shut. It was the last thing she had done this evening.

She stood at the gable, as she often did during the night. The snore of the sea across the stepping stones on the shore comforted her.

The last thin trace of the crescent moon was far away in the West, perched uneasily on the shoulder of a thick black cloud, the misshapen shadow of a false moon huddled against its hollow breast . . .

It wasn't long before the black cloud parted, letting the changeling moon fall through. All that was left was a little half-light at the edge of the darkness.

There were only a few bleary stars left, but you'd have to look closely to see them, they were so obscured by clouds. The sky was unwelcoming; cold and empty.

She listened to the Caoláire moaning. It never stopped moaning, the hard, breathless gasp of an old man on his last legs . . .

Carraig Bhuí made a hollow, rushing sound, as the undertow spurted through the bloated black seaweed below. Nóra thought she could see a bright ruff on the surface of the water, where the wind peeled back the skin of the sea and ripped it asunder with a great howl on the submerged rocks at the tip of the Scothach . . .

It was cold comfort for Nóra tonight. Even the Caoláire was against her—a ferocious dog goaded by a stiff wind from the west, barking viciously at her . . .

Strange that she should have spent a lifetime looking at the Caoláire without ever thinking, until last night, how far west it ran.

It went a long way—as far back as Na Rosa and Na Cuigéil; to a harbour where a hooker lay at anchor; to a house with a stony, fog-drenched hill and a swamp behind it . . .

And there was another woman looking out on the Caoláire tonight, listening to the roar of the sea. The other woman was thinking that the river ran a long way to the east. To a place where there was no island or inlet or narrow channel; no big, awkward seaclaws tearing chunks out of the shoreline; a place where the road ran easy and straight as a bird to its nest. He had gone out that road east along the Caoláire. He was out there now; but he wouldn't be long coming back. For her. And he'd bring her back with him—the woman who was waiting out West by the Caoláire, listening to the roar of the sea . . . A strong woman. A dogwoman . . .

Nóra started. She thought she had heard something. She pricked up her ears in the wind. But it was only the sound of the hammer from the half-open door.

The dog came up to her, wagging his tail.

'You—you—you—,' she said, and kicked him hard.

Her foot slipped on the greasy slab by the gable where she cleaned off the little shovel every day after taking out the ashes. She reached out to steady herself and touched something. It was a spade, leaning against the wall.

There were two spades, one longer than the other, leaning against each other at the far end of the house . . .

She lifted the one in her hand so she could see the footrest; the darkness clung to the gable like moss. There was no need to look. As soon as she touched it, she could feel Micil's mark on the spade, after a single day's work. There was a groove in the footrest and a softness in the metal—the softness of a hand on a baby's head, Nóra said to herself . . .

She put Micil's spade at the southern end of the gable, facing the moon. Then she threw the Young Man's down to the northern end. But she picked it up right away, and brought it over to the small fence at the end of the cowshed. This time she used both hands, hurling it as far as she could down the hill to the dungheap . . .

More of their notions, the crowd from back West, bringing their spades home in the evening . . .

27.

When she went back inside, Micil was still talking about the devastation the fox had left behind him.

'I have a double-barrelled gun at home,' said the Young Man.

'I never touched a gun in my life. No one around here has one.'

'I was on the First Battalion team, in the rifle competition at the Curragh one year. Those little lakes you mentioned, with the geese and wild ducks, are they far up the bog? . . . They'll rue the day! I'll have ye eating like kings, as soon as I bring my little beauty back . . . '

'A gun went off in a house over that direction last year. Someone could easily get killed, God between us and all harm . . . '

'Why would anyone get killed?'

The Young Man laughed.

'Why not?' said Nóra. 'There'll be no guns in this house . . . '

They ate their supper in silence.

After the Rosary, the two men sat by the fire again. It wasn't long before Micil lit his pipe again.

'Time for bed,' said Nóra.

'This young man must be tired, God bless him, after his day's work,' said Micil. 'It would be easier to dig the Caoláire than that hill out there. I tell you it's not a bad day's work for two men, to dig up "Conán's pouch" in Garraí an Tí. Herself might go over and plant some of it for us tomorrow . . . '

Nóra was getting a candle. She lit it and put it at the head of the table for the Young Man.

'I have my own light here,' he said, taking the clips from his trousers. 'It's handier . . . '

Nóra blew out the candle without another word . . . She wouldn't dream of offering Micil Óg a candle. He'd go to bed without any light, just like herself and her husband. She'd go straight down to his room as he was about to lie down. She'd look for something or other in the corner, or fiddle with the check curtains in the window. She might take away some clothes of his that needed patching. Before she left, she'd be sure to ask was he warm enough . . .

That's how she'd say good night to Micil Óg . . . how she used to say good night to him . . . the only habit she had been unable to break, for all the priest's advice . . . until tonight . . .

Tonight there was someone in the room that was no relation at all to herself or her husband: the son of a boatman from the West . . .

28.

The two men went to bed.

Nóra sat on the stool by the fire and spread her legs over the heat, something she hadn't done all day. That was always the best way to warm herself.

In the dim light of the kitchen, the fire—what was left of it—was a black and red mesh in which every imaginable shape was swimming and winking . . .

It wasn't long before Nóra's lonely eyes were hypnotised by this strange pantomime . . .

A bottle of castor oil; bread cut in wedges right into the middle; a cup and saucer and eggstand; a knife with a lip on it; a pillow without a mark; a little paper envelope; a flashlight. Flushed cheeks; black eyebrows; a mole . . .

The mole was there in the little gap in the fire . . . Nóra grabbed the tongs and raked quickly through the embers . . .

The day was over. But it was only the first of hundreds, of thousands of days the stranger would be in the house . . .

The stranger was taking shape again in the uneasy heart of the fire, his neck as thick as a policeman's belt, his back as broad and strong as the prison door in Brightcity . . . And a mole . . .

The mole was there again. It swelled till it covered the whole fire, then spread out over the house and into the yard. It was mending boots on the table, thatching the roof, planting potatoes in Garraí an Tí, in currachs off the Scothach in the Caoláire . . .

Nóra raked the fire again . . .

It was no use. Two stumps rose from the flame, two stumps that were hard and fast as handcuffs, as flexible as a chain . . . They stretched out until they had surrounded all of the Céidigh's land from top to bottom . . . They grabbed Micil by the hair and threw him face down into a currach . . . They dragged him kicking up to the roof and stood him up on the chimney, put a gun in his hand, pointing at his forehead . . .

That wildwoman emerged from the embrace of the two stumps with a flashlamp in her hand . . . She pressed a button and the light shone on Micil's heart, and on Nóra's . . . Then she laughed out loud . . .

The wildwoman kissed the mole and vomited, covering the whole of the Céidigh's house, their land and shore . . . When they emerged again, the house and land and shore were no longer theirs . . . Instead, there was a house shaped like a currach . . . The ridges were wide at the bottom and narrow at the top, like a gun . . . There was no hay or corn or ferns in the haggart, only an enormous lobster with his claws reaching out to grab hold of Micil . . .

The wildwoman and the two stumps were making a channel under the boundary fence in Garraí an Locháin . . . They made Micil take the stones from the cairn and put them along the sides and across the top of the channel . . . The stranger stuffed clumps of earth into the mouth of the channel, ripping them apart like a beaten enemy . . . Herself and Micil were under his spade . . . The woman and the stranger laughed out loud . . . The woman kissed the mole again . . .

Nóra was trembling on the stool. She heard the clicking noise inside her head and felt something heavy stirring below her chest. She grabbed the tongs and jabbed the fire until the embers glowed from one side of the hearth to the other.

She got up with a start, pushed the blanket of warm embers to the centre, and covered them over with ashes. All that was left was a sad, grey, mouldering heap without as much as a thread of smoke or a flicker of flame to be seen. She got five or six sods of turf and pushed their thin heads into the impotent heap, before covering them over with another layer of ashes.

There was nothing to see in the banked fire . . .

29.

She walked the length of the floor a few times, then gently took the basket of mangolds from the press and set it down by the back door.

She took the tin lamp from the nail in the wall, held it in one hand and opened the door of the press with the other. The noise of the hinge squeaking as she lifted the lid almost made her drop the lamp. She listened for a moment. The only sound was in her own body, in her head, chest, and left hand . . .

She started rummaging in the press, taking out a bundle of old clothes and other bits and pieces. She had to push the dull, flickering light right into the press before she found what she was after . . .

She combed her hair back carefully, gathered it in a bun, and put the high comb she had found in the press through it to keep it in place. The orange comb in her grey hair gleamed like a tongue of fire through a cloud of smoke . . .

She took off her patterned shawl and wrapper and put on the cashmere shawl and velvet dress she hadn't worn since her wedding day . . .

She put the light down on the windowsill. The cashmere, the coloured velvet, and the comb brightened her eyes and the faded parchment of her cheeks. She stretched her hand out to the light in the window, and it shone on her wedding ring — a Claddagh ring, with a heart in the centre. The dim light cast strange shadows on the gold so that it seemed more like a worm on a stalk than fingers touching a heart . . .

She lowered the lamp until it was just a weak beam lighting the holy picture on the window ledge . . .

Nóra looked up quickly at the picture . . . All she could see was the mole . . . A mole on the tip of the spear . . . A mole where the nails entered the flesh . . .

30.

She went to the door of the Young Man's room and listened to him snoring softly.

She unbolted the door of the house, went out, and closed it quietly behind her.

The moon had sunk very low and tongues of darkness were already licking the ground. Only a few dim stars remained. She covered her face in her hands as a gust of wind from the West clawed at her wrinkled cheeks . . .

She almost slipped again on the stone that was greasy from the ashes. She was still blind from the light of the lamp, and had to feel her way through the darkness that lurked at the foot of each ditch and wall, especially at the gable end of the house. She took hold of Micil's spade, gripping it tightly to her until she felt the cold iron against her thigh, through the moth-eaten velvet. Then she walked up the haggart, past the haystack as far as the high fence of Garraí an Locháin.

There used to be a gap there when Nóra visited the field. When she came out of hospital, she insisted it be closed and the whole fence built up head high. A single stone of the old stile was left jutting out a couple of feet above the ground on the haggart side. Nóra stood up on the stone just as she had done the night before to look into the field to see the pile of stones she hadn't looked at for years . . .

It had fallen . . . the rocks scattered like rosary beads given to a child to play with . . .

She tightened her fingers around Micil's spade . . .

31.

A thrush in Páirc na Buaile began calling anxiously, its voice swallowed up in the belly of the wind. It had cried out later than this last night . . .

Nóra listened again . . . Slup slap, slup slap . . . Only the plop of frogspawn in the pool. She had heard it at the same time last night. It was always like this in spring—a low, stubborn, squelching sound. For all that, there was an element of anxious happiness threaded through it . . . A motherly pain.

She could no longer see the scattered stones. The cairn was now a horrible mole pushing against the darkness left huddled against the fence by the fading moon.

She rammed the edge of the spade into the earth behind her as a prop and reached out towards the fence with her other hand, to knock it down.

Before she could attack the fence, she felt a heavy weight pressing down on her hand. A sudden thought stopped her in her tracks. What if they weren't there? What if she had been wrong about the boundary fence all those years? What if it were another lie, as insubstantial and untouchable as Micil Óg, Nóirín, Pádraig . . .

What if there was no reason at all for Micil's anger with her over the cairn, over Garraí an Locháin?

What if they had been buried all along, as she had thought at first, at the edge of a lake or in the bog, in a ditch, or a sand dune by the Caoláire? Somewhere she could never find, where they were closer to the lambs and the calves, to the wild geese and seagulls, than to herself, her house, her world. How could she know for sure?

32.

The stars had hardened to lumps of ice. The wind carried the sound of a screeching thrush from Páirc na Buaile. The wheezing chanter of the Caoláire and the moaning drone of the frogs in the dead night were a black dirge that no longer stirred her senses.

She tried to wipe away the vicious ghosts from her eyes and ears, the ghosts she had buried in the ashes, which were emerging again from the pools of darkness in Garraí an Locháin, over the high fence and into the haggart. She stood there with one hand on the fence, gripping Micil's spade in the other . . .

Micil's spade. Why had she taken it from the gable end? . . . As a crutch to lean on as she stood on this narrow, hostile flagstone by the fence . . . ! Could she, in the space of a few minutes, do what needed to be done to banish the doubts and the ghosts that had plagued her all day?

It was easier now the cairn had been scattered . . .

The first shovelful she lifted, she kept on the spade . . . She bent down and fingered through it as carefully as a girl running her hand through a lover's hair . . . Small stones. That was all . . .

She lifted a clump of dry earth that turned to dust in her fingers . . .

The spade hit something solid; something softer than stone . . . There was something else there . . .

She used her hands to clear away the earth and then began grubbing with her fingers.

A box . . . !

It budged slightly, then came away altogether . . . But it crumbled as soon as she touched it. The box disintegrated and fragments of splintered wood were swept away by a cruel wind.

'Micil Óg, little Micil, darling Micil! Michaelmas Eve of all nights. Why didn't I bring the lantern?'

She bent right down to the earth, searching with her eyes, searching . . .

A hand touched her shoulder. Micil, her husband, was behind her:

'There's no good praying for them . . . '

There was no trace of anger in his voice . . .

'They're in a dark place without pain . . . '

He was crouched down beside her, both of them sifting the earth with their fingers, their eyes searching . . .

But he could see nothing either in the faint light, nothing but mouldering earth, crumbling clay . . .

The two of them kept looking and searching with desperate fingers.

The wind too was fingering the earth . . .

She covered her face with her hands . . .

That vicious woman was throwing earth in her face . . .

She had closed her sleepless eyes for a moment. Now she opened them again. She felt the lump in her chest swelling and pushing up into her throat. She had to hold on to the fence with both hands to keep from falling. All the stars were gone, leaving complete darkness like a thick fluid trickling from the grey cup of the heavens. But she could still see. She was used to the dark by now.

She could see the boundary fence clearly, towering over her in the darkness. At the bottom, the pile was scattered—like the dead ashes on the hearth.

She stepped down off the flagstone. The spade had fallen down beside her in the haggart when she had almost blacked out. She picked it up and flung it over the fence into Garraí an Locháin. Micil's spade! She hadn't the heart to tear the earth.

33.

She sat by the fire. Her head and heart were pounding.

'I wish I hadn't banked the fire!'

The hearth was cold: a heap of dead ashes surrounded by sods of turf.

One, two, three, four, five sods. Five misshapen sods, like small fists jutting out of the ashes. Five mounds of earth.

She huddled closer to the fire, shivering.

Her heart was cold. The stones in the fence were cold. And the calves. The wild geese. The white gulls.

She rubbed her eyes. It was still there; like quicksilver in the fire. Straws of smoke were pushing their way up through the ashes. One . . . two . . . five.

One of the sods caught flame; a fumbling, hurried light that climbed awkwardly through the air, sending shadows skipping across the dark floor.

Nóra raised her head.

Her body was shaking like a leaf in the wind.

Her eyes groped through the darkness, that was now retreating from the quick flames.

She looked at the wisps of smoke, like stalks of corn emerging from the earth, then covered her head with the velvet dress and cashmere shawl.

It was no use.

The priest in confession had said faith could . . .

She looked at the window where a thin light shone on the holy picture.

She straightened up, went to the window, and looked up at the picture. She turned up the light on the tin lamp, then quickly lowered it to a flicker as a haze obscured the image in the sudden light.

She took the picture into the middle of the room where it was dark and looked again.

As soon as she glanced at it, she went down on her knees.

It was true.

The picture, too, was turning to straw, silver straw, with mist blotching the silver.

The dreary picture was taking shape before her very eyes. The point of the spear was ablaze, roses blooming where the nails had pierced the flesh; precious stones where the wounds had been; the halo a wildfire raging round His head.

The angels beat their wings as they descended on the Cross. Mary's mantle was spreading, her eyes brighter than the lightning that ripped the night sky apart over the bay to the west. The sun fell from the sky into her hair. But her face was still shrouded in sadness.

People crowded into the room. In spite of herself, Nóra stretched out her hand. There was her mother. There was no mistaking the slender fingers and fair hair; and Micil's father with his slim neck, broad back, and soft eyebrows.

Another group gathered in front of the Cross.

Sacred Heart! It was them, Micil Óg, Nóirín . . .

She couldn't see their faces. They kept them turned away; but she could see the dust cloud in front of them as they gazed at Mary and her heavy cloak.

'Mary, Mother of God, save them! Hail Mary . . . '

'Son . . . '

'They have not tasted the wine of baptism. They will go to a dark place without pain.'

'The mothers! The mothers! Look at them, Son!'

She pointed to Nóra.

'In a dark place . . . '

'I carried you nine months in my womb, Son . . . '

'You did, Mary, Mother of God; I carried five of them! Look at them! Look at them! Micil Óg . . . '

She touched the hem of her cloak:

'Mother of God, ask him to send me to the dark place instead . . . '

The stars fell in a shower of confetti upon the Cross. A million bells rang out 'He is risen.' The cloak swirled suddenly and swept up all those beneath it.

Sunlight poured through the smoke and dust in an instant. Nóra saw the rust fall from the silver straw as it became a golden ear of corn and shot off into the sky where Mary covered the right arm of the Cross with her mantle.

Mary's mantle and a baby's head; slender neck, soft eyebrows, laughing . . .

Nóra's heart leaped:

'Hail Mary . . . '

The dog whined under the door.

When he came looking for her, Micil found Nóra stretched in front of the fire with the picture held tightly in her hand.

In the flickering firelight, the wrinkles on her face had gone and her eyes seemed alive.

The wind had died down and the Caoláire breathed gently on the sleeping shore. A soft rain made pools on the old roof of the house, in the ashes at the gable end, in the fresh earth that had been newly dug today in Garraí an Tí . . .

TRANSLATED BY LOUIS DE PAOR,
MIKE MCCORMACK, AND LOCHLAINN Ó TUAIRISG

FROM *AN tSRAITH AR LÁR*
(1967)

ANOTHER COUPLE

'Laid up again. Coughing. Choking and spluttering since morning . . . '

Micil's forearm jerked, rattling the cut seed-potatoes in the bucket:

' . . . And I badly need to finish setting those couple of patches down by the sea. But instead of heading down, I have to go up, as quick as my legs will carry me to the top of the village to feed the calf. And no sooner will I be down than as sure as I'm standing here I'll have to go back up again to milk the cow. And feed the hens. And get the supper ready. And then I'll be in my hair shirt all night listening to her coughing and complaining . . . I bet Ó Curraoin doesn't have to feed calves when he should be sowing. Does Tamsaí have to milk cows? Does Peadar an Ghleanna have to feed hens? No way; but I do, and more's the pity. Máirín will take care of all that, and not a bother on her. You won't find Máirín on the flat of her back, sick from night till morning. She's chirpy as a bird, is Máirín . . . '

Micil drew a furious kick on a lump of a stone, a tongue sticking out rudely from the mouth of the hill.

' . . . Your tongue would be worn out trying to talk sense to the old pair in that house below. No matter what you said, you couldn't get it out of their heads that your one was too flighty, too airy, too unsteady by half. You wouldn't know what the likes of that one would do, they said. Whistling like a boy. Imagine! It isn't natural for a woman to be whistling. Making eyes at every man she sees; that's the kind she is. A bird brain like that wouldn't do in this house, Micil, love, they said.

Times are hard, and we could do with the few shillings. What would she bring with her to a fine farm like this? Not so much as a sniff of money, only bare as the day she was born . . . '

To keep the peace and avoid the constant rows, not wanting to face down his mother and father—he must have been struck by a dart from the lios altogether in the end—Micil married the hundred pounds, the few heifers, and Bríd. She was spluttering and groaning the night of their wedding, worn out and dizzy from the music . . . A man could get no satisfaction from exercising his body beside her in the bed. She was too holy anyway. Those chesty ones always are. If he so much as turned towards her in the bed, she'd haul a fistful of rosary beads out from under the pillow and wouldn't stop muttering her prayers till she got up the next morning.

From the day they got married there wasn't a day she wasn't sick, or a single night there wasn't something bothering her: a pain in her back, her hip, her chest, her kidneys; coughing, indigestion, heartburn, gripe, wind growling in her belly, like last night and God knows how many other nights. If your shirt so much as brushed against her, off she'd go again, complaining . . .

She was a pity. Of course she was. She drove Micil to distraction, especially in bed at night. But what could he do? No one was more deserving of pity than himself. He'd often turn around suddenly just to see if he could catch a glimpse of some flickering shadow that was trying to avoid him, or so he imagined . . .

Feeding calves. Feeding hens. Milking cows. Getting supper ready. Coughing and groaning from night until morning. Tamsaí and Ó Curraoin with their families reared, and a clutch of wrens flocking around Peadar an Ghleanna. As for that Máirín! You only had to shake a pair of old drawers in her direction when the wind was right.

Micil lashed out at another stone that grinned up at him from the side of the hill.

As for Micil himself: no balls, no son, no child. Whatever about balls, he had no son and no child. For all the oul' ones' guff, their fine

big farm had no heir. An heir, if you don't mind! Groaning! Creaking hips! Wheezing. Maybe they could bear a child for him? Would
the bundle of bones in the graveyard back there produce an heir for
his fine farm of land that was going to rack and ruin? There was only
one thatched house left in the village, and that was Micil's. Even that
was falling apart for want of regular repair. There were no thatchers
left. Every house except his had electric light. What use was it to him?
What use was electricity in a thatched house? Wasn't it better for
himself and Bríd to see no more of each other than what the flickering fire revealed at night? The endless coughing and groaning from
the chimney corner and the bed were ice cracking under your feet
on a never-ending path. A radio? A radio in a thatched house with
no electricity? Micil could identify every station in the world by the
snoring and wheezing, the hoarseness, the wind, the whining . . . The
only farming he did, sowing when he got half a chance, was to spite
Ó Curraoin. He only had the one cow. That was enough. If he had
any more, who would milk them or put out a few armfuls of hay for
them? Who'd feed the calves?

When he reached the brow of the hill, he saw Tamsaí's eldest son
coming down in the opposite direction. Micil and Tamsaí got married the same year. This lad was almost seventeen now. His bright face
irritated Micil. The young fella's manliness stung him, as though his
virility was accusing Micil of being beaten, on the way out. Seventeen! Seventeen years gone from his life as though his teeth had fallen
out or his throat shut tight and he had eaten nothing in all that time.
The sudden surge in his arm sent some of the potatoes spilling from
the mouth of the bucket. His body was tingling. He had two sons in
him yet. An ass brayed at the top of the village, sawing the air, and
another one — it sounded like his own — answered from the other end.

'That you may never taste the autumn stubble,' said Micil. His fist
was clenched, but he resisted immediately the useless childish urge
that scampered through his body — to shake his fist in the direction
of the donkey below.

The briars and brambles were harps, the land and afternoon sky pregnant with mating calls.

'Easy for the birds to be randy! They don't have to feed the calf. And every other man in the country where I should be: out with the spade.' The vindictiveness that leapt in his eyes as he looked at the fields all around him began to show in his agitated walk. As he came around the hill he met Peadar an Ghleanna: 'Fine day, Micil.'

Easy for him to be wittering about fine days. He was free to go about his proper business, like a man. Was he laughing at him? He was definitely keeping something from him, hidden under his eyelids. Was it mockery? Or triumph: it could well be that. Micil realised that Peadar could just as easily have said, 'Fine night.' Or 'Fine woman.' Or 'Fine family.' Or 'Fine bed' . . . Who could blame him? Given half a chance and the run of the forge, what man would do otherwise, only follow Peadar's lead? Her rump like an east Galway mare's up against him all the time under the sheets, brushing him from his knee to his belly. She'd have him turned inside out, in curly knots, twisted happily around her finger. You could tell as much any morning of the year you met him on the road. No matter how hard she worked him the night before, you could tell by his eyes, and the dirty big grin that was permanently kneaded into his face, like a sweet loaf from the shop, that he was thriving on his nightly exertions. Regular as clockwork he was the talk of the village:

'Going for the nurse again, Peadar! No bother to you, not like blind balls . . . '

'You're some lad, Peadar! Not fumbling around like dumb dick. Bull's-eye every time.'

'The nurse would have nothing to do only for you, Peadar. One at the first cuckoo-call, another when the oats are ripe.'

'Would you not give deaf crotch there a loan of your old drawers?'

'They're making them in ones and twos over in the wilds of Gleann. You'd never know? They were always obliging neighbours over there.'

'What are you on about? He won't let her out of his sight, sharp as a blacksmith eyeing a nail. 'Twould be a sly cat would get away with anything of his.'

'As sure as you're standing there, Peadar and Máirín have another bed broken with this one.'

It was no exaggeration. Since Peadar put the slate roof on, the Speciality's hearse had carted two new beds up there. Micil had lost count of the number of old beds he saw the last day in Peadar's haggart, and in the shed, where the hens and poultry were roosting in them. Peadar could well afford new beds with all the handouts he got: children's allowance, language grants, and dole all year on account of having a large family and only half a farm . . .

Good neighbours! In the midnight courts of the village, Micil was never the one accused of doing his neighbour a good turn! . . . The hard, agitated, venomous walk with the overflowing bucket up the steep slope had left Micil a little out of breath. No fear of Peadar being short of breath, the goat! Micil was at the top of the hill now and could see Gleann away to the north revealing itself suddenly, like a silver coin that might slip from a man's fist. There was only one house, a new house that trapped the sun in its travels with its red slates, the windows glittering like precious stones in the light. The house was neat as a new pin, as though it had just been delivered brand new from the Speciality's hearse. And there she was, Máirín, breezing through the yard, children clinging to her worn red dress so that she seemed at first glance to be a moving extension of the house, a white basin in her hands as she called out in a voice as sweet and bright as the chirping hedges and sky, the ritual cry of the countrywoman, 'Chook Chook.' Her neat little arse was as shapely as ever. The dress was short enough that the deep hollows behind her knees could be glimpsed between two children. She was as flighty as ever! She was never slow to show off her knees and her arse, round and firm as a ball. Her whole body was a ball — every last bit of it: ball-thighs, ball-hips, ball-belly . . . Her breasts, her sweet breasts were sun-drenched milking-spots, heavy and swollen. It was no wonder, with the number of children she had suckled . . . Surely she couldn't be pregnant again! All jokes aside, Peadar had put up a great fight for such a bony man. Micil could best him any day at wrestling, throwing weights, digging, cutting turf, scything, rowing . . .

When Máirín had finished scattering the leftover scraps among the hens she started singing, the kind of song she had always liked:

> Is trua nach mise, nach mise,
> Is trua nach mise bean Pháidín,
> Is trua nach mise, nach mise,
> Agus an bhean atá aige a bheith caillte.*

She had always been a bit of an outsider, coming from the West. Micil could never make out whether she was watching him out of the corner of her eye. The mission priest had threatened him with hell-fire and damnation a while back. It was always the same: threats and damnation. And still Micil couldn't resist giving his own version of the song under his breath:

> Is trua nach mise, nach mise,
> Is trua nach mise fear Mháirín,
> Is trua nach mise, nach mise,
> Agus an fear atá aici a bheith caillte.

'No word of a lie!' Micil said to himself. 'I hope he drowns, the conniving scrounger! What am I doing, only paying back the favour, returning the compliment.' It would be that all right if he only had the nerve to say it aloud. 'God put a stop to your gallop,' he said quickly, remembering the shameless ass from the bottom of the village answering the other one a while ago. Máirín was rubbing the cheeks of

---

* It's a pity, a pity, a pity / It's a pity I'm not married to Páidín, / It's a pity, a pity, a pity / And Paidín's wife to have croaked it.

her sweet arse. Micil realised she had spotted him watching her. He looked away quickly, checking for any sign of new growth in the field of oats behind him that Tamsaí had just sprayed.

He saw nothing green, only Bríd. Bríd would always be there. Tonight, tomorrow, next year, her gobs of phlegm would be an impassable tangle of briars blocking his path. The coughing fits that racked her now wouldn't kill her. But all the same, a puff of breath would blow Bríd from the palm of your hand to heaven. It would be an act of mercy to give her a leg-up on the way to her reward. Heaven was made for her. Her bright soul had been scoured by piety, cleansed by pain . . .

Bríd: a single breath would be enough. Peadar? Hard to get the better of the rock on which the church was built. He was as weak and sound as ever, planning another brood of children under his eyelids and no trace of breathlessness or anything like it on him for all their exertions . . . No fear of him unless a horse braced itself and kicked him. A newly shod hoof in the crotch! But there were no horses or blacksmiths anymore. An ass's kick could be nasty enough, especially if you were trying to keep him from a mare. But the blunt hoofs wouldn't be strong enough to finish off a seasoned campaigner like Peadar. And he wasn't exactly killing himself with work, not in the daytime anyway. If he got run over by a turf lorry, or the Speciality's hearse. But he was too careful for that. He wouldn't risk going up on his new two-storey house. If he did, he might slip, or someone could go up to give him a hand and send him flying, or take the ladder out from under him. Anything to be rid of him . . . There was only one chance, a very slim one: he went fishing with a rod from time to time on Carraig an Phoill. When the tide was in, there was a deep hole in front of the rock. A trip or a push would knock him from the slippery stone. It wouldn't even need that much if he could be coaxed and cajoled into staying on the rock; if he had hooked a fish, he'd stay on the rock until the incoming tide began to cover it. No more babies for him. He couldn't swim and he'd be drowned in the incoming back-current. Whoever kept him on the rock would drown too unless he was a really good swimmer . . .

'God forgive me,' said Micil to himself. But the next minute he was asking himself why shouldn't God forgive him. 'Don't they always say,' he said, 'that a woman belongs forever to the first man to have her . . . ' Then he'd show that shower of bastards in the village that their nicknames and mockery — dumb dick, blind balls, deaf crotch — were a mark of their own dumbness, their own blindness, their own impotence. He had the making of two sons in his strong, agile body yet, four or five maybe, twins and all, with Máirín. But without soil for planting . . .

Despite the burning acts of contrition imposed on him, by himself and others, his scheming thoughts were a sorcerer's wheel, implacable as the endless rotations of his mind, trundling up and down that village road for the past fifteen years, since the day Máirín married Peadar an Ghleanna. A single breath, a leg-up, a little push, a trip . . .

Unlike the flickering of an electric light, Micil's schemes never stopped, even now that he had yet another job to do. An ass was zigzagging its way towards him down the road, half his spancels snapped and trailing behind him, heading towards the sea, as if he had taken a sudden notion to go somewhere, and giving every indication that he was going to get there. Micil put down the bucket and began kicking the ass, driving him back up the road. He managed to drive him back a couple of steps, the ass as stubborn as the hill Micil had just climbed, as the black future he was trying to avoid. What an obstinate curse of an animal that wouldn't do what it was told! Micil was slightly breathless from the ferocity of his kicking. The ass turned his head as steadily and as unstoppable as a boat or a car responding obediently to the wheel, and headed back down the hill. Micil aimed an almighty kick at his impudent balls, but his foot got tangled in the spancels, the spancels got fouled up in the bucket, and the bucket spilt. The ass saw his chance: in spite of his hurry and the trailing spancels, he aimed a kick with his hind leg that went no closer to Micil's crotch than the overturned bucket on the road.

It was almost enough to send Micil flying. As he refilled the bucket he couldn't help thinking that the bucket tipping over was another breach in the fence of his life, another victory for fate. Even that was only another click in the relentless rotation of his racing thoughts. A leg-up. A slip from the roof. Carraig an Phoill. The incoming tide . . .

'Sook! Sook! Sook! . . . '

He was out of breath from all the sooking, but even if he sooked until his tongue turned to a sugar stick of 'sooks,' the calf wouldn't come near him.

'That ye may be the last of yer breed, anyway, ye bloody blackguards!' said Micil, as the braying of the two asses rammed his 'sook' back into his open mouth. He walked around the big cairn. It was the kind of place the ugly so-and-so might be! No sign of him there. Off he went up the hill until finally he heard the calf puffing and coughing. There he was in the farthest part of the field, up above in the hollow, huddled in the corner between two fences for all the world as if he was trying to turn a deaf ear to the sooking—to the mating calls and braying as well.

'The devil skin you alive; there you are after all that! If there was anywhere closer to Leac na Crónach for you to go, that's where you'd be hiding': Micil hurled all the frustration of his life, his wasted day, his troublesome journey up the road, at the creature in the corner.

'Sook! Sook! You lazy hoor! Sook! Sook!'

He rattled the handle of the bucket. The calf wouldn't budge. He wouldn't even let on there was anyone in the field besides himself.

'A butler is what you want, young man, or a nurse maybe.'

Unlike the thoughts charging into each other in his mind, Micil's determined stride towards the calf made it clear he knew exactly where he was going, as if, like the ass earlier on, he had finally discovered his true destination at the end of his journey up the hill. As he crossed the stream at the top corner, the calf headed off down by the fence, like a frightened child running away from a tinker, afraid he might stuff him into his sack and carry him off. Micil realised the calf didn't recognise him. It was Bríd who usually fed him. Micil followed him.

'Here, sugar! Here, pet!' Let the tongue throw off its bridle until the sweet talk had slipped out, a shared gift for the ears of birds, beasts, or any passerby who might be listening. He should be ashamed of himself. It was the sort of improper thing a person might say in his sleep. He rubbed his hardened jaw as if he wanted to tear it apart, then headed after the calf that continued to turn a deaf ear to all his coaxing. He kept retreating from him, coughing softly. The more Micil tried to keep up with him, the further the calf stayed away. When Micil was at the far end of the field, the calf was at this end; when Micil was above on high ground, the calf was below in the hollow.

Micil stood on the hummock in the middle of the field, gasping for breath. It was the best spot for keeping an eye on the calf. His forehead was like a washboard; the bottomless water of Carraig an Phoill was like that too when the tide came in, all wrinkles, ripples, and furrows. He was a man tossed about by indecision, on uneven ground in the cattle-pound of his life, who would have to go down, one way or the other, although he could no longer distinguish between north and south, a man who had to free himself from knots and locks, from spancels and taboos:

'Will Bríd and Peadar be as hard to trap as the calf? A leg-up. A push. A trip. Carraig an Phoill . . . '

The calf called out plaintively, as if on cue, terrified by this demented creature in the field with him. He was racked by a fit of coughing. Micil shook his fist at him.

'Do you think I'm going to break my balls chasing after you to make you eat what you don't want . . . You dirty hoor that doesn't hear the birds calling or the asses braying any more than my 'Sook! Sook!' Running away from me . . . '

Like the ass had run, like his whole life was running away from him, the years, the hopes of his youth, of a happy marriage . . . All running away from him, leaving him with nothing, only shortness of breath.

Micil was hardly even aware of the calf by now. He was being tossed about by the currents and eddies of conflicting thoughts. He failed, as always, to stop his conscience from sleeping. It was the same relentless rotation over and over again — 'a single breath . . . the bottomless hole . . . ' that gave him no respite or relief all those years going up and down the village road, his very own Stations of the Cross, that would never let him be no matter how many more years he managed to come up that village road; that would give him no peace even when he no longer had enough strength in his body to stir from the house; the relentless rotation was unlikely to stop even when he stopped breathing; it would probably continue in the grave, if it was true that there was another world in which people lived and moved . . . There was no everlasting happiness but Máirín. A single breath to send Bríd to Paradise. She deserved it. A bottomless pit for all eternity for Peadar. He'd had enough fun and games in this life . . .

Micil realised the relentless rotation that had been goading and tempting him down through the years, and would continue to do so until the very end, was as useless as a scarecrow in a field without a breath of wind, or passion or life to shake him, so that the birds of the air knew it was a dead thing, a lifeless toy . . . He emptied the bucket, then flung it as hard as he could at the calf. It fell harmlessly, well short of its target, like all his repeated resolutions. He was completely out of breath. He came down the hill and headed for the road . . .

TRANSLATED BY
LOUIS DE PAOR AND LOCHLAINN Ó TUAIRISG

THE BLOSSOMING, THE WITHERING

Not only did the Speciality hearse-man know every person in those parts, but, as he himself liked to boast, he knew every last flea too. The multi-tasking hearse—that's what a civil servant on the Irish course said it was. It delivered all their groceries to the locals. It was like a big disposal unit, whisking the dead away to church and grave-yard. And why wouldn't the Speciality man know everyone? He was born and bred there and had never lived anywhere else. People dropped into his shop, the Speciality, at all hours of the day, and then, more often than not, ended up there again in the hours between this world and the next.

But he didn't know this woman with her hand raised, a bit im-patiently he thought, to ask for a lift. He had never seen her around here before. She looked average enough, her figure not too big and not too small; in and out it went, forming a middling sort of shape. She was of a middling age too, not old and not young. The Speciality said to himself it could go either way: she could be a majestic beauty stepping into the blaze of the headlights, or an ugly duckling shrink-ing back into the shadows.

What surprised him was that her raised hand seemed to halt not just the hearse but also the turgid stream of his thoughts—if the pro-ceedings of his mind at that moment could even be called thoughts and weren't just some sort of chemical-organic reaction. His first im-pression wasn't that here was a hand that might turn a key to free him from his mental prison. But afterwards he realised that, in the split second between seeing the hand and stopping the hearse, that was exactly what had happened. Maybe it was because she was a stranger around here. No local woman would raise her hand to look for a lift at night. Often there were tourists on this road, right enough, and the season wasn't quite over.

He'd have to put her in the back part of the hearse. Two immediate family members of the corpse he had brought to the chapel that evening were installed up front beside him. 'The body's only just been taken out of there,' said the woman in front, in a mournful tone that conveyed, if anything, that it would be an injustice in the eyes of heaven and earth to let a living person into the space so recently vacated by the corpse.

'Sure weren't there bags of flour back there earlier today?' The man in front spoke with a low-key, easygoing nonchalance, as if he could take everything in life just as it came. 'I had to clean the flour off the shelf before the body was lifted in.'

'Now listen,' the hearse driver said, with feeling, 'you won't get a discount off me that way. A few bags of bran for Ó Curraoin was the last thing back there. He's fattening pigs. I cleaned it all up perfectly. I always do. Now, if you have a problem with me giving this one a lift—'

'Oh, not a bit of it, that's not it,' said the woman in front, somewhat snappishly. 'We practise the love of God, like everyone else. It's just that I got the idea into my head that back there would be left empty until after the old fellow is buried tomorrow. But with her being a stranger and all—'

'We won't bother with her,' said the Speciality, closing the door again.

'Oh yes we will,' said the other man, opening the door on his side.

The hearse looked ethereal in the falling dusk. Its silhouette began low in front, the midsection swelling in a gentle, upward curve and sinking low again at the back. Its length gave it a stretched look. If it resembled anything at all, with its nose down like that, it was like a currach slipping into the trough of a wave. The old people around here believed that the dead were spirited off to Inis na Fírinne. They said that they were ferried there in long, slender faery currachs.

'You're not from around here, are you, God bless you,' said the hearse driver, opening the back door to let the stranger into the part of the hearse where goods were stowed.

'No.'

'You've been walking for a while?' He wasn't so much inquiring as putting two and two together. He wasn't a man to let any detail, however trivial, escape him. At any rate, the sweat that trickled down her face, a secret script on her skin, was a clear sign of exertion. Most cars would pass by someone like this.

'Yes.'

She was as brusque as the short syllable itself. But she had answered him and confirmed his conjecture. He could think of no pretext to prolong the conversation. She began easing herself comfortably onto the back seat. In a flash of light from a passing car the Speciality noticed she had one leg up along the length of the seat. There was no whiff of drink off her and she didn't look drunk. She was probably trying to cool down and recover from all that raging sweat. 'I'd say you have your troubles, girl,' the hearse driver remarked to himself. She must have walked miles to have got into that state. The evening wasn't all that warm, and as far as he could see she hadn't any luggage with her.

The hearse-man had a litany of excuses ready to avoid accepting the invitation from the pair in front to come back into the funeral house. He had to clean and polish the hearse for the morning. His wife and the girls in the shop would be tired, but couldn't close up until he got back. He didn't want to keep the people in the funeral house from their rest: they must be exhausted after last night's wake. He'd be at their door half past nine sharp in the morning. That would allow plenty of time to bring the old boy to the graveyard, unless they were thinking of shouldering the coffin . . . That was the fashion nowadays, he acknowledged. Still, a hearse would have to show up even without a body to carry. But behind the smokescreen of his words was the clear conviction that a few fresh pints in Mike's bar on his way back would beat the dregs of the funeral barrel hands down. Tea, bread, and butter were all he'd get in the funeral house. He was looking forward to a big juicy feed of beef once he got home, which would fortify him and line his stomach for more pints in Mike's place later on.

When he let the couple out of the car at the funeral house, he didn't ask the woman in the back to move up to the front. Tongues were inclined to wag around here. The hearse driver was a bit like a priest. Anyway, he could see she was exhausted. Besides, just like the whiff that comes off fish when it's on the turn, questions were beginning to spiral up from his thoughts of beer and beef. What was he going to do with this one when he got home? Maybe he could flag down a car to take her to the city. There were always cars stopping for petrol at the Speciality anyway. He was so pleased with this solution that he started to whistle the only tune he ever whistled. 'Ancient Nora' it was called. It hadn't occurred to him to ask her where she was headed! Had to be to the city. Where else would she be going?

He recognised Séamas Bán's headlights as he came up the narrow road from Draigheanaí. When Séamas saw the Speciality, he raised a hand. In the strong light it looked about three times grimier than it was.

'Are you away over to Mike's, Séamas?'

'No my friend, I'm not. I'm saving myself.'

'I know you have to go easy on it from now on, Séamas. I heard—'

'*Muise*, if it has to be done at all I might as well get digging, as Tamsaí back the road said when his wife was nagging him to plant the row of onions. This is all working out well. You're saving me a journey. I was on my way to your place to ask if you'd bring me over that bed I asked your wife the price of the other day.'

'First thing in the morning. Well, second thing. First I'll have to bring the body from beyond down to the church again. Do you want anything else brought over, Séamas? I might as well do it all in one trip.'

'The mattress, the bed set, those two soft chairs, and the little table. Will they all fit in the hearse, do you think?'

'They will indeed, and more along with them! I took four coffins in her from the hospital the other day without one so much as touching the other. If they tried to whisper to each other you'd be able to hear them up in front! All the couples love the beds from our shop. Everyone says they're lucky for making families. It was one of our beds Peadar an Ghleanna and Máirín had when they had the two sets of twins, one after another.'

'Begging your pardon, my friend, but they broke one with the first set of twins and another with the second, but upon my soul, my friend, wouldn't any red-blooded man be happy with a setback like that. Jim and Long Jude had one of your beds too and she had twins before six months was up. The fine Speciality bed put her on the fast track. But then again, look at Micil! Nothing doing there. He hasn't the breath for it. Is that another body you have back there?'

'No, that's a stranger-woman who was hitchhiking up at Ard na gCurraoinigh. I'll be over with your and Berna's bed after the funeral and we'll have to have a drink to wish God's blessing on it . . . '

He looked over his shoulder. The woman's breath was steaming up the window. She had both legs up on the seat and seemed to be stretched out full-length on it. Making herself at home. Still, there was nothing worse than getting in a lather of sweat like that. He would have to clean out the back of the hearse for the body. They were a fussy lot over at the old fellow's house. For all that, they could easily have taken the bag of bones that was once the old fellow out the door of the church, over the wall, and slung him down on top of his wife with neither hearse nor pallbearer . . .

He switched the inside light on for a minute when he was getting out of the hearse to go into Mike's. She was lying flat, fast asleep, still soaked in sweat. He'd be time enough waking her when he got back to his own house.

The first pint had percolated down into the pit of his stomach, where it would be a good base for the beef, and the second was on its way down to join it when Scabby Stiofáinín walked in and parked his rump on a barstool. One look at Stiofáinín was enough to ruin the Speciality's appetite for drink. But it was an occupational hazard that, whether he liked it or not, he would have to ask him what he was having. Privately wishing the devil would take him.

'Nothing at all right now, thanks all the same,' said Stiofáinín.

The Speciality was astounded, so much so that the mouthful he was about to swallow slid back down into his glass. Scabby Stiofáinín refusing a drink! Maybe he was hoping to get two instead of one. He never thought he'd see the day that Stiofáinín would be so restrained. But then: 'Pour a pint for me there, Mike,' he said the next minute. Then he lowered his voice and said to the hearse driver, in wheedling tones:

'A drink loosens the tongue nicely. I'll sip away at it while I'm talking to you. What's that big lump of a woman doing in the back of your hearse . . . There was a crowd of us out there at the back of Mike's when we heard this awful groaning . . . Coming from the hearse, it was . . . Nioclás thinks—and he's a man that brought plenty of calves into the world—he's pretty sure she's in labour . . . Oh here, mister . . . what's the point in getting annoyed at me? I didn't do it. Neither of us ever saw her before, and I know you can't see much of her at the moment, but Lord, the noise she's making would bring deaf cows out of a forest . . . Another pint there, Mike . . . Oh I'm very sorry my dear man! I thought you were signalling to Mike for another round. My eyes must be playing tricks on me . . . '

The Speciality was still more amazed than annoyed:

'What's wrong with you?'

'Sick,' she gasped between ragged breaths.

'Sick in what way?'

'Baby.'

'Jesus, Mary, and Joseph! Here in my hearse? In my delivery van?'

'Your hearse is as good as a boudoir tonight,' said a mocking voice from among a crowd of loiterers that had gathered and was still growing.

'That's the way it goes,' said a mournful, older voice. 'One departs and another arrives. One goes up to heaven, another comes down to earth.'

'The worst off are the ones who are stuck here, going nowhere.'

'One going and one coming, just like when Stiofáinín finishes a pint and nods at Mike to send another one on over.'

'Oh you're all very witty altogether. But there's a body that has to be brought to the graveyard tomorrow with some dignity, right here where this big blob is bursting at the seams popping out a baby.'

'She's after taking off her belt—'

'Belt on or belt off, get out of that car, you shameless hussy.'

The moaning bundle of flesh quivered like a dog shaking water off its coat, but the legs that dangled apart over the side of the seat showed no signs of propulsion . . .

'I—I can't.'

'Here, lads! Give us a hand here, and we'll bring her into Mike's.'

But none of the crowd showed willing. You'd have thought the hearse driver was the only man present who owned a pair of hands.

'Nice of you to propose dumping her in my place. It's a pub I'm running, not a maternity hospital,' said Mike.

'How about the stable? The garage?'

'Neither of those is a hospital either. Bad cess to you, imagine what would happen to someone who got blamed for her death? I don't see you carting her off to your own house. You're the last one who'd think of sending for a doctor and nurse.'

'In the name of God, will one of you run in to the phone and

ring the doctor and the nurse and the priest as well. He might as well
come too.'

'I'll do it myself,' Mike said. 'I don't trust you lot with my
phone . . . '

After a spell of pacing up and down and wringing his hands, the
Speciality got ready to start up the hearse. But an old woman, grey
as an ancient crow, stopped him. She raised her hand towards him,
or what passed for a hand anyway, a claw of a thing, hard and hooked
and bare. At the same time a squall of wind blew a drift of withered
leaves off Mike's trees and into the hearse, some of them drifting onto
the woman's writhing body.

'Don't you dare,' said the old one. 'Leave her where she is. If you
disturb her the baby could come before its time and maybe die, and
her too. That won't do your Speciality's reputation any good. Leave
her to me. I have the skills.'

'Where did you come out of, you old witch? Still alive, are you?
Skill! Skill, my foot,' said a lame man who walked like a crab, weaving in and out of the crowd.'

'You should thank your lucky stars, Tadhg. Only for me you'd
never have seen the light of day—'

'You left your mark on me, you old hag. All your skill did for me
was to leave me with a bandy leg.'

'And the girls think the other leg doesn't match it.'

'Not in my *hearse*—': as the poor woman's contractions inten-
sified, the hearse-man's voice and gestures seemed to get wilder . . .

Mike reappeared:

'The nurse is away at a birth in Tulach a Leathair since dinnertime and the girl said that Peadar an Ghleanna—'

'Is waiting for her. God's curse on that horny bastard!'

'He's a good customer of yours. Look at all the beds he bought
in the Speciality.'

'Looks like your hearse is lucky for making families too.'

'Better watch out or they'll turn your shop into a hospital.

'On his way over to get the nurse, Peadar an Ghleanna got the doctor to go back to that Micil from his townland. What's this his surname is? Puffing Micil we call him around here. The doctor's girl said he had so little breath in his body that he could barely smudge a mirror if you held it to his mouth. And Ned Bhile's son is waiting for the doctor in the kitchen.'

'Ned himself is nearly ready to be shipped out with the sail trimmed.'

'The priest is in Clochar na mBroc. With someone who was found under a turf lorry. Old Peggy Ní Nún is nearly —'

'Listen to me, all of you! There'll be nothing but funerals between now and Christmas and all during Christmas. I have to clean this girl and polish her.' Quick and sharp, his words tumbled out, and his eyes had a steely glint as they rested on the shuddering bundle that at that moment barely resembled a woman. In his mind's eye a squadron of coffins was parading out of the hearse, their nameplates flashing in the sun like gold coins coming out of a purse, the sun's rays slipping away as they were brought across the threshold of the church, to rest quietly on the wooden rack inside. Just like the one he had delivered to the church today. He almost believed that it was his own hearse that lent them their shine, catching the sunlight and graciously bestowing it on them . . .

'Speciality, I'm warning you,' said Mike, 'don't lay a hand on that one, not without authority.'

'Authority! Whose authority?'

'How would I know? The sergeant's, maybe. As far as I know, he holds authority over everything around here. Wait a minute!'

Mike went back inside.

'It'd melt a heart of stone to look at her,' someone said.

'You couldn't but be sorry for her, the poor stranger.'

'The devil take her, and you with her. Why can't you feel sorry for me and for the bodies waiting to be moved. Pity is cheap when you've nothing to lose . . . '

'You keep your hands off her,' said the old woman. 'You have no skill when it comes to this. Or would you put her out like the man did to the Virgin Mary when she was in labour with Christ himself, praised be His name? The woman wanted to let her in, but she ended up out in the stable on the prickly straw. That was where she brought Him into this world. As they say, "the wife gentle, the man rough to the stranger . . . "'

'"And the Son of God lying in a manger,"' someone finished. Speciality could feel everyone's eyes boring into him at that moment. He was relieved when Mike came back on the scene.

'The sergeant can't authorise you to move her. He's not a doctor or a nurse or a priest or a P.C. He thinks you could take a legal case against her for compensation for causing mischief or being a nuisance in your car. But he can't get involved unless there's a breach of the peace. That's the phrase he used: "breach of the peace." As soon as that happens, let him know . . . '

'I'll breach his arse!'

'I'll breach his balls!'

'Her time is coming,' the old woman said as she leaned into the hearse. 'Bid, brush those old leaves off her: the rest of you, go and get some dry hay from the middle of a stack, and God send that you do it quick. We'll put a layer of it under her on the floor of the hearse and we'll settle her down here. That's the most comfortable way for the baby to come.'

'A baby getting born on the floor of my hearse!'

'There's no time now to be changing plans. Spread the hay here . . . You take her head and shoulders, Bid, and I'll take her feet. Don't lower her head until I get her legs stretched out apart . . . '

This talk piqued the Speciality's interest. That was just how they had gone about moving the old boy's body earlier today, one at his head and one at his feet. And tomorrow they'd put a layer of hay in the grave under the coffin.

'Hold her up as best you can, Bid, and I'll see how the baby is.'

'Don't bend its leg like you bent mine.'

'Nice and easy now, sweetheart! I'm not going to hurt you . . . '

'Missus, I'd advise you,' said Mike, 'to keep your hands off her. You could be in trouble if anything—'

'I've done this plenty of times.'

'That's for sure. Look at all the lame people, limping about.'

'I won't hurt you, darling. Be patient now! It won't be long until—'

'It's a wonder none of you thought to ring the hospital,' said a woman who had just arrived, holding a plump toddler by the hand.

'Christ, you're right. An ambulance, a bed, a nurse . . . '

'Too late,' said the old woman, still bent to her task. 'Any minute now, my little honeybunch—'

'The ambulance is being called out all over the place anyway,' said a young man whose voice took a turn upwards towards the end of the sentence like a light board across a stream springing up at one end when you put your weight on the other.

'May the head of hellfire torture them with blunt knives,' said the Speciality, and you could tell from his tone that he wouldn't have minded helping out with the task.

'There wouldn't be quite the same demand for the Speciality beds then.'

Just then there was a big commotion, and people came stamping out of the bar, across the street, around by the barn:

'I'll stick me toe right up his red arse.'

'I wouldn't dirty your foot like that, Mike, me old son.'

'I'll use me boot and this mallet to knock every drop of drink back out of his rotten blubbery body.'

'Mike'll knock a baby out of him.'

'He'll see him off to the great blue yonder . . . '

'He drank all the porter and licked the drips off the tap. He was starting on the third bottle of whiskey . . . '

'He had the run of the place . . . '

'No bother to him to sink the lot.'

'When a baby's on the way, a man needs—'

'Help, help,' Scabby Stiofáinín could be heard yelling from the depths of a hedge somewhere. 'I've a thorn in my arse.'

'Breach of the peace.'

'My God, the hedges are coming alive.'

'Alive and awake.'

'It's an ill wind that blows nobody any good.'

'I wish you'd take your hearse and your new babies to hell off my patch,' said Mike, coming out of the bar again. 'My place has been drunk dry because of those bastards.'

He was just back from a mad chase after someone who was weaving in and out of the crowd to get away from him.

'The good leg will be as bandy as the bad one when my boot is finished with it. That's a whole bottle of brandy you took . . . '

He threw the mallet at a man who grabbed a bicycle that was lying against the hedge and jumped up on it:

'I see you're good at a lot more besides helping cows calve . . . '

Just at that moment, the strangest cry of all came from the bed of hay on the floor of the hearse: a cry at once young and as old as humanity. A cry that would one day become a death rattle. Without such a cry there could be no death.

TRANSLATED BY KATHERINE DUFFY

THE QUICK AND THE DEAD

He was ensconced in the chimney-nook, the warmest part of the house. The heat from the fire was making him sweat. There were moments when he thought it was sucking the marrow from his bones. Even so, he wouldn't move out the cosy shelter of the nook. He was surprised to find himself calling it a shelter, as if he needed protection or was fleeing from danger.

In a way, he was. He felt a bit of a stranger here, being from Ionnarba, a place three miles away. He didn't really know any of the people who were standing around the kitchen of the wake-house. The young generation. Peeking out at them from the safety of his nook, he decided that that was the perfect phrase to describe them, and he had already murmured it to himself about twenty times over. The young generation! The people he did know, people in their teens, twenties, and older, were tucked up at home now, and the business of watching over the dead had fallen to this group of youngsters. It was funny, him calling them the young generation. He was barely twenty-eight himself. Still, that meant that he was nearer to people in their thirties now than to those in their twenties or teens. Of course, if he had been at the same school as them, he would have known them quite well. But he had gone to school in Ionnarba, away to the east of here.

He knew he was fooling himself. It wasn't just a matter of age and homeplace, east and west. Other things combined with those to make him feel ill at ease here, things that would maybe make him feel like an outsider in every place and among every age group. He didn't understand why, and whenever he tried to work it out, he felt he was floundering in the dark. Was it because he was a country boy?

It was true he had never been out of this country. Most people here were always shuttling back and forth between England and here. He wasn't one for going to dances on Sunday nights in town either, even though he lived closer to town than the people in this area. He preferred to stay near home and spend the evenings visiting neighbours. Plenty of people older than he went dancing in town. He supposed he had a country outlook.

All these wasters here only had to crook a finger and the women came running. They had the gift of the gab. They made getting a woman look easy, but he had never had much luck in that department. He hadn't even attempted to court one of the odd ones, even when he was in the grip of marriage fever. It was as if a vast, frozen sea, an unfathomable waste, stretched between him and womankind. Any of them who by rights should be able to see he was good husband material always seemed to prefer one of these cocky types, someone a lot younger than themselves who was only out for whatever fleeting bit of fun he could get. And the women knew it too! Gradually, Micil realised that they looked on him as a bad hand of cards, one of fate's duds.

The clumsy efforts he'd made here to communicate, to take part in the conversation and fit in with the others, had left him feeling like a bat flapping about a locked barn. They chattered away in quick, clean English that was as obscure to him as tinkers' cant. Every time he thought he'd reached solid conversational ground, it turned to quicksand. There was that simperer now chatting up Meg Micilín. 'You're all *bottled up*, Meg,' and Lord, how her face lit up like a beacon. For a long time afterwards laughter flickered in her eyes like an ember in a pile of wood.

Meg was the one standing nearest to him on the hearth. A few minutes before he thought he'd managed something funny. 'Did the *alarm* deprive you of your date last Sunday night?' But instead of lighting up like before, she stood stony-faced. She looked around in a leisurely way, her sloe-black eyes exchanging expressive glances with

those of a group of young girls: 'Did you ever hear anything so silly?'
A tall skinny one said, loud enough that he could hear: 'He's trying to
chat you up with talk of the *fire brigade*, Meg.' That damned heifer of a
Meg. If she didn't keep her sloe-black glances to herself she'd find herself high and dry, and rightly *bottled up*. Whatever that might mean.

He'd had better schooling than either of these two. But they
could casually pepper their conversations with English words that
meant nothing to him. No rhyme nor reason, although he could
understand their literal meaning. The perfect phrase, the charm, the
incantation. Over there at the wall, one little pup was holding forth to
another little pup about some night he'd spent *'out on the town.'* He
was speaking Irish, but it was littered with idioms picked up from his
time in England. Micil noticed that when he himself attempted to
spice up his own contributions to the conversation with some choice
English phrases, they always seemed to fall flat. He had tried to remark that there were 'hordes' of women over in Ionnarba. '*Whores*, he
says,' said the little pup, once again loud enough that he could hear.
'That other night when I was *out on the town—*'

'I think he was trying to say they have a good *tally* of women,
plenty of women,' said the other little pup.

He'd been schooled in both Irish and English, and knew a lot
more than they, but what was the use? At that moment he felt as if
he'd been to school not in Ionnarba nor in this place, but in a hedge-
school with his great-grandfather!

'Give us that pipe till I light it for you,' said the only fellow here
who looked to be about his own age, or a bit older maybe. It was probably the only pipe in the house. The rest of them were all smoking
scutty little butts of cigarettes, snuggling them up between their fingers as they lifted them to take a pull, paying homage to the god of
gods, the great god of smoke whose signature pall drifted close to the
rafters. One of the young girls brayed: 'Give him a pinch of snuff . . . '
He spent the rest of the night in the chimney-nook trying to get rid
of the gobs of phlegm discreetly, letting them trickle, little by little,

from the corner of his mouth into the fire where they sputtered faintly in the heat. Why on earth hadn't he thought of buying a packet of fags? He preferred the flavour of pipe tobacco. A redneck, that's what he was! He'd be time enough taking up the pipe in a few years' time when he was a married man with a woman making bread and spinning on his hearth. It was like the 'God be with you' he would say without thinking. Always forgetting to greet girls with 'hello,' always behind the times, like an eejit of a troubadour courting the pixie, as the civil servant on the Irish course would say.

Micil felt as if his eyes were bulging out of their sockets. He worried that people would think he was staring at them. So he turned his gaze on his shoes, his trousers. Expensive tweed trousers they were, and spotless, just like his soft black shoes. He had dressed for the occasion much more carefully than he would have done for a funeral in his own village. But even there, whatever he was wearing would look out of place. His scalp felt tight as a narrow shoe as he looked around again, this time checking out what the others were wearing. A lot of them wore dirty, frayed things: stained dungarees; battered, split wellingtons; weird old waistcoats instead of proper jackets; overcoats and raincoats — clothes that seemed as far from country clothes as the English language was from Irish. He felt like some relic of old decency, fallen on hard times but still due some civility. The brand-new, show-off suit screamed country bumpkin. He might as well have topped it off with a donkey's head.

A culchie, a redneck, that's what he was. Time was slipping by and he couldn't keep up with it all: the clothes, the manners, the dances in town, the quick adaptability of the emigrants. To live that kind of life you had to be ready to seize an opportunity the minute it knocked. And if there was no opportunity to seize, you had to create it. For example, you had to go out and find a wife for yourself. The day when life delivered a wife to you, like goods from the Speciality's hearse, that day was long gone. He had let years go by with nothing to show for them. At twenty-eight years old he was an old fart, a snuff-taker, just as the young girl had spotted earlier. All he was short of doing to prove himself a real old dodderer was to stick his hand down his crotch and start scratching . . .

People were coming out of the back room now after having some tea. And now the woman of the house, a cousin of Micil's, was beckoning him into the back room:

'The tailor will get the house, Micil,' she said, prattling on, seemingly unaware that Micil was still examining his clothes; 'they say the first man is neither glad nor disappointed, Micil, but then they do have plenty to say, Micil. They say as well that when the Creator made heaven and earth he made plenty of everything, and that's the way it is for us, Micil. I've a small bit of ham here, Micil. Will you have a glass of *Parliament*, Micil . . . '

He was feeling cold. Must be from the mugs of porter he had drunk in the kitchen.

'I have it here for you, Micil.' But despite her words she didn't hand him the glass she had filled. Instead, as if she'd suddenly had a better idea: 'Maybe you'd prefer a drop of the medicine. I have it here, Micil . . . The barley-juice, you can't beat it. That's the very thing'll heat you up and put the fire in your belly, Micil . . . It's up to yourself, but the old stuff will make a warrior of you . . . '

How well she had guessed that he was cold! Micil would have preferred the two drinks together. But she took the good out of it by heaping 'Micil' onto everything: '*Micil* this and *Micil* that . . . ' Tonight, more than ever, he was conscious of how old-fashioned the name was, especially when he was stuck out on a limb there beside the unresponsive Meg Micilín. Micil was a name well suited to her father, who would soon be collecting the pension. Meg was the one the woman of the house had chosen to help her in the back room with the tea, which marked Meg out as sensible, mature, and able to handle the occasion, someone who could easily be in charge of a house herself. Another sign that pointed to the same conclusion was the fact that 'a mouthful' was also offered to Meg, who accepted with alacrity. It would never have been offered to the girls out in the kitchen, even though they'd lap it up even quicker than Meg, who was someone who had never left the country and who never went near the Sunday night dances in town. Here in the back room, Micil was amazed to see that Meg was in high spirits and laughing heartily, if a bit indecorously, at things that seemed less funny than what he had tried to say out in the kitchen.

Micil couldn't face the ham. He was sitting at the near end of the table, with a clear, almost inescapable view of the corpse's face. The dead person in the bed was his uncle's wife. She had been known for her sallow complexion that had nothing to do with the sun: she was one of the Yellow Céideach family from Draigheanaí. To add to the effect, a fire blazed in the hearth, casting its light on the dead woman's face, emphasizing her sallowness and joining forces with death and decay to render it yellower than ever it was when she was alive. Maybe the drink was going to Micil's head. He wasn't used to drinking the old stuff; it tasted rough. He had mixed something with it and knocked it back. Now when he looked at the thick slices of ham on the white plate, he was convinced they were yellow. His gaze switched back and forth between the plate of ham and the bed, not lingering long on either, the ham seemed to blur into the face of the corpse framed by the white sheet.

After a few reluctant bites of the hearty portion, just enough that his hostess wouldn't think him rude, he laid his knife and fork on top of each other on the plate, as he had seen the chaplain do one day while he was hearing confessions, the curved base of the fork on the handle of the knife. He couldn't recall for sure just then if he had ever seen it done any other way. But he did remember that the chaplain's plate had been empty, and his own plate was not. It was a huge relief when Meg Micilín took his plate away, before the woman of the house could start inquiring why the meat had barely been touched.

Not alone that, but he felt that some mysterious change had taken place in the corpse, as if it had ceased trying to make him uncomfortable and was allowing him to relax.

He tried not to look at the body. Then he started to worry that Meg would notice that he was directing all his attention to her. She and the woman of the house were attacking the ham with gusto. He really didn't want to look at the dead woman. He looked up at the ceiling instead but then decided that that looked too much like he was praying. The woman of the house sat between him and the fire. There were only two places to feast his eyes — on the dearly departed or on Meg.

That Meg had a great appetite altogether. She popped a big chunk of meat into her mouth. She had a way of drawing her lips back as she chewed so that you could see all her teeth, which were eye-catching anyway, as they ground away. The heat of the fire gave a flush to her face that neither attracted nor repelled him. In fact it didn't give him pause for thought at all. What did interest him was the breadth of it. That was really what caught his attention: how huge her face looked, how it was big enough, Micil thought, to hold a world of anger, hate, jealousy, love — yes, a world of talk too.

It struck him that the room wouldn't hold too many people of her size. Strong legs that would be a challenge to any man, no matter who, if she planted them firmly. A big, curvy arse. Her flesh billowed in a way that was pleasing to the male eye, and she was womanly beyond her years. The flesh swelled from rump and thigh, rolled up her back and around to her breasts, which together formed a rampart from armpit to armpit. Micil studied her thick black hair; there wasn't a hint of grey in it. Above her upper lip was a haze of blonde down, somewhat rough and unwomanly. It seemed to proclaim the vigour of her bones, the earthy tang of her blood. Her forehead was wreathed in beads of sweat from the heat, handling the dishes, stoking the fire, boiling water. Now that was something you'd never see again on the corpse on the bed. This was a greater proof of Meg's aliveness than were the movements of her limbs, which you could say were a bit lackadaisical. In fact, you could say she only seemed to move when absolutely necessary. She raised her cup to her lips slowly and infrequently, though she took a good gulp from it every time.

Micil could see that if Meg turned to you she wouldn't turn away until she'd had her fill of you. Here was a woman who would fill a bed nicely. You couldn't be in bed with her without knowing she was there, not like some of the skinny little things out in the kitchen who looked as fragile and insubstantial as tufts of bog-cotton that would drift away on a puff of wind. In spite of himself, Micil's gaze swivelled away from the woman and over to the body that age had shrivelled and sickness withered. He was seized by a sudden longing to lay his hands on Meg, to wipe the sweat from her brow, plunge his hands into that rampart of a bosom, to fondle her voluptuous buttocks, to slap her round rump. As he gazed at the leathery yellow death's head, the thoughts kept swirling up from the depths of his mind . . .

'Is everyone in Ionnarba as short of something to say as yourself, Micil?' asked his hostess, blowing her nose on her apron after fruitlessly rummaging on her person, first down around her hips and then in her cleavage, for a handkerchief. Here she goes with the 'Micil' again! Why on earth couldn't his father, his mother, or even a neighbour ever call him Michael or Mike or Mick or Micksie or Mikeen or even Mickeen. He'd been called Michael only once in a summons to court over not having a light on his bicycle on his way to the doctor's house. At school or talking to the priest he was Mícheál. But for that name to suit you, you'd need to be a schoolteacher or have some other job like that.

He realised he hadn't said anything for a long time. He was taken aback by the question; it was like he was arriving back from a cowshed after shovelling manure out of it. Ionnarba people were very chatty . . . There was nothing shy or timid about them . . . Of course a person could be joking, even with a dead body in the room, the body of one of her relatives . . . That's how people were when they were alive . . . The dead woman had had quite a good life, after all, God bless her. If only we could all have such a life . . . Her family were grown up and well reared . . . It was better that her pain was over . . . God was good to her. . . . She was better off where she was now . . .

Suddenly Micil felt Meg's eyes on him. A wave of worry and shyness washed over him and he felt all at sea. That was how old men talked! It was on the tip of his tongue to say, 'Bad luck for her, she'll never be young again and she has nothing more to look forward to,' just to skim the grey film of age from his words and project himself as a brand-new person from a brave new world. But that line of reasoning was just as old-fashioned as what he'd said before! It dawned on him all of a sudden what the source was of all this sparkling repartee of his. His own family! His background! You can't make a silk purse out of a sow's ear. Bad luck to the woman of the house anyway. Her country talk and country ways that were making him over in the image of his grandfather, old-fashioned coat and all. Tonight he was like the Bumpkin in the Grey Coat in the old story. . . .

It had never been discussed; there was never any mention of it anywhere around rocky old Ionnarba . . . Of course he could marry, why couldn't he? Time enough . . . Up to now he'd been swaddled in a grey coat of hopelessness, so much so that he didn't care what he was saying or what conversational blunders he might make . . . His father was still hale and hearty. As for the old girl, well, there was nothing wrong with her tongue, nor with her lower half either, sometimes . . . By the hokey, another woman in the house would be a great help . . . Of course he used to think about it, marriage. He thought about it every now and then, like a tinker thinks about paying dues to the priest . . .

Just then, Meg gave a big snort of laughter, which he didn't think was very appropriate, and clapped both her hands across her mouth so that she wouldn't be heard out in the kitchen. What had made her burst out laughing like that? Micil supposed he had gone and put his foot in his mouth again.

'Lord, I don't know what I'll do with you two,' the woman of the house said, getting up from the table. Micil went to jump up as well. Out in the kitchen he wouldn't have to speak, and at least the crowd in there would be well-mannered enough not to block the heat of the fire from him. But his hostess pushed him back down into the chair: 'Stay where you are, Micil. I have to go and bring in some turf and remind them to keep the fire in below.'

'I'll go and get it,' Meg said.

'Oh for heaven's sake! You can't leave Micil on his own with the corpse.'

Apparently Micil was more nervous of Meg than of the corpse. His grey coat muffled him, trapping his thoughts in its folds, unspoken. He was silent as the corpse itself. The only signs of life about him were his eyes, darting quick glances at Meg where she sat by the fire. It was she who finally broke the grey silence which had settled around them.

'Pull up to the fire, Micil. It gets chilly as the night wears on.'

But when he moved in to the fire, she got up and started clearing the dishes off the table. The woman of the house came in with the turf:

'Leave those, Meg; I'll do them,' she said. 'I'll wash them in the back room . . . I'll get some of the girls in there to give me a hand. You and Micil can keep an eye on the fire in here. Make sure you two don't let it go out!'

You two! There it was again. Meg was sitting with her back to the corpse. Micil still faced north. He seemed destined forever to be in an awkward spot. His back to good fortune, to good luck. The dud card that nobody wanted. From where he was sitting he could look into the fire, which would be foolish; he could look at Meg, which would be fine; or—and it was almost impossible not to—he could look at the corpse. Pointless as watching for seeds to sprout in a barren field.

But that's what he did, until his tight armour of shyness was squeezed so hard that he had to smash open a chink in the silence to say something, even if it was the stupidest thing he'd ever said:

'She doesn't look all that different.'

'The body?' Meg said, not really turning around enough to see the dead woman's face.

'I don't think she looks all that different.'

'Well, there's nothing's different about her except the biggest difference of all, that she's dead now, God help us all.'

Now there was the perfect phrase! That 'God help us all' was as homely and countryish, and yet so heartfelt, that Micil knew she hadn't said it out of pity for the dead woman — a dead body had no need of pity — but for her own lot in life, her own live, vulnerable flesh, for that especially perhaps. Now he would have to throw Meg a rope, or else let this fireside melancholy capsize the small craft of their chat.

'It's an ill wind, God help us, even the big difference, that blows nobody any good.'

'Good?'

'Yes good! The Speciality hearse will be busy.'

'Oh, that!'

'I wonder if they've found out yet who that strange woman was who delivered a child in it the other night?'

Micil looked away from the sealed eyes of the corpse and into Meg's eyes. There was a strange look in them, like laughter on the point of melting into grief but then turning once again to restrained laughter. At least what he'd said hadn't annoyed her.

'Ionnarba is nearer to the Speciality than this place.'

'She was travelling from the west and this place is nearer to an Tír Thiar —'

'She was over east when her labour began. They're saying over here that nearly everyone over your way had something to do with it, and that Mike treated you all for your trouble.'

'Well, he treated Scabby Stiofáinín anyway, who ended up with labour pains of his own after all the doings . . . Stiofáinín got a thorn from Mike's hedge stuck in his backside, and Mike was hammering it home with the whacks of a mallet like he was thatching straw. That was the main thing he needed attending to. Everyone was getting involved. Between you and me, what I think was happening was that one person would pull at the thorn and Stiofáinín would start yelling, "Go on, ya boy ya. You have it now." But as soon as he did, someone else would shove it back in again, shouting that it was coming out feet first.'

Micil's face was like a big, plump-cheeked, steaming, freshly boiled potato from Achréidh wobbling on the end of a fork:

'What could they do, when they couldn't get hold of a nurse or a doctor or a priest? It was Scabby Stiofáinín that ended up in hospital.'

'The nurse was out seeing to Máirín . . . Peadar an Ghleanna's wife here, who was having twins again. Rumour has it that the stranger had twins as well.'

'Sure you could count Stiofáinín's thorn as one of twins.'

'Someone called in to Micil, Micil from round here, the following day. It turned out that it was Micil that the doctor was with the night before when the other crowd sent for him. Micil was so fascinated by the story of this woman who was supposed to have had twins in the Speciality's hearse that he was instantly cured of his shortness of breath, something the doctor hadn't managed to do for him the night before. "Where are my trousers and my new shoes?" he says. "I'm going east. I need drawers, a shirt, a vest, and a bucket. I have to get to the Speciality hearse . . . right now." One of those young fellas from out there in the kitchen, you wouldn't know him, Micil, came in just at that moment: "Your donkey's bogged down in a ditch down near the strand," he said. "I couldn't get it out." "The bloody malingerer can just stay there until I get back from the Speciality." Then another young lad starts up: "Your calf will burst from roaring up on the hill. It's hungry, Micil." "Let it burst all it likes, the accursed thing, until I get back from the Speciality. Aren't they after telling me that there's a reward for whoever recognises that stranger-woman . . . " '

'He must have been giddy after all that labouring for breath.'

'Giddy is right! Then this oul' gossip comes in. I won't name any names. "That woman up there should be ashamed of herself . . . Twins she had last night! . . . " When Ó Curraoin heard about the twins in Peadar an Ghleanna's place—I think when something is said often enough it comes true in the end—away with him over to the village beyond, with the sledgehammer, to Peadar Beag's place. Peadar is married to his daughter. They have no family . . . All Peadar could do was to jump out the toilet window, and he hasn't been seen since.'

'Maybe he went take a look at the Speciality hearse. The Speciality hasn't driven it since. Too busy drenching it in Jeyes Fluid.'

'That could well be. When Ó Curraoin didn't manage to find him he lashed out with the sledgehammer anyway, but all he hit was a cow in calf. But bad luck to the same Ó Curraoin, what had me wasting my breath on him anyhow? I'm gone away off course—'

'Off like a sailor that has a woman in every port in the world.'

'You and your sailors! So the big gossip says to Micil, our Micil from here: "It was Peadar an Ghleanna—he's an obliging fella after all—while he was on his way to the nurse last night decided to kill two birds with one stone and left word at the doctor's that your shortness of breath was getting worse." It was worse than it had ever been before! . . . Anyway, everyone round here knows that the only thing bothering Micil is that he didn't marry Máirín himself. We often hear him muttering about it to himself, outside on the path and in the fields. He never went out since. When he steps out the door the wheeze in his chest would blow you over the back wall. Unless he's trying to breathe in; then it would nearly drag you in onto the hearth . . . '

They were in full flow now, the magic words, the perfectly turned phrases, lively chat, charms and incantations. She was tearing the years off Micil of Ionnarba, like you'd scrape old paint or paper off wood or a wall when you were redecorating. As her story rollicked along she was unconsciously moving closer to him—or maybe it was he who was getting closer to her. It was hard to say.

'Next of all didn't the bloody oul' gossip come in again the following evening: "Are you feeling a bit better, Micil, you poor old thing?" You know I mean Micil from round here, Micil. "A man that has twins has luck, double the luck, three times the luck. And who was the man that went over to the Speciality, to buy a few bits for the christening . . . ? Peadar an Ghleanna, of course. Would you say he recognised the stranger woman? . . . Oh don't ask me, what would I know? Luck, that's what it was. They say he's going to get a bounty too, the De Valera prize." Micil, Micil from round here that is, turned his face to the wall, and all he said was "Where's that pack of devils got to? Away up with them now to pull that oul' blackguard of a donkey out of the ditch."'

'"You wouldn't know Ó Curraoin's donkey!" said the gossip. "Oh Daddy, oh honey, if you saw the state of Ó Curraoin's donkey!" the woman said. "If it was the Pope's donkey," Micil, Micil from round here, said, "they couldn't have said more prayers to their equipment as they were pulling him out, the blackguard. . . . " God forgive me, Micil, prattling on like this in a wake house . . . '

Despite her reservations, Meg let out a roar of laughter, clamping her hands over her broad features. She was so overcome that her right hand wandered to press Micil's knee: to tell the truth, it skirted the kneecap and homed in on the soft flesh behind the knee. His legs parted like a forked inlet, two streams carrying the bones, veins, currents, and sinews of the sea. And the force of the sea will not be resisted. His left hand seized her thigh and started to caress that yielding mass of flesh. No fabric, however thick, could have concealed the burning heat of it. He was no longer out on a limb, floundering without an answer. He wasn't ashamed that his thoughts had turned to the bed, dawn breaking gently now on it and on the leathery yellow skin of the corpse. But something much sillier flashed across his mind: that huge elephant whose picture they had shown him in school. He would love to be as big and powerful as an elephant, and he would sweep Meg off her feet and away into a wood so dark that daylight could never get through the trees . . .

The woman of the house came back:

'Aren't you the right pair, letting the fire go out! You need a fire for comfort in a house where a corpse is being waked. You'd think, once the fire's going beside it, that the person is still alive. I always think the coldest time is when night and dawn part company.'

Parting! Heat! Cold! Death! Life!

'We forgot to put "kindling," as that civil servant used to say, on the fire,' Meg said.

'It's getting light. Time for me to be heading home,' Micil said, getting to his feet.

'On your way over, slide this letter under the Speciality's door. It's just to tell the hearse to be here at three instead of at four. And well scoured out with Jeyes Fluid. The priest asked for the body to be taken out shortly after three. He forgot he had a christening at four. I'd say he wanted to have the body out of there before the christening . . . Peadar an Ghleanna's and Máirín's twins of course. They'll soon have to hire a special baptismal priest all to themselves. Those two could do with one of those.'

'Micil, Micil from round here, says that half that family aren't baptised at all, any more than Ó Curraoin's donkey,' said Meg.

Micil of Ionnarba was about to depart. His eyes wandered over to the bed. As daylight crept over the face of his uncle's dead wife, he noted how tightly the eyes were closed. Almost as if she were squeezing them shut, unwilling to see what he had been up to! Micil stole a glance at Meg. A wide world of kindling burned in her eyes . . .

TRANSLATED BY KATHERINE DUFFY

WHATEVER THE CASE MAY BE

It started out as a rumour, that two houses in Wine Street were beating each other up. Everyone laughed, of course. Some people! You'd want to put them under oath! Not long afterwards, a second rumour came from Waterside Road to the effect that another pair of houses had come to blows. In quite a frenzy they were, said a young fellow who had a job on the Heifers' Scheme. After that, it quickly went beyond being a rumour. It was in the papers. Soon, reporters from the four corners of the earth had arrived in H. and were scribbling stories about houses they stayed in attacking, or being attacked by, other houses. If you tuned in to a foreign station of an evening, you could bet on it that you'd hear H., H., H., popping out of an otherwise unintelligible discourse, sparks of the familiar out of the depths of the night.

Everyone, sage or fool, had a theory to peddle. Some of the town's old-timers were saying that it all stemmed from the old story that the Virgin Mary and St. Joseph were travelling about until they came to the eastern gate—a semblance of it still stands—but that some rude gatekeeper wouldn't let them in. When Folklore heard this, he started sniffing about. While he was taping reel-to-reel in the International Hotel, the Commercial Hotel next door began trying to push its snub nose or its chin or its elbow or its knee or its stupid grin through the dividing wall. One of the storytellers swore he spotted a hoof. The raconteurs were all thrown together in a seething heap of ancient lore. Two of them started punching each other. Another ran off with a pipe belonging to one of the two. While that fellow was berating Folklore and saying that he had never yet gone home without his pipe and that it was a special pipe that his brother had sent him from America, the whole Folklore kit and caboodle was swept out the window in an unexpected surge, leaving Folklore no choice but to exit without his bag and baggage, his umbrella and coat. The storyteller, who had to be bought a substitute pipe to tide him over, handed it in at the eastern gate and made it clear that he would never again roam in the realms of Folklore and would have no further truck with him until he got his own American pipe or the equal of it back. He ordered a pint for the road and left through the gate . . .

There were those who maintained, and the priests agreed with them, that H., with its unbroken history of boiling, monstrous, momentous sin, richly deserved its fate. An ex-nun who lived opposite the International Hotel said it was the Second Sodom. The man who had lost his pipe and who was now putting together a case against Folklore wanted to question her further, but she said she couldn't bring herself to discuss things of that nature with anyone but her confessor. The churches and the streets were heaving, day and night, with people saying rosaries. Natives of H. living in England or America were at it too, but they could hardly hold up their heads for shame. The town was given blessings, Mass was said in every house in the centre and on the outskirts, shrines and penitential oratories were erected, the Pope sent a special blessing. Everyone in town, from babes-in-arms to ancient greybeards, took a solemn vow to go to Lourdes . . .

Unfortunately, wherever virtue is to be found, vice will be there too. The types who love a bit of excitement were jubilant, asking: 'When do you think the next house will strike?' or 'Have any houses been going at it, did you hear . . . ?' Others were walking around with an expectant smirk, hoping that houses would tear the guts out of each other and that a little bit of loot might fall into their laps. Some of the town's bigwigs wanted to impose a curfew or have martial law declared. The Garda authorities were certain they would be well able to quash any sort of riots, if they broke out. Even so, they decided to cancel the annual Strawberry Festival.

The Church was being very vague on the subject. Pray, trust in God, and live accordingly: that was the sum of their advice. They were reluctant to confirm or deny, or sometimes even to admit, that anything strange was happening. Of course, when someone was found guilty they were happy to throw the book at him and blame him for the whole evil sackload of the town's sins. The story of Sodom and Gomorrah was told so many times in those days that folkloric variants were developing: that they had tried to castrate Abraham when he wouldn't lie with Jebudah's wife, and that that was what he deserved according to the law of Moses; that Lot's wife was doing business, that she was running several houses of ill repute and evading tax on them; that two yobs with daggers stood guard at the cash desk in those houses, ready to deal with any customer who disputed the bill, to make sure he paid for all his supplementary items; that she was in negotiations to buy whole towns, to create an emporium of prostitution for the whole of the East, with Abraham as patron. He would get the pick of all the women of the East if only he would keep God's favour for his own cronies . . . This is how the common people will distort any story. But it has to be said that versions of this one saturated the minds of the people of H. The blacksmith told it to the curate who told it to the Doctor of Divinity . . .

As for the scientists, you'd have needed red-hot pincers to get anything out of them. A scientist of international repute who was also a native of H. was sent for. He arrived. It was rumoured that he still owned property there. He kept shaking his head from side to side as the situation was explained to him. But the only answer he gave was to glance at his watch and say that it was outside his own field of research. The legions of other scientists who came weren't much better. All they were good for was nibbling their moustaches and blinking. One scientist asked whether voices had ever been heard from the truculent houses and then started rubbing the crack of his arse like it was on fire. But anyway, no new insight was to emerge from that particular part of his scientific person. The townspeople couldn't figure out whether the scientists were hiding something or just knew nothing.

Various people were trying to conduct investigations. Gerald Fitzgerald was making inquiries through Bargain Investigations Ltd. While he was at it the Rags to Riches Employment Agency launched a vicious attack on the Egg Packers' Cooperative, and we had it on good authority that thousands of scaldy chicks went scurrying about the place before anyone had time to lock up. Fitzgerald himself hadn't heard that particular rumour, but he penned a long series of articles. People were saying that by the time he'd finished the articles the houses would have calmed down. In that case there would be no need for a clear verdict. But since they hadn't calmed down, the last article was just a graph with two curves sweeping up and outwards, one to the right and one to the left. Some self-proclaimed expert said that this was a Freudian way of demonstrating the leanings of a particular political party and that it had nothing to do with the situation in H.

Of course there were quacks and pundits who were positively, intransigently certain that they knew what the trouble was. A poltergeist, of course, except that the town itself was the house and the individual houses were the pieces of furniture in it. The theory was flawed in only one respect. Usually there would be a teenage girl involved, although nobody knew exactly how. When she left, all the fuss would die down. Then people remembered what the ex-nun had said when the Strawberry Queen was crowned in the International Hotel last year, that the place had turned into another Sodom. Soon they were saying that the town would never have any luck as long as the Strawberry Queen was still around. Strangely, it was mostly the young girls who indulged in this kind of speculation.

One man claimed that below the ground was a mine full of flickering quicksilver and that when it began to quake that spurred the houses to beating each other up. If that mine could be found, the town would be the richest place on earth, because mercury was seven times more precious than uranium. People were going about with dowsing wands in their hands. A mining company came and excavated, but nothing unusual was found for miles around. They tested the air, the water, everything under the sun, but found nothing to cast light on why the houses were fighting. Eventually, they moved on.

The whole situation was like a distorting mirror, generating all sorts of urban legends and charlatanism. A man with two horns that curved up towards the crescent moon was glimpsed walking down Glen Street and touching one house and then the next with his blackthorn stick. By morning, those houses were hard at it. Someone saw him in Cross Street too, with a beautiful woman dressed like a queen on his arm. Jets of fire shot from his hooves. The houses continued on just the same.

Horseshoes, gold rings, sunwheels, serpents, images of four-leaved shamrock, ash branches, and so on decked the façades of the houses. Witches conducted occult ceremonies in them. It was said that the blood of a newborn piglet had been smeared on the doorpost of every house in Straw Street and that there wasn't a house on that street so much as frowned in the direction of any other house. But, without realising what they were doing, someone smeared some on one of the politician's doorposts and the house gibbered the whole night as if it was trying to tear itself away from its foundations and pitch itself straight across the road into battle with the newspaper owner's house. A dog was found, dead and disembowelled, on Main Street. Terrifying tales emerged from Irish Town across the river . . .

The Church pulled out all the stops to condemn these practices. The Monsignor solemnly threatened to impose a three-week mission by the Redemptorists. It was no use. The Church had plenty on its own plate. One of the priests of the parish got his comeuppance the night he took possession of a shopowner's house on Main Street that had been left to him in a will. Early in the night the house next door—a big dancehall—gave it three or four big, violent whacks that shook it to the rafters, overturning the laden table, breaking bottles of wine and whiskey, smashing glasses, and leaving the place in such a state that the sergeant thought there'd been a riot. He looked as if he would dearly like to get hold of the priest and make him walk the plank. The guests all fled like a madhouse was after them, trampling the priest's hat, coat, and umbrella as they went. The priest himself thought the house was caving in. He tore out of it headfirst into the embrace of the dancers.

'Serves him right,' said the wasters that were standing around under the windows, their tongues out to catch the drink that was dripping down. 'Such gluttony! Going on and on at us every Sunday about the evils of drink! Looks like we weren't the ones doing the drinking!'

The catastrophe made no distinction between cleric and layman, common and noble, nor any one part of town and another. A housing estate was built outside the town limits, but people left before two days were up because they could see the houses were warriors and always would be.

Another popular rumour held that the root of the problem was that houses were emigrating magically at night. But there was no evidence to support this. It was a poet in Wine Street who had started it. In the depths of the night, he said all the goodhearted houses up and skipped over to England or America to visit the inhabitants who had gone from them. Poetry. That was all it was. The Monsignor paid him a visit . . .

It was a hard blow that no one would insure the houses any more. And the price of life insurance on anyone in H. rose out of all proportion. But that particular cloud wasn't entirely without its silver lining. People had more money to spend on the horses and the dogs, and on bingo and drugs. For what it was worth, porter and whiskey tasted all the sweeter now. The teachers were buying loads of books. Everyone bought cars and heaps of clothes of the finest quality. This spending spree didn't go down well with the Church. They were becoming redundant. The Monsignor dropped hints about starting on a cathedral.

Now, where was the sense in that? Either a huge building like that would level everything around it or the other buildings would gang up and reduce it to rubble!

All this was going on both day and night, but more often by night. A house would attack another out of a surge of ill will against its neighbour, or from boredom with the long, relentless companionship and a burning desire to send the other house packing to a different patch.

You'd hear clattering and banging, blasting and thumping and thrashing, a general hullabaloo in fact, and it could last anywhere from five minutes to an hour. For example, the draper's shop in Cross Street spent an hour socking it to the fish-and-chip shop next door. Frequently a house was attacked three times or more. For that reason, houses that had only been attacked once would often set to whacking hell two or three times over out of the house that had attacked them. The House of Meat attacked Glad Rags on a Budget three times. Apparently the legs and carcasses of mutton were waving about on the hooks as if they were alive. Late one night, the insurance inspector's house gave the house of a clerk in the Post Office Savings Bank such a hammering that the clerk was sent spinning head over heels. The furniture was ground to powder. The next person to take the house was the man who went around selling the pools for Linn Enterprises. He got the same treatment for two nights running. He stayed put right up to the moment he saw his collecting-books being spirited off down the stairs and out into the street as if being drawn to the house of a rival pools collector. After that nobody lived in that house for a long time. One day in spring the insurance inspector was spotted moving some of his furniture in. That was the time the question was asked in the Dáil that caused all the ruckus. Someone said the inspector was a member of a Fianna Gael cumann. The Opposition declared that the town of H. was being levelled to the ground because of the government's ineptness . . .

Although plenty of adjacent houses were constantly at war, no house had actually caved in yet, and in general they seemed none the worse for wear. Of course a lot of annoyance was caused, as when Folklore's worldly goods got tipped out the window and the story-teller was bereft of his pipe. Let's not make a mountain out of a mole-hill, that was most people's motto. The townsfolk didn't let it bother them . . .

It was true that there was a lot of noise and that furniture was damaged and so forth. If any pattern could be discerned in the whole state of affairs, it seemed to be that some houses just couldn't stand each other, or had developed a grudge against each other and couldn't bear to be joined at the hip any longer. Inspectors from the Depart-ment of Local Government couldn't make any sense of events, and they admitted as much. The Guards had to move their station to Glen Street because of the continual barrage in Cross Street from the Mul-downeys' house, which was licensed to sell tobacco, wine, and spirits. It seems the Minister wasn't too pleased, but Muldowney was a big noise in Fianna Gael and a son of his was a parish priest, a nice young fellow too, in the diocese.

Something would have to be done. The Guards were all asleep on the job. A whistle was whipped off one, another had his truncheon stolen, the summons book for court was taken off a third. Another of them was seen with his fly open up to his bellybutton, his trousers saggy as a beggar's, directly across from the Monsignor's church while the Rosary was being said. One of the town councillors had the over-coat snatched off his back. A priest's new car was stolen from out-side his front door in broad daylight. It turned up outside the politi-cian's house three days later. 'Priest's Stolen Car Found at Politician's House' was the headline on the town paper that week.

A hardware and ironmonger's shop on River Road had to close up because of continual bombardment by a women's clothing shop. Subsequently, a gypsy who set up shop in a nook barely bigger than the eye of a needle, between a toy emporium and a beauty parlour, found himself so busy, with customers descending from all direc-tions, that he fled back to Irish Town. A hostel for professional women opened on Wine Street. Right beside it was a boarding house, also for professional women. It was one of the older buildings in town. Whatever sort of establishment it might have been in the old days, everyone in H. knew what it was now. It was there, for example, that the Monsignor came upon the poet declaiming his poems to a group of women who had only just got out of bed at two o'clock. But that old place could still pack a punch. They tried hard to reach an agreement, a working arrangement with the new hostel. It was a complicated one, with reference to the goodwill of the old building, how it stretched back years, and even something about antique lights. It was drawn up by the poet. He had spent some time as an office boy to a solicitor on Main Street. But the new hostel wouldn't accept it. The upshot of it all was that the two of them went at it for weeks on end, and there wasn't a girl in the place fit to go to her work, her shop, or her place of business because of lack of sleep. The new establishment had to be closed down . . .

As for Irish Town, well! A godless, lawless spot if ever there was one. The latest from there was that a tailor who had been a bit overzealous about taking one of the local women's measurements had been castrated. According to reports, it was a neat clean job, done by two qualified butchers, a pharmacist's assistant, and a doctor who had been stripped of his credentials years ago because the other doctors begrudged his prowess. The poet went over there with a poem about it, 'Abelard of Irish Town.' It seems he himself just about managed to get away by swimming the river in his clothes . . .

The people of H. were becoming inured to the situation. In fact, they were starting to take pride in H. What a special town! Name me another town where houses beat each other up! A fortune to be made from all the tourism. The insurance agent started running promotions. He did such a good job that soon he was able to buy another house—a launderette, beside the Savings Bank clerk's house, and a pharmacist's residence on the other side. He opened offices in France, Germany, Spain, Rome, America, Australia . . . There was

such an influx of linguists and foreigners to H. that the ex-nun remarked that now it really, truly, definitively had become Sodom. The
tourists swarmed into the town, and there was nowhere near enough
accommodation for them, so the place was expanding as fast as you
could pour and pile concrete. Services were laid on twenty-four
hours a day, including a special system of phone calls to wake tourists and bring them to wherever the houses were fighting. Everyone in
town was happy except the Monsignor. The Church wasn't attracting
anything like the prosperity that the town was enjoying. It was common knowledge that Muldowney had bought two new hotels for his
son, the priest, and that he was visiting the Bishop in secret, flaunting
big rolls of banknotes. The Bishop was becoming most unreasonable.
He couldn't understand why the money wasn't pouring in from H.

It goes without saying, of course, that the tourists were being
fleeced by the locals. People would believe anything in those days.
In the middle of town there was this huge picture of two tall houses
laying into each other, their gable ends crashing together. Scrawled
across it was the legend 'Best views for the best price! £1,000!' Another pair of houses was portrayed as two black men boxing. There
was one of a house in the form of a dwarf, its arse turned towards a
man (another house). The dwarf-house had one leg in the air and was
farting up into the big fellow's face. A lot of people were giving out
about this last picture. The insurance man, who could now be numbered among the filthy rich of H., said it was making people laugh
and so what if it was a little bit crude. It wasn't obscene and besides, he
didn't hear the people of H. complaining about raking the money in.

In the square there was a picture that made the Monsignor out
to be a *banderillero* when you looked at it from a certain angle. This
wasn't surprising, since the hat was clearly modelled on the Monsignor's three-cornered hat. It showed a leprechaun cobbler. He was
making a pair of golden slippers with a hammer, waxed thread, an awl,
and golden rivets. But that wasn't what made the Monsignor prickly as
a briar, while everyone else sniggered. The leprechaun cobbler had a

huge gold pouch, decorated with the letter O from the great Gospel of St. Colmcille. The cobbler was hunkered down in such a way that you couldn't make out if the overflowing pouch—which was three times the size of himself—was coming out of his arse or pouring from his crotch. The contents of the purse were another point of interest: two golden houses locked together, with a chimney, complete with golden smoke, sticking up between the two. Below it was the legend 'Seize it soon or kiss it goodbye.' The residents of Irish Town sniggered on. The poet wrote a piece in which the cobbler was God, and Adam and Eve were made out of gold, and all the apples in the Garden of Eden were golden apples, and the animals were gold, and the Fall of Man came about because God started to run out of gold because He hadn't thought to make enough of it in the first place. So He began to adulterate it with clay. That was God's big mistake. And that's how we came to be what we are and how the world came to be what it is . . . The Monsignor chased the poet up and down Wine Street, but he couldn't catch him.

A new history was invented in which Cú Chulainn, Fionn Mac Umhaill, the Fianna, Wee Bobailín and Big Bobailín, Tall Bodlamhán and Short Bodlamhán all hailed from the town. The storyteller forgot all about his American pipe, he was so busy explaining the Bobailíns and the Bodlamháns to visitors. On its menu, a restaurant was depicted doing battle with another restaurant, and everything in it was at war with its counterpart: plates, crockery, people, waiters, all fighting. Interestingly enough, there were two bishops punching each other's lights out as well: a skinny little fellow just coming in the door, and the other a big, paunchy, fat fellow on his way out. The drinks speciality of the house was called '*Les Maisons qui se heurtent*' [houses that collide] and was only third-grade whiskey even before they watered it down. On a postcard, two men were pictured drinking each other's health as they bumped their ample behinds together. The message on the card read 'Drinking a toast in H., the town of the brawling houses.'

The Great Strawberry Festival was reinstated but was renamed the Brawling Houses Festival. It was as bacchanalian as Bricriú's legendary feast. H. was made of gold and clay and it was difficult to say which was the dominant material. With the houses beating each other up, it was no time to be thinking about licensing laws. In fact, it was quite a while since any law had held sway in H. The last time the court sat, the adjacent prison unleashed a barrage of kicks — or at least that's what it felt like — against the courthouse walls. The judge gave the order to free all the prisoners. Now the prison was a kind of unofficial public toilet. Everyone was afraid to go into the old public toilet in H. because a cake factory behind it was always hammering it. The last person to use it was a man from Irish Town. He used to say, as solemnly as if he were making his confession, that for a moment there he was sure the back wall would split in two and his hole would get stuffed with cake.

Last year's queen was crowned again at the Brawling Houses Festival, although the dogs in the street knew that she had been forced to enter the competition. People got so carried away with their bacchanalian revels that they stripped every stitch off her and made her drink the health of the town naked. Most of the drink missed her mouth. She disappeared after that. The ex-nun said she saw her defiling the nearby church with her presence.

The ex-nun herself was nearly stripped. They caught her in the doorway of her house and dragged her to the middle of the square, but the insurance agent happened to be there and she had a big life insurance policy with his firm.

The night, and the weather in general, was sultry, and their blood was up. When they started taking women, willy-nilly, into the church, the Monsignor's conscience would no longer let him rest. He took off his clerical garb and went out into the street dressed like any other man. Still, he could never have imagined what he would find there. He was lifted clean off the ground and carried away on a human current into the square, his clothes were ripped off, and he was paired with a naked woman, from Yugoslavia or Greece or somewhere like that, someone with the sun coursing through her veins, a leggy, busty, voluptuous woman. She danced for him, sinuously and seductively, on a red carpet. He was ordered to fornicate with her at twilight. Someone stuck a red sparkler up his arse.

'My children . . . ,' he started to say, but nobody there was a member of his flock, or if they were, they were so drunk by now that they couldn't tell a cat from a coach. There were ten times as many strangers and foreigners as townspeople in the town now. 'Cut him,' said an authoritative voice, the voice of a leader. A sharp, narrow blade flashed under the indifferent moon. But the man holding the knife soon found his wrist caught in a grip much more powerful than polished steel. He couldn't move an inch, yet he had the strong impression that it was a woman who was staying his hand. Just then a tall, strong young man came striding through the crowd, moving like a hot knife through butter. Fists flying, feet kicking, he knocked down anyone and anything in his path. He seized the hand holding the knife, forcing the holder to let go with a yell of pain. The strong young man stood squarely between the mob and the priest. He shoved the naked woman hard, pushing her back into the crowd.

'Let this man go,' he said, laying his left hand on the priest. 'If anyone so much as calls him a name, I'll bury this knife to the hilt in his heart. Get back! Get back! Give him back his clothes.'

'But what good is the night if we don't castrate Abraham,' said a voice out at the edge of the square.

'Come out and say it to our faces, you bastard, instead of skulking about over there.'

'Who are you?'

'Me? I'm a man like any other.'

'Go on, tell us who you are.'

'I'm one of you, a visitor.'

'From where?'

'From where? From somewhere you'll have heard of, from Russia.'

'You're not from Irish Town then? They have no problem castrating people there.'

'From Russia.'

'A little atheist then.'

'I may or may not be an atheist, but if you keep on at this you'll find I'm not quite as little as you seem to think.'

'What business of yours is this?'

'Human rights are my business.'

'You'll get plenty of human rights in your own country.'

'People have them here too, as far as I know. Now I and this man will be off. Anyone who tries the same trick here again tonight will pay for it with his life. Get back! Back! If anyone raises his hand even an inch or puts a hand in his pocket, I'm warning you, it'll be the very last time.'

He was so fiery and brave, and spoke so sincerely, that the crowd's evil intent cooled. The young man had an original goodness about him.

'You saved my skin,' said the Monsignor, when they got back to the house. 'But look at that crowd . . . The Guards? That crowd would eat them for breakfast. They've sent off to I. for more of them. Now that law and order has broken down, they don't care. It was those freed prisoners who were inciting everyone else tonight. Oh, why did the devil have to turn his crooked eye on this town and make the houses come to blows?'

'The devil! I think you may be a bit deluded. Wasn't it your own hypocrisy that caused all this? But if something is true, it can be proven. I want to see the proof.'

'So it would seem. But that's not the point. Hypocrisy, eh? I'm going back into that town again even if I die in the attempt.'

'You're sure you're not just looking for a drink?'

'Why would I be looking for a drink? This place is overflowing with it. My flock.'

'I managed to save you once through sheer luck. To tell the truth you were a goner, only for some woman who held back the man with the knife until I could get hold of it. I don't think I'd get the better of that crowd a second time.'

'I'll always be grateful to you, for however long that may be, but I'm going alone this time.'

He went into the house and came out dressed in a layman's overcoat. He reached into the hedge and pulled out a big hurley stick. The flat end of it was specially reinforced. He tried to whip it along the ground, but he couldn't seem to wield it right.

'I was a good hand at this once,' he said.

'If you insist on going back there I'll come with you, but I'm warning you—'

The priest was already on his way out. Muldowney's pub was a hubbub of noise, strident music, squabbling, a woman wailing that she'd been stabbed, the street outside covered in a litter of broken glass. The Monsignor hesitated for a second but then strode on, muttering something under his breath. In the flashing light from Muldowney's the Monsignor recognised the doctor who had been struck off, now pinned on his back on the road by five men. They were brandishing what looked like a large scissors.

'Look how much he has here, plenty for three! Now my fellow tailors, let's get to work. If this devil was in better shape, he could teach us the tricks of his own trade and we'd make a better job of it . . .'

The Monsignor recognised the eunuch tailor of Irish Town: 'That robbery is one of the lesser crimes to have happened this night,' he said. 'There's plenty of wealth in this town. He was always practising as a doctor in secret . . . '

A big crowd had gathered at Cross Crescent. A doctor's house had just attacked another doctor's house. Safes, chairs, equipment, bills, prescriptions, and all sorts were erupting from the windows, and bills were flying through the air like radiation fallout. Overall, the crowd was upbeat and well behaved. The Monsignor noticed a man coming towards him carrying a safe that looked like it held a lot of valuables.

'There's something going on here that I don't understand,' he said, 'although there's probably a simple explanation, if I only knew what it was.'

Where Straw Street met Fish Lane there was a bonfire with a low wooden platform in front of it. Naked men and women swarmed under a banner emblazoned with the leprechaun cobbler. There was no mistaking who the cobbler was. He had the Monsignor's three-cornered biretta and under it the Monsignor's face. And the phallic symbol on it was as obvious as Gaeltarra Éireann's. He was tippling from a jug of the local drink, and it poured in a golden stream from the symbol.

'This is it, sink or swim,' the Monsignor said calmly and made his way in a leisurely fashion around the edge of the crowd. Suddenly, he whipped out the hurley stick and lunged angrily with it, slashing wildly about, aiming at people's tender parts. A few of them tried to grab the stick, but quick as a flash the Russian appeared, holding the knife that still dripped hot blood. The skirmish was over almost before it began. Soon, everyone who hadn't been knocked down had fled the scene, except for the cobbler, whose Gaeltarra-like symbol had been badly damaged in the stampede, and a young woman so astonished that she seemed to be rooted to the wooden platform.

'Get out of here,' said the priest. 'And hurry up and put some clothes on.'

'I have no clothes,' she said, innocently.

'Then steal some,' said the priest, reflecting that Old Nick himself could probably come across as innocent and harmless when he chose. 'Is there anyone here from H.?' he roared after the fleeing crowd. 'If so, you'll come and help me if you know what's good for you.'

Instantly, about twenty people were at his side.

'Have you come to your senses? You've often heard it said that wherever the devil might be during the day, he'd be sure to be in H. by night. Now he's dug in here day and night. We have to drive him out. What you've just seen is only the very start of the battle. And you can't always get yarn from the first thread you spin. Go and get yourselves some weapons, and be quick about it.'

Soon they were back at his side carrying a motley arsenal: cobblers' knives, butchers' cleavers, shears, tailors' scissors, penknives, spanners . . . The police had confiscated all the guns in town when the houses first started beating each other up.

At the corner of the Green and Main Street, the Munster and Leinster and the National Bank were locked in a vicious combat.

'High for Blakes and Dalys and let them get on with it,' exclaimed the Monsignor, rushing past.

In Main Street, a big crowd was running across the roofs of parked cars, dancing on them, and ramming them with other cars. 'What goes for the houses goes for the cars,' they chanted. You could barely walk on the road what with all the broken glass.

Evidently people were being rounded up to support the Monsignor, because by the time he was halfway up Main Street his following had swelled to nearly five hundred.

A crazy gang was advancing up Main Street on the left-hand side. The Monsignor was pretty certain they were coming out of the beauty parlour. All of them naked as a babe. Each one covered in colourful tattoos. Leopards, zebras, peacocks, basking sharks, and snakes adorned their skins. Compasses and circles. Fighting houses. Hammers without sickles. A tracery of tails. A trinity of penises. One had a harp above the crown. Another was patterned all over with shamrocks. A raddle of red bloomed upwards from one woman's crotch. A bull pawed the ground on another's stomach. Another had a horny fat man drawn on her back. Celtic designs meandered across breasts. A sword of light pointed towards someone's nether regions. Their skins, especially the women's, were dappled with colour: black, red, yellow, polka-dot. The air was rich with the scent of roses . . .

'Let's go to the square, Father. That's where the Father of Evil is.'

'And the Mother of Evil.'

'And the Queen of Evil.'

'You said it. The Queen of Evil, indeed!'

Down to their left, the Mercy Convent and Our Lady's National School were laying into each other. They appeared to be well matched.

'You'd think, of all buildings, that they'd be a bit more God-fearing!' the Monsignor said, but he didn't stop. He couldn't have done, anyway, as nearly everyone on the streets was following him now. People were walking on his heels as if they were racked by an impatience they could barely contain.

The square was crowded, full as an egg. A big bonfire blazed at the centre. A stage was crowded with naked men and women dancing. The dance of the Serpent, someone whispered to the Monsignor. And sure enough, they soon began to drape themselves with fig leaves to hide their shame. The uproar of the crowd was like a woodland writhing in the wind. The centre of the square was laid out for dancing too. There were hawkers going about selling drinks and sticks and cakes in the shape of the huge emblem that graced the International Hotel. The floodlit cobbler was looking down in approval on the merrymaking, wearing a slightly sinister smirk. Vying with him was the other big emblem, silhouetted in the dazzle of the International's upper window: a huge golden orchid, looking as if the cobbler might have fashioned it, with thread from a pig's bristles. The Commercial Hotel was also doing its damnedest to compete. They had a golden calf on the balcony, with a beautiful woman in golden clothes, with golden skin and hair, the Goddess of Commerce, most likely, seated beside it. She appeared to be minting gold coins and feeding them to the calf. In the eyes of the crowd, the other images paled in comparison to this one, although the dwarf was still entertaining the people of Irish Town, who sniggered on, oblivious to the classical references.

If the revels could be said to have a master of ceremonies, it would have to be the insurance clerk. There he was, resplendent in golden slippers, which were all he was wearing. His tattoo was a simple enough design: an orchid on one bum-cheek and the Tara brooch on the other.

'*Sancta Maria*,' intoned the Monsignor. 'Whether you know him or not, show mercy to no man, unless he declares right now that he's with us. Let's take the stage first.'

He met little opposition worth talking about. The townspeople fell down on their knees to beg for help and protection. The rumour went around afterwards that some of the priest's henchmen slaughtered their rivals in ceremony. Some said that the castrated tailor of Irish Town killed a pharmacist's assistant. Others heard the butcher from Gioballáin calling the general manager of Best Bargains Abraham before he gave him what was coming to him. Most of those who fell were trampled and killed as they tried to flee. The stage was shattered to splinters, and people had to be stopped from kicking the bonfire for fear of starting an inferno. A man from Irish Town put a pyramid with a yellow pint on it sticking up out of the dwarf's behind.

The last few revellers were clustered around the golden orchid on the International Hotel. Apparently they hadn't yet grasped what was happening. Maybe they thought that all this was part of the proceedings. A pair of golden slippers and the Tara brooch were glimpsed scurrying down Church Lane, but nobody could give chase because the top of the lane was jammed with people.

At this point the Guards appeared and started throwing their weight around. They challenged the Russian:

'Where did you get that knife? Who exactly are you?'

'He's Russian. He saved my life tonight, when there was no sign of you lot.'

'We can't be everywhere.'

'Tell me one place where you were.'

'We are not obliged to give anyone, even yourself Monsignor, an account of our whereabouts.'

'The Monsignor knows where you were. In the barracks. Get away back there now. You've done your bit for tonight.'

'We'll have to bring this fellow in for questioning. He's a foreigner.'

'Well if that's the case, then I'm a foreigner too. There are no foreigners in God's kingdom. If it wasn't for God and this loyal comrade here, I wouldn't be standing here before you tonight.'

The Monsignor shook the Russian's hand. He didn't even notice that the Russian was giving him the Communist handshake.

Then the Monsignor swept the Russian away with him. Up ahead, a line like the stroke of a silver pen scored quickly through the inky shadows cast by the church. The Monsignor was surprised, at least insofar as anything could ever surprise him again. Because by now there wasn't a sinner about. The house next to the church on that side belonged to the Crowned Queen of the Night. He stopped to listen. Not so much as a fly buzzing in the Queen's house.

He stopped again. The sooner he got some sleep the better. He was seeing things, imagining things. Had the Queen been appearing in various places tonight? At the wooden platform where Hay Street met Fish Lane, he had been attacked by a swarthy man with a knife. Someone had dashed in between them, grabbed the knife wielder's wrist, and bent his arm back in an iron grip, forcing the knife through the swarthy man's own temple. He had heard a voice preaching on Main Street, inciting people. In the square, a giant of a man with a huge head of curly hair had run at the Monsignor like a bull, trying to butt him with that boulder of a head. The Monsignor had got a good look at him and he remembered now that the man had been one of the freed prisoners. He'd had a hard job getting a good lash at him with the hurley stick. The giant was keeping his head low, shielding it with his arms. Clearly, this was a well-used fighting tactic of his. The Russian was battering him from all sides, but neither he nor anyone else was able to get the better of him until, all of a sudden, a woman walked up and started to lash at this would-be Cú Chulainn with a sock filled with stones. He took one arm from his head to grab at the sock. She seized her chance and delivered a clean blow to his head . . .

The Monsignor himself and the Russian were just about to go into the house when a voice behind them said:

'There's a man at the Commercial Hotel in need of the last rites.'

That was true. It was the would-be Cú Chulainn.

The Monsignor found it all very strange. He could have sworn— though then again, maybe not—that it was the same person and the same voice in all the various places. The Strawberry Queen, the Queen of the Brawling Houses! But it couldn't be her. She lived near the Monsignor. She had a bad reputation. He had been trying surreptitiously for some years now to have her put out of the house. Even tonight, the ex-nun and a bunch of other young local women had informed him that she was the ringleader of the mob that had descended on the church with intent to destroy . . .

When the Monsignor stepped into the church the following day, who should appear to him from the shadows of the belfry but the poet of Wine Street. Evidently he had spent the night there. 'By the souls of your dead' he said to the Monsignor, 'I'll have a drop to wet my whistle before I speak a word.'

The Monsignor took him around by the side entrance into his own house, even though he was half-inclined to leave him to the tender mercies of the townspeople. This nuisance had long been a thorn in his side, but the Monsignor was afraid that his death would only add fuel to the fire. His poetry was held in high regard by many people in and around Wine Street. The town's newspaper editor was very fond of him. Whenever the paper published one of the poet's satires, the politician would disappear for a fortnight. He wrote a piece about the curate of Cross Street, and attendance at church that Easter plummeted. The Monsignor himself had considered approaching him, strangely enough, on the quiet, to see about a piece on the Muldowney family . . .

The poet had once been elected to the town council. He had been full of proposals: that a temple be built to Bacchus on Wine Street; that a site be established for gypsies along the river between Irish Town and the rest of the town; that Big Maggie, madam of the Wine Street brothel, be co-opted onto the council; that rates be abolished for certain streets and doubled for others. . . .

This last one had made him very popular indeed . . .

'How come you never have any money?' the Monsignor asked. 'Could you not hold down a job?'

'My head is always full of words drifting about. They make a kind of island, a green island in an ocean of sounds. They form chains, lines, verses . . . The boss catches me daydreaming and sacks me. I do want to work, but—'

'Why don't you write some proper poems instead of always pandering to the crowd in that filthy hall up in Wine Street . . . Clean poems. Holy poems . . . If there's one thing I hate, it's bawdy songs . . . Songs about Our Lady, the Faith, St. Patrick . . . Now if it's a bawdy song . . . It's about Our Lady, you say. You wrote it yourself . . . You did not . . . François Villon, a Frenchman, that's who wrote it . . . I knew it was going to be bawdy . . . Why don't you just get a job? Now listen here! I'll give you a job as sexton here. You like the belfry, don't you? . . . You won't have much to do. Just register the baptisms, marriages, and funerals, and take in the fees for them. Give out baptismal certificates to people. Ring the bell. Check the supplies of altar wine. I'll show you the kind of poetry you should be writing . . . I want a piece about the Muldowneys, the hotel crowd. We'll discuss that later . . . Don't drink any more out of that bottle. That's all I have left. It's a deal then? The only condition is that you don't go into the bars in Wine Street anymore, or anywhere over on that side of town, and that you

stay away from taverns and women. Now, I'm going to go and lock the
church up. I'll be right back and we'll talk about wages . . .

And he did come right back. Poet and bottle were gone . . .

By dawn there was hardly a tourist left in the town. Most of the
day was spent reckoning the damages. The townspeople cleaned up
the mess and debris as best they could and renewed their baptismal
vows. Committees were formed to deliberate upon the spiritual re-
form of the town. A search party came across the insurance agent
hiding in a vault under the church. A woman with golden light shining from her face had guided him there, away from the mayhem of
the square the previous night. A man from Irish Town offered to flay
the tattoo off his behind. In the end they wrapped him in some of the
priest's old cast-offs, to cover his shame.

Some of the crowd were calling for him to be tried and punished
immediately. Chief among those were the Post Office Savings clerk
and the pools collector. The accused pleaded that all he had done was
bring prosperity to the town and that if others had exploited the situation he couldn't be held responsible for that. Any travel agent worth
his salt could tell you that when a place got a name for vice, tourists
would flock there, and that the very opposite was the case when it became known for its virtue. He couldn't help that: it was just human
nature. And business people had to earn a living as best they could
from that crooked and twisted thing. He claimed he had saved the
ex-nun from being gang-raped the night before. She confirmed that
he had but said that he was stark naked at the time.

The crowd were baying for blood, looking for a scapegoat. The
most vehemently venomous of all were those who had the most to
lose from the departure of the tourists. All they wanted was to vent
their misfortune on whoever was at hand. It was the Monsignor who
saved the agent. He would have to leave the town, never to return.
The Monsignor knew that if the crowd took revenge on the agent, it
would open the floodgates for vengeance on anyone and everyone,

innocent or guilty. He himself was still smarting from the poet and his bottle, but never mind that . . . While the agent was protesting on his own behalf and the Monsignor was talking, a fellow from Fish Lane relieved the agent of his golden slippers.

With that, the ex-nun and a crowd of young women from the town, including the manager of the beauty parlour, once again brought up the subject of the Queen who had been crowned naked the night before and who had subsequently urged the crowd to storm the church.

Someone from Wine Street said that the Queen had been stripped against her will.

'Where did she go after that?' someone else asked.

'Off carousing, where else?' said some young one.

'Carousing in the church,' chimed the young women in unison.

'Whatever else happens, that one should be put to death,' a voice said, with such certainty you knew that its owner would happily play executioner.

'My dear friends, nobody is going to be put to death until they have been tried and found guilty,' said the Monsignor. 'In this case, as in the case of the agent—'

'All you're doing is running them out of town. They'll turn round and come back before a week is out. When you put someone six feet under, they stay six feet under.'

Meetings upon meetings were organised, many of them taking place at street corners. It had taken a while, but the citizens of H. had realised that they had a store of piety and justice to protect. At the corner of Hay Street, a man whose chubby face was spattered with freckles as big as pennies was standing on a box usually used for packing fish.

'It transpires that the Mother of All Evil is still among us. Houses are still battering each other this very day. Last night we only touched the tips of his wicked whiskers. He was here.'

'He was. I saw him going down Wine Street, the two horns sticking up from his head and the woman who was crowned queen of this town wrapped around him.'

'What happened to that Queen? Why wasn't she knocked to the ground, when so many people who were causing much less harm than her were knocked down. A woman who was fornicating in public with the insurance agent on the stage in the square last night! How come nobody got a hold of her? I realised long ago that she was the cause of all the harm and that everything would come to a stop if only she was run out of town or put out of action. A fine foolish lassie, cowering behind the Monsignor's rump. I suppose he's the one protecting her.'

'She has friends. Becky from the Café, for one!'

'Isn't Miller Moran's wife a crying disgrace to anyplace? She has a man in five different streets in the town.'

'It's not only the women are getting up to no good, let me tell you. Sure Harmon the Hotelier has been holding naked parties for years, with all the best-looking women in the town screwing away in public, as if it was just a dance they were doing.'

'And that little hunchback of a chemist has been letting women in the back way to Cross Street, drugging them to sleep, and—'

'Look at the whiskey nose on that fellow over there.'

'And the manager of Best Bargains with his big belly full of blubber—'

'Full to bursting!'

'Bursting with sins!'

He was stabbing the air with his index finger, pointing out people in the crowd and elaborating on their vices for all the world to hear. His puffy face floated above the box, and he was cavorting as if on hot coals. And now his face was alight:

'But the whole town isn't like that, not at all! Let's not accuse our neighbour wrongly. That's the worst sin of all. The woman we're all agreed about, the Queen, the Mother of Evil—'

'The Bride of Evil.'

'The Bride of Evil, better again. As far as we know, she hasn't left the town. I suppose she's stoking the flames of evil somewhere, hoping to keep the fire burning brightly. Let's smoke her out of her lair. Isn't that better than doing harm to each other?'

'Let's smoke her out of her lair.'

'Let's get her!'

The gathering began to move towards the square like a river in which every drop was tightly bound to the next and moving in the same direction as if by magic. Passionate orations echoed up from Fish Lane. ' . . . And when we've got rid of her we'll invite the Cardinal, the President, and the Taoiseach to come to the opening of the fragrant garden of virtues that our reformed town will become. But first we have to make an example of her—'

The square was empty, like a house with all its furniture taken away. By now the orchid had been taken down from the International Hotel and the papal flag was foremost among the flags flying in front of it. A single motto topped the façade of the Commercial Hotel: 'Faith of our Fathers.'

The crowd made for the church grounds, where a meeting had been underway for some time.

'Whatever pieties you may be spouting right now,' the Monsignor was saying to the swelling crowd, 'your hearts are still full of bitterness. Last night the shamelessness of Adam and Eve took hold of you, and you're still in its grip. Talking about burning the house down! If you do that you'll burn the church and my house and half the town with it. '

'It shouldn't be left standing. Nor should houses of lust and corruption. Houses of chemists who entice women and drug them . . . Houses—'

'Why should they be left standing, when all they do to pass the time is beat each other up?' It was clear from his flushed face that this speaker was drunk, but a dark shiver of agreement ran through the crowd.

'If the house is wicked, as you say,' said the Monsignor, 'then listen, here's what we'll do. I myself and three or four others who can be trusted will search it forensically, from floor to rafters, and I give you my word as a priest that if we find so much as a hair belonging to the Evil One, we will bring it out here to you and then we will have evidence to base our verdict on.'

'But what about her?'

'The apple of the Evil One's eye.'

'Lot's wife who kept brothels—'

'Have patience, for the love of God. I don't know where she is.'

'Holed up somewhere with the Evil One.'

'She hasn't had a chance to plead her case. You wouldn't condemn someone without giving them a chance to defend themselves.'

'God turned Lot's wife to a pillar of salt.'

The Monsignor held firm because he knew that the very people who were least happy with the town's new direction were the ones calling for vengeance. But he hoped that in the end he could placate them by banishing her from the town, as he had done with the agent. The whole crowd wanted to follow the Monsignor and his chosen few into the Queen's house, even trying to push in ahead of them. He knew that if they succeeded, only a miracle could save the house from burning.

He held his hands out towards them. 'I see you don't trust me. You'd sooner trust a beggar on the road out there. A while ago you'd have put your trust in any Tom, Dick, or Harry, but now you won't look to me, your shepherd. You won't accept that I and these people here whom you appointed to the parish committee will bring you the truth. Will I have to ask my brave protectors to come to my aid, as I had to do last night?'

The crowd in the yard moved back. 'I implore you to be good and to have patience. You will get the truth, be it gentle or harsh.'

The door had only a latch to close it. The Monsignor closed and bolted it behind him. The first thing he laid eyes on as he walked down the hall was the Queen herself. You could see she was afraid, but there was a glow to her face in the dimly lit hall that put the Monsignor off his stride:

'The crowd out there are all riled up, so we had no choice but to do this. Four of us offered to search your house, to see — how shall I put it . . . would it be Agnus Dei or the gospel of the Evil One we would find here.'

A self-deprecating smile lit his face, but it was clear he wasn't at all at ease: 'I know this isn't exactly normal practice, but you must realise that it's all that stands between you and the will of the mob.'

'Of course I understand. Search away, Monsignor. As far as I know, this house has nothing to hide. '

The woman's polite and trusting attitude only added to the Monsignor's embarrassment. He turned to her again:

'What have you to say for yourself?'

'Nothing.'

'Nothing!'

'Yes, nothing. What am I supposed to talk about, Monsignor?'

A burbling sound came from the Monsignor's vocal cords but didn't form into words. The sound returned to his lungs as an inchoate puff of air.

'About everything' was all he could come up with, eventually.

'I was crowned Queen here twice. Both times I was unwilling to compete. The Muldowneys were the ones who badgered me into it this year. They assured me it was for the good of the town; it was what the Bishop wanted — '

'For the good of the Muldowneys and the Bishop, more like,' the Monsignor barked from the throes of a phlegmy fit of coughing.

'It was on your own advice that I put in for it last year, Monsignor.'

He had advised her to do it hoping that if she won that some crowd would take her off out of town with them and that she would no longer be such a source of temptation to his flock. She lived right next door to the church. His embarrassment turned to anger.

'Was it you I saw slipping out of the church last night and around the corner?'

'It was.'

'Where did you go?'

'To Father McKilmart's vault.'

'What took you there?'

'I guided the insurance agent away from the lane and hid him in the vault. They would have killed him in the lane. I helped him escape.'

'Why help the likes of him?'

'I'd help anyone in that situation.'

'Even knowing he was a scoundrel.'

'Let God be the judge of that! Who knows which of us is bad and which of us good. I saw him do bad things last night, whether he realised they were bad or not, and maybe I saw him do good. For a while there last night nobody was in control of themselves.'

The priest watched her carefully. What was she thinking? Deep inside himself, he could feel insight dawning. His gimlet eyes bored into her.

'Do you go to confession?'

'I do.'

'Will you make your confession now?' The priest looked out through the keyhole at the mass of people outside. 'It couldn't do any harm. That crowd's blood is up—'

'I'm not afraid of them, Monsignor—'

'All the same, be humble. Go down on your knees.'

The confession was just over when the other three came back. 'Crosses, holy water, rosaries, prayer books . . . There's no way the Evil One would feel at home in a powerhouse of holiness like this.'

'We found a bundle of letters with an interesting design on the envelope. We didn't touch them but brought them to you, Monsignor.'

'Let me guess—the devil's hoof. Hell's postmark!'

'Read them,' said the Queen, as the Monsignor was hesitating. 'I was going to tell you about them, if you had only listened. There are no secrets in this house. There are no love letters either, or rather, I hope that love letters is all they are . . . ,' she said as she looked down at the bundle.

'Now,' said the Monsignor, 'I'm going to ask you to do something for me, for my sake and yours. For all our sakes. I would prefer that you didn't live in this house for a while . . . I'm going to appeal to your sense of humility and ask you to obey me. I'll get Miss McElhinney from the house back there, you know her, to let you out the back door and take you up the lanes and in through the back gate of the Convent of the Sisters of St. Francis. You'll have to stay there for a while. I'll come and see you later today . . . '

When the two women were well on their way, the Monsignor closed the door of the Queen's house and locked it behind him and his three companions.

Every eye in the crowd was trained on them.

'The devil himself keeps holy water for his own purposes,' they yelled.

The Monsignor gave them a long spiel about how she had always intended to enter a Carthusian convent.

'As a spy for the devil,' they shouted.

'Listen, is there any chance my pipe would be in there, the pipe my brother sent me—'

'If it came from the devil—'

So the Monsignor asked for concrete evidence of her misdeeds.

She was seen wrapped around the devil last night.

'Well that's just a handful of chaff in the wind,' said the Monsignor. 'I'm well aware that the Evil One was here last night, but he took a much subtler form than that.'

'I saw it all,' said the ex-nun.

'What did you see? . . . What did you see?. . . . What did you see?' the Monsignor kept asking.

'Evil in every form but its own.'

'She was crowned queen.'

'Against her will.'

'No. Voluntarily.'

This last assertion was made by the beautician. Afterwards, a lot of people claimed she was miffed the queen had never frequented her parlour.

'I know for certain that it was on my advice that she entered last year's contest.'

'She drank the health of the brawling houses last night, stark naked.'

'She was held against her will and stripped. Not a drop of the wine passed her lips.'

'I saw her grip the hand of the man trying to stab the Monsignor, and turn it so that the man stabbed himself in the head.'

'I saw her fight with stones in a sock—'

'Yes, but I heard her egging people on—'

'And you won't make an example of her,' said the ex-nun.

'It could all happen again now that the lynchpin has got off scot-free.'

'Letting someone the devil has taken to his breast taint the holy water all day long'—the beautician's argument was getting bolder by the minute.

The Monsignor's gimlet eyes burned clean into the depths of her mind.

'Exaggeration is a deplorable practice.'

'Houses are beating each other up since morning and someone has to be made an example of, whether we like it or not. It's clear that this is the will of God': the speaker's eyes burned and his face was alight. A tremor ran through the crowd. The pressure was building in them and they were ready to explode. Most of the crowd were sided with the last speaker. Their wild babbling drowned out the Monsignor's words.

'Tell me this and tell me no more,' said an aggressive little man not unlike the cobbler, if he were to take up cobbling and don a pouch. He spoke from where he squatted in the dip between the chapel and the Queen's house. 'Can anybody here remember whether the church and this here house of the Queen's ever attacked each other, like every other pair of adjacent houses in this town have done?'

He was like a lawyer in a courtroom remarking that the man who was about to be convicted had been in another country altogether when the murder was committed.

'Did a church beat up any other house at all?' someone promptly asked.

'They did indeed, and with as much gusto as any other kind of house.'

'Sure the Capuchin chapel was at it day and night, pounding the Jesuit school back there.'

'And the Dominicans too, hammering O'Regan's store that stands between theirs and their priest's house.'

'One night the Jesuit chapel spilled all the pints that were poured in Sheridan's. My own got spilled and my lips had barely touched the foam of it. The following night Sheridan's gave as good as it got. It sent all the Jesuits' altar vases flying out into the pig yard at the top of Fish Lane.'

'It's true. The churches battered and were battered,' the Monsignor said. 'It's one o'clock in the day now. I advise you all to go home peacefully and think about what you've seen and heard. Weigh everything up. After all that's happened last night and today, anger is still in our systems like silt. And we all know that anger is a horse without a bridle. Let's all take time to reflect, to calm down, and when our minds are clear, our judgement will be keener and wiser. We will give our verdict. Everyone will have his say. Everyone, prince or peasant, will get a fair hearing. My beloved flock, my interest in seeing justice done is every bit as strong as everyone else's.'

'As long as that bitch of a queen gets what's coming to her and she isn't allowed to flee the town in the meantime. You gave us your word earlier that she wouldn't be allowed to leave.' It was the man with the burning eyes who spoke. Once again a murmur of agreement from the crowd.

'She won't be. My word on it as a priest, she won't be allowed to leave.'

'Someone will have to pay for all the shame.'

'Almighty God and his Blessed Mother must be avenged.'

'The things I've seen . . . '

When he'd got rid of the last few of them, the Monsignor sauntered as nonchalantly as he could over to the Franciscan convent. He replied pleasantly to anyone who greeted him along the way. But he did notice that some of them gave him short shrift. To many, the fact that the tourists were gone still rankled.

Passing the bottom of Wine Street he saw a crowd of men and women standing outside a pub. Judging by the shrieks of laughter they were having a pretty good time. One man was holding a bottle and between swigs exhorted:

'Did I call anyone here a fucker? If I called anyone here a fucker, let him stand up and say so . . . '

The Monsignor was overcome with a violent longing to go over and give him a boot up the arse. And to grab the bottle off him. It was the poet of Wine Street. But he did nothing. The Monsignor consoled himself with the thought that the Church had always known how to bide her time. . . .

When he reached the convent there was no sign of the Queen. A nun was going around the streets, from house to house, and people were giving her alms, even though she wasn't asking for anything. All she did was stop at each house and then move on swiftly. At first the Monsignor didn't understand what was going on.

'It was Sister Francesca's idea, Monsignor,' said the mother abbess.

'Indeed it was not, Mother Abbess, it was yours,' said Francesca.

'If her own house hadn't ever attacked the houses on each side of it, and neither of them had hit it, and yet other houses had attacked them, there must be something special about that house. From what Miss McElhinney told us, it seems the Queen herself was that special thing. We weren't able to check with you about it, Monsignor. You were busy trying to quiet that crowd down. We prayed to St. Francis and promised to do a special adoration for our intention. We had nothing to lose by sending her out dressed as an alms-sister. She's after walking all the streets in this area . . . Of course, we had to give priority to our own people. One of the houses she went into in Glen Street stopped punching the minute she set foot across the threshold, although it had been pummelling the other house for half an hour before that. The same thing happened in Fuller's Alley, that lane that runs parallel to Fish Lane. Then we got news that Riverside was in an uproar—it was like a tinkers' fair there. One by one, as she crossed their thresholds, the houses stopped fighting. She's moving southeast now. It's taking five of the sisters to carry the alms she's being given. A butcher gave her an entire sheep . . . And she got nearly a naggin of whiskey, in the bottom of a bottle donated by a drunk in Wine Street . . . '

The Monsignor tried to look noncommital.

'She's a saint, a saint sent from Heaven,' said the mother abbess.

'Oh yes, indeed she is. I knew it, I always knew. She was born and reared next door to me.'

'You knew, Monsignor.' Anyone could see from the slow trickle coming from the Monsignor's eye—a little tear of remorse most likely—that he had indeed always known.

'And Miss McElhinney tells me that she's barely out of her teens.'

'I baptised her.'

'God has been good to you, Monsignor.'

'Keep her on the move as long as you can. She should have most of the town done by nine o'clock. The meeting's not till then. Don't tell anyone who she is. If I can announce at nine o'clock that the town is as it was, with no more enmity between the houses and the lion lying down with the lamb, then I'll be one step ahead of the ill-wishers. And the tour de force will be that the very person they wanted to sacrifice is the one who worked the miracle. I'll have proved that I was right all along. And I'll ride the rush of rejoicing up to the highest echelons of the Church. And I'll see to it that a certain family whose luck bloomed a bit prematurely will find it withering on the bough . . . '

He would be able to say it. He would be the one to announce that houses were no longer beating each other to a pulp . . .

There was one little fly in the ointment. The Monsignor had placed the Russian under a kind of house arrest in the priest's house, for his own good, to keep him safe from the many disasters that might befall him all over town. But he had escaped and had just appeared suddenly on the stage. Not alone that, but he insisted on having his say:

'I don't believe in God at all. The rights of man — that's what I believe in. From what I've been told, it sounds like the houses have been beating each other up here for a while now. But what if this is evidence of the eternal, inevitable conflict between rival classes? What if it's a projection outwards from the everyday war in your minds, manifesting as another form of class war in this battle between houses? I think this conflict makes for a very interesting synthesis. At any rate, it proves that man and matter share similar inclinations and spiritual feeling, insofar as one can use that particular term. Most likely matter took a leaf out of man's book, in this case the result being houses at war with each other constantly, just like people —'

'By God, hark at you, Mr. Talking Head, your tongue is running away with you, so it is.'

'Hang the rotten atheist.'

'Tear him apart here in the square and feed him to the dogs.'

'Here's the one we should sacrifice, and not her, a beautiful woman from our own town.'

'No way,' said the Monsignor. 'Credit where it's due. If it weren't for him last night, this town would be a bitter swamp like Sodom and Gomorrah today. He deserves our heartfelt thanks. But we'll say no to his damned communism. We believe in God first and the rights of man in second place, which is how God intended it. The devil walked among us in human form—'

'He did. I saw him myself. I'd know him again, even in the middle of Muldowney's hotel, even the way that place was last night. He was Master of Ceremonies, presiding over rape and castration, and the snake-dance—'

'He set himself up to rule over matter and man in this town. Only for the good woman—'

On the stroke of midnight she entered the convent gate. The whole of Wine Street, Irish Town, and their environs escorted her, singing her praises. Young girls strewed flowers in her path. The poet of Wine Street followed her reciting poems in which she was hailed as the equal of goddesses, great queens, saints, and the heroines of history. He was hard put to say which of those four categories she resembled most. The poet was just inside the gate when the Monsignor caught him and tried to give him a belt of his walking stick. The Queen stood between poet and stick and took the brunt of it . . .

She had gone around the whole town and calmed all of the houses right down, just as surely as if God himself had sung them a lullaby. But the belt of the stick wounded her. By the third day she was raving. As is often the case, her ravings wove a strange tapestry. One thread was repeated throughout, and that was a request to see the poet of Wine Street again. Eventually, though it was against the rules, the request was granted. She wore her crown to welcome him.

It was the biggest funeral the town had ever seen. At her grave, the Monsignor proclaimed that he had known her from the day she was baptised until she died and that she had always been a saint. Her feastday has become a public holiday when the town councillors lay a wreath on her grave. All sorts of books and pamphlets have been written about her, and the story of the houses has been told in many languages. The people of H. have a special devotion to her, and many are members of a sodality formed to campaign for sainthood for her. The town could do with crowds of pilgrims arriving. But she hasn't been canonised yet. It doesn't seem likely that they'll make a saint of someone for making peace between warring houses. And anyway, she only became a martyr by accident. A savvy person might predict— and the Monsignor always shakes his head when he hears it—that she'll be beaten in the race to sainthood by the poet of Wine Street, who died a Carthusian.

TRANSLATED BY KATHERINE DUFFY

THE KEY

J. was a paperkeeper. Any honest person will admit that this is the most responsible and difficult position in the Civil Service. Because the Civil Service is paper, every size, every shape and make, every colour and class of paper. Huge bulky memos that cast long shadows, taking up space like slabs in an old cemetery. Thin tattered receipts like slime on a rainswept rock, a sign that a snail or something like it had slid past and left a trail in its wake. Acts, orders, statutory instruments side by side, armed and numbered, ready for the fray. Sacred memoranda, about which it was said that they regularly went as far as the secretary of the Department before descending again to his underlings; rumour had it that some of them may even have been touched by the Minister's hand. Then there were the labels, small pieces of named and numbered paper stuck to every document, their ultimate adornment, like lipstick. But they were far from that. They were as indispensable as the files and the memoranda themselves. For without labels, how could one file be distinguished from another? It was hard to believe the files weren't alive, or like tinned cans of flesh and blood. But they didn't have the outer attributes of living things — arms, legs, eyes, hair, tails, horns. No one had ever heard of a file that was lame or blind or short-tempered, that was ill or sinful, or of a file that was a doctor, a priest, or even a civil servant. It was as if they belonged to another order of creation, separate to ours, and dwelt among us without being noticed. It was easy to imagine that a file and its label had its own faith and afterlife. Some of them, no matter how far back they were shoved into the darkest recesses, managed, somehow, to make their way back to the light. And those that were left out in the light weren't happy unless they were in the dark. It was obvious that they held grudges and fought with each other as well. In the morning, a file might be found dented, or the head of one might be butting another. There were even civil wars between files. Especially when His Father's Government put out His Friend's Government. People swore they heard squealing, battering, thumping, and wailing of files in the cabinets. Files were found crumpled, stabbed, torn, tattered. The old files couldn't stand the new ones, and vice versa. To preserve the peace, they had to be kept apart. No one knew when a file, a particular file and not just any old file, might be sent for. If the wrong file was sent up, it was as if a civil servant had been sent to administer the last rites to a dying person. The more you thought about it, the more you realised that the files were a world unto themselves, a world that was all around us but not part of us. Every file, with its own unique label, proof of its integrity, was a living thing. The smallest puff of wind might carry a label off. They were fragile, short-lived things. A label might be swept under or behind a cabinet, down behind a file inside a cabinet, or out one door if it was ajar, then another and yet another, and finally out through the outside door. It was like the host being stolen from the tabernacle. A label could be murdered, too, thrown out a window or up a chimney or into a fire. Luckily, there was neither window nor chimney nor fire here in the files room. There was hot water in the pipes in winter and the electric lights were always on. But accidents will happen. A label might be mysteriously abducted, or any number of other misfortunes might befall it. It might end up in the wrong file, like a weed or a thieving cow, where it had no right to be. Or it might find itself mixed up in the wrong pile of papers where it wouldn't be found for years, by which time its name and title would have been forgotten. Then, of course, there were the stray files and memos, drifters which had wandered in from other departments, other countries even, and no one knew how or why they had come to be there. But they were accommodated, even though no one really knew why. Probably because no one knew who to send them back to. Or, more importantly, the correct procedures for sending them back. J. never understood how, in a place as well run, as well organised, as spick and span as the Civil Service, these cuckoos were tolerated. Paperkeepers firmly believed in ghosts—ghost labels, files, even memoranda, that were occasionally seen after they had been destroyed or murdered or thrown out years before. It was said that certain places were more file-haunted, label-haunted, than others, and paperkeepers avoided those places. The file on Secret Service monies under His Friend's Government had been destroyed years ago, but it was still regularly sighted, its red ink seeming more like the colour of blood every time, if the stories were true. Of course, there were other stories too. There was one about a label in another department a few years before. It was supposed to have been stuck to the file of a Ministerial Order, pursuant to powers granted under the Act to prevent the spread of wild herbage, weeds, overgrowth, and other unwelcome invaders in cemeteries and other places of interment, Civil Service premises and the nation's schools excepted. To pass the time one day, a paperkeeper, a junior like J., started blowing the label up into the air, flicking it around, having great fun as he watched it somersault through the air before falling, slowly, lazily, like a dead thing, to the ground . . . Suddenly it was gone and there was no getting it back. At that very moment, the file was requested. The paperkeeper owned up. He was found guilty and dismissed in the appropriate manner. Years afterward, the label was found on a wreath on the Minister's coffin. Were it not for a quick-thinking principal officer who was present . . . But that kind of thing could only happen in that particular department. The Department itself had been given a proper burial a long time ago, which reminded J. that some of the paper flotsam of the Department's Last Will and Testament had washed up in his own office. He felt his lips twitch suddenly. Why his lips, he wondered. The twitch began on the top of his head, came down his forehead and along his nose, which prompted him to blow his nose into a clean handkerchief, before the twitch twisted the middle of his lip. Bleary thoughts fluttered like bats in the belfry of his mind. You couldn't convince his Old One that a person who only handled paper had a tap of work to do. If he were handling coal or hoovers or, God save us from all harm, children. His Old One couldn't accept that it was paper that made the world go round; if a memorandum disappeared, it would be the end of department, government, law and order, and justice. It was no use telling her what the Senior paperkeeper, S., in the outer office, said: without a label there can be no file, without a file there can be no civil servant, without a civil servant no hierarchy of grades, without a hierarchy of grades no section, without a section no Department, without a Department no Civil Service, without a Civil Service no secretary, without a secretary no Minister, without a Minister no Government, without a Government no State. The label is the nail for want of which the kingdom would perish! 'Look after the labels and the State will look after itself.' One missing link in this hierarchy would mean utter chaos, humanity reduced to the level of animals. J. had read that in a magazine on the administrative officer's desk the one and only time the Senior paperkeeper, his 'boss,' had sent him over there with a file. The Senior would have gone over that day, too, if it wasn't for that woman. Bloody women! All jokes aside, isn't it amazing how they understood nothing, ever. His own Old One regarded all paper as if it were a pox in the house, unless, of course, it came in the form of banknotes. She never stopped complaining that J. wasn't bringing enough of that kind of paper home with him, for all the attention he was lavishing on paper. And he agreed with her, in a way. Paper should be kept in sealed rooms. Suddenly he realised that those bleary thoughts had been battering his skull for the past five minutes, that he had been daydreaming, as the clerical officer two offices out would say. There was nothing in particular to do. But he was in the habit of wandering around with a file tucked under his arm, or fingering a paper here and there, retrieving a file and then returning it, or looking up and down and carefully scrutinising the cabinet shelves. The closer he looked, the less he saw. Even J. would admit that it was a waste of time. What use was it to a paperkeeper to see a collection of files, a kind of abstraction, when he wasn't looking for a particular file or files? Not that anyone had instructed J. in this matter. He had figured it out for himself. The Senior, the Boss, had a habit of opening the door suddenly and sweeping into the office without warning, as if, God forbid, someone had let off a stinkbomb. J. thought S., the Senior, didn't like him. The first thing he had forced him to do was give up the cigarettes. Not that he said anything directly. That wasn't his way. He'd come in every evening before he locked J.'s office, poke about, stick his hoover of a nose into corners and between cabinets, and say: 'I seem to be getting a smell . . . of cigarettes. Almost as if . . . ' Finally, for his own peace of mind, he'd had to give them up, in case he was ever tempted to light up at work, where there was so much paper. But, by all the puffs of smoke in the world, it had given him something to do. Now, instead, he ate enough for three, and spent the whole night tossing and turning. That first night, his Old One had said: 'If it'll give my poor old hip a rest, stick that cigarette butt in your gob and start puffing. I never saw such high seas in this boat before.' Even now, looking back on it, J. was remarkably determined, crushing the cigarette butt and throwing it down the toilet. S. the Boss was constantly dropping hints, too. It wasn't enough that he had gotten in through influence. To be promoted, you had to be qualified. Minding paper was the most onerous duty in the Civil Service, because the Civil Service was paper; he hoped he wouldn't have to repeat himself on the subject. 'Watch yourself,' he said to him one day. 'Look at the state of that file, and there's every chance the administrative officer might send for it at any time. It might even be today, this very moment.' J. had let a file drop while retrieving another one. 'You're a man like any other. You only have two hands. Never take up a second file until you've laid down the first one.' J. hated the way S. hung around every morning while he was signing in, one eye on the clock and the other on the movement of the pen, like a rower lifting one oar out of the water and plunging the other one down in order to turn the boat. And then there was the day S. noticed the military service medal on his lapel: 'This isn't a jewellery museum. What kind of a fool are you that you haven't noticed that neither the clerical officer nor the staff officer nor the executive officer nor any administrative officer nor assistant secretary nor the secretary nor even the Minister himself wears a die-die like that. Next thing you know, you'll be wearing a Fáinne.' When J. answered that all he had was the cúpla focal: 'True for you. You only got in here because you had pull.' And this wasn't the only thing S. complained about: more help was needed; one person couldn't possibly look after all that paper . . . J. would be free of S. now for a fortnight, and then his own holiday would begin. For J., S.'s being on leave from dinnertime today was like taking off a hair shirt. For the next fourteen evenings, he wouldn't come into the office announcing, 'Five minutes to five. Finish up there so I can lock up.' The first part of his spiel was so listless, so casual, compared to the violent rattle of keys with which it was completed, that J. often thought that S. wouldn't mind at all if J. was locked into the office. J. would go out into the Senior's office. The Senior would follow him out and lock the door between his own office and J.'s. Then he would place the key deep inside a pocket he had specially sewn into the front of his trousers. When he'd take it out in the morning, with great reluctance it seemed, J. always thought that he'd rather put it back in his pocket and not let J. into the office at all. Even now, this made J.'s blood pound in the hollow just under his ear. He could never figure out why the throbbing was always just under his ear. Of course, he did have a habit of pushing his thumb and index finger in there as if his ear was a keyhole. He got up and danced, or tried to dance, a little jig before he realised what he was doing. This was his first year here. For the next fourteen mornings and evenings, he would let himself in and out of that office. He would be responsible for that little key, for locking his own door that led into S.'s office and locking S.'s office from outside. For all S.'s power, he wasn't permitted to take the paper-key with him while he

244 Máirtín Ó Cadhain

was on leave. But where would J. keep the key? It had never occurred
to him to get a special pocket sewn into his trousers. When he bought
his suit, he never imagined he would ever be responsible for something as valuable as that key. Someone sitting beside him on the bus
might slip a hand into his pocket. You could never rule out pickpock-
ets; the world was full of them. Could he put it in his outside pocket
and sit in the aisle seat on the bus? But how would he know where he
might have to sit? And it wasn't as if he could switch the key from
pocket to pocket once he was on the bus, like millionaires switch
women in America, if what S. said was true. What about his trouser
pocket? A woman in a pub had tried to put her hand in his pocket
once. When he caught her, she was all innocence: she only wanted
to jizz him up, that's what she said, to jizz him up, rise him, that's
right, to rise him, to get him worked up; yes, she was worked up herself, in top gear, so she was. That's what they wanted, herself and the
likes of her, a key that would open the lock to the good life, pubs, food
and drink, soft beds, the lap of luxury. Of course, that was before he
became a paperkeeper. The key might easily fall from his breast
pocket if he bent down. And a hip pocket was the easiest one to pick.
Should he hang it around his neck on a string? What if the string
snapped? He wouldn't feel it fall down his chest, along his belly, out
from under his trousers and onto his shoe. The most likely place for
it to fall would be into the toilet while he was struggling to do up his
trousers. Down the toilet, indeed! Lately, he had begun to feel itchy
as well. His Old One used to say she was suffering enough with her
rheumatic hip without J. bringing whatever rash he had caught from
smelly old papers down on her into the bargain. To grip the key tightly
in his hand, in his glove, that was the safest way. Then suddenly it
came to him: just in case anything happened, he could get a copy
made, two copies, that very evening. That should do the trick. But was
that against the rules? He hadn't heard of any such rule, and since he
hadn't heard of it, there could be no such rule. But there was such a
thing as procedure, which was just as important as any rule; he heard

the clerical officer say one day that the Civil Service had as large a corpus of Tradition as the Church did. It was all convolution. He could just as easily lose the copy, for any scut to find. The more copies he had, the greater the danger of scuts. He'd be better off putting the copies out of his head altogether and simply not lose the key. That would be the worst thing that could happen. An inappropriate, and therefore unauthorised, person might come in, do as he wished with the paper, even set it alight, God forbid. It used to make him shiver, as if a flood tide was coursing through his veins, to see his Old One lighting papers. When he asked her one day what they were, she replied, 'Old love letters from a sweetheart who betrayed me long ago,' and she stuck her tongue out . . . J. heard the telephone blare in S.'s office outside. He rushed to the door and turned the knob, but it wouldn't open. He turned it again, right and left, put his knee against it, set his shoulder to it, but the door wouldn't budge; it was as stubborn and obstinate as a statutory instrument that could only be repealed by an Act that had already been repealed itself erroneously. J. had to collect and file the bleary thoughts crashing around in his head. Where the hell was the key? He had been in cloud cuckooland all the while, sending hares hotfoot out of bushes where there was no sign of them! The door was locked from the outside, the Senior—it was always spelled with a capital S, and every time he spoke the word J. felt it fill his junior mouth—the Senior was gone on holidays to the Isle of Man since dinnertime and J. was locked in a room with no other exit, no window or chimney, no skylight or tunnel or ventilation shaft, a worm in a paper mausoleum, as an unneighbourly and far from educated shopkeeper once told his Old One when they were haggling over the price of black pudding. But where was the key? He couldn't see it through the keyhole on the outside. J. didn't realise that right away. The telephone outside rang, fell silent, and rang again, tormenting him, each ring a nail driving into his brain. There was a telephone on his own desk inside, but he wasn't allowed to use it without S.'s say-so, and S. had never said so. In fact, he had been quite

specific about it. He had given J. strict instructions that if his telephone ever rang, he was to lift the receiver, call S. into his office, go
out to S.'s office shutting the door behind him, and wait until S. returned. It was the Senior who dealt with important tasks like telephone calls: that was the procedure. J. might never have done what
he did if it hadn't been for the sudden fit of itching. God damn and
blast that same itch. Always at the wrong time. It came on him the
other day as the staff officer was walking towards him. He looked at J.
suspiciously. While J. scratched himself furiously with one hand, the
other hand reached out of its own accord and had the receiver to his
ear before he knew it: 'Mr. S.' 'He's not here,' he said. 'He's on leave.'
The tremble in his voice stirred every syllable like a poker so that his
speech ignited into an unintelligible sheet of flame. 'Speak into the
telephone. I can't hear you.' 'Mr. S. is on leave.' 'On leave! Isn't it well
for some! When will he be back?' 'A fortnight from tomorrow at half
past nine.' If J. had to write a memorandum about the conversation,
he couldn't have said for sure whether the caller was male or female.
The incident was so strange that he was completely thrown by it, like
someone who had ventured too far out to sea and was swept away by
the current. Not to mention the raging itch that was keeping his
hands busier than they had ever been when handling files. But he
couldn't mention the itch in a memorandum. Whatever else happened, nothing out of the ordinary could happen in the Civil Service.
If he had to write a memorandum or if he was questioned about the
'Isn't it well for some!' remark, what would he say he thought it
meant? When he was on the telephone, he should have said that he
was locked in. Of course, when the horse has bolted . . . he had to
catch hold of the edge of the desk to keep himself upright. His mind
was churning like a mill-wheel. He made his way along the cabinets
to the door, tried it again, examined the lock, went down on his knees
to examine the keyhole, like he used to do as a child, looking at those
crosses that had the church at Knock inside them. Although he did
have a military service medal, it was from the FCA, and he had never

been locked up before. Now, for the first time, he began to think seriously about locks. He knew very well that when you did one thing, it locked, and that when you did something else, it unlocked. But the crux, the very heart of the matter, at the end of it all, eluded him. He tried to visualise the inside of the lock, but all he could see were lobsters and crabs and claws. He felt itchy again. Had S. locked the door at dinnertime after J. left, as he did in the evening every other day? Then he remembered that S. had been in the outer office after he himself had returned from his dinner. One thigh and the side of his belly were well scratched by now. Officially, S. was not on leave until five, although he had special permission to leave that day at two. That was referred to as privilege leave. J.'s stumpy legs, the flat feet the FCA had been unable to cure — as soon as one was straightened, the other was as crooked as before — jerked up from the floor, without touching each other. S. was not officially on leave yet, he was on privilege leave, and J. had just said officially on an official telephone that he was on leave. What he had been instructed to say in such cases was that he had stepped out of his office for a moment to take a file to another office of the Department, and if the gentleman/lady wanted to leave his/her number . . . But J. had said that S. was on leave, thanks be to God he hadn't said 'in the Isle of Man' or he would have made shite of everything. The scratching had now reached the hollow of his groin, on the lee side . . . Of course, S. had been in his own office when J. came back from lunch. He went over S.'s detailed instructions in his mind: to be on time, to note the correct time in the book, to answer the telephone, to note the date and time of the call as well as the number of the caller in a little book S. had for that purpose next to the telephone; not to scratch himself or cultivate any other coarse habits in case he might be seen — if he was seen, it would be said that that was what the junior did when the Senior was absent; to watch out for matches, files, letters, the difference between a private and an official letter; for the love of God, never to answer any question the cleaning lady might ask; to turn off lights 1 and 2 when he was at the farthest end of the office outside; instructions—S.'s word—concerning memoranda, in the unlikely event that one might be requested when he himself was absent. He repeated every single word as S. had delivered it. He felt vaguely that this was the part of the religious instruction that would stamp its spiritual seal on his soul forever: Who made the Civil Service? God. What does the Civil Service make? Civil Servants. What are you? A Civil Servant. Why were you created? To be in this office. What is the purpose of this office? To serve paper. What is the purpose of paper, and memoranda? To serve the Civil Service. What is the purpose of the Civil Service? To serve the State. What is the purpose of the State? To serve the Civil Service . . . Suddenly he pricked up his ears, but that tiny bubble of memory vanished like an eel under a rock. There was something else, if only he could remember it. He couldn't quite put his finger on it . . . Hang on! S.'s final words had been to the effect that if the clerical officer, that Cú Chulainn who stood guard over the Department in the outermost office, if he got as much as a hint of alcohol—even if he only imagined it—from J.'s breath, J. would be sacked on the spot and all the friends J. had in the entire jurisdiction wouldn't be able to bring him back. J. had noticed that the clerical officer's nostrils weren't the most reliable when it came to such detective work. He had only been there a few days when the officer remarked to him that he was surrounded by a haze of rose attar and pointed to J.'s hair. The cleaning lady explained to J. what rose attar was. J. wore brilliantine in his hair. One morning, after J. had signed the book, the officer, thumb and index finger clamped tightly across his nose, pointed after him and said: 'That exhaust pipe is working overtime.' J. was a few minutes in his own office before he realised what had been said and that the officer's nostrils were mistaken as to the source of the smell; S. was the culprit, on the other side of the officer. But there is no 'provision,' no 'appeal'—S.'s words—possible with regard to an officer's faulty nostrils in the Civil Service. His Old One's nostrils were more reliable. J. would often be sucking a bullseye when he went in home to her . . . S. spoke of J.'s pay. How to make sure he got it. If J. went home to his Old One without it, it would mean the end of her hip once and for all and she'd throw him out on the street, which was unseemly for a civil servant . . . What else had S. told him? Something about leaving the office. Leaving the office to use the toilet: if the clerical officer was there before him, to beg his pardon and leave, and not go back until the officer was finished. And not to have his exhaust pipe working overtime in the toilet any more than anywhere else, in case it made the officer turn around. Not to go to the toilet more than twice a day, once in the morning and again in the afternoon. And if he got the runs . . . Yes, indeed, if he should get the runs . . . But it was unlikely that that question would arise, as S. was wont to say, in the near future at any rate. May he come to a bad end, there was something else, one more item on the list . . . And it came to him like a pay rise or a promotion. The key! He opened the desk drawer. There it was, 'a beautiful mysterious goddess,' as he had overheard the clerical officer say to S. one day about something or other on J.'s solitary afternoon trip to the toilet. He was so shaken by S.'s barbed warnings — most of them blunt — that he had almost forgotten where the key was kept. He shouldn't have said that about S.'s warnings, not even to himself: everything in the Civil Service was important. S. had hung a notice in English in his office, on the door leading to J.'s office, where J. couldn't avoid seeing it every time he entered: 'Perfection comes from small things, but perfection is no small thing.' J. was able to say it backwards, and many's the time he had. But his thoughts were so scattered that the sense of these things always escaped him. S. had left the key in the drawer, like he said he would. He must have another key, or a copy, because the door was locked. J. had heard him say before that that was the Senior's privilege. J. examined the key closely. The shaft was slender, very slender for such a powerful instrument on which so much depended. He lifted it up slowly and pressed it against his face. As soon as the steel touched his skin he shivered, remembering a story he'd heard from a relative of his from the country about the fairy lover's death-kiss. But he had the key in his hand. He strode confidently towards the door and inserted it. The lock was stiff. J. had never seen anyone oiling it. Who was responsible for oiling it? J. had never heard of such a 'provision.' He tried to turn it gently. It wouldn't turn. He took it out again. It went in easier than it came out. Was the lock broken? It was an awkward sort of a lock. You'd think there'd be some provision for oiling it. It wasn't broken. The key slid in again easily and nestled snugly inside. Please God, everything would soon be all right. The lock would turn. He turned it to two o'clock—the time S. had gone on leave: privilege leave, of course. He applied some more pressure. The key wouldn't budge past two o'clock, as if sticking there like that was an act of loyalty to S. J. was getting a bit impatient until he remembered hearing the administrative officer say to another man on the day when J. was bringing him the file: 'Patience, man! For something that can't be helped, patience is best. Therefore, patience is essential here because the entire Civil Service is full of things that can't be helped.' He'd be better off trying to coax the key. He brought it back to five o'clock. He pulled it out and tried to put his little finger in the keyhole. It wouldn't go in very far. He inserted the pencil he used for ticking the numbers on the files and rattled it up, down, in, and out. The pencil wasn't as strong as he thought; either that or he forced it too hard, because it snapped, and the stump stayed inside the keyhole. Sacrilege. Using a pencil for a purpose other than that for which it was specifically intended: ticking numbers on files. The more he tried to winkle the pencil stump out, the further he pushed it in, beyond his reach, into parts unknown, like S.'s aeroplane, which would be on its way to the Isle of Man by now. He tried using the head of the key. It went in reluctantly. The whole thing reminded him of his Old One's rheumatic hip. A bone must be off-kilter in her hip too. The two things were very alike: the hip was a large, locked, lumpy, bony, joint, creaking and groaning in his Old One. The key to women was their hips; he had heard that during those days when he used to sit beside women in pubs. He wouldn't allow himself to remember who had actually said it. He felt a hot itch right in the small of his back, where he couldn't reach except by rubbing against something. He jumped up from the floor and hit against the key so violently that it went in under the pencil stump and around it. Bang! The shaft fell away in his hand and the entire head remained inside, cuddled up with the trapped pencil stub. The shaft was a use-less piece of steel, a mere corporeal vessel for the magical part, the head of the key, the soul, that remained imprisoned in the keyhole. He had just killed a key, a living thing, murdered it, a Civil Service paper-key. He was a clumsy fool, as his wife, and S., and the woman in the alley behind the pub had said, to hell with her anyway! But he had never been this clumsy before. He broke another piece off the pencil stump. He broke the tip off the paper-scissors, something he should never have used anyway if he was in his right mind. But his right mind was away in the clouds, like the aeroplane. Otherwise, he wouldn't be emptying the contents of a file to see if the tag of the file cover could fit into the hole, if it could be called a hole anymore, it was so stuffed. Papers tumbled from the file, scattering every which way like a messy topsy-turvy haggart, like unbound sheaves of corn, unhelpful and disobliging, just like his thoughts at the moment. He stopped when he noticed that the tag of the file was bent. It reminded him of the flexibility the clerical officer kept going on about and which, he claimed, was the holy grace of the civil servant. But just before he gave up completely, the corner of the file broke off and re-mained in the choked keyhole. The word 'sack' was a constant drone in the Senior's mouth when discussing the future of junior paper-keepers. He could hardly mention the word 'junior' without 'sack' trotting along like a foal on a tether after it . . . He spent an hour re-arranging the papers in the dog-eared file. You'd think they had got mixed up just to annoy him. The dog-ear would hardly be noticed in the middle of this bundle of files. Even if it was, he could always blame the fights or civil wars that took place amongst the files. Even if S. himself noticed it, he couldn't deny that such things happened.

J. was a wretched creature—he told himself as much—tasting again the forbidden fruit. He looked at the file. Applications for army pensions, from riflemen on the side of His Friend's Government and riflemen on the side of His Father's Government. Perfect! 'Looks like the gunmen are at it again,' he'd say. 'Skelping each other's ears again.' Even S. would have difficulty contradicting that. And it would be harder again for the clerical officer. He considered showing the file to the officer and saying, 'The exhaust pipes of the civil war . . . ' The clerical officer liked a joke, funny stories, that he could repeat to the staff officer and to the blonde one. J.'s leg was inching away, itching to start dancing, when it was stopped in its tracks by the sudden insistent ringing of the telephone in the office outside. Maybe a memorandum was needed? Strange the clerical officer couldn't hear it. But he spent most of his time wandering around the section and even into other sections. J. picked up the receiver of his own telephone, but dropped it again as quickly as if he had accidentally picked up the clothes of a plague victim; then he marshalled his thoughts. Hadn't he answered the telephone before? Why else was it in his office if not to be used? He couldn't believe a system such as the Civil Service would leave useless articles in offices. And if there was such a thing in this office, would the same not apply to other offices, all the thousands, the hundreds of thousands of offices in the Civil Service? The only offices J. could imagine now were Civil Service offices, where civil servants worked during the day and slept, exhausted, at night, stretched out beside frail, protesting hip bones. Certainly long ago there was a third kind of office, but he couldn't let himself . . . The telephone outside was shrill. J. lifted his own receiver, but all he could hear was a noise like the rumbling of his Old One's stomach, an omen of protesting hips. Then he timidly imitated the Senior. 'Hallo! Hallo! A paperkeeper speaking. A junior paperkeeper.' He thought he heard an answering 'Hallo' from the corner of the cabinet—the dog-eared file, of course. He was so startled, he dropped the receiver. He looked in the cabinet, but all he could see were files. No matter where he looked, among the files, he saw neither sight nor light of any 'Hallo' . . . The telephone outside was silent. He made a circuit around the office to examine it more closely than he had ever done before. Up till now he had trained his eyes to look without seeing. Now he made up his mind to see. Walls, strong sturdy walls, as sure of themselves as his own direct gaze. There was only one way out: through the locked door. He had heard of someone else, another J.—the priest had spoken of it from the altar—who had been trapped inside the belly of a whale. But because it was God's will, he survived. God's will. But there was also the Civil Service's will. It was obvious that this lock was the one key to his salvation. The only way out, whatever about the Civil Service's will, was to dislodge the lock in one go; as easy as a hussy might slip her hand into your trouser pocket. Just to get out of this prison. Once he was out, he could find some way to solve the problem. He got down on his knees again and inspected the keyhole. A blocked hole, stuffed with his own sins, blocking the light of God. He pressed as hard as he could at the inner face of the lock, trying to push, twist, bend, wrench, pull, anything that would make it budge. But it stayed there, a huge tick with strong claws clutching the skin of the door. Was that what reminded him of the tick he had picked up one night in the pub? Maybe it wasn't in the pub at all. Bad cess to it, but he had picked up a tick and it had made a meal of his blood for a long time after. The itch had never quite gone away. That was typical. Everything dumped on the fellow at the bottom of the heap. How come no administrative officer or departmental secretary or even Minister ever picked up a big fat tick? But he shouldn't think like that . . . How had he not thought of it earlier? His Old One used to say that it never occurred to him, or that he wasn't able, to take off his trousers on his wedding night, and a big lump of a button sticking out and boring into her hip was what had started her rheumatism . . . He could try knocking. Yes. He'd knock . . . Quietly, politely, at first. Maybe the clerical officer in the outer office might hear him. His knocks grew louder. Then he started kicking the door. But the doors

and the offices were as deaf as an appeal in the Forgotten Files. What
if the clerical officer wasn't there at all? Maybe he was away on privilege leave? Office gossip had it that he gave typing classes in the evening to the blonde girl on the second floor. J. had often seen them
leaving together at five. God bless the mark, she had the same hair
and melodeon-arse as the one that had put her hand in J.'s trouser
pocket. In spite of himself, J.'s thoughts began to get the better of him.
By God, that blonde one on the second floor wasn't as young as you
might think. Her face was a suit that had often been sent to the clean-
ers. She had that same trick: the hand fondling your thigh, probably
before sliding down gently into your pocket. Damn the women anyway! It was around that time that J. had picked up the tick. The officer
was on a privilege. As strong as the door was, J. thought he was stronger,
and could probably break it down. The same broken key whose head
was stuck in this door would unlock the Boss's door outside, which
wasn't usually locked except at night. Still, it had been one of those
days. If the clerical officer wasn't in and the doors outside all locked,
there would be a whole row of doors—strong doors—to break down
before he was free. How many? Were they all locked? He didn't know.
The Civil Service's doors were as much a mystery to him as its papers.
Apparently, there were people who were authorised to lock them and
to open them, and others who weren't. Surely there must be a provision, a procedure, even a Tradition, regarding such things. It would
never have crossed the clerical officer's mind to think of J. before
leaving. Maybe he forgot that S. wasn't in his office as usual. Still, J.
shouldn't be thinking about breaking down Civil Service doors, any
more than he would think of ripping up its papers. Imagine the consequences of tearing up a single page. Such an evil deed was probably
unforgivable. It would be as bad as murder, maybe worse. The Civil
Service was a closed system, like the office J. was in, an unbreakable
nut, shelter against wind, sun, light, noise, robbers, etc. Total protection and security for paper. If he went around breaking down doors,
he would be breaking the seal ordained by the State and, therefore,

by God, as he had once heard the clerical officer telling the Senior. He had made enough of a mess of the Ten Commandments as a young man. The clerical officer attended some big college in Eccles Street. It was said, too, that the blonde woman went there. They probably sat side by side. The likes of her would offer her other thigh to some other buck and then she could prey on two men at once! Light fingers! He wasn't too far from the same college himself. His Old One was always at him to go there, to get out from under her feet so she could finish her cleaning, burning old papers and other rubbish. 'Maybe,' she said, 'you might meet some hussy who might offer you her thigh. It would give my battered old hip a break at any rate.' For all her mocking, it would be a good thing for a paperkeeper to go to college. When he mentioned it in passing one day: 'You should go to Trinity College and do Celtic Studies. You're much too good for a place like this. If nothing else, it might cure your itch,' said the Senior. 'To hell with the Senior.' As soon as he said it, J. rejected that fate as unsuitable for a civil servant and amended his curse appropriately from Senior to S. As soon as he got himself out of this mess, he'd go to college! More women than men went there, it was said. He would learn something there. Who knew what it might lead to? A promotion. Stranger things had happened . . . J. went back to the desk. His mouth and throat were dry and his lips stuck together. There was a jug of water on the desk which the Senior permitted him to bring in from the toilet every day, saying, 'He who only drinks water is never drunk.' J. drank deeply from it. Now he could start thinking again. He would have to get out. There was only one way out now: through the telephone. He'd pick up the receiver and explain his predicament to the telephonist. Ordinarily, he couldn't do such a thing, but he would have to because he was locked in. He lifted the receiver anxiously to his ear and heard a hissing sound. He would wait five minutes or so, then start calling out. He didn't notice he was shouting. Suddenly he realised there was no one at the other end of the line. She had gone out. She did that from time to time. He had heard the Senior and the clerical officer complaining. 'It appears as though the Postal Department and the Board of Works have come to an agreement and that the exchange will now be located in the toilet . . . ' 'How can there be a Department or a Civil Service with such a weak link?' 'You mean an extension, S.; a telephone is an extension. It's an extension of another kind entirely in the toilet. Well, an extension is an extension . . . ' The extension in the toilet, they called her. S. repeated what the clerical officer said, as though he had said it first. Surely she'd be back by now. He picked up the receiver again. Nothing. He'd give her another ten minutes or so; she'd have to be back by then — unless there was a major operation underway in the toilet. She had no notion of coming back . . . The thought alarmed him as much as if he had misplaced a file. She had gone home! The clerical officer had gone home, or to the college, or to a pub with the blonde melodeon, or wherever a clerical officer goes. The Civil Service had repaired to their second set of rooms, to rest. J. had often heard the Senior taking off the clerical officer, saying the sun never set on the Civil Service. Certainly they retreated, departments and offices were abandoned, in order that the Civil Service might remain as it should be, an otherworld of files. He'd seen it himself every evening at five o'clock. Did S. and the officer mean that there were microphones hidden in the walls? That was said about the police. The Senior had often warned J. not to talk to himself while going through the files, that you never knew who was listening, that the walls had ears and the whole place was an echo chamber. Who's to say the voice that had answered his 'Hallo' a few minutes ago wasn't one of those eavesdroppers? For all that was said about S., maybe he was smarter than he was given credit for. You could tell as much from the neatly trimmed little tuft of a moustache he wore. J. had started to grow one of his own in his second week as a paperkeeper. As soon as the faintest hint of fuzz was visible, S. had said sarcastically, smoothing his own between thumb and forefinger: 'Aren't you the clever one, acting the Senior already.' J. shaved it off at dinnertime. Where was S. now? On the Isle of Man probably. He was going there by aeroplane. If he'd said it once he'd said it twenty times. You'd think travelling by air was going to put him on a different level to the rest of them when he came home. But you could hardly be made a clerical officer or a Senior just by going to the Isle of Man by aeroplane. J. had an idea where S. might be by now. S. was a bit of a lad. One morning, as J. went through S.'s office to the toilet, he found S. with his fingers spread out across the large beehive breasts of the cleaning lady, the youngish one that had only stayed a fortnight. She could easily have trailed her right hand down over her impressive bosom, over S.'s hand, taking advantage of his eagerness to dip her other hand into his pocket. Hands were untangled in an instant. S. shoved his own guilty hand deep into his pocket. 'Don't you have anything to do in that office?' he demanded of J. furiously, foam flecking his lips. 'Or have you been promoted? Or maybe there's a bookies' in the toilet?' And he spent a long month in that same sarcastic vein. 'You'd better stay away from large-breasted women, with that itch of yours. The files have caught it from you. I saw a file in there the other day trying to scratch itself.' . . . Finally J. admitted to himself that there was no chance of making or taking a call; the telephone just kept gurgling like someone choking on his food. His Old One at home would never leave bits of paper around without tearing them up or burning them — receipts for rent, rates, radio, gas, or electricity. She'd be sure to ring the Guards. But he hadn't done anything wrong. Apart from the lock. That was an accident. Could they not have made a stronger key? The keys, really, were the weakest link in the Civil Service. He had forgotten, of course, that the cleaning woman would be in in the morning. It was the Senior who let her into J.'s office every day. Even if she did have a key, there was all that rubbish in the keyhole. But he could call out to her and explain everything. The telephonist would arrive soon after that. But the Senior always complained that her trips to the toilet were as much of a ritual as her morning prayers. And the executive officer, a very learned man, had told S. that to pray originally meant to wait, to sit tight. Between the

two of them, anyway, freedom was in sight. He wouldn't notice the
night pass. He'd leave the lights on and stretch out on the floor. And
even if he didn't sleep, what harm? It was only one night. Now he had
another problem. The toilet. Blast that water he had drunk. Nature
overcomes the strongest will, as S. used to say, a roundabout, lazy excuse for the fact that his hand had been caught handling something
other than paper. J. thought about doing it out through the keyhole,
letting the cleaning woman mop it up in the morning and blaming
S. for it. But he didn't need to examine the keyhole to realise that it
would come back into his own office. And even if he was sure it would
go out, he couldn't bring himself to do it. What about the desk drawer?
He could bring the drawer out and empty it into the toilet when the
doors were opened. But that's where the key had been. It was a place
where keys were kept. Even if the key was faulty, it was still a paper-
key all the same. He surveyed the office 'to that end,' as S. might say.
What about an empty cabinet? Even if it was empty, he couldn't do
it in a place that was—he almost said consecrated—to paper . . . He'd
be better off doing it on the floor, somewhere he could pull the lino
up, preferably in under the pipe in the corner of the office. If need
be, he could help the cleaning lady mop it up, but she was just as
likely to clean it herself without knowing what it was. Either way,
she'd be sympathetic. Most women were understanding, apart from
the odd one like his Old One, who regarded paper as something to
fill bins with. Even if the cleaning lady didn't understand, they
wouldn't come down that hard on him, because nature overcomes
the strongest will, or nature will take its course, as S. was fond of saying, mimicking the clerical officer recalling a scandal which was supposed to have happened long ago in some department which had
long since been dissolved and whose name was all but forgotten in
the Civil Service. J. had heard talk of a civil servant who had made a
funnel from a paper signed personally by the Minister and pissed
through it. Then he had made it into a Christmas card and left it on
the Minister's private desk. J. couldn't believe such things had hap-

pened, or could happen. What J. planned — S.'s word — was necessary but harmless. Every scrap and fragment of paper would be as safe and clean as though nothing had ever happened. He'd swipe some Dettol, Jeyes Fluid, or the like from the Old One at home. That'd put it up to S.'s dredger nose to sniff anything when he returned. If necessary, he'd bribe the cleaning lady, although that was against the rules. But it would be in the form of a tip, a gratuity, which wasn't against the rules. Was it any worse than S. being cleaned out by that cleaning lady? What had happened to S. was worse, because he needn't have done it . . . J. settled in for the night, in the corner furthest from the mess. The crosspiece of the desk was too hard under his head. In the end he had to get up, fetch a file from the top of the cabinet, the top shelf, 'the forgotten files' S. called them. He had to get a second one to make his pillow more comfortable. Ever since joining the Civil Service he had said his prayers diligently. The parish priest saluted him these days. His Old One reminded him every night to pray for her hip. She was forever lighting candles and threatening to go to Lourdes as soon as he got a pay rise: 'Our Father, who art in Heaven,' began J., ' . . . Thine art the keys. If they broke in the great lock of Heaven . . . Thy will be done on earth as it is in the Civil Service. Did Peter have a big deep pocket in the front of his trousers?' It was no use. There was a bell tolling in the back of his head, like the day he couldn't find the memo the executive officer wanted and S.'s nose trained on him like a gun. There was only one light on. He'd have to turn on the other one or turn this one off. There was a constant stream of memoranda relating to power conservation circulating around the Department. He'd turn it off. He couldn't help thinking that he was in a cave, that the filed papers were goats and sheep and that the light was the one and only eye of Polyphemus watching him constantly. An old paperkeeper who was there in the time of His Friend's Government and had since retired had recommended that he buy that 'marvellous book.' When his Old One saw it, after he came home, she wanted to burn 'that tatty old bundle of paper.' He did his best to try and explain to her that the book was a different thing entirely from files, memos, or memoranda . . . but they were all the same to her, all rubbish . . . He spread his coat out under him because the floor was cold and the lead pipes this time of year were cold, like files without covers. He spent the night tossing and turning, trying to silence the ringing in his head. The night of his second day here in this very office, it was this constant tossing and turning which led the Old One to turf him out of the bed. 'Out you go,' she said, 'you can exercise away to your heart's content on those old chairs and boxes. My hip's bad enough as it is with the rheumatism' . . . Finally he fell into an uneasy sleep. That was even worse than the tossing and turning. He had bad dreams: women sticking their hands in his pocket, stealing the keys and making off with them; St. Peter losing the great key of Heaven and the celestial Civil Service frantically searching for it while J. and a long line of others were kicking at the door trying to get in. Our Father, who art in Heaven, hallowed be Thy name, Thy keydom come, Thy will be done on earth as it is in the Civil Service . . . The Military Pensions file came toppling down on him, and paper battles, ambushes, killings, murders, parricides, civil wars raged over his head and all around him. The forgotten files cabinet bent over until it covered him, gobbling him up, until he was trapped inside it as if he was inside an upturned coffin. The cabinet lifted him up and transformed into a file, another forgotten file. He was a forgotten file, but he remembered everything perfectly, especially a broken key, a dog-eared file, and an inexcusable mess in the presence of files and memoranda. He was convinced he was a file, that he was made of paper and he had got lost when the Minister's secretary asked for the memo that he now was. Not only did he feel imprisoned, he felt every part of his body was under lock and key, and the key missing. The tongue was the last to be locked. When he tried to unlock it, he swallowed the key and a door would have to be opened in him to retrieve it . . . He woke with a start. It was as if his itch was a needle and he was being stitched up. His heart was racing, his head pounding. It took a while for him to experience himself as a living thing, then a human being, and longer again before he could get used to his own personality, let alone his own thoughts. It was a ferocious struggle to recover his identity, steal it back from a shapeless cloud where there was uproar and commotion and put it back in its proper place . . . He switched on two, three, four lights. There was no clock in the room and he had no watch. The public clocks were usually enough for him. He could remember clearly his own ravings, but nothing had changed except that he didn't hear the refrain he usually heard in his sleep: 'There's a lot of noise in the boat tonight.' As soon as he put the pillow back in the forgotten files cabinet, he imagined it had become itself again and was grateful to him for paying the appropriate fees . . . He was shivering with the cold, his heart beating as hard as it had the day he was interviewed for the job of paperkeeper. He was so worried that day, the military medal was shaking on his chest, as if his body was betraying some form of cowardice in him. And yet, he knew today was different. Occasionally on the day of the interview, his heart had fluttered like a butterfly on a grassy hillside. Today he was more like a cow he saw once on his holidays struggling to wrench itself out of a boghole. He spent a while scratching himself carefully, vigorously as a prissy cat licking its fur . . . He heard the commotion outside. The cleaning lady. He went to the door: 'Hallo there,' he yelled out through the blocked keyhole. 'Hallo there, Mrs. L. . . . ,' he said. 'Oh, my God! . . . ' he heard her scream through the door, the cleaning equipment being dropped and the uncertain scurrying of arthritic feet. 'Mrs. L.,' he shouted as loud as he could. 'It's me J. J. J. I got locked in by accident; it was an accident. I'm in here.' He heard the shuffle of feet approaching the door. 'I thought it was a ghost or something awful, God help us. It's hard to know what might be living in that dungheap of paper, God between us and all harm! By accident! Poor J. . . . Alive and kicking and locked in . . . Christ Almighty, all night! . . . With nothing to eat or drink, and nowhere to sleep . . . Were you scared? I have no key for that room, Mr. J. Mr. S. has it. He lets

me in every morning. He gives it to me so I can let myself in. When
Mr. S. used to go on holidays, Mr. V., the man that was here before
you, used to have it, and he used to let me in. None of my keys will
open this door, Mr. J. . . . The lock is jammed anyways. We'll have to
wait until the clerical officer comes. Isn't it terrible that such a thing
would happen to you, Mr. J., you of all people, a good decent man . . .'
J. had a lot on his mind, but he'd have to keep it to himself until the
officer came. He began running his finger up and down the spines of
the files in the cabinet. He took one down. Unusually for him, he
didn't put it back. He started reading. It was about an incident a long
way from the city, in the Wild West. An officer from the Department
had visited a tomato grower, and recommended a change of soil.
There was another letter following a second visit, but the soil had not
been changed in the glasshouse. An obstinate man, J. said to himself.
Suddenly, he remembered S.'s mantra: 'Don't let on you see even the
specks of dust between you and the light in this place. Hear nothing.'
He had never told him to do nothing. But he had told him not to say
anything: 'And if you have to say something, say it properly according
to the rules, procedures, provisions, intellectual acumen, and dex-
terity of mind that befits a civil servant. For your own sake, for your
own good, I'm telling you: be tough with the weak and kind to the
strong. Watch the way the wind is blowing. If your right eye should
catch sight of something by accident, I'm not saying I will order you
to pluck it out as a giver of scandal. That would diminish your ability
as a civil servant, as a paperkeeper. But let not your left eye see what
the right eye has seen. Let your mind not comprehend it or dwell on
it. And above all else, never breathe a word of it.' S. was over on the
Isle of Man, groping the large breasts of some scarlet woman who had
rifled his pockets. J. continued reading. He was consumed with curiosity about the departmental officer and the tomato man, like he used
to be about the stories of the Wild West when he was at school. The
man had threatened to hit the officer! To hit a departmental officer!
Someone like the clerical officer, or the executive officer, or the ad-

ministrative officer, or S. himself. There was even a letter from the
Minister saying how seriously he viewed the man's behaviour towards
the departmental officer and, if such behaviour occurred again . . .
By dad! By the next letter, the tomato man had struck the officer.
Another letter from the Minister. Any assault on the officer was tan-
tamount to an assault on the Minister himself. J. thought that was
worth remembering. The Minister could not turn a blind eye to such
behaviour. The glasshouse would be confiscated immediately . . .
J. put the file back in the drawer abruptly. 'Yes, sir . . . Yes . . . The key
broke . . . Yes . . . Oh, one night isn't much . . . ' The phone rang outside in S.'s office and the clerical officer answered it. A moment later
he was back at the door: 'It's Mrs. J. asking if you're here. I told her
what happened. She said it's a long time since her rheumatism has
had such a rest. She wanted to know were you drunk to make such
an eejit of yourself . . . But if you weren't drunk, J., why did you lock
yourself in? . . . But you broke the key . . . It's not Christmas, you know,
and it's not like there's been a change of government to say that
people can just lose the run of themselves like this . . . Mrs. J. wanted
to know should she bring you in your breakfast or would you prefer a
feed of moth-eaten paper? I'll have to tell her my superior will have
to decide if it's permissible to bring breakfast into the Department . . .
Okay, I'll tell her to ring back in half an hour.' He must have done
exactly that and was back again at the other end of the keyhole almost
immediately: . . . 'But if you weren't drunk, how did you get yourself
into this mess? Breaking the key in the lock! I've always said it: you
need to start young in this business. It was like trying to break in a
mule in your case — you were too old when you started. "A brittle rod
will get no budge from a mule." The young jockey is best over the
fences . . . Do you hear me, J.? My key isn't the same as yours. God
knows where S. hid his.' J. was suddenly afraid that it had been picked
from his pocket by now somewhere on the Isle of Man. Bad cess to
those women anyway, always watching, coveting what's not theirs.
Two thoughts handcuffed themselves together in J.'s mind: that he

should tell the officer about the blonde woman and (this is the one he spoke aloud) to call S. on the Isle of Man and tell him to send back the key by registered post on the next plane. J. had no intention of waiting till the key came to let him out, but was anxious that the key be safe. Who knows—if S. couldn't carry out that instruction, J. might be promoted in his place. 'There's no precedent for that,' said the officer. 'Precedent?' said J. He had often heard the word before, but he never quite understood it the way he understood what a rule or an injunction was, or a file, or label, or memorandum, or a key, hips, blondes, women's hands groping in your trouser pockets. 'Yes, precedent,' said the clerical officer. 'I've never heard of any precedent for such an eventuality, and if there was a precedent, I would have heard of it. I started here when I was young and I know the Civil Service. I have to call the Office of Public Works. They're the Custodians of the Keys, the St. Peters of the Civil Service. Petrus, rock . . . ' With all of the breathing through it, and the rush of talk, and the manhandling on both sides, it was possible to speak quite clearly through the keyhole. 'Hallo!' said the officer outside. 'Hallo! Clerical officer. Paperkeeping. The Board of Public Works please . . . ' He was back at the keyhole again: 'What was the number on the broken key? . . . There's no number on the shaft . . . We don't know about the head except that we must assume it's in the hole here . . . You don't know the number? Like I said before, there should be . . . The Board of Public Works is responsible for hundreds of keys, thousands even . . . ' He was at the door again: 'What number is the room? . . . How would I know where the number is? . . . It's none of my business. That's a matter for the Office of Public Works. One moment . . . Hallo! Public Works! . . . Look on the left-hand side above the door, J. You can't see any number there? . . . You're the one who's supposed to be looking, J., not me. Do you know how to read at all? I've said it time and time again, there should be . . . There must be a number there; if the Board of Public Works says there's a number there, then it must be there. If there wasn't . . . scrape off the paint . . . Now, madam, calm down! . . . Hey J.,

there's a woman here who says she's Mrs. J. and that she has your breakfast. In the absence of written permission from my superior . . . '
'Where is he? . . . Is it in there you are, J., my poor old coochicoo? The best night's sleep I've ever had. My hips feel so good they'll take that lice-ridden door off its hinges . . . Why don't you do it then? . . . The desk, of course! Let you ram the table against it from that side and I'll do the same on this side. I'll flatten it with my arse. What a pig does with its snout, a woman can do with her arse! Yera, what are you saying, you bullock's waters? . . . Poor J. inside there, hungry and thirsty . . . Out of my way, you heap of snot . . . What do I care, you slimeball, what the Board of Public Works will do? What are you saying, J.? Put a pile of those filthy papers against the door and set them on fire. See how quick they let you out then . . . Yera, the devil take your hooter of a runny nose, yourself and your police . . . What do you mean, be patient, J.? Do you want to die of hunger and turn into a big pile of paper inside there? So this fella could dip his pen in his dripping nose and start writing a report on you with his snot . . . So what about the job? Wouldn't you have my fine friendly hips for company to ride as much as you like. Never mind the job, J., you're coming out whether you like it or not as soon as I break down this door. Do you hear them and their hallos? Guards! Damn ye . . . ' Just then J. heard a fierce commotion in the room outside, shouts and insults flying, swearing and cursing, everyone wishing each other to hell. Through the uproar, J. could hear her: 'Ye pack of bastards, mind my hip! Ye shower of gobshites, only God can separate me from my husband, my lawful husband. The priest said we were the one flesh, although many's the time I wished there was a customs checkpoint between J.'s withered bones and my poor old hip. Ye pack of bastards, ye shower of shits. Up the IRA . . . ' J.'s mouth was parched, his lips sticking together like hot wax. He gulped down what was left in the water jug. He heard the clerical officer's voice outside again: 'Happy days! They've put her out, this woman who claims, rightly or wrongly, that she and you are one lawful flesh . . . okay then, legitimate. But I

have made provision'—another mountain of a word that J.'s mind could only climb as far as the exposed ledge in front of him—'for her violence and bitching from here on in. Begging your pardon, I can't help my language at this crucial moment in the glorious history of this office. Just because you're legally joined together in body doesn't mean I should believe that you and she are the same in every detail. The Guards will deal with the situation from here on in . . . ' 'But do you mind me asking, sir, when I will be let out of here?' J. asked politely. 'Let out? I can't make any immediate arrangements in the matter. It is now in the hands of the Board of Public Works, and that is a considerable step forward. I would go so far as to say that it represents *the* step forward. It was passed on through the appropriate channels from me to the staff officer, from him to the administrative officer, to the assistant principal officer, and then to the principal officer and unusually—a new precedent—to the assistant secretary. How's that for progress! The assistant secretary deferred the matter, quite properly, to the Board of Public Works, since there was no key and no right way of . . . ' 'How long will it take the Board to get here, sir?' 'I can't answer that question. The matter is out of my hands, out of the hands of this section. I would go so far as to say that it is out of the hands of this Department. A matter cannot be taken out of the hands of a particular department unless it is passed on to some other person or party.' In J.'s mind, the idea of matters-in-hand was like trying to pick up mercury with his fingers. God be with the good old days—he could understand what it meant to take a woman in hand, but he couldn't allow himself to dwell on such things. The only thing he could think to say was, 'But isn't this room part of the Department, sir?' 'As a result of a proper decision having been taken, and, for present purposes only, that room is temporarily the responsibility of the Board of Public Works, that is to say, in a limited sense only and for the purposes of opening the door; the room can therefore be seen as physically a part of this building, but, for the purposes of the Civil Service in this instance, a part of the Board of Public Works, without prejudice to the jurisdiction of the Department in respect of rights of entry from without and other statutory rights that are reserved by this Department and that cannot be transferred without several acts and orders being repealed. The Board of Public Works will have no entitlement to rent or rates as a result of its temporary possession of the room for the aforementioned purpose, and you yourself will be subject to neither rent nor rates. There is no precedent for such . . . '

'Sir, I'm parched with the thirst and famished with the hunger. I need to go again soon, sir, and this time I'm thinking it's a major operation.' The pub talk of the old days was shuffling around in J.'s mind, unbeknownst to him and in spite of him. 'As you know, these matters have nothing to do with the protocols of the Civil Service. As a fellow human being, if I can distinguish between my existence as a human being and my responsibilities as a civil servant, you have my sympathy. I regret, as things stand, that I can do nothing except fulfil my duties here as a Cú Chulainn of the State. En passant, I must point out to you that, in my opinion, as a human being—and this is not an official decision—in your present circumstances, you have ceased, for the time being, if you follow me, to be an acting civil servant . . . '

J.'s blood was a whirlpool, a donnybrook . . . 'It requires an act of violence to break down a Civil Service door and no individual and no corporate entity has the right to do that, except the Board of Public Works. And when they perform an authorised operation that would be termed an illegal act of violence if perpetrated by you or me, it is no longer a violent act but an appropriate intervention . . . I don't know, my good man, when they will do it, or how, but one must presume that they will do what they will do in due course and in the appropriate fashion.' J. had to sit down on the chair. He hadn't the strength to stand by the keyhole any longer. He stayed like that a long time, half asleep and half awake—half dead and half alive, he thought from time to time. Someone knocked at the door, almost as politely as J. did whenever he had to go in to S.: 'I'm the man from the Board of Public Works . . . What number was on the key? . . . Do you know who or where they got it from or when the lock was put on the door? . . . What number is the room? . . . I can't find anything in this file unless I have the details to guide me . . . I'll respond to this memo and send it on to my supervisor.' J. recognised the particular tone of the man's voice: that was exactly how the clerical officer had spoken when he said that J.'s situation had been handed over to the Board of Public Works, that it was a step forward, *the* step forward. His case was gathering momentum now, climbing up as far as the supervisor. J. sat down again. He had lost all track of time. The phone rang. He gripped it tightly with shaking hands: 'A call for you, Mr. J. . . . And please tell your wife to stop abusing me. There's nothing I can do. I only look after the switchboard . . . ' God Almighty! It was a good omen to get a phone call. A whirlpool of blood surged into his ears. J. felt as if there was a woman materialising through the receiver, skin, bone, flesh, hips, and all: 'You're not even half a man. You're nothing. I've told you before. Giving in to them snotty bastards. Throw every top-heavy filing cabinet in the place against the door and make flitters of it. If you wait much longer, you won't have the strength to do it. I'll get on to the papers, and the Bishop. May that bitch on the switchboard get my rheumatism and my bad hip—' The line went dead . . . A minute later, the telephone rang again. Today it was ringing as often as S.'s. 'Mr. J. . . . The Board of Public Works . . . Supervisor Number Nine here. What number is the key? . . . How long has the lock been there? Have you any idea of the year even? . . . The room number? All I can do is send a memo to Supervisor Number Eleven.' Slowly but surely, his situation was climbing onwards and upwards. But even the sun was slow to rise sometimes. J. had to go to the toilet again. He thought of using the jug, but the jug belonged to the Civil Service in a way that the floor didn't. The jug could be moved about like a file or a memorandum. He was in mid-flow when the phone rang. Oh my God, would it ever stop ringing! 'Is that you, Mr. J. . . . The *Little Irelander* here. Our sources tell us you're locked in. Will you do an interview with me? If we don't make the evening edition, we'll put it—'

J. informed him that no one could get in or out of the room. He was thinking on his feet, trying to find a good excuse for not talking. The voice on the other end became smooth as new milk from a cow's teat: 'But you can answer my questions right now on the phone.' J. nearly dropped the receiver. But paperkeepers were honour bound to be civil. And yet the first commandment of the Civil Service was, 'For the benefit of the State and your own peace of mind, never answer a question about yourself, your work, the Civil Service, no matter who asks, but especially a journalist.' But the reporter coaxed information from him as gently and skilfully as a woman coaxing milk from a cow: that he had been locked in all night with nothing to eat. He came to his senses all of a sudden and would give no more information, even if his life depended on it. He was sweating again. He felt as dry as hot sand from his lips to his belly, and not a drop left in the jug. He tilted it to one side to try and gather whatever few drops were left and then raised it to his mouth. The telephone rang. He was getting more calls than S. the busiest day he ever had. It was Number Eleven. He had no precise details concerning the key. Since they couldn't get the original one, they would have to try whole bunches of them, an eternity of keys, and there might be a slight delay since every key in every single key-room would have to be acquired, requested and acknowledged in the appropriate fashion. The same diligent care would be required for this operation as finding a single flea in a barrel of fleas. To hell with him and his fleas, J. was itching all over again! They'd hardly get the job done before dinner. But they'd be back by half two, three, anyway, and they should have got as far as the door by four at the very latest . . . Things were slowing down, as per usual. Although he was not very experienced in the ways of the Civil Service, J. knew there was an unwritten rule that nothing should ever be done in a hurry. This putting things on the long finger, or indeed, not doing them at all, was a defence mechanism, a guarantee that things would be done properly—eventually. Not to do something at all was to ensure that it was not done incorrectly. That made sense. A lot of sense.

It used to be said that the human element, and even the weather, could not be discounted in the work of the Civil Service. If a memo was written on an overcast day, it was usually held back until a fine day for revision and correction. There would at least be a flicker of hope in that particular version. But then that version might be considered excessively optimistic, so the gloomiest person in the office would be set to work, and still the matter would have to be deferred. J. felt, therefore, that he could hardly complain when what was happening to him was something he believed in and, in all likelihood, participated in every day in the Civil Service. The phone was ringing again. How many times was that? More than S. ever got, anyway. It was the parish priest. Who'd have thought it? The ways of the Civil Service were strange, the priest said. J. had a ready-made response—like the ways of God. The priest had phoned TDs, ministers even, and was expecting a result without delay. He was confident that J. had the necessary spiritual resolve to endure greater tribulations than this. When J. asked if his position as a paperkeeper was safe, he answered that he would see to it and that he could rest assured on that count. Mrs. J. could hardly be blamed for being a little out of sorts and telling anyone who would listen that all she wanted was to have J. back home. It didn't require much effort on J.'s part to imagine what his Old One had actually said: that it would be a great comfort to have him back in the bed beside her practising for the Civil Service sports on her hips. The clerical officer spoke to him again, on the telephone this time. That he should contact J. by telephone was a promotion in itself. It was quarter to four. Why had J. given an interview to a newspaper? A stop-press edition had been printed. A scandal in the Public Service, a service the general public thought of as efficient and considerate. The story had already travelled the length and breadth of the country. The English papers would have it tomorrow. The Opposition would exploit it. And the Six Counties. It was no use J. muttering that any damage to the Service was like a wound on his own body. For all the talk of scandal, J. couldn't conceal his desperate need: 'A drop of water on my tongue. Even a single drop . . . ' 'How do you propose that we do that? . . . Stick a funnel through a jammed keyhole? . . . Nurses have instruments for relieving patients that are constipated . . . I'm not a nurse and I'm not from the Board of Public Works. An assistant secretary came to the door in person a while ago. That was a first. He put on his glasses and examined the lock, but, bien entendu, declared it a matter for the Board of Public Works . . . ' J. hadn't heard the assistant secretary at the door. Nonetheless, he had to take it on trust that he had been there, that he had gone to such lengths for his sake . . . In the Civil Service, one had to believe certain things without seeing or hearing them. The Civil Service itself was an act of faith, as indeed was every civil servant. 'I can't hurry the Board of Public Works. It's up to them. You must appreciate, J., that they have other responsibilities besides opening jammed locks. Their responsibilities are considerable. Opening gaps. Closing gaps. Putting furniture into new offices and sections that are born to the Service every day. Providing a new desk for the Minister's office. Replacing the doors of the state prison that were broken by the political prisoners during a riot. They would have to give priority to the prison doors over all other locks and keys. And there are other jammed locks, hundreds of them perhaps, throughout the Service . . . The Board of Public Works are unlikely to be here before half past four . . . Yes, J., I do realise that that is very close to closing time . . . I don't know whether or not any provision has been made for such an eventuality . . . I've never heard of a civil servant breaking a key inside a lock before. If there were a precedent, but since there isn't . . . Keep moving your tongue; that will moisten it for you . . . ' J. decided to do something drastic. He lifted the receiver and called the girl on the switchboard. 'Number, please.' 'The Archbishop.' 'The Catholic Archbishop? Do you know his number? . . . I'll be finishing my shift here in a couple of minutes . . . There you go . . . You're through now.' He was through to the Archbishop's Residence, but His Grace was in Rome. They had been advised of his situation and were monitoring it closely. The nuns were praying for him. Mrs. J. had nearly demolished the Palace with a furious shower of curses. She could hardly be blamed . . . It would be a great comfort to everyone if His Grace were at home, but he wasn't due back until Friday. They would telephone him later. With the help of God . . . God's help was always at hand . . . It hadn't occurred to J. that the telephone would be cut off. The clerical officer came back to the door with the executive officer and the assistant secretary. 'We're trying to get the Board of Public Works to put the skids on,' said the assistant secretary. 'Skids . . . on . . . ,' J. repeated after him without thinking. The assistant secretary was still speaking: 'I think I've got them to agree to stay on after hours. They'll be here presently. Goodbye now. I'll be back later.' J. got the message: the assistant secretary was going for his tea, or a pint, maybe two pints even, to the corner pub. He had gone in to the corner pub himself after work last Christmas Eve, but as soon as he saw the assistant secretary leaning against the counter, he'd turned around and left. Who knows what the assistant secretary might have thought if he happened to bump into him with a belly full of porter? That J. might be selling files, memoranda, white papers? J. had heard of a paperkeeper who swiped from a Minister's desk an advance copy of a Government white paper on restricting the migration of swallows, sold it to those parties who were agitating for its amendment, and had his ill-gotten gains stolen from his breast pocket by a woman in a public house. The assistant secretary was gone. Tea. Porter. Water. Any liquid at all. Just the tip of a pin's worth of something wet on his tongue. He went to get the jug. His legs made their own protest, getting in each other's way, out of control. He had often had too much to drink, but his legs had never let him down in quite the same way before. He put the jug to his lips. There was some remnant of dampness trickling from it, but his arms refused to do as they were told and it ended up running down his chin. Although his finger was no more obedient to his will than his arms and legs, he ran it along the inside of the jug, then placed it on his tongue that was dry as paper . . . He was half asleep, semi-conscious, when he came to with a start. His heart skipped a beat. They were knocking at the door. 'It's me . . . Patsy Fitzprick, your local TD. You know me well, I'm Fine Fáil? I'll have you out of that hole in less than an hour, sooner, if I can . . . It's a disgrace. But it's no wonder: the Boss made one mistake, understandable enough in the circumstances, when he left a shower of Fianna Gaelers in the Office of Public Works the time we went into Government. That gave them control and since they know you're Fine Fáil—' 'But I never said . . . which party . . . I was for . . . Civil servants . . . are not permitted . . .' J. couldn't go on; every word from the other side hit him like a blow from a blade-bright sword. 'I can't believe that a man of your intelligence, who has learned the ways of the Civil Service, would be a Fianna Gael man.' 'I didn't say—' That was as much as J. could manage. 'I'll be back.' He heard the footsteps retreating like the mercy of God, who couldn't open a Civil Service door . . . The door shook on its hinges! Someone had given it an almighty kick on the other side: 'Do you hear me in there, you eejit? There I was, sitting down to my tea. Do you hear me? . . . The phone rang. The Old Lady came in to me. "Supervisor N. wants you, A.," says she. "Supervisor N.," says I. "It's a strange time for Supervisor N. to call, while a man is having his tea." "Don't look at me," said the Old Lady, "but he says it's urgent, really urgent." "Bad luck to him anyway," says I. "Look here, boy," says N. "You'd better go down to where that clown is locked in, bad luck to him, anyway," says N. "Bad luck to him is right," says I. No word of a lie. D'you hear me? "No sooner was I in the door from work," says N., "than the Chief Supervisor of Urgent Affairs was on the phone." "The Assistant Secretary from Public Works," says Urgent Affairs, "had that driveller of a TD Patsy Fitzprick on to him" . . . I'm telling you there's no Patsy Fitzprick out here. Maybe that was him I passed on my way in. "Leave it till tomorrow. I'll look into it first thing in the morning," says the Assistant Secretary for Public Works. "Bad luck to him anyways. Maybe the clown will have taken the high jump if we wait till tomorrow," says Patsy Fitzprick. "It's a coffin you'll need for him then."

"Public Works doesn't provide coffins," says the Assistant Secretary. "That would be in breach of Private Enterprise." "Well, you have to do something," says Fitzprick. "But I'm no longer on duty," says the Assistant Secretary. "All I'm asking is that someone open the lock; that's all, to open the lock. It's worth two, three, five votes maybe, for me to get that door open," says Fitzprick. "If you don't do something, and send someone down with a hammer and a pair of pliers and an axe immediately—" "An axe! God forbid! Are you suggesting that a door, a Civil Service door—" "I don't care if you do it with your prick, so long as you do it right away," says Patsy Fitzprick. "First thing in the morning." "Don't mind the morning; do it now, right this minute, as quick as a goat would shit on cow dung," says Fitzprick, "or I'll bring it up in the Dáil—and you with it." "But what kind of fool is he that locked himself in? . . . " "That's beside the point," says Fitzprick. The Assistant Secretary rang Urgent Affairs. "Bad luck to him anyway," says Urgent Affairs. "Bad luck to him is right," says the Assistant Secretary, "but it's your responsibility as Chief Supervisor of Urgent Affairs. I am formally handing responsibility over to you; it's in your hands now . . . " "But I'm off duty," says Urgent Affairs, "and I got no memo about the matter. I couldn't take a feather to that door without a memo." "With or without a memo, I'm instructing you to deal with it without further delay . . . " Bloody Patsy Fitzprick. He's about to be made a parliamentary secretary. What do you bet he'll be put in charge of us here in Public Works. We're like a hospital for every gammy leg of a parliamentary secretary, every useless eejit in the Government. He's making public statements about new brooms and all that, cleaning the place up . . . I'm revealing departmental secrets now, J. To hell with them. We're tradesmen here in Public Works, not like the fat lumps of blotting paper that pass for civil servants. We couldn't care less about those sourpuss pen-pushing pansies . . . Anyway, Urgent Affairs called Supervisor N. "A memo," says N. "Memo or no memo," says Urgent Affairs. "The first job on the list for tomorrow," says Supervisor N. "Immediately," says Urgent Affairs. "Patsy

Fitzprick, the next Parliamentary Secretary in the Works . . . " That's when Supervisor N. rang me, A. That was what had the Old Lady in a tizzy and me in the middle of my tea. "What sort of eejit would lock himself in?" says I. "Eejit is right, you can say that again," says Supervisor N., "but go over anyway, A., and take—" "No one said anything to me about it," says I. "Things have to be done right. What's the world coming to at all? Soon there'll be no memos. I'm going to the Bingo tonight. First thing tomorrow morning . . . " "Look," says N., "this Patsy Fitzprick . . . " "Bad luck to him anyway," says I . . . No word of a lie . . . "But where will I get the tools?" says I. "The tools are locked away. That fella with the gap between his teeth, U., will have to open the store. He'll need written permission from B. to do that. Not only is he deaf, he's the kind of fella who, if he had the pen, he'd be missing the ink, and if he had both, he'd be missing the necessary forms. Anyway, the pens, ink, and papers are all locked away since five. In order to obtain permission—" "Look," says N., "you'd need at least a day to wade through the shitload of forms and the whole shebang." "This is an emergency." "I thought the emergency finished at the end of the war," says I. "This is an emergency," N. exploded like a megaton bomb. "Urgent Affairs. Patsy Fitzprick. Get a screwdriver and a hammer, I don't care if you have to steal them, A. Take off the lock. Let the clown out of the locked room. Break his neck for all I care once he's out, or drill a hole in his back and give him a good kicking, unofficially of course. We can cover it up in the memo by saying you were helping him out of the room when he fell and broke his neck. There isn't a doctor in the Civil Service who will contradict you. We'll all go to the funeral. A half-day in the Office. Only put back the lock again so it looks like it's been fixed. It doesn't matter a damn if it falls apart again as soon as someone touches it with the tip of a wet finger, so long as it can't be said it was the Board of Public Works that broke it, or left it broken after them . . . You'll have to go over there right away, A. Patsy Fitzprick! . . . " Can you hear me in there, J.? I won't break your neck, but make no mistake, if you insist on staying in that room, I have the authority to use all necessary force to evict you from a place that is, for present purposes, appropriated by the Office of Public Works. Do you hear me? . . . ' A voice as harsh as a saw cut through A.'s voice outside. 'It's me . . . your local TD, Benny Fartling, Fianna Gael, who else? Yes, another example of Fine Fáil's incompetence . . . When we were in Government, no individual, no matter how hard he tried, could lock himself in like this. It's no wonder! You only have to take one look at that Patsy Fitzprick . . . Let's see now. I'll put this in the public domain. I will. You'll get compensation. I'll see to it that the Dáil and the Seanad are forced to sit within four hours. An emergency sitting . . . But this has gone beyond politics. It has nothing to do with you personally, except to the extent that your welfare is now inextricably linked to the welfare of the country. Leave it to me . . . ' It seemed as though Benny Fartling and A. had both left. Fartling must have chased A. away as soon as he arrived. J. was trying to collect his thoughts, like someone trying to make out a shape shrouded in darkness. Benny Fartling had got rid of A. so that no one else would share the credit for getting J. out. J. had lost all control of his limbs by this stage. He groped his way as far as the pipe. As soon as he touched the cold living lead, his whole body began to tremble. It was summer and there was no water in the pipe. Maybe there was, only it was cold water. He could break the pipe. No, he couldn't. Breaking a pipe was an even worse crime than breaking a door. Anyway, how could he break it? The pipe ran through the whole service like a transport system, an artery that circulated authority. He felt helpless as a fly caught in the grip of that strong pipe. If it had anything resembling horns, J. could well believe he was in the same room as the devil; it was black as hell. He began picking flakes of plaster and paper from the wall and sucking them to try and keep his mouth moist. Then he remembered that there must be a wet patch in the corner. He had heard it was poisonous. At that moment he would gladly have swallowed anything wet, even poison, if only he could bend down far enough to reach it. Why hadn't he relieved himself in the jug? There wasn't a drop left in his body. He thought of the hair oil on his head, but it had dried out and his hair was a mess after the night. He chewed the mildewed cover of one of the forgotten files in the corner of a cabinet, leaving only the label with its title on it. He felt reckless—tempted—the pipe was the cause of it all—in a way he had never felt before. He started on a second file that wasn't as mildewed as the first one, except that this time the mildew was on the musty papers inside the file. The commotion outside drew him back to the door. 'I'm Paschal Lambe. Your Independent TD. An intolerable injustice has been done to you and I give you my word there'll be hell to pay . . . You want me to break down the door from this side? . . . I'd be delighted to, only I can't . . . It's like one of those huge rocks you see balanced on a hillside back home. The slightest touch will topple it, but a small army wouldn't put it back where it was. It's typical of the Government and the Opposition, a way of trapping people and undermining them. They'll have bribed the coroner's court to say it was an accident and that no one could be held responsible. Then the Government can say that emigration figures are dropping. I've raised numerous questions already in the Dáil about these inquests. The last one was about the big wall the Board of Public Works left . . . The Minister said it was a dirty black lie, that I had spoken strongly against moving the wall last year, that tourists wanted to see it. Of course, what I actually said was that moving the wall would be dangerous, a public hazard. But the Minister twisted my words, saying that wasn't what I meant, and that he didn't have the statutory power to grant the widow a pension . . . This door is a job for the Fire Brigade. I'll call them right away . . . Could you not set the place on fire? Can't you set a match to a bundle of papers, and the whole place smothered with paper . . . Now, now . . . a little fire will do you no harm, and you'll be rescued right away. The Fire Brigade is fully authorised to rescue people and property. It's the easiest way through this "chevaux-de-frise" of protocol—that's the term the Minister kept throwing in our faces last year, trying to pull the wool over our eyes on the Archaeology vote . . . A plague on this paper! It won't light. Too damp. Government neglect . . . God almighty tonight, J., do you know what it is—the Record of Dáil Debates with my speech about the wall. No wonder it wouldn't light. May God preserve the truth, now and forever . . . I'll call the Fire Brigade. It's all the same, so long as there's a smell of burning. As soon as someone smells burning, the Fire Brigade can take action as quickly as if there was a conflagration for all to see. They can smash windows, demolish walls, break down doors . . . A smell is only a clue, a kind of philosophical attribute. What stinks to heaven for one person is perfume for another. They say that what the sensory perception of one person's nose deciphers as foul-smelling according to its faculty of discernment, the next person's nose will translate as sweet perfume . . . I'm surprised you never heard that, J. The Dáil Bar is a great education. I'm not saying the drink now . . . '

J. crawled on his belly to a damp patch on the wall that had been left behind when a cabinet was moved. He began licking the spot frantically, all the way up the panelled wall as far as he could reach on his knees. There was a knocking at the door again, and he crawled back to it: 'Your corporation alderman Ernest Bellowes here. They weren't going to let me in. The Minister had to be called. There were only twenty votes between me and his own yes-man at the last election. Do you see now, J., how little respect they have for you in this miserable little country. And you a martyr to your duties. In any other country, you'd be a hero. In Russia—and believe me I'm no Communist, I'm a Catholic—you'd be made a hero of the Soviet Union; they'd give you a hundred thousand rubles as a prize, a pension right away, a villa in Moscow, and free time every day to visit Lenin's mausoleum. I'll raise blue bloody murder. I'll go out on the streets, door to door; I'll get you a full pension right away . . . Well, okay, a promotion at any rate . . . We'll make you a Senior, no problem. I'll be in the Dáil after the next election, or by-election maybe. Mr. Silver-Tongue, the Fianna Gael candidate in our constituency, has a dodgy ticker. Every voter in the place knows that Buckley, the Fine Fáiler from the east of the city, will kill himself some night with his drink driving . . . You want a priest? I'll bring him in myself. What would you prefer? A Franciscan? A Carmelite? A Jesuit? I prefer the Jesuit myself. He always notices the blisters on the working man's hands and looks at them closely, sympathetically you'd think . . . Yera, fuck that for a game of soldiers, they'll have to let the priest in to you. If they don't, I'll shout it from every rooftop in Ireland that this is a pagan country, with a pagan Government, worse than Russia, that its soul is blacker than Africa, and it has twice as many sins as that cesspit London . . . Oh, you don't want to create a fuss? You get nowhere in this place without making a fuss; it's the last refuge of the poor and the weak. It was by making a fuss that I scared the shit out of that Sullivan fella in the paper scandal. As you know, he had the market cornered and sold half the paper in the country to the Jehovah's Witnesses for books of sermons . . . Well you're the only one who doesn't know it then. If you knew anything at all, you wouldn't be turning to dust inside there. D'you know what I'll do? I'll go out into the highways and byways; I'll leave no stone unturned, no possibility unexplored. I'll turn your predicament into a national emergency. They'll have to bring in the Army like they do when the buses are on strike. . . . Yera, there's a fear of them . . . The Army's engineer corps. They'll have it sorted in half an hour, an hour at the most. Nelson's arse was a greater challenge, and it didn't take them long to blow him up. There you have it. The Army.' J. stayed exactly where he had fallen by the door, clutching the handle with his left hand like a drowning man. The voice of Deputy Rush, from the Sweat Party, shouting at him was like the distant crash of a wave against a cliff: 'You give them the last drop of your sweat and they grow fat on the back of it. Big houses, big cars, big women, big jobs, big bellies from the sweat of the underfed. That's it: fat cats pay no heed to famished mice. They're up there right now in the Castle eating and drinking on the sweat of the poor, and their wives beside them with their big bellies, big arses, big hips, big breasts, big thighs. Would it happen anywhere else under the sun besides this

misfortunate country of ours? I brought a bill before the Dáil to protect workers from catching colds from their workmates. Do you know
the latest thing that medical research has discovered about colds?
That the smell of sweat can spread it, or the smell of a fart. The Minister claimed there was no evidence for it and threw out the bill. I
introduced another bill to control the prices charged by prostitutes
and asked that the matter be referred to the Fair Prices Commission.
Between ourselves, it would help to provide equal opportunities for
the man who earns his living by the sweat of his brow, but I had to say
the opposite in order to get what I wanted. What I said was that as
soon as illicit pleasures, traditionally the preserve of the well off, became available to everyone, demand for such dubious delights would
decline. Do you know what the Minister said? That there were no
prostitutes in Ireland, and if there were, the police could deal with
them. All they want is to keep all the perks for the rich. Look at the
injustice that is being done to you . . . You want a priest? With all due
respect, the bill I proposed would have benefitted the clergy. As soon
as prostitution had lost its attraction, the priests could divert their
energies into opposing something else—communism, for instance.
I'm telling you, it's not just you that's suffering from injustice, but
others like you as well. The last time your wife came to my clinic complaining about her rheumatism, she said the worst nights were when
you started twisting and turning in the bed like Christy Ring scoring
a goal. Wouldn't it be a great relief to your poor crippled wife if every
now and again you could get out of a Friday or a Saturday night, into
a public house, like they do in Spain, another Catholic country . . . A
priest, you say? Do you know how many priests there are in Spain?
The most Catholic country in the world, they say, and the one with
the most prostitutes. I'm not speaking from personal experience here,
because I was never in Spain . . . Of course, you're trying to get out
of here! Didn't I read it in the papers and hear it on the news? I was
very sorry to be out when your wife called in to me at home. She
nearly killed my own missus, chasing after her with her walking stick.

Is it any wonder she was spitting and cursing, the poor woman. Look, you'll be out as quick as a whore would rob a drunk man, the kind of thing my bill would have put an end to. Wait till I go down to the Liberty Lounge, the party's drinking hole, and get my brother Mickey Rush. He was a locksmith by trade before he was elected secretary of the union. He opened the lock on a door for a friend and colleague of mine the other day. Just between the two of us, it had nothing to do with politics. There was a woman with a room on the other side of the wall from my friend, same as if she was in this room here now and you on the other side of the wall. A lock can close or open all kinds of things, as the fella said. I won't be—' J. slumped down against the door. He raised his knees but got little relief from the pain . . . He was sufficiently conscious to hear the shouting and abuse outside. The Sweat Deputy had come back with the locksmith Mickey Rush and all his equipment. He was laying in to the door when the Guards stopped him, on the instructions of the civil servants who had taken advice on the matter: 'A private locksmith cannot interfere with a door such as this unless requested to do so by the Board of Public Works. Do you have written authorisation from the Board of Public Works? No. Where is A.? If you give the equipment to A., he can do it . . . A. is not available?' The outer room was a watchtower sounding all kinds of alarms. For a long time Sweat Deputy's voice nestled comfortingly in J.'s ear, but even that didn't last. The Army was the best and least complicated solution, all things considered. The Government issued an emergency order that was taken to the Minister for Defence in the Castle to sign and pass on to the Chief of Staff, who had to be followed from Headquarters to the Castle. He, in turn, informed the Director of the Engineer Corps, who was found in the Castle after he was discovered not to be at Headquarters or at home. The engineers were either asleep, on marital leave, or on other forms of leave. Telephones were ringing, messengers on motorbikes going back and forth, transport being arranged. A warrant was issued by the Board of Public Works that kept a tight grip on that part of its authority until the bitter end. Two Senior Supervisors were present which meant that the secretary himself had to be woken at an ungodly hour as he slept like an old ruin after his day's work in the Castle. It was said that Patsy Fitzprick was mostly to blame in the end for the delay. He was deadweight, in the way, an obstacle to the urgent matter at hand. He insisted to anyone who would listen that if it wasn't for him, the Army would never have been called in and that J. would have died in that hole for want of assistance. In the heel of the hunt, he managed to slip into where the action was, in between the two Senior Supervisors, something no other public representative had managed to do. Dawn was breaking when they finally reached J. His knees were raised up as straight as was possible for a man with flat feet and stumpy legs, his dishevelled hair covering his eyes, his head to one side against the bottom of the door, and the cover of a file in his mouth as if he was kissing it. It is rumoured that it was one of the forgotten files and that they were unable to get it out of his clenched mouth without cutting it. The priest gave J. conditional absolution. Patsy Fitzprick said a Rosary single-handed and produced four masscards that he always carried in case of such an eventuality. It was the considered opinion of the independent doctor that Sweat Deputy, Benny Fartling, Paschal Lambe, and Ernest Bellowes insisted be admitted that coronary thrombosis was the cause of death, precipitated specifically by hunger and thirst, along with palpitations brought on by anxiety and trepidation. A Civil Service doctor disagreed with those findings but demanded permission to reserve his evidence until the coroner's inquest. The Board of Public Works managed to salvage something from the episode: the two pieces of the Broken Key.

TRANSLATED BY
LOUIS DE PAOR AND LOCHLAINN Ó TUAIRISG

FROM *AN tSRAITH DHÁ TÓGÁIL*
(1970)

RELEASE

Tomás was on his way home. He had to cross a river, canals: they reminded him of fresh graffiti, a cruel tattoo disfiguring the pale arms of the city. The image scuttled along the path, the right-of-way it had beaten into his brain.

The slapping water whispered suggestively in his ear. He imagined something much worse than any picture or tattoo, than any familiar sound: great slimy creatures in heat coupling in a steaming swamp. The water was ahead of him. When he could no longer avoid looking, it morphed horribly again; the sun on the water was a gold dish covering fruit rotted to a stinking pulp . . . What a place to go swimming! In water so sluggish he thought at first the man was swimming more strongly than he was. It was almost obscene to Tomás that human flesh should touch the stained skin of that filthy water. It was definitely a human being down there. What was visible of him above water—slender back, shoulder blades, neck, and head—was a bright candle celebrating this festival of sunlight . . .

There was a time, not so long ago, when Tomás would have enjoyed this feast of youth and sun. He heard a man with a posh accent remark to another man that the splashing of the water below was refreshing, and consequently a tonic, for anybody. A dip in the water was a new lease of life for young and old, said the other man in a flatter, more country, accent. This timely marriage of sun and water was sending a fountain of laughter tinkling by him, said the posh one . . . Tomás looked at them—it was a relief to look at something other than the man in the water—but he did not tell them how their precious water had fastened a tight lock on his own laughter with no key to open it . . .

His wife had explained this in private to her friends by saying Tomás was a poet. There were poets for whom waves lapping on the shore, waterfalls, streams and riverlets were the greatest of all things. It seems there were other poets . . . well, we all have our hang-ups, she said. Lots of people are frightened of loud noises, unnerved by rasping sounds. The slap or gurgle of water was enough to set off Tomás's twisted imagination. More than that, the tingling it aroused extended to every inch of his body. He could have said to those two that for him it would be a sovereign remedy, a new lease of life, to have the water out of his sight and hearing even if it was still there waiting under the hood of his mind . . .

He heard a cry, like a rabbit or some other small creature might make, a sound he could hardly describe, but clearly a cry of distress. The swimmer was among the reeds and weeds, in a stretch of water where it was hard to make out right away if what was there was some natural growth or discarded human refuse. He was on his side now, his shoulders and slender back submerged. The one who had been like a new god performing miracles of sun and youth a short time ago was now no more than a drooping, wilted thing, his head down, unable to keep it up. His body was a key, reduced to a stump, rattling impotently in a lock that wouldn't budge or let him go.

'Keep going! Keep going, son!' The shouts fluttered like a frightened bird from the quickly gathering crowd.

'Throw him a rope! Here! Quick!'

'A rope! It's as bad as the sea for drownings, this shithouse of a river.

'When I think of the rates we have to pay for water.'

'I've said it before and I'll say it again: they won't do a bloody thing about it until someone plants a steel toe-cap in the Mayor's hole and fucks him into it.'

'And the Minister with him . . . '

Tomás quickened his stride and lengthened his step. There were always people delighted to have the pain of some other unfortunate to stoke the fire and turn it to a blazing row. The rest of it, too, he had seen before: anxiety turning to horror and then despair—like punters studying the quickly scribbled, quickly changing bookies' numbers, as the race came down to the wire . . .

One man stood dangerously close to the edge. Amazing how he had made a signal station of himself, facing the crowd and the swimmer by turns. The shifting of the crowd almost knocked him into the water. Instead of the silly, slightly creative gestures he had been making until then, his body gave an involuntary twist to make sure his feet stayed on dry land. The abuse he got from one of the crowd was an epitaph to his naive efforts, drawing Signal Station's eyes reluctantly back to the weeds:

'A pity you didn't trip over your gammy leg and fall in arse over tip, you gobshite! Who asked you to get involved? Right arm forward, left arm back! You wouldn't be half as quick to put your own right arm in the water!'

Tomás's eyes did not follow the terrified look the other man cast out on the water . . .

'God help us! Is there a single excuse for a man among ye who knows how to swim?' The middle-aged woman was so exercised that every trace of her personality was obliterated, reduced to an engine of concern, for death and life.

'He hasn't gone under yet.'

Tomás had turned his back on the water when the swimmer sank. In spite of himself, almost, he imagined the gentle grip of that still water, relentless as the soft, insistent embrace of a shroud. His twisted imagination saw clearly the water smoothing away the man's wrinkles, closing over him, the bubbles rising one by one like a difficult report being written, each one of them bursting at the surface more flatulent and contemptuous than the previous one. An obscene ritual, said Tomás. And other unharnessed words that were trotting around in his head began to see that this was the bridle they needed: an obscene ritual . . . death's door . . . the mouth of the grave . . .

'Fuck the lot of ye! A man drowning! Wimps! If I have to do it myself . . .': the man took one sprightly step on his crutches towards the water. The other foot stayed put, as though it had a mind of its own, some secret knowledge the rest of the body knew nothing about, and no intention of moving. People like that infuriated Tomás. Easy for him to make brave with his bold words. His conscience did what he told it to do, as did his crutches, pretty much, and the medication he received for the gammy leg, free gratis from the State. He was uselessness personified, the old fart, with his stiff shanks and his pair of crutches like two big nostrils torn apart sniffing the danger ahead of them cantankerously, but cautiously.

The rest were no better. Tomás was certain the reason they were hanging back was they knew full well, now that things were coming to a head, the best they were capable of was to be loudmouthed windbags outside the unhearing walls of destiny. To console themselves for doing nothing, they became even more agitated, more anguished. That they had no way of reaching the poor wretch in the water didn't stop them shuffling about among themselves. Unable to reach the swimmer, they found plenty to occupy their empty hands: planks of wood from the path, branches on the edge of the water, left over ice cream wrappers, orange skins, empty cigarette packs and matchboxes, handles of buckets, saplings yanked from the riverbank: things they were subconsciously drawn to because they were as useless and ineffectual as themselves. As soon as they picked them up, they threw them away again in disgust. No sooner had one person thrown something away than someone else picked it up . . .

One of the women stood out from the rest. Her voice was so shrill, so sharp and penetrating, that Tomás had to look twice at her to be sure that noise was coming from a human being. As if the voice needed some kind of accompaniment, she clapped her hands fiercely without taking her eyes from the edge of the reeds where the game of bubbles was still going on.

'Leon! Leon, my darling! My only child. My little lamb! Let me out to him! . . . I don't care if I drown . . . '

Tomás thought the people beside her weren't holding her back so strongly that she couldn't have broken free. After a while they let go of her altogether, as if they wanted something else to occupy them. As soon as they released her, she fainted.

The women were going demented.

'You coward! You regimental bastard!' said one half-blind one to a stocky middle-aged man who was moving away from the water ahead of Tomás. Her accusing finger was pointing past the jut of his hip towards the clear outline of his crotch. All he could see was the shrug of the man's shoulders as if to say he had enough troubles of his own. He spelled it out for her too:

'I have thirteen of them at home,' he said, turning towards the woman. Tomás had to face her too.

He heard another man respond irritably to another shrew. Tomás was too preoccupied with making his own way through to see the man, but it was easy to imagine his face creased in a sour smile as he laughed bitterly:

'Would he jump in for me if he was in my shoes and I the one drowning?'

A woman with dishevelled hair was on the path in front of him trying to push a well-built young fella she had cornered down towards the bank:

'Too fond of yourself and your big balls.'

There was no mistaking where her hand was pointing. Other women clustered around her, their eyes like magic lanterns following her hand as though it were pointing at the battle-halo over a warrior's head.

'I haven't worked in two years,' he said, pushing her away, making it clear that if anyone was going to end up in the river, it was her. 'And I won't lift a finger today either, my dear woman, not for him anyway. The man whose balls are safe and sound should give thanks for them: what other comfort or luxury is there for a man on the dole? I wish a few more would drown . . . He's a construction worker! That shower—'

Tomás didn't hear the rest. A woman was pawing him all over. Wasn't it amazing how excitable women were? Especially in situations like this, in the midst of danger and disaster! Or anywhere trouble was brewing—they were in their element! It occurred to Tomás that there was good reason for this: women were closer to life than men. They were shackled to it. For his part, hero or not, the man should be as gallant as a soldier. But the woman had to wait, watch, and suffer, guiding and comforting. No wonder it was her destiny to be a high priestess wherever the cruel contest, the deadly game of death and life, was played . . .

'In the name of God and His blessed mother'—the woman's words hammered into him like nails. 'Don't refuse the mother of God. What if it was Jesus Christ—how do you know it's not? You'd never forgive yourself for letting Him drown. It's not even deep out there. A man as tall as you could wade out to Him. The rest of your life will be all the better for our prayers. I'll go to Lourdes for you. He's an only child. You have two choices: the widow's curse or the widow's blessing. Come on! Imagine it was your son, your daughter, your wife. You're a married man. I pray God and His blessed mother it never comes to your door—'

For a brief moment Tomás heard the gentle rustle of pages being turned as an angel searched the Book of Accounts for the good deed that would secure him a place in heaven! That deed was nowhere in the chronicle of his life.

A man next to him was saying to another that it would be a good idea to say the Rosary: 'Not yet,' said the second man. 'There'll be plenty of time for that later.' As much as to say the drowning man was about to meet his maker. 'He hasn't drowned yet and God's help is closer than even the Rosary.'

Tomás turned around quickly. He couldn't deny that he, like every man, felt a spark of hope in spite of himself. Suddenly the word 'rope' was on everyone's lips, its single syllable a greater mouthful of consolation than any call to arms or battle cry. People had started saying the magic word slowly, quietly, solemnly. For a while before the thing itself materialised the word moved among them: a living thing, a miraculous being, a Christ-man appearing and disappearing at will . . .

Then:

'Give it to me here! Here, mister, my lad!'

'I can throw it to him from here, Bigmouth . . . '

'You'll need a weight on the end to pull it down in the water.'

'Here we go again! Ye'll let your man drown with all yer antics . . . '

The magic of the word unravelled as soon as they started pulling on the rope to make a noose on the end of it. It was like a cruel game of chance — a game for fools — with a big prize for the winner. That's why they were playing pairs. Not only were no two pairs working together, no one person had his arms and legs on the same side. Somehow the rope got tangled under the knees of the man on crutches. They were milling around him, in each other's way, twisting the rope even more, threatening to shove the cripple in the water, where he deserved to be more than the other poor fella, and 'let the waterhorses trample you and your seven-league legs that should have been sawn from your arsehole long ago . . . '

Next up was a man with a ladder on his shoulder. Tomás shook his head sadly. It was like a pantomime. As if the yielding, submissive, pliant water would support a ladder, as a house or a wall might! They'd be as well off reciting the Litany of Lifebuoys, like people in fishing villages do.

'Here!'

The strong, strapping young man's left hand on his shoulder was enough to turn Tomás back towards the water. The young fella was pulling off his shirt with the other hand: 'A comrade in distress. Here, have you a knife on you? Quick as you can, you old woman, cut the straps on my sandals . . . '

Tomás did as he was told, then turned away from the young man and the water. He heard the plop of soft skin splitting the water and wished the loud cheer that lifted the roof of the sky was a spark from the forge of human virtue. It was certainly a relief, a let-off for the bystanders. In the water, in the skin of the young man, every one of them was performing feats of courage and bravery in the deadly contest. Tomás could not suppress a warm surge of excitement or hide his curiosity: the strong strokes of the young man who said he wanted to rescue a comrade in arms were swimming in the depths of his eyes. He heard the echo of that declaration more clearly than the insults hurled by the women behind him:

'This one won't leave his tick-ridden balls for any blackwater snake.'

'Fraoch will go home, safe and sound, balls and all intact.'

'Home to his darling! His dearest, dearest darling!'

'She must have taken out insurance against your balls getting wet!'

'What is that fat fuck of a brother giving out about?' said a man when everyone had quieted down again. 'Are those two students of his?'

'Students, my hole! Are the ducks his students? Apparently some slut put her hand on his crotch when people were pushing a minute ago. Now he's fuming and you'd swear he had a dispensation from the Vatican Council to put the hard word on every woman here.'

'That's a very serious matter! Putting your hand on a man's crotch, especially a man of the cloth. Someone went rummaging in my flies as well.'

'Your flies? She must have been an archaeologist.'

The rush of excitement had subsided. Everything now was a tangled rope—the people, their voices, the volleys of abuse fired at him and the other men. It was the tone he remembered rather than the abuse itself. Not so much the voice of another person, a fellow human being. More like two candles struggling, a bright candle from God, a dark one from the devil, a fight to the death between light and shade, between two shadows inside himself, if truth be told. As if to prove it, he could no longer tell the difference between the first swimmer and the one who went to his rescue. If he was summoned to give evidence in court of what he saw and did from the time he arrived here, he could hardly say for certain, never mind on oath, that he had slowed down at all except to undo the young man's sandals. When he had wiped away a dribble of snot, his face was so composed, so untroubled, anyone would have sworn he was the most easygoing man in the city . . .

It wasn't long before he had to brush the familiar sweat from his face. He was dripping like the king of all candles, thick splodges raising painful blisters on his neck. There was no denying he had turned his back on the water and his duty, on the crowd and their humanity, however thin and corrupted the dregs of human nature were mingled in their veins. More than anything else, he would have liked to have gone to the rescue. He had no excuse other than a reluctance to get involved. He could swim. There was the rub. That was why he was sweating like a candle. Too easy to say he wasn't a strong enough swimmer, that the blackwater snake would beat him to the prize no matter how bravely he entered the fray. Water was tricky— the weakest element and the strongest. Recently he had declared a truce with it and determined to avoid it altogether. Better to live in the middle of a desert without a single drop of the stuff. He often thought of going to live in some other town. He would, too, whatever the cost, only he couldn't think of a place that had no water. The shittiest, most backward village had a stream of some sort pissing through it . . .

Still and all, he was happy to imagine himself entering the water, diving, grabbing the eejit by the hair, and dragging him to the shore where any number of willing hands would offer to take over. He'd be a hero. He wouldn't care. He wasn't looking for thanks, even from the one he saved. To see that warm fresh living thing on dry land, the water pouring off like an enemy releasing its grip! How Tomás would have relished that.

The incident was too close, too recent, to shake it from his mind. Chances were it wasn't over yet. If it was, he hoped to God it had a happy ending. The details, the moving pictures, he had erased from his mind. What was left was a shapeless lump, the drowning as an abstract death, a body flush with life reduced to a sod of black earth; or the body missing and nothing to be done except imagine its destruction: how the drowned man might look with underwater creatures swimming in and out of him, fish spawning in what was left of him . . . The thick gobbets of abuse he had swallowed had cooled in his veins. He was back in the ring, locked in single combat. The splash, the swimmer going under, the bubbles on the surface gradually subsiding as the water closed over as gently, as silky-smoothly, as a cat stretching after swallowing a bellyful of fish — as obscene as a lascivious mouth kissing. He felt again the pull on his neck, the sudden jerk, the primeval dragging down of hands and legs on soft treacherous ground, the dizzying edge of a cliff, the cold updraft from the abyss . . .

For all that, the gadfly of fear had not stung him under the tail today any more than any other day. He used to tell himself he was no more a coward than the next man. He had some of the skill and experience that steady a man when danger looms. He'd been a good footballer; he'd worked as a fisherman; he'd spent time on high buildings. He'd had no more fear of water than the next man until that day last summer when he saw a woman drowning in a seaside town on the west coast. It was a blustery day; she'd gone out too far, got caught in a current and dragged out. It was all too simple. Death should be solemn. Not just the moment the soul departs the body;

the whole thing with all its trappings from beginning to end should be incomprehensible, inevitable, slow, ritualistic. It was inconceivable that it should come so nonchalantly: no sabre rattled or battle-dress donned, no bugle blown, no gauntlet thrown. The whole thing was so ordinary. There was a big enough crowd — her husband among them. Neither he nor they made any real effort to save her. Let the man who owns the cow grab it by the tail, said one man peevishly. Maybe her husband wasn't a strong swimmer. As far as he could tell, Tomás was the best swimmer there. The weather wasn't that bad or the sea that rough. He had little interest in who or what she was. A mother, apparently. He saw two kids in hysterics with her husband . . .

That day and again today, pity sank its fangs like a blackwater snake into Tomás. What upset him most was that the best of that pity, the champion's portion, was reserved for himself. The woman's drowning was like a new marriage consecrated between him and Bríd. A secret, too, he'd have said, but that word made him angry and ashamed; he preferred to call it a mystery, a sacrament — a conflagration too, he told himself, burning him alive . . . It was also a cold sword in their marriage bed, ripping the seamless garment of their wholeness. How many times had he asked himself the same question: what if it had been Bríd, his own beloved wife, who was out swimming that day on the west coast? She had often gone swimming in the very same spot that summer. Those days had been blustery too — a voracious wind whipping up the waves. Back then, his pleasure unclouded by worry, he used to love watching a wave stretch and arch its arms like some giant silky sea-cat as if there were a creature in its womb determined to overpower Bríd and carry her off. What a pleasure to see her master the sea as if she had it on a leash. How many days had he stood there, a happy fool, at that same treacherous spot that might have become her death bed at any moment . . .

To see her trying to reach the shore. Struggling against a receding wave that knocked her back. A moment on the surface. The waves rolling and swelling as if bales of sheepswool were being hurled at her, smothering her. To see her dragged out. Going under. Rising again. Then sinking again for the last time . . .

Tomás had no doubt at all as to what he would do: tear himself apart, every inch of his being. Of course he would! They'd have to hold him back. He'd hold on to the seawall and break away from them. All the frenzy of combat, the warp-spasm of despair, would be in him just then. Out he'd go, head first, into the lap of the gods, without stopping to strip off. He'd feel the tingle of cold brine against his skin, whispering to him wetly from the depths of the sea. As if the hungry belly of the ocean had just roused itself to devour him! Where would Bríd be at this stage? . . . Since then, he'd often woken at night, swimming furiously in the bed, those bales of wool smothering him and no sign of Bríd . . .

No word of a lie. Tomás was absolutely certain what he would do—at first. That was nearly a year ago. It was clear to him now that, in certain circumstances, his sacrifice would be in vain. Death can be so sudden. A clap of thunder. A runaway car. A fall from a cliff. In cases like that there would be no time to do anything. It was those occasions where there was time to react, a choice to be made, that kept tying Tomás's mind in a serpentine knot that could not be undone: a mad bull in a field heading straight for Bríd; a maniac lurching towards her; the whole house ablaze and Bríd, oblivious, upstairs . . . Tomás had teased out every detail of every possible scenario. Often, he had grabbed the bull bravely by the horns; other times, he was afraid the curved tips bearing down on him had sent him scurrying away. Sometimes he took the axe from the madman. Sometimes, he crouched and let the angel of death slip past him. He didn't have to race upstairs against the flames . . .

How often had he grabbed the horns, snatched the axe from the madman? Tomás had rehearsed so many horn and hatchet pantos on the scaffold of his mind that year. How did he know he'd grab either the horns or the hatchet, that he wouldn't always run or hide rather than confront danger head-on? There would be no 'always' if he ran or hid even once . . . The drowning woman confronted him today like a body in the freezer at home waiting for a postmortem. It was obvious there was plenty of time to decide what to do, from the moment it first became obvious the woman was in difficulty until the sea finally claimed her. That was Bríd in the freezer . . .

When it came to Bríd, he was a man with a contagious disease kept secret from everyone, as if to reveal it would be to expose his soul, his whole being. Like any hidden disease, he couldn't wait for it to run its course. That's what sent him rambling alone in Phoenix Park and a few other places like that on days like this. Bríd disliked these solitary excursions. She offered to go with him a couple of times. Once, he gave her the slip and left the house without her. Another time she followed him without his realising. She never stopped till she got a look at him on a small backroad in the Park. All she saw was the expression on his face. She had no idea what caused the facial contortions that seemed to be drawn from every corner of his body. She had never seen his face screwed up like that. It reminded her of the old poets in her schoolbook. It had to be poetry because she never understood poems. He was on his way home today after one of these excursions when he happened on the man drowning . . .

Today of all days, he had gone to communion to stop Bríd nagging him. 'Another reason why I should have no fear of the water,' he told himself without conviction as he hurried on. He unwrapped every fold in the poultice, picked away every flake of scab from the wound. The priest had tried to suppress his laughter, but the smothered snigger kept flapping around like a trapped bat in the confessional. His voice was very nasal as he spoke:

'No one lets go of life until he has to . . . Even those determined to sacrifice themselves. There is little or nothing that clutches a human being tighter than that mysterious grip of life. It's deeper than love, the love of wife or child, deeper than charity, deeper even than faith. You've heard of the drowning man's grip? A man will destroy what is most precious to him to save himself. There isn't a single thing in this world more dear to each and every one of us than the glowing ember of his own life . . . Other people? You know the proverb: "No matter how close your clothes are, your shirt is closer again" . . . If that's all that's troubling you! You're too scrupulous by half . . . I tell you again, no one knows what he will or will not do when danger rears its head . . . In a way, keeping your conscience on too tight a leash is as bad as giving it free rein. Give yourself a break, man. Next time you get a chance, drop in to see Dr. Mullins . . . '

Dr. Mullins! Let the fucker cure himself! He had a fine lump of a wife. Not wishing him any harm or anything, but what if he saw her drowning someday? What good would his bottles and potions do him then against the all-conquering flood? There wasn't a doctor alive who could tell Tomás he wasn't as fit and healthy as the next man; as steady too. Despite that, the priest hadn't healed him yesterday: the wound was as raw as ever. Just as well it wasn't a physical ailment or disease, more a spiritual unease that time would eventually heal. And yet, worry had strapped his legs to his waist, manacled his hands in lead, and spawned a repulsive stain in his and Bríd's marriage bed . . . He reminded the priest of what Christ said about the man who would lay down his life for his friend. Easy for the priest to soft-soap him: Christ was not like the rest of us poor human creatures, bare carcasses made up of flesh and blood and the milk of human kindness. As much as to say that kind of bullshit was fine for Christ! The moral of His words in this morning's sermon was that he who would lay down his life for his friends was the dearest of all God's children . . .

That was a snarling mongrel of a question the woman by the river had sicced on him: would he try to save his own wife? Or Christ Himself? A wife was surely more to a man than any friend or comrade. Tomás felt sure Jesus would agree with him on that score: she was more deserving of rescue than anyone else, including Christ if He were the one floundering in that foul swill, going under, in the final twilight of breathing life . . . She was as close as could be to you, as close as yourself, the other half of your soul. Tomás remembered again the cold Shrove morning he solemnly swore to grant her all his worldly goods and possessions. The priest said they were one body forever after. It would be like losing an arm or a leg to see her beaten about in the womb of the water, or torn apart by some ravenous fish, God forbid! . . .

But why get upset, as the priest said, echoing a question he had often asked himself? It might never happen. Please God! But then again it might! Then what? Then he'd have to choose, one way or the other: to plunge into the snaky blackwater or stay on the bank, high and dry, nursing his precious balls, reaping the rewards of cowardice, 'shitting himself sevenfold with fear' as the women had accused him of doing earlier. He was surprised to feel the vomit rise in his throat, a dry retch, every time he thought of it. And yet, he couldn't help thinking of it every time he saw sea or lake, canal or river, any kind of water. The day had turned blustery, the cold breath of the breeze rising off the water behind him. Birds—seabirds, he thought—had landed in the front garden of a house ahead of him. The screeching flock that descended on the shore when that woman was drowning were etched in his memory . . . Was today an extension of that other day, like Eve created from Adam's rib? . . . Disaster had no preference for one day over another. Any day could be the final day. Tomás banished that thought with an almighty green gob of mucous over his shoulder. He was not a superstitious man. He knew that seabirds would keep coming ashore on blustery days in saecula saeculorum . . .

He still couldn't free himself from the hook of his own question. Let's say she worked it out that I was in two minds, uncertain, trying to stay upright on a submerged stone, half in, half out of the water; that she guessed I wasn't all there, split down the middle, the lesser part of me in the snaky blackwater, the greater part . . . Women are a scourge, he thought, a word he was fond of that stiffened his resolve to bring things to a head. She knew something was up. He had half a notion she'd followed him once. So what? He was clean as the Pope's whistle as far as that went. But the way she looked at him! Like being questioned by every cop in the country at the same time. Over time, he had stopped going to the seaside and strolling by the river with her. He knew well she knew he was lying when he said it was to avoid meeting her friends. It was an excuse to cover up his fear of perished bodies and his reluctance to go swimming. It was obvious she didn't believe a word of it when he told her he'd had a bath while she was out visiting. Anyway, she knew he hated water. One of her gossipy friends came to the house one day while Bríd was out. There was no beating about the bush:

'I forgot to ask you, Tomás,' she said, 'are you still scared of water? Never mind: it's a strange thing, poetry. Next thing you know you'll be growing a beard and letting your hair grow long! Our Muiréad hated the sea. No word of a lie, dear! She wouldn't even set foot on the boat to England or America! And not a line of a poem to show for it. Not one word. Now how do you feel?'

Bríd teased him about it from time to time. 'The cat got your fish again today, Tomás,' she told him one Friday. Sure enough, he was there on the doorstep, sunning himself, a big silky cat, his back arched, with a bellyful of fish. Tomás drew an almighty kick on him . . .

It didn't bother him that she knew that much about him. Fear of water! So what? Some people were allergic to fresh-cut grass, others to certain types of food. Others again were afraid of flying . . . All he revealed to her about himself was no more than if you were to pick up your lover's phone and hear the engaged tone at the other end: all it meant was that you weren't the only one who spoke with her. No more; no less. Afraid of water! But what if she guessed his secret! If she managed to reach out with those paws as far as the lonely perch inside him, to touch the wound and pick at it! . . . He wouldn't put it past her to condemn herself to the dark briny bitter brown water some stormy day. She would too—to test him! And it would be the end of her! She wouldn't care. She'd do it anyway. Women were like that.

What the world saw was the honourable man, the respectable

appearance of one whose house looks marvellous from outside but has hens nesting and pigs snoring around him in the bedroom. The same old question was pulsing through him, demanding an answer. A full and final answer . . .

Tomás was shaking, as if there was an engine throbbing inside him. What if she did throw herself in? What then? What would he do? What exactly would he do then? If only he knew. If only he knew for sure hc would not go to her rescue! At least then he'd have good reason to hate himself. Who knows — it might even be a relief after all this time plastering over the ugly wound on his skin. The cord that was binding his brain would finally give way. He wouldn't be at war with himself, playing cat and mouse by turns any longer. Better to be the most timid mouse in God's creation than pretend to be a cat just to prove he wasn't afraid! He could end the civil war in his soul, confiding the secret that Labhraidh Loingseach had the ears of a horse to the first tree he came upon. To bleed the wound, the mother of all infections: the wound would be healed, for good. To go home then, stepping across the threshold of his own house more lightly than he had for a year. He'd no longer be afraid to take a bath, to scour the film of filth from his skin. He could look her straight in the eye, daring her. To do what? To stay away from him, of course! She'd ease his disgust with a feast of kisses! For now, those kisses tasted bitter in his mouth. They made a coward of him, preventing him from telling her the truth, or blurting it out to himself. If he could shed his secret, let the clean air in among the hens and pigs. Instead of pledging his deepest love, of swearing a false oath again, he'd show her the dead tree where his secret was hidden. They'd come to an arrangement, a fair and reasonable settlement, with no more spiritual or noble a bond between them than a contract of joint possession. Even that would be a release. Anything that snatched the cold sword from the marriage bed would be a release . . .

There was a cool breeze, but Tomás was sweating, his hand clammy from clawing his handkerchief. He felt weak in the knees, his head addled, thoughts howling to each other like dogs stumbling on a carcass. He could no longer tell if he was heading for home or not. Would he tell her or not? All he knew for sure was that there was a tormented wailing in every corner of his head and every howl a dangerous question. Would she be better off not knowing? . . . She wouldn't believe him if he told her the bitter truth after all the years of sweet talk. He'd swear to her that was all it was: the sweet nothings that love demands. He had to tell himself she wouldn't believe him: she'd say that was only more of his sweet talk! Women! She'd never credit it. Until some blustery day when she was out swimming and got pulled under, the warp-spasming sea holding her tight. The last she'd see of him would be there at the water's edge, screaming, tearing his hair, a signal station, rending the air with his hands like a mime artist . . . anything other than going to her rescue . . .

For once, Tomás didn't notice that he had reached another stretch of water. He moved across the humpbacked bridge as unaware of his surroundings as if he were fondling a woman's breast. His thoughts consumed him, wearing each other out as if this was some kind of lewd game. It was hard to say if what was going on in his head now could be called thinking or deciding. What was in his mind was a physical thing, a rock, left high and dry after a flood, that would require the strength of Hercules to hide before it crushed him like a millstone, smothering him under its stoniness, killing him more surely, more precisely than all the snaky blackwater . . .

The driver didn't see him: his face was buried in the seaweed-red hair of the woman beside him. The hump in the road was his excuse. When he finally saw Tomás, he swore he had no way of knowing what he was going to do. He couldn't believe he'd do nothing at all, only stand there, erect as a sword, halfway across the bridge . . .

TRANSLATED BY
LOUIS DE PAOR AND LOCHLAINN Ó TUAIRISG

FROM *AN tSRAITH TÓGTHA*
(1977)

BECOMING PAPER

Yea, right so. Nothing strange about that. Don't tell me you don't get what I'm on about. I could just as easily say that I became paper, or that I changed, or that I was being set up to be made into paper. But it didn't happen to me like somebody from Muskerry, or even as a civil servant. To me myself, a true son of Conamara, God save the mark. I got it just like I would get any other disease. Like getting lice or a rash, or TB or cancer, don't even think about it. This kind of talk is just the leftovers of my old life. To tell you the whole truth, it is done, I did it. Now that it is over and done, it is easier to talk about it. When something is over and done with like that, it's easier to talk about how it started and developed. 'Cos the end explains how it came about and how it started just as easily as anything else. So that it's, like, always changing, reinventing itself like the universe. So that, like, if I hadn't become paper in the end, I couldn't say that I had started in any particular way despite how precisely I had actually begun. How it was anyway, when I started becoming paper, was that I always knew it was a right and proper and even a correct transmogrification or even change. A change in the leather-bound volume, or even in the file of my person—or to put it in clumsy pleb-like talk, in my pre-paper life—the kind of stuff in which I took economic, social, cultural, sometimes spiritual circumstances into account—the circumstances of normal ordinary humanity in which we are locked, that wrack of life which whacks upon us until that day when the undertakers of the Corporation of Corpses, the Bailiffs of Breath, come and take us away. There are those, of course, like my pal M. for example, who are hell bent on believing that beauty is entirely random. Maybe that's how he sees it. We'll soon see. But there's no harm in saying, even if I am getting ahead of myself, that the cold clip of savage beauty didn't tickle me until I became paper. Which reminds me, of course, that I did actually become paper. For this simple reason: despite the fact that I was becoming paper, and am indeed paper right now—and it's me, as paper, that's telling this now—I didn't entirely banish the old man, as Saint Paul himself said who only actually became a Christian, nor did I entirely garb myself in bright brilliant paper propriety entirely. There was always a kick in the old body, the original body (that was me too)—I felt like saying the 'urbody,' the basic fundamental thing as the Germans have it—and this despite all.

I was lucky that it didn't take millions of years for the change to happen. In that sense there are no reconstructed forms or putative versions as models for the likes of me. This is a synchronic account by my own hand on my own paper. There isn't that much left of my old existence that would raise more than a faint echo from a life that has vanished beyond the mists of yesteryear, a ghostly presence haunting a later life.

I already said that I became paper. Believe me, I am not trying to piss you off. Why would I? Don't think I'm making this up or throwing shapes. It's not like I had done anything that others hadn't done and wanted to crow about it. The change that happened, that I done, was enough to banish any uppityness that I had. I examined myself, right through, just now. That is to say, I examined the kind of person I was, the way that I am made completely of paper. If something like that had happened to me in my other life, I would have had to invent an account, and a duplicated account—the duplicated account most especially—and to keep it most appropriately. And this is totally beyond my ken and competence. I am not a scarecrow in the middle of a field plonked there just to frighten the birds. I am somebody who became paper, a civilized being: paper is culture. Don't even bother to try to make a better case, I'm not trying to claim a special privilege for the few pennies that paper might garner. No more than anybody else who put his spiritual life on the line, it would be criminal now if I were to say nothing, to keep my mouth shut.

From the get-go, I have to say that it is a serious thing to even hint that somebody became paper. It is no joking matter, no way. I have my own plan for the layout of the theology of the world—both original and as a copy. Instead of inventing Hell and Purgatory and Limbo—torments that are waiting just around the corner—God Almighty All-powerful All-knowing screwed up by not making the punishment—whether pain or burning or even just discomfort—by not making it an immediate reaction in the most appropriate part of the human body. For example, if you had constantly gone on the piss with the booze, your tongue, your throat, your stomach would know about it straight away, and the same thing would happen to the expectant part after too much fucking and whoring. I'm not recommending anything extreme—a fine on the spot, something like that. If that had been the case, it's not likely that I would have become paper. For all that, and be that as it may, I'm not taking the piss when I tell you I became paper. There's no limit to what else could have been learned by science or written down if it wasn't for the constant silly giggles by those whose values are already a bit skewed. Becoming paper, after all, maybe it isn't such a big change—God help us—as big a change as becoming a devil or becoming the farting champion of the world, or even—like that famous politician—just becoming a phornicator.

Just regarding this last one, you would have to examine the precise language. Was it done efficiently according to the rules or actively according to the law? One way or the other, it doesn't concern us here: phornication we will always have with us, just like the poor, despite the best and worst efforts of the Labour Party. But if, however, he happened to be involved in phornication passively, the whole case will have to be assessed in its proper context, as we do not know was phornication his precise purpose or simply a result of wild improper speculation, so that it might have come to pass that he was a being who had taken on other qualities and those qualities were his only ones and could not be any other.

But hey, I still know what I am talking about. It's much worse to say that somebody was involved in phornicating than that he got a rash or fleas or tuberculosis or cancer. There isn't another living thing who would visit any of those rules or regulations on the human being, or certainly puff him up, rather than bring him down and insult and treat him like shit. That is why I have kept some grip on myself, in this matter of the paper. It's not that extreme, actually, just a kind of prejudice that my countrymen never left a jot or a smidgen of behind, it's like that ever-new philosophy of Aquinas which asserted that Western Man didn't invent the person in the likeness of an angel, but neither did he think that God made him in the likeness of a whale, not to mention akin to some aborted evolutionary thing as a rabbit. What would a beast be doing with paper anyway, you well may ask? I hope I am getting there. That's the way it was, or so they said about philosophy ever before I became paper—although it was a very surface-skim study, I have to say. But that's what happened to me completely: absolutely and totally, from beginning to end, from top to bottom, from alpha to omega, beyond arse to elbow. I was there, always reinventing myself. It was a cosmological transmogrification. I could see the opposition as clearly as the spires of cathedrals arising out of holy cities.

Be that as it may, there are some advantages in becoming paper. If you were losing your personality, it's not exactly death, but more precisely another life. Just like, say, the change from the Irish sun, such as it is, to the dull distant sun on the Russian tundra, for the sake of argument. And people noticed it, especially dubious women. But I was losing interest in them, and it wasn't just physical.

But of course, if that wasn't the end, this wasn't the beginning either, not to even think about if this was the beginning . . . How much of the beginning is in the actual finished product, me being a paper artefact? Or its opposite—like what else, the same always?—to give a kick in the arse to the whole business of evolution going backwards this time, the evolution of a highly cultured man in this second half of the twentieth century, he in the midst of his paper empire, all that paper which defined who he was in this civilisation, a critter who was indistinguishable from the paper he was: trace him back from the file age, through the modern age, the stone age, the bronze age, the deer age, all the way back to that monkey up in the tree licking the arse-possibilities from which he descended. Or was it just the opposite of all of this? It might be, who can say? If it was man who evolved, as clear as that Easter is on Sunday, then the monkey got it all wrong. This is not in direct contradiction to the fact that the monkey was the driving force of evolution. Nor that we didn't come from them. Or even the other—God help us. We often heard the saying that a good father often raised a bad child—and I don't think we ever heard the opposite of that. It's entirely possible, therefore, that there's me hanging out of the tree and my lad of a monkey all dressed up stuck in the office wrestling with all kinds of paper, shares, income tax, admin stuff, reports, orders from above . . . until he became paper. Or was he just tired of it and wanted to return to his own patch, the field of his fathers, so that he could fancily Freudian manicure his arse hole in the best possible way until life came around again. But it's not my intention now to decide which of us pulled the short straw.

I'm sorry, but I think you must have some patience with some-one who has become paper. After all, it's not everyone who becomes paper, even at the pinnacle of the culmination of civilisation, nor in the paper paradise where God is a file and is prayed to through refer-ence numbers. I have my own story: I became paper, that's it. It's much easier now to talk about the change, now that it has happened. This philosophy we have in the Western World is all exactly about the beginning, middle, and end of everything. Its frame of reference is so thick and so tight that it doesn't allow for any ambiguity, suppositions, or for two premises to exist simultaneously, like two St. Brigid's Days in the Spring, or like that it's necessary now for Western Man to try out so many women before he's married—I didn't say to get them up the pole, although there's some merit in thinking he would be better off having a lot of experience for the sake of what he was facing into afterwards—or at least to have had relations with them, the official version, before he finally lands in the harbour of his desire.

If it happens in the future that the monkey could be our paper slave, even provisionally of course, like in place of the negro who even got work in offices throughout the world, I am absolutely certain that he who knows both the ways of worldly informality and the demanding strictures of jungle life will not be too happy to be confined within the tight straitjacket of Aquinistic syllogisms. A youngster could do worse than to clasp one of the most massive volumes in the library to his bosom and to start Freudian manicuring himself with it . . . That doesn't mean, of course, that I am not a true son of Western Philosophy, even though most people wouldn't believe that. I was bought and sold with Roman gold to the Catholic Church even before I was born. I saw all the changes in my lifetime, I saw them all with my own two eyes. It's possible that there may be a Black Pope in the Vatican before long. But I don't believe there will be a monkey, nor do I believe that a monkey will be in charge of the archives in the Vatican. I'm not happy to divest myself completely of the detritus of Aquinas until I am certain that there is some other acceptable monkey to do the work. Okay, so, I wrote that before I completely became paper. In my new existence I wasn't able to accede to any one philosophy, or any philosophy able to accede to my new existence. The only way I had to explain to someone who hadn't become paper was to describe what happened from the beginning to some end that we may suppose. Here comes another monster humping a bloody wild boar on his shoulder proclaiming that it is all about relativity, relativity is the beginning, the middle, and the end. You need some kind of methodology to pin down this work. Therefore, we must assume and even emphasise that intelligence and discernment requires a beginning, a middle, and an end in this matter of change. So, there's a line going through this mess, and I have it on file! A file is not just a paper orphan. It has reached a certain perfect or fulfilled state, like it might have been happily married and died in bliss, that is to say, it has reached its final and appropriate destination in paper paradise.

Now I can really begin my story, begin at the beginning and drift nice and easy through it to the end. There is no other way to write a short story, really. Of course, that's not what I set out to do. I just wanted to describe the change that came over me. I don't mind pleading the great God of Relativity as a protector. If I get accused of breaching the convention of the story, I simply say that all change like this in the course of time is simply a matter of relativity. Be sure of it, I didn't become paper in the course of just one day. But they were very special days, those days when I was becoming paper, a special measure of space-time, like that time when God himself set about creating the world. Therefore, don't, don't even misunderstand me when I say that I remember the first day, I clearly remember the first day when I began to become paper.

That, in itself, is a bit weird. I suppose it wouldn't have been if the change hadn't been so exact as a result. Unknown to yourself, like the thief in the night, like the inspector sussing out unpaid television or communication licences, unknown to yourself the various diseases get you. They are there gnawing away at you before you get any warning. Unfortunately, you are often too neglectful. Me too. I hadn't the least clue that I was becoming paper. It just might be that some strange spiritual situation or disease was coming about because of the philosophical bullshit of Western Man, like a cowering dog who always licked up to you. This hit me so often that it didn't bother me anymore. It appears that I might have been predestined for this, what the Western philosophers call an inclination or a trend, or even a fundamental necessity maybe, that I would eventually just become paper. It appears also that I was a most suitable subject, as some pseudo-science or other would aver—and it's likely that others would say it too, but I don't want to get tangled up in small pissy things like that. After all, it doesn't really matter that much about inclinations or tendencies. It was there, after all. The dead didn't leave the field: I did become paper.

Maybe the most important feature, the most relevant feature of God's critters is that the ability to think never leaves them. In point of fact, they get new revelations and epiphanies as they are about to kick the bucket. But I'm just telling my story. It would be much easier to bang on about it if it was only a big gut-busting dinner or a huge feed of porter waiting to be welcomed by your appetite. I'd better not rabbit on splitting philosophical hairs. The only thing that has to be assumed was that there was a time when I was unmade paper, that is to say, that I wasn't becoming paper. But as I said, Einstein turned everything into relativity, and regarding this matter I can't say was it before I started becoming paper (I can't say unmaking paper, as that is an applied situation like doling out lashings of cash) — or afterwards or at exactly the same time. I don't want to be too hard on him. Who knows, maybe I would end up proving that I never became paper and that it was never so that I was becoming paper in the first place. That is to say that I was simultaneously in my paper paradise and not in my paper paradise, in my republic and in my non-republic. I had to lie down with the ugly monster before I arose in the sunny uplands of the paper principality. To cut to the chase, speaking as a lay man: I became paper.

I realise that this narrative is a bit dull, no sauce to give it a tang. But the hard, precise brick of truth is far better. I have enough cop-on to offer the observation that dullness is the best gift of the poet. Something that will reveal that this compulsion to become paper is as wide as the air itself. I know in my heart of hearts that I was never as dull as when I became paper. I once had a neighbour who said to me that he never understood the urge to have children (I know we're not talking about the same thing entirely here, as having children is both practical and active) until he had some himself. And now that all of post-Cartesian philosophy is no more than an examination of language, don't even begin to think your man's body transmogrified into a child and more children like I entirely bodily transmogrified into paper. His body changed all right, that's certain. He made a kind of arrangement, a 'fixed engine' as the law has it for those purposes, but it is a mysterious process that I am not competent to discuss right now.

I have said one thing up to now, that is, that I started becoming paper. This wasn't the worst start in the world, that is if we accept that it was a start at all. But as we have said, methodology demands that there must be a beginning, 'Let there be a beginning' as God said in the Book of Genesis, even though not everyone thought that Adam was a great start. But there was a beginning and an end. I have no idea how the beginning came about. No more than that neighbour of mine I was just on about who hadn't the least clue what happened to himself. He was totally disgusted and pissed off when his wife chucked him out of the bed to go and look for someone else. What for fuck's sake did I do that God would be so cruel? But then he got used to it and wouldn't have it otherwise. I mean, like he said, what other pleasure does a poor man get? You'll get used to it too, he said. Maybe it happened just at the psychological moment. I craved a file. I think I might have said, 'Isn't it a great pity that I am not a file.'

I stretched out my hand, just one of them, in case there might me whisperings or hints in my ear, or my windpipe, or an itch in my nose or in my coccyx, and my other hand ready for the file in which there was a copy of the letter that was going to the Head Office which I was writing just now, the first link in this live chattering paper chain. I had to hold one hand back, as there was a more serious emergency looming. I hope God sends me some good tidings here or there, I says to myself. That might be a strength at the right moment. I remembered that Kitty was the one who was coming and that I'd give her a lash of my tongue. Do a fixed engine job on her on the couch! A guy has to shake himself out of being the old fellow who is writing these accursed letters.

I have to admit, if I was being precise about it, that there was no need for the alertness of the hand on the left since there was no emergency or threat from the right. The left hand made a swift movement on the same latitude across the southern hemisphere to a place which I can't call my hip anymore. Paper has no hips. I was pure paper down there, paper which was soft, brittle, silky in some places, paper I thought was greasy in other places, like it was leaving slimy slobber on my fingertips. I felt badly that I didn't find anything weird about the change. I felt I could grope that part of my anatomy just as well as I might Kitty. I could almost say that it was hardly a change at all. I'd really have to think hard about it in order to see that it wasn't a natural state, what has happened since I became like this. There is a good chance that this thought is self-contradictory. If it was the nature of the universe to be constantly creating itself, then why couldn't I just go on creating myself just the same? And isn't that just what every alive and thinking person, every fully formed soul, is doing all the time, either that, or there isn't any such thing as a live thinking person or a full formed soul at all. And if that was true, then it is also true that I wasn't becoming paper at that time or afterwards. There was no such thing as afterwards, before, or during. Whatever was happening or not happening, it was all putting my head in a spin.

I'm talking as a layperson to other laypersons. Anybody will understand me when I say 'my hip has turned into paper.' The wonder of it didn't hit me all at once—you get used to everything. To tell you the truth, the change was so complete that it would have been difficult not to get used to it. The paper was well practiced in its place, snug in its own way by all appearances, settling in quite nicely as paper does, like the way that a car learns the way of the road having been driven for a while. It might even have begun to stiffen and begun to get a bit mouldy. Just like, I said to myself, just like a string of letters on a file that were just being kept there on the off chance they might be needed. Or what else?—young old wans that never gave up hope of marrying so long as there was a sign of some class of an old wreck of a man still hanging around somewhere in the whole wide world. I often thought that God gave us the Ten Commandments, the Bible, the law courts, and the whole shooting gallery for the sake of files. I noticed the odd smudge on it. It wasn't actually ink, more like a greasy stain which left its own spiritual seal on the paper like it would on a dispossession notice. But that greasy stain wasn't the only thing. Inside in the crotch of two folds of paper there was a scribbled signature, and if I wasn't mistaken, it belonged to the boss!

This was much more serious than just a change. This paper was one of my limbs, another file, like from now on I was all of my limbs plus or minus a file. But I could only imagine it like my neighbour when his wife was in labour.

'What's this then,' he said, 'every misfortune follows the poor man. He has to wake up in the middle of the night to get a wink of sleep.'

I saw this rare and unusual event as a kind of disease, a stroke of bad luck. Insofar as I complained at all, I am ashamed to say, that I really moaned like shite. Why would this fall into my lap? Me, who neither deserved it nor saw it coming. Why me, why not them? That soft lump inside in C., he always puts a tape recorder running before he speaks. And I saw M. the L. carrying as many files as a beggar has curses. And then there is R., who has a sideload, a backload, an arse-load, a gutload of files. It wouldn't surprise me a bit if some part or other of him made more paper by screwing and bonking. Any office is only really a file community and a few bits of clerkish furniture as support. But after all, the clerks don't turn into paper. I was the one sent out into the storm.

But I had to finish my answer. I took out the carbon copy that I needed without bothering my butt to climb up to pluck the original from the top shelves, nor did I want to put the file in danger of being disseminated or discommoded by continuous handling and being opened. I felt a kind of freedom that I'd never felt before. I would no longer be a slave chained to the top of a desk in a file. A buzz went

right through me, that kind of feeling you get on a fine spring morning when every corner of the air is a feast of music. The kind of freedom which is only the external manifestation of a health that is bursting forth, health of the body and of the soul bonded together in one
great uplift. A person wanting to dump all that old stuff, every petty
thing, every unworthy and trifling and flippant thing, and to take off
out up and away just like a butterfly who has cast off its corrupt caterpillar chrysalis to fulfil its destiny. That is why I wrote a letter of a kind
I had never penned before to the Head Office.

'Sack her, that lady is not to be trusted.'

Before this I would have made a serpent's knot of clauses out of
that, each one adding its own link to the one that followed, while reflecting back some thing or other to the one that came before. Linguistic flourishes, that is all. And to put it up to your man over in the
Head Office to see what he'd ever do about me recommending that
the lady should be fired! Normally I'd be full of scruples, thinking
that your man was having it off with the lady unbeknownst to anyone,
and I'd tag on a heap of addendums to the letter, addendums phrased
properly but uncertainly, 'Do you wish to assess whether it would be
to the good of the company that she should be given extended leave
under the guise of ill-health if this was desirable or agreeable in order
that it would be weighed against the good of the company in the long
run and taking every possible contingency into account. Or, on the
other hand . . . '

Bit by bit I began to see the change as not really a disadvantage
at all. I didn't have to be getting up and stretching myself, putting a
strain on my heart by lumping heavy files around the place. And they
wouldn't be scattered about the place like seaweed on the shore, generating dust and mildew, making me gasp for breath.

But these thoughts didn't come to me altogether in one fell
swoop: the conclusion I had reached right now was that if this was
not a part of my parts, then it had the function of a locum tenens, a
kind of substitute.

As regards Kitty she'd have bags of space on the couch from now on. I had to admit to myself that I had gone off her a bit in the last while. I wouldn't let her into the room that often. She really got a thrill out of taking down the files and reading them. Didn't she suss out a copy of that letter I had sent about the lady and didn't she start reading it, until I whipped it from her. She is far too thick to understand it, of course. From now on, I could bonk her away at my leisure and pleasure without giving a moment's thought or a toss about the files.

After a couple of days it happened that I got a letter from your man over in the Head Office informing me that they had noticed my recommendation in the letter dated ——————— and that that lady had been dumped without any hope of return, but that they would be very grateful to me if I could inform them what had resulted from the case of Business XYZ file dated ———————. The first part of this letter was okay. The XYZ thing was no worse than any other and the file which I had was very manageable, so manageable in fact that I had a reply written and a copy ready by 11 a.m. and was off to get it in the post by 11.30. The spring morning was like stepping out into a newly decorated boudoir. I happened to meet Miss J. I would have invited her in as we had half an hour to spare, which was quite unusual this time of day, but what she was on about wasn't to my liking, but so it goes. Do you ever feel a huge weight of guilt about dealing with all that paperwork, she asked? What are you on about, Miss J., I answered. It's like this, she said. I suffer from depression. I'm absolutely certain now that that's what I have. You're there on your own, do you get it? I do, I said. And nobody near you at all so that you think that you are useless . . . Me useless, I said. If you like, Miss J., we still have half an hour. It's about me, she said, not you. I should have been born a man, like you. Then you wouldn't be talking like that, I said. But that's it in a nutshell, she said, just as a man has no shame, no depression. Freud had a patient in Vienna, some banker's wife, and I know for sure that I have the same symptoms as her, the same prob-

lem . . . What made you start thinking like this, Miss J., I said. A book
I got from Kitty. Oh, Kitty, I said. Yes, from Kitty. Kitty told me she
would have no cure from her own depression until she got a man . . .
A Man . . . a Man. A lad she would be so proud of just as if she was a
man herself out and about and having it off with women . . . screwing
and boning and boffing and dipping the wick . . . she said she never
understood that until she had read letters . . . Letters . . . Yea, that's
it, letters in your files, when she was waiting for you sometimes. She
said they all amounted to, or so she said, women writing to you invit-
ing you to contact them, for God's sake . . .

God help Kitty. That piece of chicken shit would read anything.
And that's what she was up to now, dirty books. Signs on it. Let her
lie down on the couch with them from now on until she sees what
kind of crap they are. I'll have to get a different cover for the couch.
But I also think I'll have to give my limbs a rest for a while. But there's
a great danger in taking any sonofabitch to where there are files. If I
live there will be no need for files anymore in a short while. I am becoming paper. It crawled up and below my hip these last few days. I
think it is in my chest now. I noticed a weirdness in my hip at first. I
didn't think it was anything, and yet I knew it was. I wasn't ready for
it. The body doesn't change that much when somebody feels that it
is weird.

'That wouldn't bother me,' my neighbour said, 'but sometimes
I think that it is only me who carries the family. I get small, nice,
kindly pains . . . '

Your man over in the office was happy enough with my answer
about XYZ, but now he's asking my opinion about PQR/2 and how
would I differentiate between that and the new offer, reference
VW/W? And as a postscript: 'That lady Miss A. was here this morning.
She said she is pregnant because of you. That time you were over here
and the office was empty at lunchtime, you brought her in, laid her
on the couch, and took a book about Freud from her. If you have any
details about this matter, please forward them to me before ———'

It wouldn't surprise me in the least if A. was up the duff. She kind of knew it was coming. She had spread herself around. There's hardly any one in the office who hadn't had his go. Your man over there trying to pin his blame on me. It's too true that I would have gone all the way if it wasn't for the porter. He was spying on us. He's trying to use what the porter told him to scare the shit out of me and to keep my pay down. Also looking for an excuse to get A. back to the office. Every chance that's he's not getting women as handily as hc uscd to. He's getting old and his bit of a gut is getting in the way.

A. has a lovely cute arse. But it's not a patch on Kitty's. Hers is like something shapely that has just come out fresh from the oven. You could see her two slits and down her thighs with that skimpy skirt she was wearing this morning. An urge came over me to invite her over to the couch but shc had a face on her because of what I had said to F. about her. Fuck F.! Maybe I should breeze over to her all the same. If I knock one of them up, so what? I can't marry both of them. I swear, though, that neither of them is bothering me that much. There is not a great deal passing through my body right now, but that's not bothering me much either. That's because as I am becoming paper I am losing my appetite. It doesn't appear that paper limbs require much training. I was never on top of my work more than now. It's like a gift from the Holy Ghost. I only need to stretch out my hand. I have taken care of HIJ/J. Another note on the latest letter from the office: 'A. has informed us that you will hear from her shortly. I would imagine it is a solicitor's letter . . . ' In that case, bring it on. It is only paper. For the very first time I will be able to give paper a warm welcome. It's food and drink to me, really. But I have noticed that the biggest change that has come over me is both feeling and disgust. Human disgust is leaving me and paper disgust taking its place. It's probably a relative thing, as paper has its own disgust. Not the same thing as real live blood. A bit morc like a dead fish, a cold-blooded fish. F. told me a story she had read somewhere about some women in a town who smelled of fish. F. the shit bag is able to tell them! The man who is engaged to paper, she said, is only like a whore's pimp. I think, all the same, that paper could be a lot more conservative than real live limbs. Not only do paper limbs not have their tongues hanging out for unlawful liaisons, but they are not like real live limbs when they are, so to speak, neutered, without any juice. I wouldn't say they have any passion, no more than in a lump of wood, even though F. said that she had read somewhere that there was as much passion in wood as there was in a woman but we don't have the science yet to measure it. It looks like the Russians are getting somewhere. They measure the amount of passion there is in a prison door.

I was thinking about this today when I had finished all of my letters. I thought—I'm interested in science as well as being interested in philosophy—you would have to admit that it was only in units of fabula that those who thought they could measure paper's passion could work. I don't know if there is any passion in blank paper. You can't presume that there is. It certainly has the ability to take passion in. It gets its passion from what's written: satisfaction and dissatisfaction, pride, worry, discomfort, human living disgust. This shapeless cloud must be converted into a piece of writing, and it is this in its own time which organises itself into a most definite, measurable, foreseeable passion. There is a huge differentiation between paper passion and people passion, because people passion is just one big disorganised inchoate mess without rhyme or reason whilst paper passion is more akin to a well-organised republic, with soviet regularity, or like one that a government commission would lay out in one of its reports. At the end of the day, what is a report, only paper? Yea, you would think that the maggots died because the paper was tasteless. Maggots only exist on watery passion, the earthly spent passion or that of the human. It's a depressing thought that there is the human being busying and bustling himself and all the time part of his body is renting the grave.

Kitty put her hand on my knee today, but I didn't take any notice of her. She told me that she is pregnant and that I would have to fend

or fuck off. A guy who is becoming paper. You can get used to everything no matter how bad it is. My old personality, the one I got from
my father and mother, from my relations, and from the community,
that personality which served me well, I have banished it, or at least I
am in the process of banishing it as I am bit by bit becoming paper. It's
not simply like a tadpole becoming a frog, or a caterpillar becoming
a butterfly, or a person turning into an angel. In every single one of
those situations it is presumed to be a movement from a lower to a
higher order. There I was becoming paper and of course I was thinking of this when Kitty earlier today was trying to coax me onto the
couch and telling me that I used to be full of jizz but had lost two-
thirds of it recently. Some kind of holy fit, I think.

I imagine that a bit of the tadpole always stays in the frog, and a
bit of the caterpillar in the butterfly, and a bit of the person, the puri-
fied person, in the angel. For me it is a change in appearance and in
substance. It appears to me that insofar as I have changed, changed
in shape and looks, that it could be said that not a jot nor a tittle of
the old me remained. I have three afflictions now: my human parts,
or living body; my paper parts; and a soul. And I think that the difference between the human parts and the paper parts is deeper than
between either of them and the soul. Because I am surmising that I
have a fourth substance, a spiritual soul which belongs to that part of
me that is paper. Up to now, my soul never had any objection in the
way it expressed itself with my sleeping with women, with Kitty, or
F. or A. But right now, those paper parts of me—a fair chunk of my
body already—have no interest in women at all. It actually gives me
the shivers to come near them. The only sense I can make of this is
that those parts of me that are organically paper have no tolerance of
any organic parts of a woman. And that there is no tolerance either
for that which was acceptable before to my soul, or any soul or body
anymore. The sense I make of this is that my soul is contracting just
as my bodily parts are being reduced, all relative again, but as I still
can feel my personality it stands to reason that I have to concede that

I have a new soul, a soul that is loyal to paper and paper only and is a cover for this new personality. And this is a personality that has no place for her, as I said to the woman. Maybe if the woman turned to paper just like myself it would be a different story, but I don't know any who has done so.

Another miniskirt on Kitty today. The whole town was gawking at her up and down the street. But the paper part of me is far more interested in paper. I have to say, while this change is still very spotty and macular, that there are great advantages accruing to someone who is becoming paper. I can carry my files around as part of me instead of always handling them, taking them up and down from the shelves and out of the cabinet and spreading them out on the table. Your file is safe with you everywhere, eating, sleeping, on the bus, in the pub, with women, and even when you are praying. It is a sleeping pill for worry. You don't have to torture yourself was it stolen during the night. Or did I leave it in some place I have forgotten. That little hussy of a servant-girl moved it again. They were private letters. A. threatening your man in the office that she will squeal that her bump is his if he doesn't put the screws on me to marry her. They're in it together now, and bad luck to them! Let them sue me! That's what I'm good at. More paper!

Is it possible that I would never get it? Did that young strap of a girl swipe the copies out of the file and give them to Kitty or to F. so as to blackmail me? That letter from the boss QRSZ/s.d., informing me that because I had relations with A.—the porter saw me—that I would have to marry her, or that the two of us would lose our jobs—but I couldn't access my latest reply, that is to say TUVXV.omega/d. I remembered the evening before when I was typing that I brought the file down where the heat of the fire was in the sitting room. The old cold still buggers those bits of me that are not paper yet. I was also a bit wary that Kitty might turn up and I might have to go through the motions—lie her down anyway. The sitting room is a bit too exposed. Kitty is getting a bit uppity, even demanding. She insisted I'd have to marry her. The package was beginning to show, she said. But you're not becoming paper, I said. I said that it was permitted now, all that stuff, since the Vatican Council. If I had to make the best of a bad lot, I would rather keep my job and let your man in the office deal with A. How long more has he got before his time is up? But I'll play the two sides yet. Kitty never came.

Doing that, working away on official papers beside the fire in the sitting room, was so unusual that I had forgotten that I was allowed to do it. Next morning I found my file down there and the servant girl was lighting the fire with copies of letters that had fallen from it. How could I prove that I had answered—the walls of the house shook—without those letters, or that I set up W., me the Wheeler Dealer, W. with the prognathous chin from Kilcornan, according to the provisions of Y., of the monstrous flagration, Y. of the sods and the lumps of turf . . . until I wrote the memorandum.

But do you see how it wouldn't be long now before I could dispose of or burn my old files, my cabinet, my shelves of files, or to stack them with training manuals, something I never had. When the shelves and the filing cabinet would be cleared out or got rid of, there would be a breath of fresh air in the room and bags of space to stretch my limbs, or what was left of them, not much now. I had begun to notice bit by bit that the worries of the world or people's own problems weren't impinging on me much. As regards my work, which I would have died seven times over being harassed about before now, I found I was able to do it as a doddle. But as the worry went, so did my interest in it. I'm not sure I would have had any interest at all in it only for the paper, my own corporeal paper being there and written on. Because there was a new kind of interest and indeed worry arising in me, that is, an interest in the very paper for its own sake. Everything is relative, I know. When it ebbs on one side, it must inevitably flow on the other and so on.

Kitty found me, her skirt up to her crotch, but I started holding forth about paper. You might call it passionate talk. I started reading

her a piece of poetry which I had just composed entitled 'The land-
scape of that page which I have just penned.' She tore it from my
hands. I heard it wailing, like the otherworldly scream of a little child,
its being torn as it was ripped apart, and I think I will write another
poem about it. I am now neglecting those parts of me which haven't
been fully enpapered yet, even as regards eating, drinking, and just
sustenance. My tongue is on the way already, but I prefer to read the
lines of paper on my lips than to listen to talk. I am deaf already to
Kitty and F.

I actually believe that my talk is becoming confused. I have far
more interest now in the part of me that is paper. I give it full priority,
with the gentlest handling. There is a division of compartments, a di-
chotomy in me. The non-paper part of me can't get a handle on the
paper parts. There is a kind of unbridgeable gulf between them. My
right hand, my writing hand, is already paper. My left hand, which is
not my writing hand, is still a thing of flesh and blood, a limb that can
romp and play and make love, and therefore an entirely human limb.
You'd never guess now that they ever had any connection with one
another, that they had more or less the same purpose, not to mention
that they were both joint limbs. Almost unknown to me I have begun
to call my right hand a quill. There is a new reaction in me: the paper
part of me is reacting against its own parts in its independent places
and the rest have retreated completely.

My paper part, that is most of me by now, has a great need to
seek out the company of other paper and ink, any kind of paper, news,
letters, magazines, books, even wallpaper and paper on the ceiling. I
foresee whole art galleries dedicated to wallpaper and physical land-
scapes plastered to the ceiling. I follow bits of paper being whipped
away by the wind on a wild day, and the best thing I have in my possession now is that which I had hated before, the file of my income
tax. The reference numbers there are very interesting. I had written
to every goddam place that could provide me with paper, especially
letters: the translation department of the government, the universi-

ties looking for old examination papers and scripts, memorandumbs from anywhere, publishers, works that had been dumped, and even refuse . . . I love books, but I don't read too many. I love handling the pages with my quill-hand—never with my left hand—to stroke and rub them with my fingers, to let them stand up straight upfront and gawp at the wonder of paper, of writing itself. I buy a lot of newspapers, too many. I collect every kind of old paper that I can, food wrapping, stuff from bins or anywhere I would get a scrap, and they are all in heaps around the floor. They are my bedclothes, my tablecloth, my cushions, heaps of them. I tried to make a suit of clothes out of them but failed miserably. I'm still trying to do my best. I never tried to dispose of the files, to dump them, as I thought I might have to once. I actually gave them an extra lease on life. I stripped them out of their covers and I spread them out so that the writing would be visible and clear. My wife tells me that I have to cop on and not be deluded. Those copies of letters of hers to the office about Big A., I really love to be getting off on them, something I hate to do with Big A. herself in the flesh.

I think this is spirituality, or some or other version of spirituality anyway. Those letters have all been laid out in proper order just as if they were human and I was keeping a record of something human. I have laid them out. I go through them one by one. I think about them. I examine them. I write them love letters as one does and I write love letters in reply all the way back to myself. And I keep those love letters in a special place and I take them out fairly often and give them a fulfilling paper kiss, as my mouth is nearly all paper now. And I'm having an *affaire de coeur* with a bundle of income tax forms that I discovered in my search for paper. I took a fancy to them, they were so suitable for filing, unambiguous letters dressed up with suitable ref. numbs, precise dates, my reference, your reference, you couldn't help loving them. I pet them and rub them and hug them and give them a big hug, and I write to them appropriately with ref. numbs. and so on and tell them that I love them and entreat them to have pity on me, that this is unrequited love, a gracious gentle love . . . They informed me they were jealous of that lady, her paper spirit still in the room, and that I'm flirting with her on the quiet.

You'd never guess who came in on top of me? Are you better now? That particular lady. Her butt bigger than ever; she disgusted me. Her tiny skirt halfway up her arse. She sneaked in on top of my papers and brought me and the papers down in a heap, and me underneath. She made sure that I could feel her pregnancy all the way from her floating rib down to her belly button as I fumbled with my left hand—I made sure I didn't go near her with my paper quill. She started rolling about and pressing into my crotch murmuring all kinds of endearments, 'O my love, my darling, my precious.'

'Do you have any heart left at all?' she asked.

'It has turned into paper,' I said.

'A paper heart.'

'A paper form, you silly twit,' I said, and I stretched out my paper quill scrabbling for the income tax form as I have become paper through and through finally and completely, heart, crotch, the whole lot . . .

TRANSLATED BY ALAN TITLEY

MARBLING

Waking up in a public hospital ward at three o'clock in the morning. Whether or not it was the strange music that awakened me, I certainly blamed it. The well-defined nostrils next to me were wheezing and sucking, whistling and blowing turn and turn about like the folds of a melodeon being played. The only light in the ward came from a dirty yellow bulb very uncertain of itself. Nonetheless the ceiling of the room was clear enough that I could see it was an arch. Clear enough that I started to imagine without any good reason in this twilight of the ward that I was under the sea in the company of seals and pleasant ripples tickling me all around. Somebody else might call it a lullaby. I imagined it more like nasty stormy weather bashing against the weakened shores of my feeling and disgust . . .

If this didn't beat it all! The Wheezer woke up on the spot—he was lying half on his side in his own bed, and every bit of his rant was like telegraph poles on a deserted rode whanging away above me.

' . . . I'm telling you now that I wrote about it in the papers already. We are not people at all, only statues. The system wasn't devised to look after you or me any more than the nurses who were trained to tend to people. The beds, the lockers, the whole lot, they are all got up as statues. Look at the holy stuff! It takes precedence over everything else, like a prominent promontory sticking out on its own into eternity and beyond. She covered up every single shred of that miserable locker as the priest was about to come! She was on her knees saying prayers between eight o'clock and thirteen minutes past while our stomachs were crying out for something to eat since six when we woke up! It was obviously all the same to God to say the prayers before tea, or even after it. Signs on it—cold tea all the time. And God knows there was no other way it could possibly be, only cold—no matter when the tea came after the food. Do you hear the way they say "Jees-ass"? Like sinners calling out to God for vengeance . . . '

I tried to make those poles trip him up. No way.

' . . . Didn't I tell you that, didn't I? Your bed is wet . . . A mistake with the bottle! No chance of a mistake. It might be. That bitch of a bottle was in the baggage that the wench of fate had packed for you before you were an uncertain ticket in the waiting room of pre-creation. That's how I put it in the paper. The guy who answered me said it was a load of crap . . . Remember the old chamber pots, do you? The bottle was overflowing. One drop of a wren's piss would be too much. You'll have to change the sheets and nightclothes now, and your sleep is ruined anyway. If there was a wisp or a hair out of place the nurse would notice it, but leave the bottle up to the brim and she'd never see it, never mind take it away. We are not poor watery creatures—the paper wouldn't print this kind of language—nor human beings, which we're supposed to be, but rather bright polished marble, and if we're not completely there yet, the sooner we are the better. I intend, as I leave this place—but of course I never will except as marble—I intend having a question put in the Dáil, to banish the cobwebs from the question once and for all, a question during the estimates for the Department of Health—'

A nurse interrupted the rant. She looked after me and threatened the Wheezer that she'd dump him out. After a couple of dissatisfied grunts he slid back into his snoring cocoon of sleep, which was for all intents and purposes the antechamber before becoming marble, clean pure crystal marble.

I could only manage that intermittent waking and dozing which is usual at the dawning of the day. That bit of the mind that is half-alert starts slurping on the sweet pleasures of dessert and won't allow any full-throated meat or lunch into its ken. My own girl one, she always took her lunch in some gallery. My most comforting memory was a memorial I saw in Avila where the Grand Inquisitor was buried. But it actually wasn't really his. Nor do I remember any stone or burial chamber for him in Spain, and I have been there a few times. Nor did I see any memorial to Savonarola in Firenze! They were people, or so you'd think, that marble would be just waiting for with open arms, who you would think would march straight out of the shroud and into a suit of marble. Ireland is run by people in suits of marble . . . That suit and scarlet shirt that would put ancestral memory in its place very quickly . . .

You might say that that statue walked up and plonked itself without ceremony on its own plinth. Dare anybody knock it down! He wouldn't recommend how the bold Nelson was brought low from his own crow's nest. But he was for knocking him off his perch. But just in such a manner that was done appropriately and properly according to the norms of righteous war and as long as no innocent person would suffer. There should be another statue right next to you — without the widow's patch round about, Willie Smith O'Brien . . .

You were really the bellowing slave. All signs on your statue, it's kind of collected up into your arse like an apron on a fish wife. And Daniel O' Connell, does your statue understand English? . . .

Anybody would know by your smug satisfied supercilious smirk that you were destined to be here and like this for ever and ever. Baggage that you got in the pre-created world! And then, that covering, that dust-wrapper that left you there drinking up the rain, Theobaldy Matthew! . . .

When they stripped you for burial, all they got was marble. You had been marbleised for ages, you Tom Moore . . .

You'd almost think they had stolen you from another plinth! You were a kind of fairy statue that had slinked in through the back door after closing time. Where will I lay my head, as Paddy said . . .

He wouldn't shut the fuck up, even as a statue. Me crouching there listening to him for all eternity! The marble itself melding into a poisonous whinge! God forbid . . .

I woke up suddenly because I was scared shitless. The bottle was lying there on its side on the chair, its neck pointing to another bottle. I thought that water was needed to bestir the raw marble. Prayer itself was a dead duck. That 'Jees-ass' with its braying emphasis on the second syllable wasn't an out-and-out blasphemy, but just a kind of link in the litany of prayer.

A shaft of summer sunlight keeked through the window. It was sucked into the room and was being kneaded into marble by the doctor's bright sacred jerkin, and by the nurse's sparkling snazzy get-up, even by the walls themselves, especially the big high arched one that reminded me of a gallery, some gallery or other that I saw on my travels. Even the Wheezer's own clean bedclothes up as far as his chanter's windpipe stuck out, it was all marbled by now. And his whole neck's chanter too. And all the way up and down, all marbled too. And my own hand down as far as the sheet. I started searching down in the farthest recesses of the ward that was just a gallery now, searching just to see could I find a plinth, a vacant plinth, or any kind of a plinth at all that I could plonk some kind of statue down on . . .

TRANSLATED BY ALAN TITLEY

MÁIRTÍN Ó CADHAIN was born in an Cnocán Glas, Cois Fharraige, Conamara, in 1906. He was educated locally, and a scholarship allowed him to become a National School teacher. On graduating from St. Patrick's College, Drumcondra, Dublin, he returned to Conamara, where he taught in local schools, including Camas and, later, Carn Mór. During the Second World War he was interned in the Curragh camp in Kildare for membership in the proscribed Irish Republican Army (IRA). He subsequently became a translator in Dáil Éireann, and Trinity College Dublin appointed him lecturer in Irish in 1956, naming him professor in 1969. He died in 1970. He is best known for his novel *Cré na Cille* (1949), published in the English language by Yale University Press as *Graveyard Clay*, translated from the Irish by Liam Mac Con Iomaire and Tim Robinson (2016), and *Dirty Dust*, translated by Alan Titley (2015). His short story collections include *Idir Shúgradh agus Dáiríre* (1939), *An Braon Broghach* (1948), *Cois Caoláire* (1953), *An tSraith ar Lár* (1967), *An tSraith Dhá Tógáil* (1970), and *An tSraith Tógtha* (1977). Another novel, *Athnuachan* (1997), and a piece of continuous imaginative prose, *Barbed Wire* (2002), were published posthumously.

LOUIS DE PAOR is Professor of Irish Studies at the National University of Ireland, Galway. His publications include *Faoin mBlaoisc Bheag Sin* (1991), a study of narrative technique in the short fiction of Máirtín Ó Cadhain, critical editions of the work of Michael Davitt, Liam S Gógan, Máire Mhac an tSaoi and Máirtín Ó Cadhain, and a bilingual selection of twentieth-century poetry in Irish, *Leabhar na hAthghabhála/Poems of Repossession* which was among *The Irish Times* Books of the Year and a Poetry Book Society Recommended

Translation in 2016. He was Visiting Professor at Sydney University (1993–4), Fulbright Irish Language Scholar at New York University (2013) and the University of California, Berkeley (2014), and Burns Scholar at Boston College (2016). His monograph on the work of Brian Ó Nualláin (Flann O'Brien/Myles na gCopaleen), *'An té a bhíonn ag gáire': Brian Ó Nualláin — Scríbhneoir Gaeilge Béarla,* will be published in 2022.